C000156627

UNDERGROUND GUY

by

Kyle Michel Sullivan

KMSCB, Buffalo, NY
Published 2018 by KMSCB

This book is a work of fiction meant for adults only. Names, characters, places, incidents, and situations are purely the result of the author's imagination and are used fictitiously. Resemblance to any persons, living or dead, is purely coincidental. All rights are reserved by the author, including the right to reproduction in whole or in part in any form, manner, or concept.

Cover design by Jamthecat
Photographs courtesy Shutterstock.com
Copyright 2018 by Kyle Michel Sullivan, dba: KMSCB
ISBN: 9780578436661

— Acknowledgements —

Thanks to Vicki H-J for helping me make the book as good and accurate as it can be. Without her assistance this would just be another story.

Additional thanks to The Depraved Minds Club on GoodReads.com for giving me so much support. They help me keep real.

UNDERGROUND GUY

Table of Contents

ONE

I saw him on London's underground, looking tired, sad, alone. Sleepy gray eyes under honey-colored brows. Thick hair covering a classic skull and cropped close enough to see he had a couple of scars in his scalp. Aquiline nose. Taut lips. Strong neck under a clean chin. Smooth cheekbones. Mid-twenties. His shoulders broad. His chest full and round under a threadbare red hoodie. No gut to him, even sitting sloped over. He got on at Knightsbridge and grabbed a seat near the rear door of the carriage close to where I was standing, his focus on his cell phone — excuse me, mobile phone — the whole time. His dark cargo pants were smudged with white paint and his legs filled them just right. Smallish feet in basic tennis shoes splashed with more paint counterpointed by powerful hands. A workman's hands. All the complete opposite of what I like ... and of me.

I look as Italian-American as they come — with a Roman nose in good proportion to my face and chin, a wrestler's build that's stocky but tight thanks to running five miles a day, dark hair everywhere there should be, eyes so brown and wary they're close to black, clean-shaven, and sporting a suit and tie instead of casuals. Very Brooklyn, even in London.

My preferred type was like this one man who entered just before my underground guy at the same station and stood right by the door — tall, dark, good-looking in a Jewish way. Either side of thirty, which put me about my age, and wearing a sleek suit of brushed wool — a lot sharper than the one I got on sale at Macy's. Probably Savile Row. A neat goatee, trim body and no briefcase added to the sense he was someone whose life was perfectly organized. What was even better? I caught him casting my guy a low-key look of appraisal. The second I saw that I knew it wouldn't have taken much to get him out of his suit, and under normal circumstances I'd have found a way to strike up a conversation with him, get him back to my hotel and spend a few hours in bed because I really needed a fuck.

But nothing was normal for me, right then, and for some reason the sad guy kept drawing my attention. I can't explain it ... except I noticed he wasn't happy about a text he got. He made a reply, waited for an answer and took a deep breath at what he read. The vague lines in his forehead drew deeper and his eyes darker. The news was obviously not good and I felt for him ... which was weird because, to be honest, fair-haired Englishmen never really interested me. But even Savile Row's dark perfection and calm control couldn't drag me away from the little drama unfolding before me via text as my underground guy tensed and shifted and leaned back and scrunched and shifted upright, each movement increasing my awareness of his beauty.

We were on the Piccadilly line, westbound, and it was getting to be solid with evening commuters, every damn one of them the typical English sort. I was standing not three feet from him just a bit to his left, and I'm not embarrassed to say I was gazing upon him like some needy puppy seeking a treat or scratch behind the ears. He finally noticed as we pulled into Hammersmith, gave me a couple of quick confused glances then scrunched deeper into his seat. He shifted so I could see his left hand held a thick gold ring on his third finger, and he pulled up a photo of a woman and some children on the phone's screen. Then he got into another serious back and forth via text.

Him sending me a *subtle hint* that he's *not into dick* is no problem for me; I've had lots of straight guys. But I was way too impatient to take the time needed for a decent seduction, so I decided to adjust my gaze to Savile Row ... only my underground guy leaned forward to rest his arms on his lovely thighs, still focused on his phone, and in his reflection in the window I noticed he had a tattoo of some Asian character on the elegant nape of his neck. Japanese, it looked like.

Beautiful.

Heartbreaking.

I'd seen it before ... something like it ... and I got caught in one of those moments where you almost glimpse what the memory is but can't quite grasp it. Then he leaned even farther in and the hoodie pulled lower to expose the frayed collar of a faded green t-shirt and the beginning of yet another Japanese character and —

My heart began to pound. My breath went soft and sharp. I totally forgot Savile Row, forgot the mess in my brain — hell, damn near forgot that I was headed back to the States, tomorrow.

All that mattered was him.

He was my prey ... and it was all I could do to keep from reaching over just to ruffle his hair to let him know the chase was on, I was so overwhelmed by the idea of having him.

I snuck some photos on my cell phone, which only made him lovelier.

And lovelier.

And lovelier.

My focus became so intent he tightened even more. Oh, he knew I was interested ... hell, a blind fuckin' poodle would've known. But he wasn't acting like a man who's freaked out by my attention; it was more like he was surprised. I wondered if he was wondering if this might be the way to make a bit of extra money. Let the fag suck him off for a quick fifty. Looked like he could use it.

I watched him work his texts. Work through confusion ... then wariness ... finally ending with a weary stubbornness over some decision he'd made. I figured it was *marital trouble*. Maybe telling the wife he'd be late for dinner and she was pissed. Which hurt him. Made him sadder. And more beautiful than anyone I had ever seen.

My heart pounded stronger. Son-of-a-bitch, I had to have him. Had to be with him. Completely. No matter what it took.

He glanced at Savile Row a few times. I almost thought my guy expected something to happen between them, but that man was too lost in his own contemplations, so he cast one more half-glance my way, sent a last text then put his phone in his hoodie pocket and, as we were pulling into Hounslow East, stood up.

I stopped breathing for a moment, because those legs flowed into what was promising to be the most perfect ass ever in existence. Then as he worked his way to the door he brushed against me — his solid arm rubbing mine, almost like he was saying *Here I am* — and I fell headlong into animal mode.

And followed him.

Okay, that was a stupid thing to do. Period. Like I said, not one real, honest, serious ping on my gaydar. The most I could even have hoped for was the cash-for-access scenario, and while the thought of making an offer did dance across my mind it died quick ... because I wanted more than that would give me. A hell of a lot more. But getting a straight guy's no problem for me; it all depends on how far you're willing to go.

And I'd learned a long time ago that I had no limit.

I hopped off the train and watched him stride down the platform, and his legs did *not* disappoint. The right length and shape with just a hint of footballer's bandiness to them and a soft suggestion of being pigeon-toed. Hands shoved in his pockets. Ass rocking with the promise of solid smooth symmetry. Even his bit of swagger was nothing more than that of a guy who's used to being athletic and in charge. I prowled after him, soft and stealthy.

He used an Oyster Card to exit, not once noticing he was being followed. Outside, he cut left into an area of typical English shops, and I sauntered after him. People were out and about shopping for dinner or walking their kids or dogs or just taking a stroll. Cars and trucks whizzed past as jets roared into the sky, Heathrow being just a few stops further down the line.

Man — getting him wasn't going to be easy.

He jaywalked to the other side and hurried down a long narrow street of homely row-houses that led to a modern high-rise block of what I think were apartments. A cube truck took up one lane as it unloaded goods, and there were cars parked along both curbs ... but none were actually coming or going. Low fences blocked in tiny front yards. All very depressing.

Now for all I knew this guy was a black belt in Aikido or had years of experience in street fighting. And looking at how strong and sure just his walk was, I knew he wouldn't be an easy mark. Plus I didn't know the area so had no idea if we'd get to a place that was isolated enough for me to make a move — but none of that mattered; all I cared about was finding some way of gaining ownership of that ass, and if the right location sprouted up and I had half a chance ... I could do it.

How?

Easy — I wrestled in high school and college, and I'm still in top shape. Also, he wouldn't be my first ... oh ... let's call it *conquest*. Hell, not even my tenth. On top of that I have a roll of packing tape in my briefcase. You can carry that crap anywhere in the world without question and it's perfect when you need to subdue a guy who might know how to fight; it's too sticky to slip out of, hard as hell to tear and also makes a great gag. Finally, I had a little tub of Vaseline, very nondescript and perfect as lube.

So as we walked I slipped the roll out, shifted the strap of my briefcase so it hung behind my back and got a length of the tape started. All I needed was the right spot to make my move. That was always the tricky part.

We passed a slim passageway between two sections of houses that provided access to a narrow overgrown strip of foliage running between them and the underground's elevated tracks. I had noticed it from the depot's platform and figured it was to minimize the noise of passing trains. If we came to another passageway ... yeah, that might work. And if another train was rolling by, it could cover any yells he might make.

But then some people came out of a house across the

street and strolled towards the main drag, enjoying the final decent days before winter. Okay, witnesses would *not* be at all conducive to a successful endeavor. Still ... they were facing the other way and no one was ahead of us, and reality was something had to happen soon; we were closing in on that apartment block.

Then I saw a house was being remodeled, up ahead. It had scaffolding around it and piles of refuse filled the yard. And it looked like there was another small passageway between it and the next section of houses. Even better, the windows were dark.

And a train was coming, headed back to town.

So this was it.

Now or never.

I lengthened the strip of tape, slow and quiet as we neared the house. Got closer and closer to the scaffolding. My heart raced. My breath was short and sharp. My dick twitched at the idea it might be having some fun. The feel of my boxer-briefs on my balls and thighs was electrifying.

And sure enough — there was a small alleyway there, half-hidden by a full dumpster.

The train slowed as it neared the station so the second he reached the alleyway I jumped him and whipped the tape around his body to trap his arms — right one bent up to his neck, left one just above his elbow — and all he had time to yell was, "What the fook?" before I whipped tape around his mouth to muffle him and slammed my own arm around his chest and yanked him behind the materials. He tried to flip me but I dropped and rolled, still holding him, then whipped more tape tight around him to secure him even better. He struggled but he had no leverage to fight back.

I crushed him to the ground, face up, and finished the gag with a couple wraps around. He kicked at me so I twisted around and sat on his thighs to secure his ankles with the tape then jumped to my feet. I had him and it took twenty, maybe thirty seconds.

The house had a side door that was slightly open so I rammed my hands under his arms and dragged him inside. He bucked and fought and tried to gasp out cries for help and demands to know what I was doing but the tape muffled him. He was also working at getting one hand loose, even as he kept trying to talk and keep my focus on his face.

I kicked the door closed. A quick glance showed the place was completely empty — stairs to the left, hallway back to the kitchen, open double doors for the living room to my right — so that's where I dragged him. He really began to buck and kick and curse and fight to get away from me, sending some pretty loud cries out even through his gag, so I whipped more of it around his mouth a couple times to completely muffle his cries.

Then I forced his semi-free hand up to the other one, taped his wrists together and jabbed the tape around his torso with my fingernail clipper's file to break it. He tried to smack me with an elbow but I flipped him onto his belly, yanked both his hands over his head to the back of his neck and secured his wrists there by wrapping more tape around the gag. Then I rolled him onto his back.

Now I could stand up and put my briefcase aside — it had jammed into me a couple of times so I'd be bruised, in the morning. Still ... I stretched and savored the moment. That's when I finally realized my dick was hard as a rock. He must have felt it, even through my boxer-briefs, because when he looked at me he had those big wide eyes a guy gets when he realizes he's not being robbed but something else is going to happen. Something worse, in his mind.

Man ... seeing him like this ... I couldn't move he was so fucking gorgeous. The line of his body from his shoulders to his hips. His arms pumped and straining under the frayed cotton hoodie. The left sleeve had torn at the seam to reveal the underarm of that ratty green t-shirt and part of a bicep that was defined in all the right ways. The fullness of his pecs was enhanced by his arms being held behind his head, and they were matched by the fullness of his crotch and thighs and even his calves. I think I stopped breathing for a moment, and I seriously wished I'd had time to work my way into his bed instead of this catch and grab crap.

And I *have* talked straight men into bed plenty of times. Depending on the guy it could be a long-term process of days or weeks of nudging and leading and hinting and subtly building in his mind that *he's just trying it out to see what it's like* kind of shit-talk. I'd only gone through that much trouble a couple of times, and then only because it was so much fun to watch their faces as they realized they not only got off on being with a man, they damn near passed out from the sensation. I got repeats off every one of them and I'd made damn sure they got the full experience every time.

Of course, it could also be the right number of beers or puffs on a joint to make them open up. Those types were always one-timers because they'd blame their enjoyment on the mind-altering crap and never on the quality of your involvement. Not that I minded; they tended to be good-looking enough to have fun with if you're horny, but not necessarily someone I wanted twice.

But my underground guy? Just looking at him, the way everything about him fit together in damn near perfect symmetry ... I didn't want a one-time thing with him. I wanted something I've never even thought about before — days ... weeks ... months.

Which made absolutely no sense. Aside from the fact that he wasn't my usual type what did I think I was going to do? Take him back to the States in my luggage and not declare him at customs? Keep him locked in a closet of my Brooklyn condo? Bring him out when I got the itch for some English beef? Yeah, that'd work.

I had to shake myself to return to the moment's reality ... and remember that breathing is good if you want to stay conscious. But it was hard to keep my mind on that because the bottom edge of his shirt and hoody had ridden up to reveal some of the soft swirling hair on his belly. A gentle light filtered through a tiny part of the bay window that was not hidden by the scaffolding and trash to lie across it, causing it to gleam like down, elegant and pure. I pulled out my phone and snapped a couple of images.

I noticed he was wearing a back brace so asked, "Did you

hurt your back?"

He seemed not to hear me.

I knelt beside him and he shifted away, scared, so I whispered, "Listen, don't worry; I'm not gonna hurt you. If you work with me I'll make you happy, even." At the same time, I let my fingers drift over the soft hairs spreading across his exposed belly.

He flinched and shook his head. He knew what was up.

I stood and removed my suit coat, undid my tie and unbuttoned my shirt to reveal my own nice set of pecs to him. I strutted a little as I hung my coat on a nearby doorknob. Yeah, there's some beef on me, but it's solid while my ass — let's just say I've been told it would turn the straightest man queer when he saw it. So let's put that to the test. I turned away from him and glanced back over my shoulder as I slipped off my shoes and undid my pants.

"Be happy I'm not some fat bastard clown in Chicago doing this," I said as the pants dropped to reveal my good solid legs. I stepped out of them, my raging hard-on pressing against the boxer-briefs' cotton. Since that needed some relief, too, I dropped the briefs, lifted the tail of my shirt and smacked my cheeks with the other hand. Then I turned to stand before him in all my glory.

My dick's not the biggest ever — my older brother, Colin, got the better deal in that — but I've had plenty of men tell me it's worthy of being worshipped ... who then proved it by doing it. Pun intended. And right now? It was at its height of perfection.

He shook his head and tried to back away from me, but all he could do was push with his legs or roll. Can't go far that way. I yanked off my socks and dropped down to pin him on his back and sit on his crotch, my dick pointed straight at his face.

"I mean it," I said, almost giggling. "You're too pretty to hurt. I'll even leave the brace on. Just work with me — play along — everything'll be fine."

Then I slowly unzipped his hoodie, inch by inch, to reveal the thin green t-shirt had even more tears in it. Recent ones that must have happened when we wrestled. It lay across his chest like silk drifting over gentle hills, showing the barest hint of nice pointy nipples. I ran my hands over them then pulled the front of the hoodie open, let my hands whisper down his sides then up his belly to his pecs and finally the shirt's collar ...

And tore it open.

I didn't mean to, because that made him flinch and struggle, but it added so damn much to the moment of revelation. He had exactly what I expected in the way of a chest — firm and nicely developed with just the right spritz of hair swirling over his skin and around a pair of elegant tits. I flicked at them and he almost yelped and I realized I still had my socks in one hand and —

A car slammed up, outside. Blue lights flickered through the exposed sections of the bay window.

Shit, it was a cop.

****

I whipped a sock around his throat and held it tight as I covered him with my body, growling, "One word and I'll break your neck."

I could hear police chatter on a radio. Shit. Someone must've thought they saw something and called them. Shit, shit, shit. I knew it was going too damn well. And while the window was pretty much hidden by the trash and filth, someone could still see in if they tried. A flashlight beam shot through to search the place and someone rattled the knob of the side door, but it had locked when I kicked it shut. One of the great things about British doors is they normally do that when closed; that was probably why it'd been left open — so the contractor's guys could get in without a key.

"You sure it was down 'ere?" said one man's voice.

"Yeah," replied another.

"But that don't fit what Reg said, and this door's tight. Should we break in?"

My guy started to shift and groan but I only held him tighter and glared into his eyes. He began to shiver.

"Call Boss. See what he says."

"The mood 'e's in? Fook that. Maybe Reg did make it down the ASDA. There's a walkway leads to it."

"Right, better get on it. Bugger, I'd 'ate to be him, right now."

"'Is idear, wan'nit?'"

My guy shook his head. He knew they were leaving. And sure enough, the car drove off. He began to shake.

I loosened the sock and smoothed my hand over his head, tickling my fingers through his hair. "See? We're okay, now."

He just kept shaking his head.

Man, I loved just lying there with him. Feeling his breath entering and leaving him. Accepting the warmth of him. I ran my hands over his shoulders and across his chest and down his abs, wishing he was doing the same to me as I whispered, "I mean it. Really. You got no reason to be scared of me."

He was fighting to keep control. His eyes were slammed closed, his face trapped in a tight frown.

It hurt me to see him like that so I made myself sit up and whisper, "You think I'm gonna fuck you, don't you?"

He looked at me, unable to do anything more.

"I'm not. I don't want to." I shifted to make certain my naked ass was on his crotch. "I want you to fuck me."

That made him blink and for good reason. First off, what kind of rapist wants his target to fuck him instead of the other way around? Second, he was nowhere near thinking about getting hard enough to even consider the possibility of jacking off let alone pushing into a man's hole. And truth is ... it's a crazy thing to say to guys like this. But that's why I say it. That shifts their focus away from their virgin ass and onto my anything but virgin one and they begin to think, *Maybe this won't be so bad if I can just get myself hard enough for a minute.*

Of course, it was just a line of bullshit. Oh, I'm not averse to being fucked by the right guy — especially if it's one I've spent weeks cultivating — but I love fucking men and my dick was going inside this guy, and soon. But to get to that point without having to fight, non-stop, this bit of subterfuge works wonders.

Besides, I also love sucking dick.

I pulled the rest of the t-shirt away from his neck to reveal good clean muscles, not overdone but just right and pumped and ready to fight if given the chance. They electrified me at how elegant they were, even with the bit of a Celtic design I could see that was tattooed around his right one. I let my fingers drift over it and the smoothness of his skin was heart-stopping. He jolted but still stayed in the same position. Then I noticed rough patches under the ink. I let my fingers follow the roughness.

His breathing grew more shallow but he didn't struggle. Not even as I shifted him onto his left side so I could pull the hoodie up out of the way and tear the shirt completely off to get a better view of the tattoo. It extended across his shoulder and down part of his back, keeping its distance from the Japanese characters. Rough scars alternated with its smoothness.

"You've been hurt," I whispered. "Motorcycle accident? Hit by a car? Fall off a bus?"

He just kept fighting for control.

I lay him back down and ran my fingers around the back of his head and into his hair. I felt the little scars I'd noticed in his scalp. Small and uneven. Like little bits of metal or rocks had torn into him.

"Were you caught in an explosion?"

He wouldn't even look at me.

It usually makes me angry when a conquest won't even try to respond to my questions. I'll start growling and get rough. But this time? I just sat up and let my fingers whisper down his neck and over his shoulder and into the soft hair on his pecs to toy with his nips. Caress them. Flick them. Give myself time to think. To wonder what he'd been through. Wonder what sort of trauma he'd experienced. Could he be a soldier home on leave? Or was he caught in one of London's terrorist bombings? Something I couldn't even think of?

The thoughts confused me. But I loved the sensation of his light hairs on my fingertips. Felt joy at the quivers of his skin as I caressed his sides. My heart was so light it seemed ready to float away. I had to keep reminding myself to breathe.

I was losing focus ... wanted to just stay there like that and touch him for hours ... days ... months. I finally had to make myself regroup and unbuckle his belt.

He squirmed and shifted under me, more by reflex than anything, and that set my dick to raging, again. I drew my hands down his belly. Fire exploded through me as they drifted over his skin. Shivers from his muscles added to the beauty of my caress even as I let my fingers dance through his treasure trail and across the strap of the back brace. Holy Jesus, the tender kiss of his hair was so elegant.

Then I unbuttoned his pants.

He shook his head *No*, over and over, and gave a soft wail but only squirmed a little.

I had to shift down his thighs to unzip him and open the fly to reveal he was wearing a pair of striped briefs. Man — I loved how its colorful lines emphasized the shape of what they contained. I could focus on that for hours but all I did was drag my fingers over the hump of his dick, enjoying how the material stretched over him so comfortable and easy, before sliding back up his honey-colored pubes and hairs and returning to barely touch his nips then flick them and let my fingers tickle around them, over and over, and whisper out to dance through the hair on his chest and down his sides and over his belly to toy with his navel and down to his pubes and up and around, again and again.

"Why do you have the back brace?" I asked, looking closer. "Accident of some kind? Work related?"

This time he looked at me and sort of nodded. That was a good sign.

I kept caressing him, giving him a chance to calm down

some more. After a few minutes his nips were even a bit perky. That's when I guided the pants down his hips and pulled them under his ass and along his thighs to his knees and oh-my-God his legs — light hair swirling up them as if to emphasize their perfect shape. His briefs were worn but not in bad shape and obviously he wasn't hard, but just as obviously his balls were fat and in desperate need of a milking.

Well that was about to be remedied.

I stopped to gaze upon him for a moment ... and take more photos with my phone ... then began groping him to get the feel of him. The first touch is always the best because this is when you find out the heft of his balls. So I rolled them with my fingers. And rolled them. Loved how oval they were. Even through the taut cotton they felt fat and alive and wonderful — and what's better? My tender non-stop caress was making his dick respond. I could feel his shaft just beginning to thicken and extend itself along the line of the briefs, drifting to the left, so I traced the length of it while still fondling his balls and whispering around them and back up to his dick and back down, over and over and over, loving how the cotton felt like a second skin on him until I stopped thinking and just tore them open at his left hip, making him cry out and try to jolt away.

What I now saw was smooth creamy white skin between the gentlest of Speedo-like tan lines as the briefs floated back into place to cover most of his balls and part of his shaft. I forgot to breathe, again. It wasn't till I leaned down and kissed that creamy white skin that I could draw breath. I'd never felt like this, not once, not even with the men I'd cultivated into bed, building anticipation to the breaking point before gaining access to their hidden treasures. He'd become my beginning and end. My alpha and omega. The universe in one and I was no longer in control of myself.

I lifted the torn material away to get a good look at what I had to work with. It wasn't the biggest cock I'd ever seen — and the one drawback was he wasn't cut; I prefer guys who look like me. But I was right to figure it wouldn't matter because the way his dick lay across his groin, his balls bouncing around just below it, his honey-colored pubes framing everything and fanning out so beautifully — it was eroticism defined.

He tensed and froze as I played with his foreskin, ignoring his grimaces and how tight his muscles got as I slowly pulled it back ... back ... back to reveal he was clean and had a lovely head. He'd have made a perfect helmet instead of this anteater.

His stomach quivered as I drew my fingers down the length of him then let them drift around his balls and along his inner thighs, and I leaned in close to whisper, "I want you to get hard then I'll ride you. That really is all I want. I want to be able to say I was fucked by someone as beautiful as you. And when you cum I'll be done. But I want you to cum in me. You understand? I want you to fuck me and cum in me." It took him a moment but he nodded. "Can you do it?" He took in a deep breath and sort of grimaced a *Yes*.

Of course I was still lying, but by this point even if he didn't believe me he knew he had no choice if he wanted to have even the slightest chance of keeping his ass virginal. So he lay back and closed his eyes.

This was part of the deal — getting him to fire his wad. I don't do it out of any sense of obligation; like I said, I love blowjobs. Giving. Receiving. To me they're more intimate than fucking. You've got your teeth next to him and your tongue caressing him and your lips sliding along him and your breath exploding the nerves in his head with your fingers to help bring things along. And you could tell when to hold back and drive him crazy with a need to bust his nut. Fucking is great and I love that, too, but to truly control a guy give him a blow job; that'll show him exactly who's the boss.

Only something funny hit me as I nuzzled his pubes in preparation; I wanted to impress him. Wanted him to know how good I was at this. So I huffed my hot breath onto them then licked his shaft like he was the tastiest of lollipops. I sucked on his balls, soft, careful, tickling them with my tongue and letting them slide in and out of my mouth. Jesus, he tasted so damn sweet. My fingers toyed with his nips and caressed his sides and across the hair on his belly and all over his thighs, and I kept my own dick out of the way as much as I could so the reality of it wouldn't intrude on him. I put everything I had into pleasing him — and after a few minutes he began to grow.

And grow.

And grow.

His foreskin all but vanished as his shaft thickened and expanded. He wound up long and sloped and so perfectly shaped he could have been used to illustrate what the male penis should look like, erect. I couldn't help but circle him with my lips and ring him with my tongue and take all of him in my mouth.

I worked him steady for the next few minutes. Up and down, my hands exploring him, my tongue swirling around him, soft and easy then faster and harder and more intent and on and on and on, nonstop. I didn't forget his balls or nips, either, pulling at them and massaging them, left then right then left then right. I went for the whole package, planning to make him scream for me to let him shoot. The beast in me growled and snapped, loved how he felt as my dick and balls bounced between his thighs, making me harder and more sensitive. It was perfection.

Despite himself he got harder and harder and began to squirm and clench his ass and groan from the overwhelming sensation of it all and buck into my mouth. Sooner than I'm sure he thought possible — hell, even than I thought possible — he was close to letting go.

So I pulled back.

Which confused me. Normally I let the guy fire his load and then say, "Fine buddy, you don't wanna cum inside me? I'll cum inside you." Then I flip him over and fuck him, telling him the whole time this was really what he wanted. That messes with them, massively.

But this time — something about this time — I don't know why but I gave him a chance to hold back his ejaculation. Let him calm down a little before I pulled out the Vaseline and slathered it over his dick, slow and tender and vicious in my playfulness, making him hard as a rock again, then smoothed some into my hole — good and deep, with two fingers — and knelt across his hips to straddle his crotch and sat back and ... and with the feel of his solid dick lying up over his belly, his balls tight and pushing against my own scrotum, need took over and I held him in place with my knees and positioned his dick against my hole and sat back and let him slide in, slow and soft and easy and so fucking exquisite, holy fucking shit, it was like he was built to be part of me.

And I wanted to stay like that forever.

Shit, me doing that was a first. But with this guy — even if I had wanted to stop myself I couldn't; I was out of control.

So there I sat for a moment, savoring the fullness of him in me. Unbelievable beauty and emotion whispered up in me like an uncharted world. I almost laughed at how right it felt. Then I clenched him tight. Pulled at him. Rocked up and down on him. Did everything I could to feel every inch of him. Worked his nips. Bent down to kiss his face. Ran my hands along his sides and hips. Rubbed my balls against his pubes as much as I could. Every movement sent screaming lightning into every corner of my body. I touched my own nips and fire enveloped me. I ran my hands down my own thighs and came close to madness from the intensity of it. I never wanted it to end but to keep on and on and on ...

But then he began to breathe faster and groan and his tits grew hard under the play of my fingers and his moans shorter and sharper and he growled and grunted and pushed himself into me, deeper and deeper and faster and faster and harder and harder and I rode him tighter and meaner and used every muscle I had in my ass to pull at him and roll him around in me as I caressed my own nips and thighs and humped him faster and faster until he grunted and bucked and —

He fired into me.

I felt him shoot into me.

Son-of-a-bitch, I felt him.

His first shot was sharp and full and made me gasp at how strong it was. I kept working him and working him, tighter and tighter, draining him until he was whimpering and trying to twist away and I started to lie down on him, my brain a blank, but my dick was so needy and ready and primed just that hint of brushing it along the hair on his belly made me jolt up and explode. I didn't even need to touch myself with my own hands; my orgasm was spontaneous and mind-blowing and screaming through me as my cum shot over his chest and onto his face, over and over, and I cried out and I couldn't stop it and in seconds I was shivering and groaning and I ... I seriously think I went crazy for a moment.

When I finally finished, I wilted down to lay my chest against his, my ass still gripping his softening dick. My right cheek pressed against the stickiness on his right cheek. I couldn't move, it was so beautiful. I hadn't cum like that in years. Hell, maybe ever. There was not one fiber of my being that didn't tingle. My hands trembled. Even my breath was ragged. I was too weak to move; all I could do was close my eyes and whimper and hold him tight against me.

****

I don't know how long I stayed like that before I was able to make myself rise, slow and in stages, then stand up like someone drunk or stoned. I looked around, lost, then down at him. My cum was smeared into his chest hairs and his cheek and chin. Confusion and shock filled his eyes. His dick gleamed from his semen. His thighs were spread just enough to let his balls drop and his torso curved just a little and — and the whole image grabbed me so right I fumbled for my phone and took yet another photo of him. And another. And another. And another. From every angle I could think of.

Then finally I stopped, drunk on the images of him, then used my briefs to wipe myself off, my hands back to shaking.

I knelt beside him. He wouldn't look at me. I rolled him onto his stomach. Pulled the hoody up and away to reveal the whole of his elegant back. There were three Japanese characters in a column down his spine. A perfect line that looked just right. I ran my hands down them then shifted the remains of his briefs away from his ass. Oh my God, it was so lovely. The skin so smooth and clean. So perfect even with the dimples of soft scars on his right one. I caressed it. Kissed it. Slipped my fingers along his crack, making him squirm. Lay my face against it. Heaven's pillow. But did nothing more. Something within me refused to even consider violating this exquisite part of him, as if it would be a desecration of what we'd just experienced.

He finally twisted around to look at me, his eyes hurt and wary. I think he suspected I still meant to make use of his perfect ass so now he was waiting to see just how much of a father-fucker I'd be. And the truth was, up until now once I'd fucked the target of my inner-beast I'd just wiped myself off and left. So I couldn't understand why I'd set out to own this man but wound up being owned by him. I felt — shit, I felt close to him. Felt tame and at rest. The beast was curled up and sleeping — and something in me said it wouldn't reawake. My soul had shifted a little, which scared me.

And brought me nirvana.

I looked back at him, my cheek still against his butt, and stroked his smooth skin. My voice shook as I said, "I'm not gonna. I'm not. You were perfect. You were — all I needed and — and — "

I began to weep. I couldn't stop myself. Everything just exploded over me like this had been a religious experience and the only sacrifice that seemed appropriate for the moment was my tears. Through them I could see him frown at me, even more confused.

I didn't blame him.

I made myself rise to get dressed ... but I had to make

myself remember what comes after what. Pants, first — no, briefs. Wait, not the briefs; they go in your briefcase. Ha, briefs in my briefcase. And with his still wrapped around his right leg. His right hip. His. Already torn. He can't use them, anymore. Did I want them?

Yes.

I knelt beside him, again, and tore his briefs completely away. He clenched and jolted but he couldn't do more. I ran my hand over his exquisite ass one last time and kept weeping as I slipped both his and my underwear into the briefcase. I made myself pull on my socks then rose to button my shirt. Oh, and shoes. Good idea to wear your shoes. My tie and suit coat joined the briefs.

I didn't look at him again till I was done and in better control of myself. He hadn't moved. His eyes were focused on a dirty blank wall. I knelt down, rolled him onto his back, sat him up and tried to pull the hoodie back down over his shoulders, but it had also torn and was ruined. Damn, probably the only clothes he had to work in. Then his cell phone fell out of the hoodie's pocket. It was smashed and turned off. I started to weep, again.

"I'm sorry. Didn't mean to do that. I'm so sorry."

He didn't respond. I looked at his face. He had a thousand yard stare going on. Probably in shock. That hurt me.

"What's your name?" I gulped.

Still no response.

Of course. He was still gagged.

Idiot.

I dug his wallet from his pants. It had a UK Driving License in it with his photo. Reginald Brewster Thornton of Twickenham. Twenty-six years old. Born September third. There was also a photo of a pretty English girl and four young children, the oldest maybe six. The only other things in it were an Oyster card, an ATM card and some pound coins in the pocket. I pulled six fifty-pound notes from my wallet and stuffed them into his.

"I — I hope this will help replace everything." I leaned

him forward and used my nail clipper to cut a bit of the tape around his wrists. "Now you can get free. Once I'm gone."

At least that made him look at me. His expression was so lost and childlike I straddled his lap and held him close, tender, like a lover. I nestled my face against the right side of his neck and drew in a deep breath of his scent. Nothing foul or unwashed but manly and human, and to add to my confusion I whispered to him, "I know you're straight. And I'm sure this is freaking you out. But we don't have as much control over our dicks as we think. A guy can get any man to have an erection and ejaculate, no matter how into girls he is. It's a physiological reaction, that's all. Don't let yourself get lost in confusion. Please. I only needed one thing from you. And I took it. And I — I mean it. Don't let it become anything more than that."

He gave a vague sigh.

God, I did not want to leave. I wanted to keep him with me. My fingers ached to dance through the hair on his chest and belly down to his groin. My lips screamed to brush over that creamy skin. I wanted to remove the gag and kiss him, deep and with meaning and be with him like this, forever. But it wasn't possible.

It was nuts to even think it. Hell, maybe I *was* fucking crazy.

I held him for a few more minutes, breathing him in, feeling the strength in him, loving that he had owned me for these few minutes, then made myself get to my feet, grab my briefcase and leave — letting the door remain open as I went.

I vaguely remember some kind of commotion on the streets. Blue lights flashing by. Sirens wailing. People watching and talking. I pretended to pay attention ... but in reality I ignored it all.

I'm not sure how I made it back to my hotel. I must have got back on the underground and got off at Hatton Cross and walked, it's so close to the station, but I don't remember doing it. My mind was lost in trying to figure out why I'd never felt this kind of connection with my previous conquests. Why I'd been so shattered by it. I looked at the photos on my phone. Okay, he was definitely good-looking but not what I would have called male model perfect or even godlike in any way before this. And yet ... he was beauty personified. I ached for him. And for the first time I was both happy with what I'd done and horrified by it, if that can make any sense. I mean it, the encounter had been exactly what I'd dreamed about and given me absolutely everything I'd wanted and I was overjoyed about it, but I was also deeply ashamed that I'd forced him to participate.

I didn't undress. I just flopped on my bed and fought to keep his scent on me. I savored his sweat and the awareness that his cum was still in me. I draped his briefs over my lips. Held my phone over my heart. More than once I came close to returning to that house to see if he was still there. See if we could repeat what had happened. I don't think I slept; just wandered in and out of a lonely dozing haze.

I was back in control by dawn — which was well past seven. The chaos gone in my head. Feeling more refreshed than I had any right to. Ready to face anything. Since my plane wasn't till one, I set my photos to downloading into my laptop and took a long leisurely dump followed by just as leisurely a shower. And as I washed my crotch I smiled in remembrance of caressing him there. And when I washed my ass my heart jumped at the thought of him having been inside me.

Which still amazed me.

I wasn't hungry till I remembered I'd skipped dinner, so I paid a ridiculous price for an English breakfast and two cups of coffee and checked out. Since I'd already turned in my rental car I had the hotel call a taxi; I didn't have time to mess with making sure I got the right underground train to my terminal. A black car zoomed right up and I slung my bags in and followed it without a thought, saying, "Heathrow. Two."

Then a pair of rough no-nonsense men in suits piled in with me, one on my left, one on my right.

"Wait, this cab's — " was all I got out before the chubby guy to my right held up a police ID.

"Robert Devlin Pope?" he asked, obviously knowing damn well who I was.

Before I had a chance to do or say anything a third man sat in the front passenger seat and looked back at me. It was my underground guy, dressed in crisp navy slacks, black Polo shirt and a fake black leather windbreaker, looking a thousand times better than I remembered. My heart exploded with joy ... until I realized his eyes were hard, cold and touched with hate as he said, "That's 'im."

And my world froze.

TWO

I was driven to the back of an ugly modern building a few miles from the hotel; yanked out of the car; stripped of my luggage, wallet, phone and passport; and slung into a brutally white interrogation room that held nothing but a table, four chairs and the inevitable two-way mirror-window that fooled no one, anymore. Then I was left alone to contemplate my fate for a solid three hours under lighting that was harsher than hell.

Needless to say...I missed my flight.

But the worst part was — Mr. Reginald Brewster Thornton refused to look at me, again. He just got out and walked away the second the car stopped. Watching him go nearly tore me in half.

And finally let my brain shut down my dick and catch up to reality.

Reg was a cop.

A fucking undercover cop.

I fucking hated cops.

The guys who almost caught us, last night, had appeared fast, like they were waiting for a signal and thought it had come but figured they they'd gone to the wrong location.

And had even referred to him as Reg.

"But that don't fit what Reg said ... "

"Maybe Reg did make it down the Center."

Reg.

"Bugger, I'd 'ate to be him, right now."

Shit.

And what about that hint something was going on between him and Savile Row? Is that what clued me in, maybe subconsciously, and got me locked on getting to him? But then why was I hurt at what I'd done and reveling in the memory of him and — and son-of-a-bitch, why didn't I make the connection till now?

Jesus Christ, did I hate cops. Fucking despised them. Have since I saw how they'd take the side of my Dad whenever he beat my Mom, me and Colin.

"What'd you say to make him so mad?"

"Can't you be more careful about your words?"

"Y'know, if you were good boys, this wouldn't happen."

Same for the fucking priests who'd come by. They'd give dad a joke of a warning and go on their merry way, then Colin and I would stay home from school till the bruises and busted lips were healed while mom just never went out unless she had to ... like for groceries or dental appointments.

She vanished when I was eight. Saw me off to school one morning and when I came home, she was gone — along with all of her clothes. My father filed a police report, but even at that age I knew they wouldn't look into it. They'd been called to the house too damn many times and done nothing to change things. I found out later that my not-so-stupid father had made some very nice donations to their pension fund and the church coffers and they didn't want to kill the golden goose.

Motherfuckers.

So sure enough they shrugged it off by deciding mom had abandoned both me and my brother to my father's lack of mercy. Even chuckled about *crazy bitches*. Meanwhile I was sitting in a corner wondering what dad did with her body and Colin was standing by the front door, staring outside, silent.

I made Colin spend the night with me at a neighbor's then forced him to share my room for nearly a year. He never caught on that I'd wait till he was asleep before I'd slip over to the bedroom door and pile my toys in front of it so if dad did come in angry and needing to beat someone up we'd hear him and would have a decent chance of waking and avoiding him. Didn't do much good; he just started drinking in the afternoon and would fire up before our bedtime. Colin got the worst of it, but the only thing I was completely spared from was anybody giving a damn about what was happening.

Since then I'd made it a point to stay the hell away from cops. If I had a problem I'd take care of it, myself. Or have it *taken care of*. I'm half-Italian and from Brooklyn; I *know people who know people*. But I also thought I was sharp enough to smell *cop* on any guy, no matter how good-looking they were.

So why hadn't I seen that on Thornton? Had my inner beast been so focused on its meat it ignored the signs? Were British cops all that different from American ones? Of course he didn't have a badge or policeman's ID on him so maybe he wasn't with the Met ... but no, it was too obvious he was, now. Hell, it was obvious that those texts were probably to his superiors to let them know something about —

About me?

Were they targeting me?

No, that didn't make sense. I wasn't under arrest — I mean, not like how it goes in the US. Read you your rights and book you and all that. No mug shot or fingerprints or demand for information or anything. Plus he got on the tube at the station after me, so unless someone was tailing me and handed me over to him it was too much of a chance encounter. And he didn't start getting tense with his texting till Hammersmith, long after Savile Row got on. So was he waiting for someone else? Waiting for a contact and he'd seen the guy and I'd screwed everything up by being so focused on him? Was Savile Row his guy? Did he think I'd made him as a cop? That I was working with the guy? Had I ruined some secret drug operation or sting or whatever they call it in the UK? Damn, if I had I was deep in it because no matter what country you're in cops do not like you to mess with their fun and games.

Jesus Christ, what a stupid, stupid, stupid fuckin' move

I'd made. And I wouldn't be able to lie the situation away; no matter what I swore or claimed, he'd be believed.

Well ... there was nothing I could do about it till someone came in to try and make me make un-lapse my Catholicism and do the *Bless me father* crap, so I waited and had a nice long bout of calling myself a fucking idiot. Then I calmed down enough to remember that if this was just in regards to our sexual encounter it would be a case of his word against mine. I hadn't fucked him, thank God. In fact I'd insist they check his ass to prove he had *not* been violated, then I'd harp on how it'd just been some kinky fun and games and all I'd done was given him a blow job. The bondage and torn shirt were just a part of it all; that's why he'd worn some old ratty things. Even if they didn't believe a word out of my mouth, that would throw a curve to any prosecutor thinking he or she could make a name off me.

The more I thought about it the more I figured all I'd get is yelled at and they'd keep quiet about what he'd done with me. Cops don't like to be seen as incompetent or stupid or weak enough to be taken advantage of. It might take time to calm them down but I was fairly certain I'd get released.

Except — I'd taken those fucking photos of him bound and gagged and exposed. And they had my phone. My fucking phone. The security on it wasn't all that great so they'd be able to break in. Shit. That gave them proof of kidnapping! Okay, that could even mean a trial. I might still get off but it would be difficult and damned expensive, something we did *not* need.

Oh, we were making it okay, even with all of the economic gains going to the rich. Maybe even because of it. My company makes silver or gold plated pins with colorful inlays to cover any situation, fit any company logo. We worked with your design, whatever you needed. The company was founded by my father thirty years ago and Colin and I took over after he died. We didn't sell direct to the public; we facilitated the manufacturing of the pins for a network of dealers who offered our product to their clients. That's why I was in the UK — to meet with our dealers here and offer our services to a few others, see if Brexit was causing us much damage. Instead I found it had helped our business because the one-percenters were hoarding their cash like Scrooge McDuck instead of letting their employees have it. Now they just handed out little symbols of thanks for their good work as opposed to actual money.

Typical cheap-assed rich scum who think a nice token of gratitude was better than a check.

I'd been en route back to my hotel after a long meeting with our best dealer, Ghadir Baranzi, in Canary Wharf. Him, I'd saved for last ... half because he was our best dealer and half because he has a son who is to die for — Jamil, black eyes, black hair everywhere it counts, olive skin, trim but not skinny with a smile to promise heaven. The three of us had an all-afternoon meeting of too much wine and too little food, so when I headed for the underground I was more than a little tipsy.

Perfect time for the world to slap me around, because just as I reached the station I got a phone call from the States with news about my mother. They thought they'd found her body and wanted me or Colin to come in for verification. Twenty-two years after she vanished. Twenty-two years to get used to not thinking about her and BAM! It shook me up, so I'd hit a pub and had a couple more drinks and ... and I'd fuckin' lost control.

In England, of all fucking places!

In New York I had a damn good lawyer who could muddy the water so much I'd never see a day in jail — unless I killed somebody and only idiots commit murder. Hamilton Larrimore; he'd already saved my ass once against a motherfucking cop in Chicago who'd come after me after I'd had some fun and games with his ass ... and dick and mouth and everything in-between. But Hamilton was in New York and I was in England so I was screwed until I found a London counselor to fight and snarl for me just as viciously as he could. Only they had this weird system of solicitors and barristers that I didn't even try to understand since I'd never had to make use of it, meaning it was probably double charges for everything.

Shit.

What's funny is how calm I was in the face of this annihilation, like a panther lying in the brush waiting to see if the creature approaching it is to be feared, feasted on, attacked or ignored. No turmoil in my gut. No nibbling of nails. No nervous ticks. No, I was as cool as ice.

And ready to run the second I could.

****

Just after the beginning of my fourth hour in that pitiless room an older man entered, tall, brisk and efficient, his uniform as impeccable as his posture. His cap and coat were littered with insignia, meaning he was high-ranking and had a big dick, and he planned to smack me around with it. Normally I'd say, *Fine, motherfucker, bring it on*, only this man's eyes gleamed not only with intelligence but anger, which strongly indicated this was war.

He was joined by that pudgy cop who'd busted me. His hair had gone floppy but his clothes were still neat. His piggy eyes and chubby cheeks made him too damn typical an English lad for me to take any real notice of because he was lowest of the low. Just someone to carry Mr. Insignia's folders. Now he was here to listen in and back Mr. Insignia up in court, as needed. To say this did not bode well would be an understatement.

They took seats opposite me and set two folders on the table. No tape recorder. No note pads. Nothing.

"So," Mr. Insignia spit out in his upper-crust manner, "Robert Devlin Pope. Junior. It's unusual for the second son to be named after the father."

I shot back with, "I need to take a piss."

He eyed me for a long moment then pulled a photograph from one of the folders and set it on the table. It was of a man's face twisted in agony, eyes half closed, mouth drawn tight. A wire cut into his throat. Blood trailed around it and more blood foamed at his lips. I jolted despite my plan to play Brooklyn Bad-Ass because for a second I thought it was Reg, he looked so much like him.

"This happened last night," Insignia said, his voice vicious in its cold hollowness. "Martin Perriman. Married. Two children. A business in Feltham near your hotel. He was raped and stabbed several times in the back as well as being garroted. Was your assault on my constable to help with his murder?"

I was too locked on the horror of the photo to even think of a word to say.

He took in an irritated sigh then slapped my cell phone on the table and pointed at the image of Reg bound and gagged on the floor, my semen gleaming on him. "Explain how you knew this man was a constable. How did you know he was on surveillance? How did you know we had this operation underway? Do you have a contact in our office who's feeding you information? If so, what is his name? How long have you been working in tandem with the killer? Was that your plan — to create a citywide diversion so your *other half* could have fun at his leisure?"

I looked at the image of Reg, again. I still couldn't think of anything to say.

"Robert, answer my questions!"

Him using my first name was like ice water slapping into my face. "I ... I ... I don't answer to ... to Robert," whispered from me, like an afterthought. "It's Devlin."

His voice grew even harsher, if that was possible. "How did you know about Thornton!?"

My brain was about to run screaming from the overload of realization. I had to close my eyes to even manage to croak, "I want to speak to someone from the American embassy."

"Of course you do." His voice dripped with flat-out hate.

That made me look at him. He was pure stone. "Lawyer?"

"No."

"Isn't that illegal?"

"Depends on whom you ask. But since you are not under

detention the point is moot."

"So I'm free to go?"

"No."

My heart just about stopped. "You got a Guantanamo Bay, too?"

"We have no need for one."

"You just gonna throw me in jail?"

"No. You will remain in this room until you answer my questions to my satisfaction."

"So you can fuck me over with them? Why should I?"

Mr. Insignia calmly opened one of the folders and laid out three more crime-scene photos of what used to be fair-haired men. Guys who could have been brothers to Reg. All killed in the same way, their faces showing different levels of agony. Eyes open. Blood on their lips. I cringed.

He pointed to the first one. "Etan Conescieu, twenty-one. He worked in catering and attended computer classes. His wife just had their first child, back in Romania. This one was Liam Hanlon, twenty-eight, from Belfast. He worked in The City. Investments. Divorced with two children, another en route with his girlfriend. This was Stuart Goughan, thirty-five, born and raised in Ruislip. He was a livery driver, married three months, only. His second, her first. One child by his previous wife. And now we have number four, thanks to you, and six children without a father, soon to be seven. Fortunately, we also have you."

He made a mistake showing me those pictures because they had dates on them that showed they had all happened within the last two months. That poked my inner beast so I sat up as straight and cold and hard as Mr. Insignia and snarled, "I haven't been in England for six months and I've only been here a week. What the fuck're you up to?"

Normally going on the offensive with a Brooklyn attitude makes your opponent take pause to regroup. Mr. Insignia didn't even tighten his jaw as he said, "Do you really not understand what has happened, here?" I didn't answer so he made the obvious assumption. "Well it's my mistake for assuming you capable of rational thought. And since I haven't time to play your childish game, I shall lay it out in detail.

"Prior to yesterday evening we had three men murdered in the same manner. They look somewhat alike and all are or were married, with children, but the only direct links between the three are the manner of their death and that each rode the same route on the underground at one time or another.

"Then we found another connection between the deaths and initiated surveillance in hopes of catching this killer before he struck, again. Well ... last night Constable Thornton noticed you held a great deal of interest in him so led you off the train, but then you both vanished and the GPS application in his phone ceased to work. This put the entire Metropolitan police force onto alert, focused on East Hounslow. It was while we were distracted that Perriman was murdered. Close to your hotel. Shortly afterwards, Constable Thornton was released unharmed except for torn clothing, bruises around his neck, wrists and ankles ... and your semen on his body."

"How d'you know it's mine?"

"Your suitcase contains a pair of torn underwear identified by Thornton as being his. Do you insist those are not your ejaculatory fluids on them, as well?"

Man — there was nothing I could say against that.

Insignia nodded and continued in his cold, hollow voice, "I'm sure you understand why I do not even begin to believe these two events are not directly related."

The smart thing to do would have been to shut the fuck up, but mental and emotional chaos took control so I said, "There's nothing in the news about a serial killer."

"We'd been able to keep it quiet — until last night, thank you very much. Now the bloody press thinks they have another Stephen Port situation, so we must inform the public of how these unfortunate men met their deaths. Publicity which will cause even more distress to their families. We must also find a viable excuse for our racing about East Hounslow at the same time as the latest murder, one that preferably does not include Constable Thornton because those bloody hyenas would tear him to shreds if they caught one hint of this. So I want you to explain to me what part you played in this diseased adventure before I face them."

Instinct finally caught up with my mouth and shut it, solid. I just leaned back and stopped looking at either man. No matter what I said it wouldn't make any difference.

Mr. Insignia eyed me. "We have CCTV cameras throughout England. You also use an Oyster card to travel the underground. You've had the same one for quite some time and you always top it up with your American Express. Now that we have that account number we will be able to work out every movement you've made in the UK for the last five years. And trust me ... if there is any situation in the areas you've been to that is even remotely similar to what's happened here, you will be held responsible for it. You can make things a great deal simpler for yourself if you just answer me one question. If it's satisfactory, it might even assist you in proving to me that your meddling was *not* a deliberate attempt to help cause Perriman's death." I looked at him. He almost smiled as he asked, "So ... why did you choose Constable Thornton?"

I didn't move. I learned a long time ago when not to trust someone. Learned the hard way by getting fucked over not just by Dad but by people I'd been willing to think were on my side, and this bastard was anything but.

He must have seen it in my face because he filled his voice with fake weariness as he said, "Mr. Pope, do you insist on suggesting that, in order to satisfy some overwhelming carnal desire, you inadvertently mucked up a police operation at the same time a serial killer decided to strike, again? Do you honestly think that is the least bit believable?"

I remained still. Then his shadow slapped another file on the table. Mr. Insignia opened it. I took in a deep breath before I let myself look at what he was looking at, expecting to see that

Chicago cop's picture.

Instead it was a photograph of a man named Griffin Faure.

Griffin fucking Faure? Shit!

He left it in the folder, once he was sure I'd seen it, and pulled out a printed e-mail then continued with, "We've been in contact with the Justice Department in America. They are aware of at least two claims of sexual assault against you, one by another police officer. Neither one taken to trial but both remarkably similar in their circumstances. They are now looking into the possibility that there may have been other victims, some perhaps even murdered. As your modus operandi has already been established imagine how it will sound when we bring it before the Crown's Bench."

He picked up the phone. Reg's photo was still on it. His voice took on a gentle measured tone as he said, "This young constable's name is Reginald Brewster Thornton, formerly of Their Majesty's First Armored Division and now serving with the Metropolitan Police. He's been with us for not quite eighteen months. Has a wife and four children, two girls and two boys. He will turn twenty-seven on his next birthday. We believe he has a bright future with the Met because he has shown himself to be not only intelligent and resilient but also willing to take on difficult or dangerous assignments. He even put his life on the line in our attempt to capture a serial killer after multiple attacks that are remarkably similar to what occurred here, your grace. His bravery caused him to be kidnapped, terrorized and sexually abused. He is under the care of a psychologist, and we sincerely hope he will soon be able to return to his duties and regain the path of a brilliant career." He leaned forward just a bit, his voice back to harsh and cruel. "Now do you understand what kind of trouble you are in?"

"I'm gonna spend a long time in a jail in England. Right?"

He sighed, and for the first time I started wondering what the hell he *was* talking about. "No, you will spend your time in this bloody room until I receive a satisfactory answer to my question, and you will give it to me as soon as possible so we waste no more resources than necessary on determining what sort of vile actions you've perpetrated!"

"All you wanna know is why I chose him?" He gave me a hint of a smile in answer. I took in a deep breath. Something about this was all off and my usual tactics when confronted with my ... oh, let's just say, *less than legal actions* ... weren't doing a damn thing except pissing this guy off. And as much fun as that could be, I didn't have the focus for it. That damned photo of Reg was all but screaming at me. So I let, "The tattoo on his neck," sigh out of me.

"What. Of. It?"

What of it? What of the beauty of it? The beauty of him. The chaos in my brain? The need to do something to make it quiet down? The animal in me that needed to hunt right then? To own someone? To see those tattoos closer? To try and understand why they seemed so familiar? To want hold him close? If I told this guy any of that I'd wind up in a crazy house. I had to work up a story. One I could stick with.

One the son-of-a-bitch would believe.

I finally let myself shrink a little and decided to keep close to the truth — well, as close as possible.

"I was standing," I said. "He was seated. I saw a Japanese character on his back ... his spine ... just below his neck ... in his reflection in the window. He's got a good clean neck. Smooth skin. That ink — I'm not into tattoos, really, but it — it looked right on him. Then I noticed another one below it — and I — I got fixated on getting a better look at them. See if he did them all the way down his back. So I followed him. To ask him about them. Invite him for a drink. Seduce him."

That brought a frown to Insignia's face.

I smiled and kept on with, "C'mon, you want to know how many straight men I've gotten just by talkin' to 'em? Buyin' 'em a beer? Sometimes all a guy's looking for is someone who'll listen as he vents. Couple of drinks and he's got an excuse to just

... *let things happen*." My gaze shifted to the wall behind the man. "But the way he walked. Thornton walked. The way he *looked* as he walked. Things sort of snowballed from there."

"Snowballed?" The disbelief in his voice made me look back at him. "This was not premeditated?"

"I'd never seen him before, not till I got on the subway."

"That is immaterial. You carried the means to subdue him."

It took me a moment to understand what he was referring to. "Packin' tape, that's all. I always have some with me."

"In case you wish to assault someone?"

Yes. "No. It's just somethin' I carry in my case, with my samples and other supplies. It's really useful."

He snorted. "Why not follow through with your plan to — *seduce* him?"

"He was walkin' too fast. Wasn't gonna give me time to work up a conversation."

"And you refuse to be denied, is that it?" His look of condescension was brutal.

"In this case," I said, and I made myself look him straight in the eye.

"So you claim you kidnapped and sexually abused him because of the tattoos on his back?"

He shifted the image to one of Reg face down, the tattoos visible around the shreds of his hoodie, his ass naked and so goddamn beautiful. The memory I was trying to find kicked at me, again, then flittered away.

"I didn't abuse him; I used him. I told you, it snowballed. Having him like that, I got horny so I got him to fuck me — "

"Wait — you convinced him to have anal intercourse with you?"

I couldn't tear my eyes away from the image on the phone. The memory made me weak so I dug my fingernails into my palms, sharp and painful, and forced myself to snarl, "Yeah. And I came all over him as he came in me. How you gonna explain that?"

"Why need we explain anything?" Man, not even the slightest hint of hesitation. But he'd leaned back a little, giving me just enough room to think he'd been surprised by my claim.

"Because my family knows I'm gay," I said, "and I'm on the Cloud so those images are on my desktop in New York. My disappearance is gonna cause issues with them; I'm due back for a very important meeting on Monday. They'll raise hell."

"They know of your appointment with the New Jersey State Police?"

I blinked. *He* already knew about that? Of course. They broke into my phone. Shit.

"You received a call from them just over an hour prior to Thornton's disappearance," Insignia continued, still cool, calm and collected, "so we've been in contact. They found a body in the Marshlands and think it may have something to do with a twenty-two year old missing-persons report. Concerning your mother. Was that your trigger?"

BAM! The tattoo on his back — it *was* like Mom's. On her shoulder. I saw it when I was seven, just once, when I got home from school and went to take a piss and she was soaking in the tub, half asleep and hurt, and I thought it was a bruise but it was something in Japanese or Chinese and ... and —

The beast in me howled, *We're being attacked*, and it roared up to take over. My voice dropped to a growl as I said, "You really want to know why I chose him? 'Cause I knew I could buy him. He's got three-hundred pounds in his wallet for lettin' me shoot that image — the image of a British cop with semen gleamin' on his chest, his dick out and still kind of hard and dribblin' more cum. I pay guys to let me tie 'em up and take pictures, and my brother and sister-in-law know. And that image — that'll bring 'em straight to Thornton. And you, whoever the fuck you are."

"You'd destroy this young man to protect yourself?"

"Back me into a corner, bet for trouble. And don't think

you can get rid of that picture; my IT guy can make your IT guys look like babies playing Pokemon. Then there's his wife; what's she gonna think when she finds out he fucked a man and got off on it? For money. Like a whore."

"The only semen we found was yours."

"That bullshit won't even begin to work. And my family, we know people who know people. If you pull this shit on me it's not gonna be a quiet story. So if I don't show up they'll raise hell with the State Department and — "

He cut me off with, "If your State Department and our Ministry of Justice take it upon themselves to care about the disappearance of a man who rapes men ... " He took in a deep breath and continued, " ... Well, it is our duty, of course, to make every effort in locating you or determining what caused you to vanish. But we cannot be held responsible when each avenue of investigation meets with a dead end. Can we?"

"I was arrested in front of the hotel — "

"You entered an unmarked car with some unknown men. As for this photograph, why on earth would anyone think this is one of our constables? He's not dressed as one ... though he does resemble many of our lads. Vaguely."

So that was how it was going to be, huh? He must have read that in my face, because he let his mouth grow tight and his eyes sharp as razors as he quietly said, "It would behoove you not to fuck me."

My beast growled back, "Don't worry; you're not my type."

He cast a glance at the phone and said with condescension, "Oh, I think we know your type. And I think we'll find Thornton is not even the second officer you'd done this to. Or third, or fourth." Then he and Pudgy grabbed up the folders and headed for the door.

"Hey, I still need to take a piss," I called after him.

Mr. Insignia turned to his shadow. "Bring a bedpan from the dispensary, a roll of tissue and a bottle of water."

"No bread?" I sneered.

"It's not tea time, yet."

Then they left.

Okay — no question but that I was in deeper shit than I'd ever thought possible.

THREE

I peed, drank the whole bottle of water and forced myself to sit back at the table. Finally I had something to focus on besides my situation.

They knew about Griffin Faure.

Griffin fucking Faure. A self-indulgent Upper East Side asshole who figured, *Hey, life's easy for me, so it must be for everybody.* And daddy being worth billions thanks to his sleazy real estate work — and having installed Griffin, his brother and his sister behind fine desks in a private office in his eighty-story headquarters in uptown Manhattan — was beside the point. He honestly thought that was normal. Same for wearing ten-thousand dollar suits, working out with a personal trainer before he hit the office, going to all the right clubs and restaurants and being lusted after by every avaricious bimbo there was — half because he was divorced and they thought he was richer than Solomon, and half because ... well ... he wasn't too bad-looking. Dark hair, sharp eyes and kissable lips, but atop a weak chin and short neck. Still if I'd run into him at some super-chic club I might have tried my song-and-dance, maybe even done a roofie on him just to get his ass.

Except I hated that fucking ass. Despised it. Loathed it. You name it.

He'd set up a huge conference in Dubai to trumpet daddy's move into oil; one of those *Spare No Expense* things meant to impress rich low-class idiots into investing. Part of the package was a lapel pin of the company logo, two-hundred-and fifty of them, 18 karat gold (not plated) with a sapphire stone in a curling part of the F and each with its own silk-lined jewel box. Meaning NOT cheap to make.

Dad had checked with Mr. Mihn to see if it was feasible — he owns the factory in Thailand that we use to make the pins — and he'd said, *Yes*. Dad also discussed it with Ghadir, who'd filled him in on the kind of jewelry people in the Middle East would go for, hence the sapphire stone. Our cost would be over three hundred thousand bucks, so our bid was five hundred thousand, with Dad making it clear we'd require fifty percent of the estimate up front. We got the order.

But Dad died before the deposit was arranged.

A couple of big dealers who were his buddies stopped using us when that happened so this job became make it or break it for the company. Then ten days after Dad was in the ground and a week after his Will had entered into probate, Griffin Faure met with Colin and said he'd pull the order if we insisted on the full deposit. The pins were already in the process of being made in order to meet the deadline, so Colin caved and let him put up ten percent.

He didn't tell anyone, not even his wife, Diana; he figured once the pins came in we'd hold onto them until the invoice was paid. He didn't expect Faure to bribe our shipping manager to ship them soon as they arrived, before we'd even been able to do a quality check. By the time we realized what happened, Faure was saying they were bad quality but offered no proof of defect and ignored the contract he'd signed.

We sic'd Hamilton on him and learned this was part of Faure's negotiation process — *Don't pay till they sue you then make a settlement offer in exchange for not letting this drag on through the court system.* The implication being it would take years. Faure's offer? An additional fifty thousand.

Mr. Mihn was holding back on our other orders because he needed to be paid and US Customs wanted the duty due on the shipment or they were going to kill our bond, so Colin suggested we agree to the settlement, thinking a bank loan with it would tide us over till dad's insurance paid. But I was pissed as hell at what Faure had pulled, so even though I was still in college I was also half-owner of the business and I flat out refused.

Hamilton arranged for a meeting Faure and the little prick's five attorneys — four male, one female; we left Colin out because he was pretty shaken up by it all. We faced off in their cheesy-ass gold-plated conference room and the second introductions were done — and they'd stopped snickering at how *some kid was there to negotiate with them* — I looked Faure straight in his black condescending eyes, dove into my harshest Brooklyn and said, "Pay the contract in full, right now, or we go after you in court, plus damages."

The little bitch didn't even have the balls to respond to me. The attack dog to his left said, "That could take years to settle and — "

"Fine," I shot back. "Choice is yours."

"Hamilton," said the smirky attack dog on Faure's right, "shouldn't you be handling these negotiations? Young Mr. Pope doesn't seem to understand the delicacy involved in this."

"Fuck you, bitch," shot out of me before Hamilton could even let a smile cross his face ... and did that send a ripple around the room. Even the female attack dog got her back up. "I told you what your choices were — you pay what you agreed to or we go to court, and once that happens no more negotiation. It'll be all or nothin' at all, plus damages."

The female popped in with, "For substandard quality?"

"Fine, send 'em back. I can melt 'em down, sell the sapphire stones and recoup some of our costs."

"But your company is not in a position to make a demand of that nature — "

I asked Hamilton, "When does that conference start?"

He smiled as he said, "Two weeks."

"It true the pins're already couriered to the participants?"

"That's my understanding."

I shifted my eyes straight to Faure's. "Then you really

wanna use that tactic? We provided you with substandard items but you sent them to potential partners, anyway? Really?"

I finally saw some human emotion in those soulless black pupils ... and it wasn't love. "We had a real jeweler correct the issues."

I shook my head. "Those pins have our seven-fifty stamp on 'em, so no matter what, they're ours. You tell people we crapped it up, we go after you for libel."

"I think I may let your company shut down."

I shrugged in answer. "That'll help us in court."

The dog to his left leaned in to whisper something. Faure nodded, in response. Then the mongrel straightened up and said, "Seventy-five thousand — in your bank by tomorrow morning."

I shook my head. "You owe us four-hundred-and-fifty-thousand."

"Which we will not pay." And I could tell he meant it. They all did.

Hamilton leaned in at that point and said, "Make it two-fifty, so my client can at least recoup their costs."

The woman piped in with, "It's not our fault you spent too much to make the pins."

"Specs agreed to, lady," I snapped back at her.

And the mongrel growled, "One-twenty-five."

"One-seventy-five," Hamilton shot back, and the look on his face screamed, *Don't push it.*

Faure gave the slightest of nods and the mongrel said, "Deal."

That's when I jumped in with, "But if it's not in our bank account by 4:55 today, deal's off. Okay for that, Hamilton?"

He nodded. "Someone will be at the courthouse ready to file the papers."

They paid at 4:56, just as Hamilton was calling his clerk to tell him to go ahead.

That took care of a lot of the trouble but we still had seventy-five thousand in bills and our bastard bank wouldn't extend us credit. We would have done a crash and burn anyway if I hadn't postponed grad school for a couple years and let the company use my half of dad's insurance to keep the cash flowing. Money that would've paid for grad school. It gave us space to work our way back up to solvency and I made damn sure some of our extra bucks from then on went into Treasuries — no return but good collateral on a loan. Plus we never took another job without enough of a deposit to cover our costs. I also shifted us out of that fucking bank and into a credit union, which pissed off our bookkeeper/receptionist, Marci, but I didn't care.

Of course, Colin felt responsible but I did *not* blame him for this. He'd enjoyed dad's slaps and fists two years longer than me and they'd left their mark. Not just in emotional scars but physiological ones. He would get blinding headaches that put him on the floor and had trouble remembering things clients told him or appointments that had to be kept. On top of that his mood could do a one-eighty like you would not believe, sometimes even in mid-sentence. After a dozen doctors told him he was just overworked or too stressed out or eating the wrong food or just imagining it, Diana forced through an MRI. That showed lesions on part of his brain. Which gave them a clue as to how to treat it ... which was basically to leave it alone and suggest he see a therapist on how to control the symptoms better. Diana hooked him up with a guy who worked with people suffering from PTSD and he was finally on the road to actually seeming recovered.

No, it was Griffin Faure I held responsible, because he either knew about Colin's issues or sensed it and used it to his advantage. Apparently destroying my brother meant nothing to him. For months after the debacle it took a lot of work by Diana and me to keep Colin from doing a dive off the GW Bridge when he got down, and I loathed every ounce of Faure's being for it.

But it didn't come to a head till about two years after. I'd just reworked one of Colin's pin orders for the factory when he came in and sat on the floor behind my desk, his back against the wall. He was weaving and breathing hard and his hands were clenching each other. I stopped work and let him take his time to speak.

"You'll need to call Ghadir," he finally said, his voice thin as tissue paper.

I nodded. "Okay."

"I — I called him a fuckin' raghead. I can't believe I did that."

"Considering he's a Persian Jew ... "

"Yeah. Yeah." He finally sighed and said, "I'm never gonna be whole, am I? I'll never be complete. I keep screwing things up. Like that thing with Faure — I nearly killed us."

I took in a deep breath and said, "Colin, considering what you've been through, you're doin' great," as I hit a button on the intercom — my warning signal to Marci to get hold of Diana. Then I sat on the floor with him. "We got robbed by a thief. Not your fault. Dad's the one who set us up with that prick, not you. Faure would've pulled the same shit on him."

"Don't bet on it. Remember what dad always said?"

"I try not to."

He almost smiled. "He said not to put your eggs into one basket, *all* your eggs in one basket ... but that's what I did."

"Um, I don't think that's the right saying for this."

"Doesn't matter. I killed your school fund — "

"Colin, I got four more years to finish my masters and no idea what I'm gonna do my thesis on, yet. Workin' here gives me real-world experience, a chance to think about it and — "

"You sound like a fuckin' college brochure!" he snapped.

I put an arm across his shoulders. "Y'know, I wouldn't sound like anything if it wasn't for you."

" ... You ... you were always gonna do fine ... "

"No, I'd probably be dead or in jail or a junkie. You got between me and Dad a few too many times for your own good but it protected me and I love you for it, bro'. Now look at what we know. Dad ... he damaged you like — like a car's damaged when it's broadsided or a boat'll sink if it's got a hole that isn't fixed.

Griffin fucking Faure used that against us. He belongs in jail like any thief. Once you're fixed up you'll see that."

He didn't move for a few moments then he whispered, "What if we can't fix me? What if I'm always a drain on you?"

"You think Diana'll let that happen?"

He looked at me, almost smiling, again. "I got lucky with her, didn't I?"

"No shit. If I wasn't all about dicks I'd take her away from you."

"Shit, you gotta talk about that?!"

"I am what I am."

He nodded, fighting himself. "More'n I ever will be."

"Diana won't let that happen."

He looked at me, near tears. "Why does she put up with me?"

"I hear she loves you."

He rested his head against his knees and choked out, "God, I want be right for her. I want to be a man for her ... "

I pulled him tight to me and said, "Colin, you got another kid on the way. I think you've been a man with her."

He just started to sob. We sat like that till Diana arrived and guided him back to his feet and into his office.

I didn't get up. If I had, I'd have stormed out, tracked Griffin Faure down and broken his fucking neck. He damn near crushed us so he could buy himself a new car or a second house or a thousand dollar bottle of wine. So what if it drove a man to lose his mind or take his life? All that mattered to that motherfucker was his own happiness and I hated him so goddamn much, right then, it scared even me.

So I sat in that corner for at least an hour before I had control enough to stand and go to my computer and open the Faure Companies folder in our archives. The beast inside me roared as it sensed a hunt aimed at having a cruel casual form of revenge to bring that whole fucking family to justice.

Starting with motherfucking Griffin Faure.

****

We already had the company specifics and details of Faure's involvement in them but I needed information that was not ... oh, let's just say not *business oriented.*

I started by flirting with an older woman I knew at the Hall of Records, who had access to notices of complaints against The Faure Group — even the ones that had been sealed. I'd gone to school with her son and was half her age but she had a thing for me and I played it. She wouldn't get me copies of the actual files, but I did find out that we were one of dozens of small businesses that had done work for the Faure family and been forced to accept partial payment on contracted deals. All I needed was their names ... which she gave me for dinner, a decent wine, a couple of long slow kisses, some grabbing of my ass ... and a dozen selfies she *snuck of me* as I lounged on her bed and slipped into the bathroom, naked, to prove to her girlfriends she *still had it in her.*

I *think* the pun was intended.

Then just to cover my ass I *sounded out* Hamilton about going after Griffin *through the courts* for the rest of the money we were owed *since the statute of limitations was approaching.* He knew the world the little asshole came from and told me that it would cost more to sue him than the losses were and there was little guarantee we'd see the money or even get legal expenses.

"You've met the assholes who represent him," he said. "And they will be assholes more from pride than legal reason. They will tie us up in court for the next ten years just to prove we have no right to even think of justice against *America's Gods of Enterprise.*"

I'd *sighed and agreed*, said we'd have to chalk it up to bad luck and did it all with a tear in my eye so he'd think I'd given up. I also told him Colin's health was our main concern now. No need to let him even begin to suspect my real goal.

Something the *Gods of Enterprise* fail to understand is,

like I said, when you're dealing with someone from Brooklyn you should assume they know people who know people. Which I did. I got hold of a friend from high school — Rio, not his real name, of course. I filled him in, gave him the names I had and in the space of three days he gave me not only the full story on over two-dozen local businesses that had been taken by The Faure Group, I had Little-Sir-Asshole's life jotted down to the minute. Seems he'd recently done a few beloved grandparents and uncles the same way as us and the current discussion was over whether to break the little shit's legs, arms or back. I asked Rio to let them know they needn't get their hands dirty. He came back with their response — I had two weeks.

Then he added, "I know some guys'll help ya."

I barely kept the surprise out of my voice. "You don't know what I'm plannin' ... hell, even I don't know yet."

"Bullshit, Dev. I know who you are an' I read all the info. I can see which part you honed in on. These guys'd ... oooooooh, they'll fall in line with what I'm pretty fuckin' sure you're plannin'. They're professionals."

"I'm not killin' the little fuck! Only idiots do — "

"I know that! Shit, gimme some fuckin' credit. I also know about some shit you pulled in your fancy-ass college ... "

"You only think you know — "

"Don't bullshit me!"

"Okay, okay, okay, okay, you know what you know. Is this a choice?"

"Meet with 'em and decide," he said. "An' you lay down the boundaries." But the look in his eyes was, *You want my help, you accept theirs*.

That's the only downside of *knowing somebody* — there's always a price tag.

So I met with the guys at a leather bar in The Village — three men aged 21, 34 and 45 who were so big, bad, butch and buff I felt like a fat-ass dork next to them. Piercings and tattoos everywhere I could see, hair cropped short, showing off the kind of leather and latex that was barely legal on the street but which each of them filled in just the right way, and with smiles that would scare a hyena. Oh ... and they had a porn company in an old house in West Nyack. One I'd heard of.

I felt like I was meeting celebrities.

Still, the second I saw them I had to fight a laugh because they all had mustaches. In fact I nicknamed them after their level of mustache — young was Neat, middle was Thick, and the old guy was Walrus.

Thick took a serious liking to me. Sat close enough to touch me whenever he could, his hands drifting here and there and everywhere like he was testing me, and he never took his eyes off me. I let him do it, even built up a nice boner for him to *accidentally* caress, bringing a nearly tender smile to his lean face ... for an instant. What made it fun was I liked him enough to think he might be fun for a future session, especially since I figured he was a total bottom-pig.

(FYI — I was right.)

Neat and Walrus noticed and seemed a bit put out. Maybe they thought I'd be their next puppy, I dunno, but they were made happy when I told them who our target was; they knew one of Faure's victims, too. They suggested use of their basement but it was too far to drive and I didn't want anything that could be easily connected to them. The rest of what they brought to the table was more than acceptable, including wearing masks so he couldn't identify them, but I did put up three limitations: no marks on Faure, no drugs in him and no tearing of his clothes. They agreed and we worked up both a deal and an outline for immediate action.

First course of action was to find out where he planned to be that weekend. Cross-referencing by Rio and his friends' friends' friends took us to Le Francoeur, a French restaurant off Fifth near Central Park where he had dinner reservations for Friday night. Eight pm. For two. Saturday and Sunday he was slated to be at daddy's place in the Hamptons, so Le Francoeur it was.

The info included the glorious detail that he was dating a

certain supermodel so he'd be all about projecting a Joe Cool image the whole evening — well, as Joe Cool as a divorced thirty-five year-old asshole can be. He also had a couple of bodyguards, which needed to be taken into consideration. But I figured the focus of attention would be on Little Miss Swizzle-Stick and that helped me figure out just what to do.

Flip 'em off.

Griffin drove a black too-cool-for-you Porsche Cayenne. Cost over a hundred thousand dollars. Talk about something to feed my beast's fury. Colin and Diana had a four-year-old CRV; I rode the MTA. But this little fuck had ripped us off to buy a car that was ludicrous in New York City.

The rental companies apparently agreed. I searched the five boroughs and Long Island for a black Cayenne to rent, finally finding one at an upscale boutique agency near Stewart Field. Five-fifty a day. Damn.

Thick gave me a ride — his hand on my thigh the whole way, his little finger caressing my crotch, and acting like it was part of the deal. I didn't refuse; it felt nice.

I picked the car up at noon then drove straight to the restaurant and haunted the area for the right parking slot. After an hour I was able to grab one at the end of the block and within sight of Le Francoeur's entrance. It had permit parking but Rio wrangled me a few temporary tags from the area. I chose the one I needed to hang off the mirror then wandered up to and around the building, like a tourist.

It was in the first level of an old brownstone, up a few steps and all newly refreshed. Some paparazzi were hanging about, so I altered my plans a hint to deal with them and took note of where the valet took the cars. Round-trip was about five minutes at a run. It was a warm day so they wore plain white shirts, black pants and slim black ties. I already had similar clothes back at my apartment, so I headed on.

Back then I lived in a garage unit near our office. It was just over an hour each way on the subway, so I was able to get there, have a good solid meal, shower and dress, and return to be sitting in the Porsche by 7:50.

I watched the usual snob-crowd come and go. Photographers snapped a few pictures of the nobodies with money who were willing to blow four hundred each for a meal that cost a buck-ninety-eight to make.

Then Faure's black Cayenne roared up and he got out, looking sleek and fit in one of his ten-thousand-dollar suits. The valet opened the passenger door for this tall woman in a near-nothing dress who was so thin and sharp her long legs looked like they could cut slivers from bricks of cheese. Not that I give a shit about what women look like, but since when do straight boys like stick figure caricatures of females instead of Marilyn's tits and curves? The paparazzi loved her; hell, they went nuts at seeing her ... and Faure once he joined her. Then two hulking bulldogs in suits came out of a Mercedes behind them and escorted them past the cameras as their cars were raced off to a nearby garage.

I called Neat, who had a cargo van ... and who'd provided me with an automatic pistol. I made sure it was unloaded; no way did I want to accidentally kill anyone, not even a worthless piece of shit like Faure. Then I put half a strip of tape over part of the rear license plate. Within an hour I was chomping to go and my boys were on stand-by.

Just after 9:30 I got a call that Faure and date were paying their tab. That meant the valet would be alerted to have their cars ready and waiting when they exited the restaurant, so I called Neat.

He parked his van so the valet couldn't get out of the garage. When I heard the honking and screaming in the near distance I started my Cayenne. A moment later Griff and Swizzle-stick came out, the bulldogs with them, the paparazzi firing away. I called the Maître d' and asked for the model to come to the phone. *Very important; didn't have her cell phone number but heard she might be dining there and it's a family emergency* kind of crap. The maître d' appeared at the door and she went back up, followed by one of the bulldogs, the photographers focused on her. Griff waited at the curb, the other bulldog keeping a watch.

I ended the call, drove my Cayenne up to the restaurant and hopped out. Like any good valet I left the car running; no one even looked at me. He offered no tip, the prick, just strolled over to the driver's side, paying more attention to the restaurant entrance than me ... and looking amazingly hot. He got in and —

I kicked his bulldog in the knee, sending him to the pavement with a howl, then jumped in the passenger seat and stuck the pistol to Faure's side and said, "Drive. Now!"

He jolted. "What the — ?"

I jabbed the gun at him, snarling, "Drive, bitch!"

He put the Cayenne in gear and drove off.

I heard photographers crying out and in the rearview mirror saw flashes chasing after us. Then his real cars pulled up as Swizzle-stick came out. The second bulldog jumped that valet as more people exploded from the restaurant, but by the time they realized what was going on we'd turned up Madison.

Faure was shaking as he said, "You want money? Fine. I have money. Lots. You want the car? Take it? We can stop at an ATM and I can — "

"Shut up. Take the next right."

He did.

I saw Thick down by a fire hydrant and hit the horn. He waved and pulled a balaclava down over his face.

"Stop here," I snapped. He did then I pushed him against the door, sharp and sudden, keeping the pistol at his throat.

Thick ripped the driver's door open and yanked him out then wrapped packing tape around his arms. Griff managed to cry out, "What the fuck're you — " before Thick wrapped tape around his mouth to shut him up. He'd already opened the back passenger door so slammed Griff inside, face down, and piled on top of him. I jumped out, ran behind the car, grabbed the tape off the license plate then kicked the passenger door closed and scrambled behind the wheel, slipped the Cayenne into gear and headed for the 49th Street Bridge.

Griff whimpered the whole way. Considering Thick was in loose gym pants I figured he was feeling something hard and round against his ass that he didn't want to be feeling. That's why I finally said to him, "Don't worry, we're not gonna kill you. No one is. Even though you deserve it."

We whipped over the bridge into Long Island City. One of Rio's friends' friends had some kind of machine shop there with well-padded walls, lots of space and plenty of fun toys to work with. The only stipulation was that it had to be clean by Monday, 6am.

That would be no problem.

FOUR

I found the machine shop and called Walrus; he was already inside. He rolled up the door and I drove the Cayenne in. He was in a leather mask that hid his full face. Neat had beat me there with the van and was pulling on his own mask. I started to park behind the van but he shook his head.

"Put it in that other corner," he said. "Out of the way."

"Get him out, first," I snapped back.

Neat opened the passenger door, helped Thick out, then they dragged Faure over to an office chair, slammed him into it and used padded leather cuffs to lock his feet to a loop fixed in the floor. He tried to kick at them but it did him no good.

I backed the Cayenne into the space and got out to survey the situation. Man — as metal shops go this place was perfect. There was an overhead pulley with a hook chain on a rail that ran the length of the building. Two pallet jacks and a forklift were parked near the front entrance. Some massive barrels were full of metal junk, but a couple of them were empty and sat next to rectangular bins on wheels. Nearly a dozen massive machines were in their own little work-stations — lathes, drill presses, some I had no idea what the hell they were, each of which had a bench set up next to it. It was so damn porno-hot I began to think we might shoot footage for two-hundred videos.

Which looked probable since five high-end video cameras were set up on tripods at various heights, with two more ready to use as hand-held. Lights were prepped, as well. On top of it all, there was a portable rail of hangers holding all sorts of clothes and suits and restraints and a trunk packed with toys off to one side. This was going to be a major production, a bit more major than I was expecting.

The boys were already feeling Faure up big-time, pinching his tits through his thousand-dollar silk shirt and groping his crotch and kissing his neck. He was squirming and grunting and trying to cry out but the tape was working. Same for how it was wrapped around his torso ... and now you know where I got my idea to use it. It was fun to watch, but we needed to get on program.

"Okay, guys," I said, "slow down; we got all weekend."

"I wanna se what we got to work with, now!" Neat snapped as he grabbed at Faure's shirt.

"HOLD IT!" snarled out of me so fast they all jumped. "We got an agreement — we don't tear his clothes."

"Fuck that," Neat laughed. "Three of us and one of you? He's dinner; you're dessert."

Neat tore Griff's shirt open as Thick and Walrus advanced on me.

My beast roared. "What the fuck? I gotta play alpha dog with suburban brats? My guy vouched for you. Pull this shit and he never will, again."

"He gonna believe you, knowin' what you like?" Walrus smiled, caressing my cheek.

"Yeah," I smiled back. "'Cause he and I agreed — no drugs, no marks and we don't tear his clothes. Wanna know why? So he's got no proof he wasn't a willin' participant in the *fun* we're gonna have."

That made them hesitate. Walrus's smile weakened and Neat turned to look at me, wary.

I shoved between Thick and Walrus to go to Griff. He watched me, his eyes wide as he fought to maintain control of his breathing. His shirt was torn completely open, half shredded where it was still caught by the tape, revealing a hairless chest and oval nips that had been tanned in a salon, not on a beach. I took in a deep breath and glared at Neat.

"You fuckin' idiot," I snarled. "We're gonna undress him, now. Carefully. Then you're gonna leave with this shirt and find another one exactly like it, and I do mean exactly. And if you can't, don't you fuckin' come back. In fact you better leave the fuckin' state. You got me?"

"This is bullshit," he snapped back. "We always give our guys new clothes — "

"From where? Walmart? You think you can find a shirt like this at Macy's? What the fuck's wrong with you?" I grabbed Faure's hair and yanked him forward. He squirmed and squealed, but I had too good a hold on him as I pulled back on the shirt's collar. No label. "See that? I bet this shirt is custom made. You know a good seamstress who can duplicate it?"

Neat finally began to see what I was talking about and began to back away.

"My wife," said Thick.

I looked at him. "Wife?"

He nodded. "We ... we have an agreement ... on many things. She's good with sewing. Made some costumes for us."

I chuckled. "Okay, then let's see what she can do. First we undress Mr. Faure. Carefully. Undies included. Did I see some CKs mixed in on those hangers?"

"Better," said Walrus. "FTL boxer briefs and a Speedo and ... and a jock and ... "

"Then let's get to work," I said, releasing Faure's hair. "It'll take all four of us and — "

"Wait," said Thick, "let me get all the cameras started."

Griff let out a howl at hearing that and struggled to get free so I straddled him to sit in his lap and leaned my arms on his shoulders, grinning like a hyena.

"I bet you're wonderin' what this is all about, ain't you?" I asked. He didn't respond. "Don't you recognize me, yet? Or did you pay so little attention to me my face didn't register?" That made him stop struggling and look closer at me. The frown in his eyes told me the later suggestion was true, not the former. I smiled. "That's all right. It's been a couple years but it'll come back to you." I patted his cheek. He shook his head.

I glanced over my shoulder to see all the cameras were being focused on Griff. They'd been plugged into six kick-ass CPU towers by slim cables while the handhelds had batteries, no cables. They turned them all on me as I continued with, "Now don't worry, Griff, like I said, we're not gonna kill you. That would be too easy and, in reality, counterproductive; I don't want anyone to see you as a victim. Plus I am gettin' somethin' out of this. How far I have to go to get it depends on you. And you will give it to me. Whether you want to or not. 'Cause I know what you hate and I'm makin' that your punishment."

They turned a couple of lights on, shining on him and glowing on my face. I finally saw him thinking, *I know this guy from somewhere.*

Then Thick said, "We're live."

I chuckled and caressed Griff's ears then trailed down his chin to the base of his neck, saying, "I heard an interesting story. That you were in one of your big bad board meetings and actually said somethin' like, *I don't have any fags workin' for me. Same for dykes. Soon as I find out they're queer I order human resources to find an excuse to fire 'em. And there's always an excuse.*"

I rose and stepped back, pulling off my tie and shirt to reveal a tight white athletic tee. With my full chest, even less of a belly back then and hair peeking over the shirt's neck, a small gold chain draped over it, and hair on my head slicked back ... I looked sooo-very *Guido*, which I knew would look great on film.

I walked around him as slow and easy as I could. Rocking my hips just a little as I continued, "You see, this is about you rippin' people off by gettin' them to do work for you that you were never gonna pay for." He shook his head. "People who couldn't afford that kind of hit. People like my brother, who's close to suicidal thanks to you.

"Apparently the cops and today's judicial system can't be

bothered about your kind of crime. *Too complicated to take to trial; really a civil matter.* And when some DA does bother to get ambitious enough to hit you, you just pay a couple bucks in fines and walk away. Never-mind how many people you destroyed. People who worked all their lives for what little they had while you were born into wealth. And ease. And a diseased attitude that you're self-made. Well, there's other ways to get justice."

He watched me, pressing back into the chair, his eyes growing wider and wider. I advanced on him, stopping when my legs straddled his. I swiveled my hips a little. Took a grip of his floppy hair and pulled his head back. That's when I lowered the zipper to my pants ... slowly ... slowly until I could reach in, pull down my boxer-briefs and guide my dick out. I was full but not completely hard ... not yet. I smacked him in the face with it. He squealed from shock.

"This is goin' in your mouth and up your ass. And when I suck you off you're gonna cum. And my guys here — they're gonna have *allllll* kinds of fun with you, and we're gonna record every minute of it. And when it's done, if you want to keep it secret you'll buy back every episode we make for a hundred-thousand each. I'll text you instructions on how to pay. I figure there'll be about a hundred of 'em."

He looked at me with hate and shook his head and managed to grunt around the gag, "I don't have that much money."

I smiled. "You'll get it," I said as I drifted down to my knees, undid his belt, unbuttoned his pants and unzipped them as slowly as a lover. "If you don't, I'll crush your father. Your mother. Your grandfather. Your sister. Your brother. Your associates. Your asshole attorneys. Even those motherfuckers who attended your party in Dubai. I look like I could be Arab, don't I? Imagine the shock in the Middle East when they learn wealthy Muslims have consorted with a male whore well-tested by a vile man like you? Imagine the gossip and questions and innuendo about what kind of kinky crap they're into. They'll be so busy divesting themselves from your company and any contracts they have with you, you'll drown in the paperwork."

He squirmed and tried to fight me as I pulled the flaps of his pants apart to reveal he was wearing designer briefs with a major soccer star's name on them. He cried out and struggled, making the chair move slightly, but I held him in place as I reached in, trailed my fingers over his hips and thighs and fondled his crotch. Nice enough balls but not a lot of anything else there. Yet.

He was nearly in hysterics as he fought to get free, so I grabbed his face and held him still and snarled, "Calm down or you'll choke on your own vomit and we won't do anything to keep you alive if that happens. So cut it. Now."

The glare he gave me was nuclear in its heat but he made himself stop fighting me. He breathed in grunts and gulps as I guided the elastic waistband of his briefs down to reveal his dick. It was small and scrunched up and uncut and his pubes were manscaped to a triangle around its base while his tan-line was so obviously fake, it was laughable.

I maneuvered the elastic to behind his balls and began to whisper my fingers around them and up and down him, over and over and over as he flinched and squirmed and his skin shivered and he shook his head and shifted in the chair ... until, bit by bit, I had massaged him into a vague normalcy. Took about ten minutes but he started to prove he was a grower. Still more of an anteater than a helmet but that could be taken care of.

I kept swirling my hand around him in ways that were gentle and demanding. He tried to move away. Fought to free himself. Cringed and shivered and jerked whenever my fingers caressed up the length of his dick, but all that did was prove how well bound he was.

Finally, he started to get hard — just enough to look good but not ready to explode. I pulled back his foreskin, making him squeal, saw he was clean and nice, and played with it, soft and easy, making him clench his ass in horrified reaction to how good it felt ... and how it made him even thicker and harder. Then I surrounded his head with my lips and used my tongue to caress him.

It was a nice-enough dick. A bit too straight and simple for me, and it being uncircumcised was a letdown, but I could take the whole thing in my mouth without a bit of effort. His balls were the kind that liked to travel up into his scrotum when he's hard so it took some care and effort to keep them low enough to where I could make use of them ... and work him and work him and work him ... over and over and over and over ... until he gasped and I could feel the first real jerk of passion in him. Then I got to really sucking on him ... and pulling his balls ... and tickling his pubes ... and running my fingers up and down him. He grunted and groaned and grew harder and harder. His whimpers began to sound more like questions and he clenched and grimaced and gasped and shivered and pushed himself into my mouth and finally ... finally ... fired hard into me.

I let the next two shots of cum fall back onto his briefs — and there was a lot of it, to my surprise. A couple more caresses of his balls even brought forth another spurt that landed on his pants. I even sucked a bit more out of him and spit that onto his suit jacket and tie.

I stood up, my dick now hard as rock, and looked around. My three guys were looking at me in awe. The main cameras were pointed at Griff's dick while the one Walrus held on his shoulder was focused on my face. I wiped my mouth, felt the cum that had trickled past my lips and smiled. "You get it all?"

Walrus nodded and gulped.

"Now for Act Two," I said, then I carefully undid the tape around Griff's mouth.

He coughed and gasped and spit and said, "You fucking son-of-a-bitch. What'd you do to me?! You can't do this to me! You don't know who I am. What I'm capable of. What my father'll do to you! Cocksucking motherfucking faggots! You think I'll go along with this? Shit, motherfuckers! I'll get you all killed!"

He kept snarling and spitting out words along those lines as I stroked myself harder and harder, got myself close to the edge, then I grabbed his jaw and his nose and held his mouth open and pushed myself inside and released him and made two more thrusts before he could wrap his brain around what was happening then I fired down his throat. I pulled out so the second spurt hit his face and then made sure some of my cum joined his on the suit and designer briefs. He choked and more cum dribbled from his lips. When I saw the video later it looked like he'd actually given me a blowjob.

He choked and retched and howled in anger and horror. "What the fuck!?" was followed by a full range of curses and hatred of fags and queers and how we were going to get our dicks cut off and rammed up our asses and on and on to the extent I began to wonder if he'd really actually enjoyed what just happened.

Thick didn't care. "Got it all," he said. "Beautiful."

I chuckled and backed away from Griff. "Okay, let's strip him and hang his clothes up. Nice and neat. Especially his briefs. Then you can dress him ... or not ... and do what you want ... within the boundaries laid down." I turned to Neat and added, "Except for you. You'll take that fuckin' shirt and bring one back exactly like it before we let you join us."

He hesitated but said nothing.

So we got to work at undressing Griff. He hurled all kinds of abuse and threats at us mixed with cries for help, his voice echoing around the building. It did him no good; the walls were double-thick to cut down on the machine noise. Still he kept fighting, I'll give him that, wiggling and squirming and twisting as best he could.

First off were his shoes and socks ... and Walrus had a lot of fun with his rather nice toes. Then Thick and I held Griff in the chair as Walrus pulled his pants down to his ankles, followed by his briefs, at which point Neat wrapped his knees together with cellophane ... mixing in a bit of his own groping and fondling. After Griff's ankles were released from the padded cuffs, his pants were removed then the restraints put back around his ankles before the cellophane was cut away.

He kept twisting and turning and spitting out crap like, "You can't do this! I'm straight! I'm fuckin' rich! I'll get you all fuckin' killed for this! Sent to jail and fucked to death by some big black dicks, you motherfuckers! I'll have you fucked up the ass with red-hot pokers for the rest of your fuckin' lives!" All punctuated by more screams for help.

I laughed and made the occasional comment of, "Griff, we're father-fuckers, okay?" and "How can you be so straight if you came in my mouth and then sucked me off? Hmm?"

"That's not what fuckin' happened! People'll see that."

"Bullshit, bullshit, bullshit, baby."

Then Neat and Walrus connected the ankle cuffs to the hook chain linked to the railing so we could hoist him upside down. We cut off the tape around his body and arms and he flailed at us, but he could do nothing as we pulled off his jacket and torn shirt. I found his cell phone in one pocket, put that in the Cayenne and tossed the shirt across its hood. Once he was completely naked they forced his hands over his head and put his wrists into padded wrist cuffs.

I got to say ... seeing him upside down twisting and turning like some trout caught while fishing, his pumped-up chest heaving, his dick and balls bouncing around, his abs looking even more taut and lovely ... it got me going, again. I turned him around to look at his butt. It wasn't quite as nice as I thought it'd be but I still squeezed it ... and he screamed bloody murder.

"You get that first, too?" asked Walrus.

I stuck a finger into Griff's hole. Felt how tight it was. He twisted away, grunting in fear, now. I slapped a cheek.

"No," I said. "I think I wanna be the last one in him, so he'll remember me." I smacked him again, not hard but he still screamed. I laughed and said, "Cool with you?"

They nodded then Neat said, "Okay. Hey, listen, I ... I'm sorry. We thought we were dealin' with some bullshit kid, full of himself. A cute guy we could use. Have all kinds of fun with. We won't go up against you, again."

I grinned and pulled him close and kissed him, and as I pulled back I whispered, "Taste that? It's his cum. That's what a bullshit kid from Brooklyn does to motherfuckers who fuck with him — he fucks them up in ways you wouldn't believe. Don't be a motherfucker like Griff."

Neat licked his lips and took in a deep breath. "I'll be back by ten. Save some for me." He split with the shirt as Thick called his wife, then I stepped back to let them start their fun.

Son-of-a-bitch, what their fun was ... let's just say I learned a lot of new shit on how to use a man, that night.

What's funny is ... the thing I found the most fun was how they pulled a fucking *bed* out of the back of the van, set it up, shoved it in a blank corner and stretched him, face down, on that, chaining his hands to a ring in the cast iron headboard then spreading his legs to a two-foot bar. After that they changed into matching outfits of jeans, chaps, boots and harnesses and spent an hour just groping his ass and caressing his legs and back and arms and pulling on his dick between his legs. When his screaming and cursing got to be too much, Thick shoved a dental spacer into his mouth and, basically, gagged him. Then they took turns rimming him and forcing him to blow them. Thick had a good-size dick but with a head on the small side so he was able to use Griff's mouth easily and shot all over the guy's face. Walrus was pretty damn big and he unloaded a mouthful into the bastard. It splashed back and dribbled out. Griff stopped trying to cry for help, after that.

When they flipped him over his dick was semi-hard again, so both of them worked on it with their mouths and vibrators and electro-toys and penis pumps for twenty minutes until he shot another wad. Not as much as with me but still a couple of nice spurts. Then the bar his legs were attached to was connected to the hook and his legs raised, and Thick started rimming Griff's ass before lubing him up and casting me a glance.

I motioned for him to have at it ... and he pushed deep into Griff, careful, easy, as the bastard struggled and tried to scream around the dental brace. Walrus straddled his chest and pinched his nips as Thick slipped in and out of him, long and slow and elegant ... until he began slamming into him over and over and over and harder and harder ... and he came.

Shit ... I never knew watching live porn could be so ... so damn glorious.

By this point, Griff was letting them do whatever they wanted. So next they put on cop uniforms, dressed him in those FTLs, shorts, thick socks and mountain boots and an athletic Tee, bound him back in the chair and felt him up ... then ripped the clothes off him and went through the same thing again.

Next came them in suits and Griff in workman's shirt and pants that got shredded before they slapped him over a lathe, naked, face down, as first Walrus then Thick then Walrus then Thick fucked him. And came again.

And more as cops and businessman perp.

And more as workmen binding a boss and raping him.

And more.

Again.

And again.

Man ... I was in awe. I owed Rio for this, big-time.

It was 5 AM before they were spent. Walrus had found a shower and bathroom in a corner of the shop so they forced an enema up his ass, let it come out in the shower stall as they pissed on him (something I have zero interest in), all of it recorded. Then they washed the basin. When it was clean (probably cleaner than it had been in twenty years) they positioned Griff in the stall and set the water to going and had him soap himself up ... then got in the stall with him ... and gave him probably the most erotic washing I've ever seen, with hands going everywhere and soap trailing over wet skin and groping and pinching and two hard-ons bopping against a limp dick and each other till they shot ANOTHER wad.

Jesus, were these guys superhuman or what?

At long last they wrapped Griff in a robe and handcuffed him to the bed. He passed out. Then Thick and Walrus unrolled a foam mat in the back of the van and crashed for some sleep, holding each other tight.

I was too keyed up so sat in the chair the rest of the night to watch Griff lie as still as death, his chest barely moving. He looked sweet and sexy like that, almost innocent, so I found some copy paper and did a sketch of him.

And another.

And another. Each from a different angle. And in each he looked almost like a child.

When I finally lay down beside him, he didn't stir. I put an arm over him. He kept sleeping, steady, easy. I pulled out my phone and took a couple of selfies of us lying together like lovers ... side by side. Me nuzzling his neck. Smelling the soap on his body. Kissing his cheek. Toying with a tit. Then I finally drifted to sleep.

****

Neat woke me when he arrived at 9:45, holding a shirt that was exactly like Griff's torn one. I hung it up as he kicked his buddies back to life. He also brought coffee and donuts. The aroma enticed Griff into having some, too, his movements vague and uncertain as an old man's.

When they were done they dressed Griff in briefs, shorts, tee-shirt, thick socks and boots that were too big for him but looked good, then had him stand by a drill press as they snuck up behind him and grabbed him. He jolted and started to struggle so they gagged him, bound him with soft rope to the press and let Neat have his rip-n-strip fun.

It went like that all day Saturday. This scenario, that scenario, these toys, those clothes, taking thousands of still picture, with Griff just going along with it. I went out for pizza and sandwiches and beer, and Griff ate and drank with us ... but in a mechanical way.

They put Griff back in the shower to wash him and

wrapped him in a towel then the three of them dressed as prison inmates and jumped him. He started crying with that one so we agreed it was time to end this.

Time for me to have my go at him.

They still had a red Speedo that hadn't been used so I asked about it.

"We got video of a lot of guys in that," said Thick. "On the beach. In a pool. Y'know ... a couple of 'em could pass for him from behind."

I nodded then had them douche the douche as I changed into a pair of jeans, and they bathed him with lots of fondling then put the Speedo on him, tied him with the soft rope and put him in the back of the van with a knotted bandana as a gag. I lay behind him, spooning him, and wrapped my arms around him so I could play with his nips.

He tried to shift away and muttered through the gag, "Please. Please stop. No more. Please."

"I'm the last one, baby." I don't know why I said it like that but I did.

"So ... you gonna kill me, now?"

"No," I said. "I told you ... "

He didn't seem to believe me.

I rubbed my hand along his abs then pulled at his tits, twisting them slightly. He shifted against me so I kissed his neck. He sounded like he was crying. I didn't care. I spent half an hour feeling him up while rubbing against his ass through my jeans ... then through my briefs after unbuttoning my jeans ... then releasing my dick and pushing it between his legs, hiding how I was using my finger up his ass to force him into yet another hard-on. The Speedo looked like it was still on him, not pulled down away from his butt. Finally, I pulled it partway down his hips to let his dick fall out. He was only a bit thick, still I lubed my dick up and rolled him onto his back with his legs over my shoulders and pushed into him and fucked him hard as I yanked on him, just as hard. He grunted from pain and shook his head and almost began to struggle but I had too good of a hold on him so worked him and worked him and worked him until he came and tightened around me and I fired into his ass.

I stayed inside him a minute more, playing with his nips and abs and dick and balls before pulling out and rising. Then we dressed him back in his clothes, all nice and neat, put him in the back seat of the Cayenne, covered his face with the balaclava, drove him back to Manhattan and dropped him a couple blocks from his condo. We'd planned to get closer but there was a huge police and media presence by the front entrance. When he got out he just stood there, looking like he was drunk. We drove away without a glance back.

It was about 3 AM, Sunday.

****

We came back to the shop and spent hours cleaning up then my mustaches headed on. Soon as a car wash was open I got the Cayenne detailed and returned it to the rental agency, *very happy with the service*.

I called Thick to pick me up at the airport to bring me back. He must've driven at Mach Ten to get to me, then his hand on my thigh from the moment I entered his car.

"You're a maniac," he said.

I chuckled. "Pot calls kettle black. Jeez, you guys ... "

"We'll have to try it out sometime. Just you and me."

I gripped his crotch. "Don't forget who's top dog."

I think he'd have cum if he wasn't already spent.

He dropped me by Terrytown to catch the train. I found a Macdonald's up Railroad and ate breakfast as I watched the news on my phone. It had exploded with stories about the kidnapping of Griffin Faure thanks to that high-profile disappearance and no word from the kidnappers all day Saturday. The FBI had been called in and there was speculation of ransom notes and threats of death, but no one even thought to wonder if this was payback from someone he or his dad had ripped off. It was all, *Those poor little billionaires*. Sickening.

Until *The Post* ran a story suggesting Griff had just suddenly shown up at home and no one could figure out how he got in ... till they discovered there was a delivery entrance behind the building and he'd gotten one of his father's assistants to open it for him. This got them to wondering if the kidnapping might have been staged, or if his shady dealings had brought it on and the ransom was a form of payback.

That's when the family's lawyers came out in force and shut the news down. By Sunday evening, it was being treated as old news. Rio's friends' friends let me know that Griff was being cared for by the family doctor while stuffed in his father's penthouse, so no one thought he was physically hurt. It was perfect.

Until Tuesday, when some tabloid photographer got a shot of Griff being driven out of his parking garage in his Cayenne and it looked like he had a black eye and split lip. That brought up headlines screaming his kidnappers had beaten him so it hit page one, again. I asked a couple people I knew about what was going on and they said his father had tossed a massive fit over the whole mess and punched him around. Word was it wasn't the first time.

That almost made me wonder if I'd hit the right target.

Almost.

Because the little asshole ignored my text about payment — sent from *his personal phone* (since I'd kept it) to his corporate one — I contacted my Mustaches and they posted a nicely edited video on Griff's *new Men-For-Boys escort account* to let people know he was seeking more kinky pleasure. And gave his father's direct line as contact.

I hear things got really dicey after that.

Somehow Daddy's bloodhounds tracked it all back to me a week later, and we had a lovely session in that same conference room as before ... but without Hamilton; the less my lawyer knew of this the better. His attack dogs threatened to take my company away and have me jailed for life for kidnapping and rape while I kept telling them *Griff* had wanted what happened.

"I connected with him after your company ripped us off," I said, "and we fucked more than once. He was horny and Swizzle-Stick wasn't interested so he shot his wad all over me."

Then I played one of the videos showing him covering my face with it.

That made them squirm — a couple from finding it a turn-on, I'm sure — but the threats were still wild and vicious and their demands were backed up with lots of legal mumbo-jumbo. Thing was they had nothing in the way of evidence except his claims as to what happened. That was voided by his own cum on him mingled with mine, no marks on him, and Thick's wife had done such a great job with the shirt he couldn't even convince anyone it had been torn.

What was better? I let them know I'd told a friend of a friend about Griff and me and said that if anything happened to me they were ready to spread proof about how *slavishly devoted* Griffin was to his rich Dubai friends and would *do anything to please them*. Backed up with a few choice screen-captures labeled *Mohammad and Griff*.

Then I let the attack dogs know I had ten more videos and said I'd sell them for a million. Each. I also pointed out their expansion into Middle-Eastern oil would be hurt by this non-stop scandal. Sheiks don't want their people to hear about such things or to wonder if their leaders aren't really good and proper Muslims. Might even kill their business completely.

All said with a snotty grin.

That's when Papa Faure burst into the room. I saw a look in his eyes that I hadn't seen since the last time my father hit me and I readied myself for him. But three of his dogs stepped in, so he just kept that glare on me through the rest of the meeting. I'm sure if we hadn't been in a room full of people he'd have beaten me to death. Happily. And gotten away with it thanks to his money. I almost started to feel sorry for Griffin, again.

Almost.

I let them settle for eighty percent of my asking price in exchange for the masters of every minute of video recorded. Never mind my boys had backup masters and I had ninety more videos, as insurance. They gave me 800 bands of hundred dollar bills instead of transferring it to my credit union. Where they got it — I didn't ask, nor did I care; I just took our money out of the pot and gave the rest to Rio to share with his friends' friends' beloved uncles and grandmothers. I'm told it helped a lot of people. I snuck ours back into the business in little bits and made sure half of it went into a safety fund just in case something like this ever happened, again.

The last I heard of Griffin Faure, after being held in seclusion at a health spa that was really a crazy house, he'd been shipped off to Singapore — on a private jet. Gossip swore it was to hide another beating. Then he got himself married to an associate billionaire's not-so-beautiful daughter, by whom he had three kids. So far as I knew or cared he was still there *doing great and wonderful*, and making them all richer than rich, I'm sure.

I often wondered if he was dumb enough to try his bullshit business tactics in a country that had refined them to an art. I almost hoped he was that stupid.

Almost.

****

Okay — so that was six years ago. It was now pretty obvious Papa Faure was keeping track of me, had heard about the arrest and still held a grudge, and never-mind what his little boy had done to so many people. *You fuck with me, I fuck you back.* A perfect case of *Do unto others and keep doing and doing and doing.*

I'd learned that from my dad, too. I wondered if it was a necessary trait to achieve that level of success. One of my business professors once used Balzac's claim that *behind every great fortune was a crime* as the basis of a long lecture about capitalism and how two-faced it could be when not held in check. The likes of John D. Rockefeller's bullshit with Standard Oil, Joe Kennedy's rum-running during prohibition, Henry Ford's violent union-busting and Jay Gould's murderous actions for his railroads backed him up. The Faures' deal was mild in comparison — simple fraud to keep building on their bank balances and screw anybody who tried to find justice or just get even — but it still fit. So if they were helping in this then I could be in for one hell of a beating. And while I didn't like it I could understand it — they'd done to me so I'd done to them, and now ...

Now that mental back-and-forth slapped a question into my chaotic mind — So why did I do that to Reg? Why did I attack a man who'd done nothing to me? Who I had no excuse to go after? What had made him my target? Had it just — shit, had it just been about the sex? No, because he's not what I usually go for and ... and I didn't ... didn't make use of his lovely ass.

Had I sensed deep down that he was an undercover cop on a surveillance job? Did the bit where he was focused on Savile Row call attention to it? No. No, it was too big a shock to me to find out who he was and there wasn't enough interaction between the two of them to indicate anything more than just a casual notice.

Was it control? I did take a sort of control over him; there's no better way to prove you own a man than to force him to cum when he doesn't want to. Only it wasn't that either, because if that's all I'd wanted I'd have just sucked him off. And reality is it was more of a case of him controlling me, if that makes any sense, and a huge part of me was sorry for what I did. Not just sorry — ashamed.

Man ... that was a first for me.

I laid my head in my hands and closed my eyes, trying to block out the unbearable whiteness of that room. Find some way to control the shattering thoughts in my brain. Understand why I'd felt a ... a connection to him. Something I'd never felt before, not even with Thick, despite the number of times we've been together.

Why there was a ... hell, a *need* for him. To be with him. Why I'd held him so tenderly and wantonly. Why I'd felt a hunger for him.

Why I'd wanted to touch the tattoo on his back. The one like my mother's.

Damn, she was pissed at me for walking in on her. But she'd never taken baths in the afternoon before. That I knew of. And she was always in a shirt or full blouse; better to hide the cuts and bruises; that was the only time I ever saw her out of one.

Son-of-a-bitch, was Mr. Insignia right? Was that my trigger — seeing that tattoo? I had shut down everything else once I saw it. All I wanted was to touch it. Just touch it. But then I'd spun out of control ... because I wanted it to be part of me, again, and somehow being with Reg in a way that ... that was just being with him and not really raping him was part of it and ... and ... and ... SHIT!

I bolted to my feet to walk around the room, because all of that sounded stupid. But it's the only reason that would come to me that sounded right. Mom had been tender and caring and human in the face of Dad's horror and I ... I wanted to touch that, again ... and for it to touch me because I knew it wasn't in me and maybe never has been.

Oh, God, now *I* sound like a freshman in Psych 101. But it's the only explanation I can come up with that makes any sense. Because if all I'd wanted with Reg was control I'd have fucked him and left his lips dripping with my cum, like I did with Griff. And that cop in Chicago. But I didn't do any of that. I'd made a ... a sort of love to him, and truth was ... shit, being with him had ... it had comforted me ... calmed me ... settled me ... touched my soul in a way no one had since my mother.

And him now hating me was tearing me to shreds.

Damn, this shit was giving me a headache. I wanted nothing more than to just go back to being a happy cat in the jungle prowling to its heart's content, but suddenly I knew I couldn't. This beast had met his beauty and he was tame as a kitten. And it flooded me with a weird sense of relief.

And fear.

Because wasn't it Beauty who killed the Beast?

FIVE

I'd have kept stalking about, but even though no cameras were visible in the room I was pretty damn sure I was being recorded. Of course, once you've got a recording it's impossible to keep anything completely secret. Then there was Mr. Insignia's shadow; he looked like the type who wouldn't mind acting like he had the inside scoop, so word would still get around about Thornton and me. And that bluff about claiming to be able to claim he did not know whose photo was on my phone was horseshit; a freshman journalist could ferret out the truth.

So what was Mr. Insignia up to? He knew I wasn't in London when those men died and I hadn't killed anybody. Was there some other game he was playing and using what I'd done with Thornton as the centerpiece?

Man, I hated myself for spitting out *consent* as my excuse. All that would do is fuck up the guy's life. He didn't deserve it. He was innocent.

Fucking innocent.

That word tore through me. As much as I hate cops I still know not all of them are scum. That some do believe in fairness when they serve and protect, and it sounded like Thornton — no, he's Reg.

He's Reg.

He was that kind of cop and I'd probably trashed his career. Mr. Insignia didn't seem like the type who accepted failure. In his limited brain, if Reg had turned the tables and busted me Martin Perriman might still be alive. Which was bullshit but never let reality get in the way of a self-serving meme. It would've been better if I'd knocked Reg out and fucked him and snuck away. Better for both of us.

But I didn't, did I? I fucking didn't.

I made myself sit back at the table. Forced myself to become still, at least on the outside. I needed to Zen myself back down to calmness. To awareness. To understanding. So let Mr. Insignia come back in with his shadow. I wasn't gonna say another word to the fucker.

Only he didn't come in.

Reg did.

Alone.

And I damn near stopped breathing.

He was still in that black Polo shirt that looked so damn perfect on him and pants that fit him so right, with his wedding band gleaming under the hideous light, trying so hard to look professional and in control. But little tremors in his hands gave lie to that. He held the same type folder as Insignia'd held and sat across from me in the same chair, his eyes cold and hard and fighting to keep from looking into mine. He did not want to be anywhere near me.

Oh my God, I was so pissed at Mr. Insignia I damn near wanted to cry.

Reg gripped his hands together to keep their shaking from being too obvious. He fought to keep his breath even and his eyes locked in a stare. It took him a few moments to work up the voice to speak.

I hurt for him every second, still barely breathing.

"Why'd you pick me?" he finally asked, his voice barely even.

I made myself take in a deep breath and let it out as a sigh. "That's already been asked."

"Not answered," Reg shot back, anger coloring his words. "Millions of lads have ink like mine. Why me?"

I couldn't tell him it was like my mother's because the

truth was, I'd only seen it once and that's when I was seven, for Christ's sake. For all I really knew it could have been a birthmark or a stylized dragon or another of Dad's bruises; I just know his reminded me of hers and that was too much to admit right then. Too much to say.

He pulled Griffin Faure's photo from the folder. *And here we go*, I thought. Then he pulled two more out — one was of Ryan Orriagio, that Chicago cop I'd had *fun* with after seeing him smack his wife around; the other was of a guy named Armando Guardinos, also dark-haired and good-looking and a conquest of mine. But he didn't count ... hell, he'd never pressed charges, so how did they know about him?

"Look at 'em," Reg snarled.

His voice cut into me. I jolted then blinked. "And?"

"Now look at me."

I already was. His expression was raw. Close to hysteria. I had to lock my fingers together to keep from reaching for him.

He continued with, "I don't look like 'em."

No shit about that; they were darkness to his light. Shadows for me to hide in.

He kept on with, "They look more like you than me." I nodded. "So I'm not what you're after. I'm not what you go for. If this is what you — you — you like so fuckin' much when you choose your — your *playmates*, why'd you pick me? What's it about my tats that made you want me? There's got to be more to it."

I took a deep breath and turned away from him. I refused to let myself look at the two-way window. Mr. Insignia and his twerp were sure to be watching and listening in and I'd be damned if I'd give them any indication that I gave a single solitary fuck about this diseased game they were playing.

Or how they'd made Reg a pawn in it.

His voice was anguished. He wasn't trying to hide the shakes, anymore. I could feel the table move. Even his breath was ragged like it had been, last night. "Please, why'd you choose me?

I do something to make you think I wanted — wanted what happened? That I — that I'd like it?"

My voice cracked. "No."

"Then why!? Was it just to mess up the operation?"

"I didn't know about that." I had to close my eyes to keep from turning back to him as I whispered, "I just ... saw you get on the subway and you were beautiful and you — you were sittin' there and you were — there was somethin' goin' on with you and I couldn't figure it out and I saw the figures on your back and — and shit ... I thought you were hurtin'."

"What?!"

I opened my eyes and looked at him and saw pure confusion in his face. I sighed and the words whispered out, "I thought you were in pain. In turmoil. Like right now. And it's easier to gain control of someone whose mind is lost or ... or who's wanderin' 'round ... in confusion."

He leaned back a little, disgust growing in his eyes. "Do you know how evil that sounds?"

I felt like I'd stripped before him, again, only this time I was ashamed of my nakedness. And it pissed the shit out of me that Mr. Insignia was hearing it all. That woke the beast.

"Would you call a lion who takes down an injured gazelle evil?" I growled, fighting to keep it low. "Does that word even apply to a hawk snatchin' a field mouse that's just a little too slow in gettin' back to its hole?"

"Those're animals."

"So is man."

"They kill for food."

"I don't kill."

"But you're still a beast?"

"Sometimes."

"King of the jungle? Takes his pick and choice?"

I just nodded.

"Those other men. The dead ones. Is that how you excuse what happened to them?"

I shook my head. "That's a waste. Only a fool does that. You never know when you might want to — " I stopped. I didn't want to say what I was about to say.

His look grew wary. "Want to what? Want to what?!"

Dear God, I looked into his eyes, fought myself ... but I couldn't lie to him so the words came out. "Feed, again."

He recoiled. "Again?"

I nodded.

"You — you've done this to these men more than once?"

"Just one of them," I said, trying to be defiant. The horror in his eyes crushed any possibility of that. I had to look away.

"You're bloody mad."

I shrugged. "You're not the first person to say that."

"What about the killer?"

"Told you — he's a fool."

"Are you — are you aligned with a fool?" he asked.

I actually felt insulted by the question. "I wasn't here and that prick with the insignia knows it."

Reg snarled. "His name is Sir Monteith St. James."

That made me chuckle and the beast roared a warning that enough was enough. "So what do you call him — Sir Monte? The fun I could have with a name like that."

"I call him Boss! And you got some bloody nerve sneerin' at him considerin' what you've pulled."

Before I could stop myself I turned to him and hissed, "The only thing you know I pulled is your dick."

Reg exploded to his feet. His chair crashed back against the wall. He'd have punched me, like dad used to when I'd hiss at him, but some quick loud raps on the mirror caught him. He gasped and shook and gulped in air and glared at me then grabbed the folder and stormed from the room. He could go now; he'd gotten the maniac to reveal more than he'd ever intended.

Soon the real games would begin.

****

Now it was my turn to shiver. Not from anger or fear, but from shame. Last night I'd slipped a knife into Reg's back and just a moment ago I'd twisted it. And I hated myself for that. Hated how it happened so easily. And I was even more amazed at how awful it made me feel.

God-awful.

This had to stop. I hadn't used that metaphor lightly; when the beast took over I really was like a lion hunting for food. Nourishment. Something to end the howling hollowness in my heart. Something to prove I was *King of the Jungle* and they were nothing but my meat, every fucking pun intended.

But I'd only gone that far with guys who'd challenged me. Who'd fucked with me — and not in a fun way. Men who deserved some sort of punishment and the courts weren't doing the job they were supposed to. Men like Griffin. And Ryan.

And Armando Guardinos.

Sort of.

Shit ... no, not really ...

Armo. A tight taut surfer-boy with sun-bleached hair. He worked for our biggest competitor, a born-again couple whose factory was in Shanghai and office in Southern California. They did okay work but on the cheap-assed side and couldn't fill orders on the magnitude we could.

I'd gone to LA to talk with a couple of dealers who had stopped using us and learned Armo was promising them the moon for half the price. I did everything I could to show them that our quality was better and the other company couldn't be trusted to deliver, but they'd placed good-sized orders with them and were waiting for the results. Of course the first batch would be damn near perfect to keep them in the fold. It's after that when things would deteriorate. I made both promise to contact me when that happened.

A year later, a source in another dealer's office told me they had *had* wound up with crap a couple times. One even ruined a client's function but the dealer was too embarrassed about me being right to ever admit it. That made me decide never to trash another supplier to a dealer; just bite the bullet and natter something like, "Maybe we can work together again, some time."

Thing is, they'd dumped us while we were still struggling to get over the Griffin Faure mess. Now that we were done with him and back on track I'd pushed Mr. Mihn to expand his workforce for what I was sure would be a flood of new business, some of which would come from the return of those two dealers. But neither would see me when I went out to LA a year later.

That got me to growling but not really angry. Yet. I decided to check into the competition and see what I could do to counter the inroads they were making into our client list.

That company's owners liked to post bible sayings on their website along-side employee photos and their names. Armo's was 1 Timothy 4:12 — *Let no one look down on your youthfulness, but rather in speech, conduct, love, faith and purity, show yourself an example of those who believe.* So not only did I know what he looked like — Brazilian, bright smile, hazel eyes, bushy brows — I knew at least one of his bosses was crushing on him.

I decided to do my seduction thing. Just drinks, no roofies or anything; I got the impression he would not be averse to enjoying a good-looking man's attention and that could make bringing him into my stable a lot easier. Maybe hire him as our West Coast rep. Use him to get those two dealers back and spit in the face of the born-agains.

So I went to their office in Torrance, parked down the street and waited till everyone left from work. Mostly Asian women and a couple of shlubby Anglo and Latino guys. Then out came Armo. Skin that tans with just a hint of sun. Aviator style mirrored glasses. Tight shirt on his taut torso. Colt-like legs under cargo shorts. Getting into a Jeep with a surfboard in the back. He chatted with some of the women, who acted girly when he smiled, then headed straight for the ocean. Sun wasn't due to set for another couple hours and he was going to get some awesome wave-time in.

This wasn't going to be quick or easy; I've never surfed so had no idea how to get him to talking before he was out on the ocean zoning over his next curl, and I wanted this done now.

I followed him through Palos Verdes Estates till he parked at the end of a residential street. Nothing but million-dollar bungalows overlooking the ocean, not so far below. No one around. A small gate in some hedges led to old wooden steps that took you down to the beach. He hopped out and pulled off his shorts to pull on a pair of Boardies. Damn, bitch free-balled it. I got a good look at a nice ass and honest tan-line as I parked behind his Jeep.

He looked around and was about to say something but I popped out of the car and said, "Armando! Hi!"

"Who're you?" he asked as he pulled on the boardies, his voice carrying a hint of an accent.

"Willie Hays Maze of Glitter and Gold," I said, taking off my suit coat and leaving it in my car. "I saw you pass, a few streets back, and followed you. I need to ask you a question about some pins."

"You should call the office, tomorrow. Everything I know is there. And it's Armo; that's how everyone knows me."

"Yeah, right, thanks," I said, approaching him, my critter growling. "It's just a quick question about gold plate flaking off an order."

He yanked at his shirt. "Oh, for that, you need to talk with Rocelyn. She knows more about the process."

His cool dismissal in a voice reeking of condescension irritated me so when he pulled the shirt up over his head I grabbed its tail and smacked him three times in the gut. He cried out and doubled over. I bunched the shirt and tightened it around his neck, his wrists trapped in with it, then slammed him over the hood of his Jeep and jabbed my nail file behind his ear, pressing it hard against his skin as I snarled, "Quiet or I'll cut your fuckin' throat."

"Please," he gasped, "I don't know anything about gold

flake or anything — "

I twisted the material tighter. Felt how solid his ass was against my hip. Holy fuck, it was nice. Got my dick hard in a nano-second and my other thoughts about him flew out the window. I shifted to grind myself even harder against his cheeks and grunted as the beast took over, so I yanked the boardies down his hips and groped his ass with my left hand, my right one still holding the file to his neck.

"What're you doing?" he cried. "I haven't done — "

"Shut up!" Followed by a jab into his neck.

Skin so smooth. So cool to the touch. I found his hole with my fingers and slipped them in. He jolted and struggled but I held him tight with my legs, pulled my dick out and pushed it against his hole before he could even think about what I was doing. It wasn't easy getting in because I was doing it dry and he was fighting me and gasping, "No," over and over ... but I made it ... and I fucked him as he choked and gulped in pain.

Damn ... every nerve in my body fired up. And as if the feeling of him wrapped around me wasn't enough, the sensation of my balls rubbing against my briefs and my pants caressing my legs and my shirt whispering over my nips and the sweat trailing down my back — man, nothing short of a 9.5 quake could have stopped me just then. It didn't take me long to fire and it felt so damn good. Too damned good. Like heaven on earth good.

But you want to know the best part? He shuddered and grunted as I pulled out, so I reached around to feel him up and found he was just as hard as I was and of a decent size — and that he'd cum. Without me even touching him.

I released him and stepped back to put myself away, out of breath and feeling all was well with the world. He rolled over the fender and slipped down to sit on the Jeep's running board then dropped to his knees. His lips parted. His breathing hard. His eyes looking at nothing. He didn't even try to untangle his arms from the shirt. His boardies were down around his ankles, showing off his slowly softening dick. Yeah he was uncut but at that moment I didn't give a shit. He was beautiful. Without thinking, I bent down, pulled his head back by his hair and kissed him — and I'll be damned if he didn't kiss me back.

"You liked it," I whispered.

"You — you raped me," he murmured.

"You came in your boardies, bitch."

"You raped me."

I fingered one of his tits. "Don't steal any more dealers from *Perfect Pieces*. If you do, I won't come back for more."

He looked at me. Licked his lips. Said nothing.

So I kissed him again, long and deep, then left.

We lost no more dealers to them.

I saw him at a manufacturers convention in Las Vegas a few months later, looking hot as shit in a trim navy blue suit. He licked his lips at me ... and I took him again. In a stall in the men's room. And it was just as good as before. He whined about being raped, again, and went back to his hotel to change because he got his own cum on his suit's pants.

I saw him every time I was in LA after that. I'd send him an email to let him know when I'd be around. He'd answer with some cryptic message like, *I work from home on Wednesday*. Then I'd show up at his apartment. He'd open the door wearing those boardies or a towel or a Speedo and I'd grab him and drag him into the bedroom and he'd struggle but never cry out, then I'd have at him and he'd cum every time without me touching him. It's like he stored it up for those moments of fake-rape. Soon as I was done, he'd go into the bathroom and I'd leave. We'd say maybe five words to each other over the space of half an hour, and never once did I even think to sketch him.

This kept on even after he got married. I don't know what he did with his wife when he set up our encounters. In fact the only reason I knew he had one was a wedding photo on top of the TV and he started wearing a wedding band. He even had a kid, if I was right about a toy I saw in my last visit to him. He was a crazy puppy but a lot of fun.

And secretive to the extreme.

So how did anybody know about him? He wouldn't have shared. Hell, the last time I saw him was at a convention in New York, back in March, and we had a lot more fun over those four days. I even brought Neat in during one session and Armo seemed to like him just as much. Maybe even more. Shot his wad twice, that night, to the extreme. So how did they fucking know about him?

Dammit, this was dragging me back into freak-out mode.

****

An hour later, Sir Monte strode in with another man in a suit, one of those modern four-button types that managed to look both Victorian and SyFy cool. He was probably ten years too old for that style and too many pounds underweight to look right in it but his eyes were as sharp as Sir Monte's with an expression that was just as condescending. They sat across from me. I said nothing. What was there to say?

After a few moments, Sir Monte started the conversation. "Have you had time to consider your situation?"

I shrugged.

"And?"

Before I could raise my filter I blurted out, "I think you're a mother-fuckin' son-of-a-bitch for sendin' Reg in here to mess with me, and if there's any way possible I'm gonna fuck you up for that."

That almost brought a smile to his face. "Thornton's been in Afghanistan, Pope. He's handled worse than you."

"You're a fuckin' idiot," I shot back.

"Now that's clear shall we get down to business?"

"No."

"The question was rhetorical."

"So fuckin' what?"

"So fucking this, to respond in your vernacular. You are here. We have you." He looked at his partner and continued, "Who else knows of this situation?"

Four-buttons said in his most condescending manner, "No more than six men, with ourselves and Thornton, all affiliated with the Metropolitan Police Special Unit and none giving a damn because we want this investigation to come to an acceptable conclusion without further loss of life. We did have one inquiry from the press concerning an arrest near Heathrow. Easily brushed aside by saying it was merely a low-level drug courier. Rather boring to them."

"So how long may we keep him here?"

Four-buttons looked straight at me and asked, "Keep whom?"

Sir Monte looked back at me. "Are we now clear as to your current situation?"

"No," was all I managed to say.

"Pope, obstinacy is not an option at this point. You have proven to be the brains in your family, as opposed to your less-than-capable brother — "

"Leave Colin the fuck out of this!"

"I will leave no one the fuck out of it until I receive a satisfactory answer to my question."

I kicked back from the table and paced around the room, livid. "You know fuckin' well I didn't have anything to do with those murders! And Reg got the answer for why I grabbed him!"

Sir Monte was unmoved. "Yes, you are but a lion and he was a wounded gazelle. It had naught to do with the operation of which he was a part. That a man was being viciously murdered at that very moment not far from your hotel is completely beside the point. That Thornton resembles the murder victims in more than just looks is the merest of coincidences while none of your previous victims — at least, the ones we know about — resemble him in the slightest. Yes. Makes perfect sense." Then he folded his hands, leaned forward and let ice fill his voice. "I told you — do not fuck with me. You will tell me who the son-of-a-bitch is that's murdered those men or you will never leave this room. I will not have you able to contact your partner, again, in any way, form or fashion!"

"Again?" The beast growled then sat back to purr in a calm cool voice because I finally caught on, "You have a suspect and you think I was there to back him up. That I made Reg as a cop and pulled this shit to let him slip away. Son-of-a-bitch, no wonder you're pissin' your panties."

"Pope, I am morally opposed to the utilization of enhanced interrogation techniques, but in regards to you I may suspend my objections!"

I leaned against the table, cool and calm and in control. "Cut it out. You broke into my phone. You know who I've called and when. And who called me. Texted me. Everything. And you're probably already into my laptop. You've got my Oyster Card and my credit card charges and company business and know everything about me down to the size of my dick and you've got nothing — *nothing* — to connect me to those murders except I raped one of your cops." I rose and slapped my hands together, back to palm. "There, I said it. I kidnapped and raped one of your cops. Try me for that. Lock me away for life, motherfucker. Do whatever you fuckin' want. All you're doin' is fuckin' yourself up because you damn well know that by focusin' on me you're the ones screwin' up your blessed operation."

He didn't even flinch. "Whilst it could be just as possible your associate is now en route to the States to assist you in your own escapades there."

"What — you think he might've been on the same flight as me? Is that why I'm being held here? To give you time to check everyone on it? Keep me from sending any message to him?"

"You're rather limited in your concepts of what can and cannot be done," said Four-buttons.

I sat down and said, "Right. You're lookin' for consistency with the other male passengers on the flight. Same guy showin' up when I show up. Nearby hotel. Because that guy, Perriman, was killed near where I was stayin'." I looked at Sir

Monte. "You're wastin' your time. I've made dozens of business trips all over the world."

"We need only go back over the last three months."

I shrugged. "So? I've also had dozens of hook-ups."

"I would hardly refer to sexual assault as a *hook-up*."

"These were all happy butt-buddies."

Four-buttons straightened up and asked, "Then why did you decide to assault Constable Thornton?"

"Why do you keep harping on that!?"

"Your responses and explanations make no sense."

I laughed, and for the first time I got Sir Monte to frown.

"You think I don't fuckin' know that? So what d'you want from me? Lay it out."

Four-buttons took in a deep breath and said, "We merely had hoped you might spare us some time in our investigation, if only to spare others besides yourself."

I did not like the sound of that. "What d'you mean?"

"One of your dealers is of Middle Eastern descent, isn't that correct?"

"No, Ghadir's a Persian Jew," popped out of me before I realized what he meant — they were going to mess with my dealers. Screw over the company. Aw man, that was not what I wanted. I had to get back to using my brain instead of animal instinct. "Oh ... oh, you've got DNA. The killer's DNA from his cum. Another way you know it's not me."

"What makes you think that?"

"You know his ethnic type. Ghadir's not the guy you're lookin' for." Sir Monte was anything but impressed so I added, "Besides, he's never been to America so that'd kill your theory of him bein' my helper."

"What about his son, Jamil?" Shit, they were gonna focus on Jamil? Beautiful Jamil of the black hair and doe eyes and sweet smile? "Has he been with you, whether he wanted or not? He appears to be the sort you prefer."

I looked straight back at him. "Ghadir's too important to

our business here, and he wouldn't take kindly to me fuckin' his son, no matter what the circumstances."

Four-buttons almost smiled. "So you do have some form of control over your animalistic urges."

"Don't fuck with me? I won't fuck with you. Pun intended."

Sir Monte leaned back. "Then you're saying you picked up on some form of interest from Thornton."

"No." Then I saw his skeptical glare and snapped, "No!"

"You attacked him despite knowing him to be hetero-sexual? And yet somehow you managed to force him to participate in his assault via anal intercourse?"

Oh you son-of-a-bitch, you really will trash Reg if you can't get what you want from me. Make him the fall guy for your fuck up. I looked straight at the prick. "Did you do a rape kit on him?" Sir Monte looked away. I didn't know if that meant yes or no. "If you did, you know I didn't — I — I didn't — never entered him." I shifted my focus to Four-buttons. "I — I was gonna. But I couldn't. I couldn't hurt him."

Four-buttons did not appear to believe me. "You kid-napped and bound him but you *could not hurt him*? Why not?"

It took me a moment to say, "The ... the men I ... the men I took ... they'd crossed me in some way. Or ... or done something I ... shit, that I thought was wrong."

"And if they do cross you, *in some way*, you become judge and jury?"

I nodded.

"But Thornton did nothing to initiate this aspect of your persona?"

I shook my head.

"Has this happened before?"

I let out a long deep sigh. "Never."

Sir Monte leaned forward. "You view homosexual assault as punishment?"

"If I know you hate fags, yes."

Distaste curled over Sir Monte's lips. All I did was look away from him and focus on the mirror. His condemnation meant nothing to me.

"You have a photograph of Griffin Faure," I said. "He never filed a complaint so how'd you connect me to him in any way that matters to these murders?"

"Our methods of securing information are immaterial."

I gave him a shrug. "He's the perfect example of what I'm talkin' about. He defrauded my company of hundreds-of-thousand dollars and nearly drove my brother to suicide." Four-Buttons glanced between me and Sir Monte so I focused on him. "Mine was just one of dozens of companies he did that to. And the courts blew us off. So I got the homophobic little bitch to pay us back by showin' him he wanted exactly what he claimed to hate. He got off on everything that happened between him and me and I can prove it."

"Got off?"

"Ejaculated. Hard. More than once. And he kept that quiet, so why do you have his picture?"

For the first time I saw a question in Sir Monte's eyes. "And these two?" He pulled out Ryan's photo, and Armo's. "One's a *former* police officer thanks to your handiwork."

I looked at the ice-cold son-of-a-bitch and said, "Good. I saw him smack his wife around when I was in town for business, so I smacked him around. You want details on him? What I did and when I did it? Want 'em on every one? Think your virgin ears can handle it?"

Four-Buttons leaned forward. "Have you been evaluated by a psychiatrist?"

"Isn't that what you are?" He said nothing. "I told you my M-O — you fuck with me I fuck you back, times ten. I don't take guys who haven't done something to me or mine, and I don't kill people; that's stupid and a waste."

Four-Buttons quietly said, "Or could it be because your father might have killed your mother?" Then he pulled a photo of the fucker from that fucking folder. A mug shot of dad when he was young. Face like Colin's. Dark eyes like mine. Black hair like both of us. Then came a photo of mom with a black eye and bruises. Her lip split. Taken the one time a rookie cop had thought about being decent and doing something about him — only to have his superiors let it slide.

Again.

My late and very unlamented father. Who liked mixing beer with his Bourbon. And loved being free with his fists and words. Even after mom was gone. Especially after. But he'd been gone eight years. Dead and buried. Unlike mom ...

I relived that fucking phone call. From more uncaring cops. Cold and callous.

"Mr. Pope, we got your cell phone number from your receptionist. We've found some human remains that we think could be your mother's, but we need more information."

"What makes you think they're hers?"

"There was a locket with the photo of two boys next to them, their names engraved into the cover. And that missing person's report came up."

"Where? Where were they?"

"The Marshlands. They may have been uncovered by a recent storm. Can you come by today? Give us a DNA sample?"

"No, I'm in London."

"When're you back?"

"I return tomorrow afternoon."

"Newark?"

"JKF."

"Monday, then. We'd like to get this cleared up ASAP. I'm sure you'd like us to get the remains back to you."

"Yeah, sure. I — I can be there."

"Morning's best."

"Okay, I — I'll try."

I was glad Marci had referred them to me, because I didn't want to let Colin know till it was certain. But my brain was exploding. If I'd been home I'd have called Thick for some emergency diversion. Even had him bring Walrus and Neat along to make it a major event. Instead I'd gone to a pub and had a Guinness and a shot of bourbon. Then a second shot. Then I aimed to get royally drunk on the overpriced booze in the hotel bar and stay drunk all the way through the flight.

But then I saw Reg.

And whether it was factual or not, his tattoo was mom's tattoo and the creature inside me took over. And now I was facing years in prison. What's crazy is, for some reason I was relieved.

But that didn't mean I was going to stop fighting.

I looked at Four-Buttons and shook my head. "That was a dumb move."

"Was it?"

"My father doesn't look like any of the dead men."

"But he does look somewhat like these men." He pointed to the photos of Griffin, Ryan, and Armo.

"And not like Reg! So I'm not killin' men to get even with daddy."

"Merely assaulting them, sexually."

"Having sex with them. Makin' sure they get fucked in the ass and cum as I fuck them. Every one of them 'cause I always cum when I get fucked. So what I'm really doing is makin' them into me. How does that work into your fucked up theory?"

Four-Buttons looked at Sir Monte, who looked at the mirror and waved his hand. An instant later Reg came in. I bolted to my feet. Went white with anger.

"You made him listen to this!?" howled out of me.

Sir Monte ignored me but Four-buttons' eyes were locked on my face.

"Thornton," Sir Monte snapped, "you've been closer to this man than any of us." Reg barely kept from flinching. "Do you believe his ravings?"

Reg looked straight at the wall behind us, at parade rest. "I don't know, Boss," he said, his voice under tight control. "All I know is — he appeared ready to — to do more than he did. But then he started to weep and — he left me in a way so I could unbind myself. Did nothing more than what I've told you."

"He claims much more than that."

"I — I don't know what that could be, Boss. I — I've been examined. You know what the doctor's determination was."

Sir Monte nodded. "Yes. Very good, lad. Now go home to your wife."

Reg looked at him, confused. "But, Boss, we're still — "

"Go home to your wife." And the tone of his voice screamed that it was an order.

Reg hesitated then nodded and left the room.

It wasn't till he was gone that I realized my hands were tight fists and I was quaking inside from anger. I had to whisper, "My first description of you was too kind, Sir Monte. You are a motherfucking devil. An asshole in the extreme."

"Who deserves punishment?" he responded with a cold sneer. "I should consider myself fortunate I don't resemble the sort of man you chose for your *pleasure*."

Then it hit me and before I could censor it I blurted, "Savile Row."

"Sorry?" I'd thoroughly confused Four-buttons.

"Son-of-a-bitch, he's your suspect. Good-looking guy, dark, high-end suit. Reg was there to entice *him*. Get the guy to go for him. That's why he had the back brace — to keep from bein' knifed." I dropped into the chair, weak from understanding. "Son-of-a-bitch, that's why you're pissed. Reg was a decoy but I kept your suspect from goin' after him ... may've kept him from gettin' killed ... "

A growl whispered from Sir Monte. "Pope, I will not have you making wild accusations — "

BAM! I was back on my feet.

"You fucked it up!" I snarled. "You sent Reg in without backup! He was your sacrificial lamb and you're pissed because he's still alive."

That brought the first hint of human emotion to Sir Monte's eyes. "I would never let one of my men go into a situation like that without support, and for you to suggest I would is depraved beyond measure!"

"There were no other cops on that train."

"How would you know?!"

"They'd have followed us off and jumped me when I jumped Reg!"

Sir Monte glared at me then snarled, "You made it appear that we were mistaken in our assumption but we could not risk losing our man, so I had them stay on him and sent cars to intercept you. When traffic delayed them I texted Thornton to abort ... but by that point you had already destroyed his mobile phone."

"So you *are* focused on Savile Row," I snarled right back. "And Reg was textin' you 'cause the guy wasn't takin' the bait. But I did. And you goaded Reg into leadin' me off! Then your other guys lost your suspect anyway. Lost both of us."

He rose to his feet, back to calm and cold, sighing, "And to think I considered you intelligent." But I could tell I'd finally landed a good solid blow.

That's when I noticed Four-buttons' eyes were still locked on me and while his expression had not changed I got the feeling he was satisfied. He also rose without a word then he and Sir Monte left the room.

I stood there for I don't know how long before I grabbed one of the chairs and slung it at that fucking mirror. It bounced away, leaving only a soft scratch. The damn thing was Lucite, not glass. Of course.

Dear GOD, I wanted to tear into something, anything, hell, anyone right then. I paced about like a caged animal, grunting and growling into myself for I don't know how long before I was able to regain control. I'm sure it made Sir Monte happy to see me acting the part of a beast. The son-of-a-bitch had shredded me — fucking shredded me, and it took all the effort that it might take to peel an orange. I was bleeding inside from the pain in Reg's face and from the reality of the danger I finally understood he'd been in. It's like he was my child and someone had tried to hurt him and that bastard had to die to make it right again. Like I'd felt about Colin over Griff. Like I'd felt a couple times about my nephews when some teacher had criticized them at school or when a bully had thought the twins were too weak to fight back.

I'd shown them some solid wrestling moves from my high school days, a couple not strictly according to the rules, and they'd taken him down after school, one day. Done it tag-team style and let him know if he ever tried to get them alone to get even they'd both come at him.

Diana wasn't happy with me about that, but at least it convinced her to enroll all three boys in Aikido classes. "To learn control," she'd said. But I knew deep down it was also about making sure they could fight back without mommy, daddy or *Uncle Devil* there to help.

Uncle Devil. That's what they all called me. Easier to say than *Devlin.* More formal than *Dev.* Three great kids who accepted me for who I was. Like their mother and father did.

Remembering them calmed me down. Helped me stop breathing like I'd run a hundred miles. Let me grow casual enough to pick up the chair, put it back in place and sit in it, my feet propped on the table. I could now see that in reality I'd done right by Reg. Not intending to but still I'd protected him, in a weird roundabout way. Because if the man who'd killed those guys had jumped him that brace wouldn't have kept a knife out of him and backup would have been worthless. He'd have been dead before they could stop things. I knew it. I was actually his hero. Hell, if I'd had a hat I'd have put it over my eyes like a too-cool cowboy in some old western.

Of course my self-congratulation was still colored by what I'd done to him and the situation he was now in ... but my own? That I could handle, now. I'd saved Reg's life. I knew it. Let Sir Monte and Four-Buttons pile it on. Inner kitty was rested and ready to rumble. Even looked forward to it.

So naturally the bastards set me free.

SIX

Well ... not completely free. I was released on bail, meaning they kept my passport so I couldn't leave the country, and I had to check in with Sir Monte's shadow once a day, or else. But with as much efficiency as when I'd been brought in everything else was returned to me. In a complete mess but there. Except for my phone. When I asked about that and my passport, a clerk said, "The Boss has those." Then he handed me a receipt, adding, "If anyone asks to see your documents give 'em this." Then the great Sir Monte, himself, drove me away, with Four-buttons beside me in the back seat.

My plan was to ride in silence and let my brain focus on a way out of this mess, but my seatmate opened a folder and a surveillance photo was shoved in front of me; it was of Savile Row in another snazzy suit, same goatee, hair wind-blown as he got into the back of a Bentley. Even from a distance he radiated wealth and calm. A man the size of a tank and built just as strong was holding the door open for him.

"He is what you normally talk into your bed, correct?" Four-buttons asked in a way that needed no answer.

I sighed and nodded. "That's the guy I saw on the train. Almost went for him instead of Reg."

"How unfortunate you didn't. His name is Tafiq al Qasimi. He's an Arab Muslim and has a connection to all four dead men."

I shrugged. "Then bring him in."

"We can't. The evidence is, at best, circumstantial and he

has ... diplomatic protection."

"He's young to be an ambassador."

"He's a bit more than that ... "

"Okay ... so why're you tellin' me this?"

Four-buttons took the photo back. "We have discussed some rather *incredible* claims you made whilst being interrogated. Claims which, if we read the prior accusations against you carefully, do not ... actually ... sound improbable."

This made me rather wary ... no, let's be real — my critter was crouched and ready to run as I said, "Thanks for the vote of confidence, but — "

"We wonder if this might be of some use to us?"

"Whoa, whoa, whoa, you guys want me to jump him and fuck him? You think that's how to get info out of him?"

"I seem to recall you mentioning seduction as one of your chosen methods ... "

I nearly laughed. "Oh, right, I'm Mata Hari — *She makes love for the papers*."

"Pope," Sir Monte snarled, "stop being so damn thick." Then he took in a deep breath and muttered, "We merely want you to do whatever you can to get information we cannot."

"C'mon, don't you have a gay *cop* who can do that?"

"We tried."

"He was the same physical type as the victims," said Four-buttons, "but al Qasimi proved ... uninterested."

"Like he did with Reg." I took the photo back and looked at it. "So it's not like he actually prefers straight guys. Do you have other pictures?"

He showed me a couple dozen more. All surveillance. They'd been shadowing him for a while.

"I don't get it," I said. "If you were watchin' this guy so tight how was able to kill anybody?"

"We began our surveillance after the third victim," said Sir Monte, "when we discovered the one other consistency between them — that all are tenuously connected to a certain foreign embassy. He's the only male whose whereabouts cannot be accounted for on any of the nights of the murders."

I let a breath escape me. "Oh, come on, guys, you watch this country so hard you even know when someone don't wipe his ass right. So how could he get to Perriman and you not stop him?"

"You, thank you very much," Sir Monte snapped. It took him a moment to continue. "When Thornton vanished that put the entire Met on alert. The two additional men we had on your train were collected at Hatton Cross and brought straight back to East Hounslow as al Qasimi continued on towards Perriman's office. They wanted to follow him, still, but they had seen you so could help search for you while we scoured CCTV. And to be honest we thought we had been mistaken about whom to suspect. Obviously we were both wrong and right."

"Okay, point taken," I said. "But this guy's awful neat to be plannin' to kill anybody. Tell me — your gay cop, is he out and proud?"

" ... Yes," said Four-buttons.

"Then this guy *wouldn't* want him. He wouldn't want anybody who might talk about him." Four-buttons' eyes locked on me. "That's why you shoved Reg in front of him." I got a half-smile, in answer. I shook my head. "You sure the victims weren't hidin' their interest, too?"

"We've found nothing in their backgrounds to indicate they enjoyed homosexual encounters."

"But hasn't this guy been with other men?"

"There is only so much investigation we can do!" Sir Monte snapped. "Not without arousing problems with the Home Office. And MI5. And Foreign Office. And the entire government of another country. Questions have already been raised regarding our surveillance of this embassy. They don't know who we're keeping an eye on, yet, but they will find out. Sooner rather than later. Once that happens who knows what obstructions will arise?"

"But if he has a connection to four murdered men ... "

"A tenuous one ... "

"Okay, how tenuous?"

Sir Monte and Four-buttons exchanged a glance in the rearview mirror then Sir Monte nodded and my seat-mate pulled more sheets from the folder, including good photos of the victims. All bright and happy and heartbreaking.

"The restaurant Etan Conescieu worked for catered an affair at the Embassy," he said. "He helped move everything in but he was not one of the servers. Liam Hanlon was employed by a broker who was handling a business matter for a corporation al Qasimi's connected with, and while he was not on the team controlling it, al Qasimi has been to their office on many occasions. The livery company Stuart Goughan drove for would on occasion collect visitors and diplomats for the embassy from the airport or wherever but al Qasimi, himself, does not use them; he has that Bentley and a bodyguard who drives him." I pointed to the guy holding the car door in the photo and Four-buttons nodded. "Abdel Fayiz Naifeh. He's a third generation bodyguard to the family. That said, our suspect does greet every important visitor at the main entrance so would probably have seen Goughan dropping them off."

"But if Tafiq's got his own car, why take the train? Especially at rush hour?"

"It is faster though not as convenient."

"But it's not like he's drivin'. Sit in the back. Have some Dom Perignon. Contemplate ways of screwin' more people out of more money. Think about how good life is. Drop him off a block from his appointed rendezvous." Then I kicked myself. "Except he doesn't want his bodyguard to even suspect what he's up to with guys. Get a grip, Dev."

"Yes, that would make for a potential witness," Sir Monte snapped. "One who might not agree with his ... *peculiarities*."

Four-buttons continued with, "Last night's victim, Martin Perriman, owned a courier service used by the embassy. Normally it was one of his drivers who transported the diplomatic pouch, but on two occasions he brought the pouch personally when a driver was unavailable. There may have been other deliveries he made; we are still researching his records."

"Yet none of them had direct contact with this guy."

Four-buttons nodded. "Which makes it damn near impossible to anticipate his actions — without him telling us."

I said nothing. Four-buttons kept watching me like I was something under a microscope while Sir Monte's eyes stayed on the road. It had started to rain, not hard but steady, and the windshield wipers ticked to the same rhythm as my heart. I looked out the window, barely able to breathe. I could now picture the whole sordid situation.

They'd followed al Qasimi non-stop, then when it looked like he was sneaking away from his bodyguard had offered Reg up to see if he'd jump. But it didn't matter how lovely Reg was, this guy was locked and loaded on Martin Perriman. Now they wanted me to take him to bed. Fuck him, whether he wants it or not. See if he has a diary on his nightstand that details his fun time. Sneak it off in the dead of night to find out if he was focused on anyone else he had a *tenuous connection* to. And maybe prevent another death.

Shit ... that made me responsible for preventing another man's death.

I noticed we had stopped in front of the same hotel I'd checked out of just hours before. The rain still pouring. I wanted to be anywhere else but there, but Sir Monte led me in by the arm, had me check back in and made sure he knew what room I was in by escorting me up to it. I had nothing to say because my mind was still bouncing against every corner of my head at how fucking crazy the whole idea was.

Then Sir Monte made it worse.

"I dislike asking this of you, Pope," he said as I opened my door, "but Herries-White thinks it's our best chance to — "

"Herries-White?"

"The man in the rear seat with you," he snapped. "He pointed out that when dealing with a devil you can't always play by the rules. Sometimes evil must be used to defeat evil."

I smirked. "And you think I'll be your evil slut."

Sir Monte's glare would have sliced through steel. "You're a gamble I'm willing to take, within limits, in order to try and save another man's life. Serial killers tend to get away with their crimes for years, even decades, before they make enough of a mistake to end their slaughter. I don't want to wait for luck to play a hand and have to face God knows how many more dead men's families, in the meantime."

"But ... can't you just keep him under surveillance?"

"Were he anyone else he'd have been in that room instead of you, long ago. Now? I would like to have something more than mere supposition to counter any objections raised by the Home Office."

"Who else knows about you pimpin' me out?"

"You, me and Herries-White. And that is how it remains."

"And if I get killed?"

He almost smiled. "If your death helps us stop a killer you will be given a hero's burial."

"What if I tell you to fuck off?"

"I suggest you find a solicitor and barrister for Crown's Counsel to be in contact with." Then a cold cruel gleam entered his eyes. "And we will send Thornton back out to try and decoy him again. Find some excuse for him to have business at the embassy. He is what this killer likes — straight, good-looking, fair-haired. It wouldn't be much trouble to provide al Qasimi with a *tenuous connection* to him. This time since you won't be around to inter-rupt ... we might be successful."

Ice shot through my veins and I clenched my jaw to keep from shivering but the bastard still noticed.

I let out a long deep breath and murmured, "You're right; I should never have fucked with you ... because you are one mean-assed cold-blooded motherfuckin' son-of-a-bitch."

This time the smile filled his face. "Nice to have that understood. We'll be in touch." He handed me my phone. "We have your number."

Then he left ... and I was stuck trying to figure out what the hell kind of shit I'd just got myself into.

****

It was the same damn room I'd had before. Shit. Now I was stuck with paying the equivalent of over $150 a night till this was settled. Sure, I'd gotten some decent orders on this visit, like one for a thousand *Rule Britannia* pins for some anniversary thing, but we couldn't keep up this kind of expense forever.

Man — I was kicking myself. I haven't been a saint, as should be obvious by now, but for this to come crashing down in a foreign country? Bigger than big mess. And Sir Monte — I wouldn't be surprised if he'd blocked my departure to give the FBI time to meet me at the plane with a warrant six miles long, probably at the very insistent urging of Griffin Faure's father and a number of Middle-Eastern oligarchs.

Not that it mattered. I had a solid defense for every one of the guys I'd taken. *How can it be rape if he cums?* And I had photos of cum dripping from their dicks. But that meant I'd have to play the *it was consensual and now he's embarrassed* card. In a courtroom. Make my private life fodder for the news weasels, *kill the fags* scum and blue-haired-blue-suited-anti-homosexual league. Hurt business, since most of our dealers are conservative. But what's worse is, it would mess with Colin's barely controlled life and the wellbeing of his kids. The anti-fag filth love to take out their hate on everybody they can, especially children who can't fight back.

And it would hurt Reg. Might get him divorced.

Shit.

I tried to call the American Embassy but was told it was after hours so call back on Monday. Very curtly, too. I guess they'd already been forewarned about me, something vaguely verified by the way the receptionist called me, "*Mister* Pope." That did not bode well.

So I called Colin to tell him I was staying in London *a few more days*. Fortunately, I reached him before he realized I wasn't on my flight.

"Dev, we've got problems with the Thai factory," he said before I even got a word in. "They used a cheaper gilt for the pins and it flakes off before it's been handled twice. I can't send this order out. And Eastern Mutual's ignoring my demands for payment on their account. And then there's — "

"Don't worry, Colin," I said. I always called him by his full name because sometimes he didn't recognize being called Collie or Lin or anything else. "E-mail me the info and I'll handle it from here. As for the flaking, see if Paulie in shipping has some spray fixative — "

"No, better if you come by the office; there's other — "

"Colin, I'm still in London."

"London? I don't understand. Aren't you home?"

"Yeah, yeah, yeah, that's why I'm callin'. I'm stickin' around a few more days." I hoped.

"You're telling me NOW? Your plane arrived an hour ago and — and I'm just now finding out — ?"

I cut him off with, "I got caught in a meeting and I didn't want to bust it up because it's a solid in on a new client. With the UK government. If it comes through we'll be set for years. They want to use pins to ID people and keep track of employees and on and on. Somethin' with a nano-chip in it that's small and protected. They been havin' trouble gettin' their current supplier to understand what they're after and I was with one of the top guys in the bureau and he likes five martini lunches and then high tea and — and I have to work it careful."

This wasn't a total lie; Ghadir'd let slip that a group who supplied pins to Her Majesty's Army had screwed up another order and the Palace was *perturbed*. One of their majesties had been pinning one on a loyal subject's uniform and half of it dropped right off. He didn't know exactly who we could talk to regarding it, but this forced delay would give me time to find out since I knew a guy who knew a guy who knew a guy; that even worked over here. It might actually be better because it meant I could start making my inroads in person instead of starting online. I could also get Ghadir's feedback on alternative pin factories to back up Mr. Mihn and find out if the UK had a problem with letting chips be fixed into something made in Thailand or Korea.

Colin's voice grew calmer, though not by much. "It'd be a lot of business?"

"Ten thousand just to see if we'd do a good job."

"Can the factory in Bangkok handle that? What about the crappy gold leaf?"

"I'll discuss it with Mr. Mihn when I call tonight. We may need to look into gettin' a backup factory. Like in Taiwan or Korea."

"Mr. Mihn won't like that."

"He took himself close to capacity by takin' on other business — like from those assholes in Torrance. He probably mixed up their instructions with ours on that flaky pin. If he can't expand or keep the quality issues straight he's got no complaint if we look elsewhere."

I didn't want to screw things up with Mr. Mihn, but if we did get this order he'd have to double his workforce and that takes time. Having a stopgap group would be a good idea. So long as they turned out quality work. It might mean taking special care and probably a monthly trip to whatever country it was in to make sure things went right. You don't want to lose a potential client by screwing up the product or taking too long with it, either. And if it turned out they did better work than Mihn's guys ... well ... them's the breaks.

Of course I was acting like my current situation wouldn't make any difference. I figured until it did ... why worry?

Yeah, yeah, yeah, very nihilistic ... and not at all realistic.

Colin was still ruffled so I put everything in an e-mail and made sure to cc Diana. She knew how to calm his nerves, which was usually by giving him a blowjob. I don't know what tricks she knew; I just knew whenever Colin got freaky she'd come in and take him away for fifteen minutes, and he'd come back acting like Joe Cool. So I trusted she'd see the upside to the extra business and soothe him the only way any man really understands.

The reason I know she does that to calm him down was ... well, I saw her in action. My office adjoins Colin's and after the Faure mess I had a little speaker system hooked up to his space, one he doesn't know about, so I could keep an ear on him when he's on the phone. I'd hear him starting to growl so could get next door before he exploded. Saved us more than once.

Well, just over a year ago he was having a rough morning. Not able to concentrate and getting frustrated, mainly due to a very complicated job that had just come in. Why he didn't tell me about it so I could work up the instructions, I don't know. I just heard him huffing and puffing and slamming pens down and snapping at anybody who came into his office and all that, so I called Diana and *suggested* she drag him out to lunch. She said she'd be there shortly.

Twenty minutes later I heard Colin's door open. Then close. Not a word from anybody. I heard some shuffling about and his chair creak a little. It made me curious so I slipped over to our connecting door and carefully peeked around it, halfway thinking I'd see this big blond dumb-cause-she-wants-to-be associate trying some shit with him. Instead I got a perfect side-view of Colin stretched across his desk, legs hanging over the edge, pants around his knees, hands gripping his hair and his dick curling up to the sky with the lovely Rubenesque Diana going to town on it like she was a gay man.

I think that's what startled me most — that she actually seemed to enjoy giving Colin head. I knew he'd like it; what man, gay or straight, doesn't love a good blowjob? But not all that many women are into it; at least that's what I've heard. So watching her lips and tongue worship my brother's big dick as her elegant fingers caressed his pubes and thighs ... I got the feeling I'd been misinformed about girls and boys' toys.

I made myself quietly close the door, but I don't think either of them would have noticed a six-point-nine earthquake. Then I sat at my desk. I could just hear their moans and a hint of slurping through the speakers. Damn she was good. And it got me going. So I pulled out and whipped off and finished up just about the time Colin's grunts grew too fast to be anything but him firing his load.

I wondered if she swallowed or spit.

Didn't matter. They slipped out and when he finally came back to work, alone, he was all sweetness and light.

I'm still trying to figure out how to ask her where she'd learned to do what she was doing — and if she'd teach me some of her tricks.

Anyway, now I was checked in and trapped out by LHR and I needed a drink and a decent dinner. I can't concentrate on an empty stomach, but I didn't want the okay food and acceptable beer in the hotel's restaurant so I headed for a pub. On Faggs Road of all places. Of course fag in British is cigarette, but it's still funny. So I walked since it wasn't far and I liked being outdoors after — what? A whole seven hours in lockup? How the hell did people handle that for seven years?

How could I and not turn into a caged animal?

I had a decent steak with a couple pints of Guinness and almost felt human when I got a call.

From Sir Monte.

"Where are you?" he snapped without even a hello.

"Having dinner on Faggs Road, sir," I chirped.

"Al Qasimi's returned to Feltham. He's currently en route to Hatton Cross."

"Whoa, whoa, whoa, you want me to start this now? I've got things to do and —"

"He's on Green Road about to connect with Faggs."

"But why would he come back out here?"

"Good question. Don't ask him. Just see if you can get to

him now."

"Wait a minute I — "

"Pope, the sooner this is done the sooner your situation is resolved."

"Shit. Okay, okay, but no promises."

"Nonsense." He hung up.

I slipped out and looked around. It was dark but I could still see along Faggs and saw no one. If he'd already rounded the curve into the A30 no way could I catch him before he got to the underground station without running. So I walked. Nice and slow. If I missed him ... *well, sorry, Sir Monte, maybe next time.*

Faggs was directly under a runway approach where jet after jet roared in, smooth and easy, carrying people who had cares so different from mine they might as well live on another planet. I thought of how I'd arrived on one just last Sunday and how long ago that felt. Like months or years. Wondered if I'd ever get to make trips like this again.

I reached the crosswalk for the A30, threatening to drift back into a blue funk, when a guy in a dark gray suit joined me. Damn he fit that suit good — broad shoulders, trim waist, nice legs under what promised to be a fine ass. Not big, just the kind of body that looks perfect in a good suit. He waited patiently for the light so I snuck a look at a profile that was sharp and clean, with dark hair, a goatee and golden tanned skin.

It was Tafiq al Qasimi.

I pretended to look past him at the oncoming traffic, but really to get a view of his face because those surveillance photos were a travesty against his beauty. That goatee framed amazing lips and gave a nice counterpoint to thick eyebrows and eyes with lashes a mile long. And that suit was not off a rack; you could tell by the quality of the brushed wool, threadwork and how perfectly it fit him. No wonder he stood silent and still with the complete assurance of someone who knew who he was and how he looked; in a killer suit like that I would too.

The light turned but I pretended not to notice so I could

watch him walk as we crossed to the little island in the center of the road ... and the way he walked — if it hadn't been for Reg, I would have followed him all the way to wherever the hell he was going. Chat him up. Some careful maneuvering. Get him curious about me and my intentions. My usual shtick for reeling in a new conquest.

But then he glanced at me, cautious but casual, and I decided, *Sir Monte wants fast; he's gonna get it.* I saw my in — a lapel pin on his suit. I leaned over to him.

"Excuse me," I said, "but do you mind if I ask you where you got that pin?"

He looked at me with big dark eyes and a hint of a frown crossed his elegant face.

"Sorry?" he asked, a gentle British lilt to his voice.

"The pin on your lapel — it's good work; where'd you get it?" I wasn't lying, either; it was a nice Cloisonné, the dragon-like design filled in with translucent blues and greens that were surrounded by a white-gold trim.

"Oh, this?" He looked at the pin, still a bit confused. "It was given me by my embassy. No idea where it came from."

"Which one? I'm lookin' for a new factory for a big order and I'd like to check them out. Maybe someone there can tell me who the dealer or manufacturer is."

That focused him on me ... and me on how the amazing beauty of his face was made perfect by a smile worth heaven and hell. It cut into me like a blinding laser. This guy was a killer? No fuckin' way.

"Um, I've no idea with whom you should speak," he said, his voice sounding even more calm and cultivated as he pulled a business card from his wallet and handed it to me. "Try the cultural affairs office."

Nothing but a seal, an address and a phone number on it. In Knightsbridge. Not far from the underground station. My inner kitteh growled.

"Nice area. Harrod's is there, right?"

He blinked and took a step back. "You're American."

"Yeah. Sorry, don't mean to spook you."

"You haven't."

"But I am keepin' you from gettin' home — "

He glanced me over in a way that sent my gaydar to Mach Ten. "You're not. I was merely trying to reach someone but they appear to be out of pocket."

"You don't work in this area?" I asked *in all innocence*.

"No." And that was spoken with polite amusement. "Do you?"

I looked him straight in the eye and said, "I'm at that hotel. It's become my center of operations. I can get out to see clients without any trouble and they can come see me."

"Clients?"

"I manufacture pins like the one you're wearin'. Got my sample case and everything. In my room." Said with just a hint of emphasis.

"You really make pins similar to this one?" He unfastened it and handed it to me.

I checked the back of it and saw a familiar design stamped into the metal — those born-agains in Torrance. To be honest, I was surprised at the quality of the piece ... but I still wouldn't mind stealing a client from them.

"Okay, I know who did this," I said, then I latched my eyes onto his. "Not bad work but — um — I like to give my clients *more* than they expect. A lot more."

He almost smiled. "Sounds like the proper way to do business. May I see your samples? Perhaps something will pop up in future. If you are not preoccupied."

"Naw, I was just comin' back from dinner. All that's left for me to do is wait for some emails; stuff I need to do before I head home."

"Where is home, for you?"

"New York."

"That is an amazing city. Very exciting." And he looked

me dead in the eye when he said it, his head cocked to the left.

Holee shit, did kitty-cat yeowl inside.

"C'mon up. I'll show you some real quality."

"I should hope so."

SEVEN

I didn't make anything like a move as we returned to the hotel and rode up the elevator and strode down the hall to my room. Even once we were inside all I did was offer him something to drink while continuing the banter.

"What do you have?" he asked.

I showed him some little bottles of red wine sitting by the ice bucket, glass stemware beside them. He nodded. I poured and made sure that when I handed him his glass one of my fingers caressed his. His smile threatened to widen. That's when I knew I had him.

"Let me pull out my sample kit. Give you an idea of what we offer. Then if you want I've got WiFi; we could track down your friend that way."

"I am not certain I should," he sighed. "There is a great deal of police activity around his office. I heard a lorry driver mention something about an assault and break-in, and that the authorities have been there all day. They were there yesterday evening, as well."

"Yesterday?"

"Yes. Must have got something of high value."

"In this area? Like what?"

He gave an elegant shrug. "A great deal of freight moves in and out of Heathrow. It may have been something he was handling. I tried to ring him but he does not answer his mobile and the office phone's message is they are closed pending further notice."

"That why you came out to look for him?"

He nodded. "We were supposed to have met last night but when I arrived his office was dark. And he has not answered my texts. Now I understand why. I hope he's well."

This did not sound at all right.

"Good friend, huh?"

"One could say that."

"Steady friend?"

The way his eyes danced when he looked at me and how he gently sipped at his wine screamed, *He doesn't know Perriman's dead. And he's been with the guy more than once.* That didn't fit what Sir Monte and Herries-White were thinking, at all.

So I did something I probably shouldn't have. I sat on the bed and said, "I like having good steady friends."

"Have you many?"

"Some. Back in New York. But I'm always lookin' for a new one."

He sipped more wine, still standing. "Do you make friends easily?"

"Depends," I said, then I leaned forward to rest my arms against my legs. "Could you be one?" I asked, almost whispering.

His breathtaking smile came back. "You are not very subtle. Or patient."

"Would you rather play games?"

He leaned against the desk, his pants tight across his legs and crotch. He looked like sex incarnate and his voice was just mocking enough as he softly responded, "What else have you to offer?"

I slipped over to him and set my wine down and ran my fingers up his lapels. "That's a fine suit. I'd hate to ruin it." Then I slipped the coat off his shoulders.

He set his wine beside mine and let me caress the coat down his arms. Nice arms. Strong and lean, not over-built. I hung the coat in the closet then he guided me back to face him and put his hands on my hips and we kissed. A nice kiss. Nothing needy or greedy but elegant and surprisingly satisfying. Surprising because I did not want it to stop.

He pulled back a little and whispered, "Ah — you taste of Merlot. My glass held a Cabernet."

I kissed him again. And again. And again. And I could have lived my life on those kisses. My hands holding his face, soft and gentle. His hands caressing from my hips up my back and down again. His legs spreading just enough for me to fit between. His pecs breathing steady against mine.

I have to say ... undressing him was one of the loveliest experiences in my life. And he let me do all the work. First undoing his tie and whisking it away from his neck. Then unbuttoning his vest and sensing his torso was well-shaped but not overdone. Then working my way down his silk shirt and feeling him quiver under my touch. All the while nibbling kisses around his ears and face. He wore an Armani t-shirt, thread count in the ten-thousand range and molded just tight enough to show his pecs were lovely and he had nothing in the way of paunch on him. I flicked his tits through it and he giggled a gasp. He let me guide both shirts off to reveal dark hair swirling up his arms like a flowing river and a chest fanned with just the right amount of fur around a pair of perfect brown nips that were born to be kissed. So I did.

He took deep breaths in reaction then slipped out of his shoes. My fingers tickled down his sides to undo his belt and pants and they drifted off his hips to reveal Armani briefs. I snapped the elastic.

"Man has good taste," I murmured.

"That is the merlot," he chuckled ... and made no move to undress me.

I lowered his pants and he raised one leg after the other to step out of them. I hung them up then turned to look at him. He was leaning against the desk, his elegant legs spread just enough, the hair on his flat belly diving behind the undies and happily dancing out calling for me to come and play as they whispered down his thighs and calves. And from the way the buttons on the

Armanis were straining ... oh, he was as ready as I was for fun.

He looked me over, too, so I grinned and whipped off my shirt and slacks to show him I wore Jockey briefs with y-fronts. He grinned then hooked a finger in the elastic of mine and pulled me into another kiss. I ground my crotch into his and slipped my hands down to cup his ass. Not as full as I expected but I got the feeling it would fit him, perfectly.

He ended the kiss by saying, "Anticipation is so important to a moment like this but I must be back no later than ten."

"Or mommy spank?" I growled.

"Something like that."

"Right you are," I said in horrible Cockney.

I grabbed him and slung him onto the bed. He bounced onto his back, laughing, and I jumped him, yanking at his undies and socks with as much fervor as he yanked at mine. And when they were off I got a good look at a dick was just as lovely as he was. And cut. Looked like I was getting a good substitute for my Persian guy's son.

Oh, man — the way he grabbed my ass, his fingers kneading into my skin as he rubbed his pubes against mine — and his balls against mine — and his dick against mine as his legs wrapped around me ... it was perfection.

I lifted him up and dove down on his long lovely sloping dick and made him nearly scream with the use of my tongue. My own dick danced between the cheeks of his ass. I could tell he had some hair there because it was electrifying. He caressed my legs and my sides and my arms and my back and pinched my tits and grabbed my hair and damn near drove me nuts with need. But as I was about to slip my fingers into the holiest of holes he twisted away from me.

"Do you have a condom?"

I laughed. That's something I'm never without. I grabbed one from my briefcase, wondering for half a second why I didn't use one on Reg, then bounced back on the bed beside him and held it up like a dollar bill.

"You wanna put it on?" I asked smirking like a lewd Madonna.

He did.

On himself.

I was so taken aback I didn't even think to say anything before he grabbed me by the hair and rolled me onto my back and was lying on top of me, his dick rubbing against mine, the latex adding to the sensation of it all. Then he whispered in my ear, "I don't know you well enough for anything but this."

He grabbed my ass with his hands and leaned back and hoisted me onto his crotch and without even a knock on the door plunged into me. No lube except what was on the condom.

I cried out from the shock and the pain. He put a hand over my mouth then leaned in and bit my left tit. That made me damn near scream from the jolt of need it shot down my body, and I clenched my ass tight around his dick.

"Much better," he chuckled as he began to rock into me, his hands still massaging my ass, his lips jumping from one tit to the next, his nose dancing through my chest hair, his hips rubbing against my thighs, his pubes washing over my balls like waves on the sand. By the third thrust I was overcome with need and grabbed his ass and pulled him hard against me and dove my face into the hair on his head, biting at it and grunting my hot breath into his scalp.

He went harder and harder, his hands jolting up to grip my face as he dove in for more kisses. Animal kisses. All but growling. Almost biting. I wrapped my legs around his waist and encircled his torso with my arms, all but forcing myself to meld with him because I felt like I was joining with God, the feeling was so right and perfect. In what seemed like only moments of an eternity I exploded, my cum shooting onto my face and chest as he grunted and whimpered and thrust deeper and harder and I would swear I felt his dick pumping through me.

He kept pushing — pushing — his arms wrapping around me, holding me tight. Still pushing. His hips grinding slower and slower. Still pushing. His lips whispering from my right shoulder up my neck to my ear to nibble at the lobe then back down to my shoulder — and back again. His beautiful nips rubbing against mine. And still he pushed — and pushed — and finally lay atop me, sweating and as hot as August in Manhattan.

I nibbled his ear and let myself whisper, "Fuck."

He chuckled deep and elegant as he murmured, "Exactly."

And we just lay like that, loving every minute of it.

****

He finally rolled over on the bed and looked at the ceiling as if it were Heaven and he was in awe. Neither of us said anything, even as my left hand drifted over to make contact with the hair on his thigh and trail up it. Then I shifted onto my side to look at him and trailed the fingers of my right hand over his pecs and down his treasure trail to his pubes to remove the very full condom and toss it to the trash can.

I missed.

Then I said, "My name's Devlin. What's yours?"

"You may call me Tawfi," he said in a voice so soft it was more like breathing.

"Like the candy?"

He chuckled and spelled it you for me. "My true name is Tafiq but that is too formal for a moment like this."

"Interesting. What is it?"

He gave me a cockeyed look. "What is what?"

"Where's it from? What does it mean? Your name."

"Oh. It is Arabic for good or fortunate."

"Fits."

He smiled. "What meaning is there for Devlin?"

"My sister-in-law says it's Gaelic for fierce."

"Sister-in-law?"

"Brother's wife."

"Back in New York?"

I nodded. "But we should switch names. You were fierce and I was fortunate."

"My self-indulgence did not trouble you?"

I dove in to flit my tongue over his right tit, then I snarled, "Lemme put this a New York way — bitch, you're the first guy ever got me to shoot my own cum in my own face."

He laughed. "You are delightfully vulgar."

I caressed his elegant throat, making him sigh. His long lean body seemed stretched to its fullest length. His dark hair highlighted the beautiful curving lines from his adorable nips along the flow of his belly to where it filled his crotch, half-hiding his sweet dick and balls, then fanned out over his lovely thighs and solid calves. Even his feet were long and lean. Seemed the only thing fat about him was his dick.

Damn, I loved how he looked — the light scruff on his chin emphasizing the goatee under his hawk-like nose as his un-sculpted brows let his eyes seem softer and more inviting, giving him a surprisingly masculine grace. I drew my hand slowly down his body, making him smile — almost giggle.

"Be careful," he murmured, "you know not what you do — "

"Don't I?"

"I was a man in need. It is not right to take advantage."

"Needy? You?" I was being facetious.

He sighed. "That is, perhaps, the wrong word to use — "

"Yeah," I joked, "I'd have said greedy." Then I tickled his pubes and sing-songed, "And I got more condoms. One for me this time?"

He squirmed a little, still not looking at me. "As I said, I do not know you well enough for such intimacy."

"You fuckin' me wasn't intimate? Felt that way to me."

"Yes. Yes." Sudden tears drifted from his eyes. He took in a deep breath. "Sorry. I should not be so emotional."

"This what you missed with your guy?"

He nodded. "We used to meet every Thursday — but I've

not seen him in weeks."

"So that's why you were so hungry."

He looked at me. "You and he are not similar in looks, nor will he ever be thought of as fierce. He is a hesitant man. With a wife and children. Unfortunately that bespeaks a need to keep this part of his world in shadow."

"Didn't that bug you?"

"No. I quite understand. I am rather similar in that way."

"Married?"

"I have yet to take that step. But some day I shall. No, it is only that when we are together it is as if no one else matters in the world. I miss that contact with him. Miss how our assignations were a game to be played. Like little James Bonds, so no one would ever suspect. I never left him unhappy." His voice trailed off and he coughed a bit. "You say you return to America soon?"

"Next week. Still lots to do."

He rolled onto his side to look into my eyes. His hands drifted over my eyebrows. "Are you booked up, Monday?"

"Uh — not really — "

"Come by about tea time. Afternoon. I'll find out who arranged for that pin and introduce you to him. If you are still interested."

"I'm always interested."

His hands drifted down my body. Soft. Tender. Almost afraid to make full contact. "Brilliant. There are some excellent restaurants in the area. And — and I have a flat not far away."

My lips touched his. "But you haven't told me your full name," I whispered.

"I tell no one."

"Ashamed of it?"

He shook his head. "My family is too high-ranking."

"Really? You mean you're like my king?" And I pinched one of his tits.

He yelped and gave me a shocked glare then burst into a smile and snuggled close to look into my eyes. "Then I suppose what we just did makes you my queen." His dark eyes twinkled and his perfect smile grew and he shifted himself to lie on top of me and kissed my nose. "Is that all right for you?" he murmured, his fingers playing with my nips and his dick telling me he was still hungry.

I wrapped my legs around him and grabbed both ass cheeks, nice and rough. "What do you think?"

He kissed me, hard, his tongue slinking into my willing mouth as he ground his fast-growing dick against my already ready one. When he finally came up for air he said, "You are a very dangerous man."

"So I been told."

"You mentioned you have another condom — "

"Dude — I got a box-load."

He laughed and said, "I will need but one more — for now."

I rolled him onto his back and pinned his hands above his head. "Why use any?" Then I kissed him as deep and French as he had me, but with a lot more insistence before I started working my way down to take him in my mouth.

He was big but not too big for me and in moments I had him squirming in ways that damn near made me weak with need. But what's crazy is not once did I think of forcing the issue, like I had so many times before with other guys. I wanted him to say, "Okay," before I fucked him. I wanted him to be completely willing and a part of it so I could drive him as crazy as he was driving me.

Which was totally unlike me.

He gave a deep throaty chuckle and said, "I do not think I will leave you unhappy."

I came up for air just long enough to say, "Not if I got any say in it."

And he didn't.

****

Tawfi headed off about nine. I hated to see him go, even though all he gave me was a glorified hand job, because for the second time in twenty-four hours I'd been fucked to within an inch of my sanity.

Yes, yes, I know — Reg wasn't a willing participant, that in reality what I did with him was rape and I'd be lucky if I didn't go to jail for it, but being with him had cut deep into me in ways no one ever had before. Now ... having Tawfi here and using me like a sex toy ... like I'd used Reg ... and me letting him do it — it's like my whole world had shifted in ways I was just beginning to see and still did not understand.

For example normally I'm the first guy out of bed and into the bathroom. Instead, Tawfi had rolled onto his feet and taken a quick shower. As I secretly watched. And sketched him. I never did that with my one-nighters but this time I just grabbed a pad, sat on the toilet and started in. And I made it nice. Nothing lewd. Just from the chest up, water pouring over his head and face and chest in a way that was brutally erotic. Quick and simple.

He didn't notice me working till he grabbed a towel. He blinked and asked, "Have you been watching me this whole time?"

I nodded and showed him the sketch.

He hesitated before he said, "You did that as I washed?"

I shrugged. "Just a quickie for our quickies."

He smiled and I melted. "You are quite good."

"It helps with the job I'm in. You want it?"

Surprise came over his face and he nodded. "Thank you."

"I'll put it by your suit coat." I went back in the room.

He finished toweling off and followed me in to dress. "Do you design all of your pins?"

"Naw, I just clean 'em up. Sketches like this are for fun."

"You are better than that." I grinned and sat on the bed to gaze at him. He looked at me. "Devlin, what are you doing?"

"Watchin' you dress."

He chuckled. "Shall I do a reverse of the *Dance of the*

Seven Veils?" Then he held his Armanis up to his nose and wriggled about and turned to pull them on and I lost control and pulled him onto the bed with me and kissed him.

"Wish you could stay the night," whispered from me.

His elegant fingers caressed my chin as he said, "Next time perhaps."

"Then I'll walk you to the station." I started to get up but he pulled me back down.

"I would rather you not," he said, gazing upon me. Then he rose to his feet, his eyes never leaving me. "I want this to be the image I hold of you — naked and wanton — not waving bye-bye on a cold platform. All right?"

And so it was.

I could just see him as he left the hotel and headed for Hatton Cross, sketch rolled up and in hand. Even from the fourth floor and in the dark you could tell he was in complete control. And I liked that about him.

Two minutes later, Sir Monte called.

"Bloody hell, you weren't exaggerating about your ability to seduce men," he said.

"It's what you wanted."

"What did you learn?"

"Weren't you listening in?"

He hesitated then said, "Your voices were often quite soft. Unrecordable."

For some reason, knowing Sir Monte had heard the unimportant stuff and it made him *uncomfortable* gave me a tingle behind my balls. "Okay," I said, "I don't think he's your guy."

"That's not for you to determine."

"He doesn't know Perriman's dead yet. He came out here to look for him. And he's been with him more than once. Usually on a Thursday. That don't fit what you told me."

Sir Monte hesitated again before saying, "We'll look into it. Anything more?"

"Dinner date for Monday. I'm meetin' him at his

embassy."

"Did you manage to collect any of his DNA during your escapades?"

I glanced at the used condom on the floor and said, "Yeah, but I've already taken a dump." I went to it and put it in the trash.

"I don't understand."

"It cleans you out."

"Oh. I though you used a condom."

"I did; he didn't. Sorry. Didn't know that's what you wanted." I fired up my laptop and signed into the Wifi.

"Do so next time. If we have his semen we might be able to eliminate him."

Or frame his ass, I thought. "Yes, Boss."

"Oh, stop. Are you planning to leave your room, at all?"

I checked my emails to find one from Colin listing the problems of the week.

"Just for a little bit, Boss. I gotta print up some emails."

"I'm having housekeeping change your sheets. We may be able to glean some DNA from the ones you just used."

Shit. "Okay. I'm back in 15 minutes." I ended the call.

I pulled on my jeans and a t-shirt and went down to the business office to print the emails. That's how I keep track of what was done when and where. A bit old-school but I didn't care. I rode back up alone and there was no one else in the corridor as I walked down it. I got to my door and unlocked it and —

I was slammed against the opposite wall. My wrestling kicked in and I grabbed the guy and we tumbled down the hall and a searing pain ripped into my left arm and I cried out and crashed to the floor then caught the slightest glimpse of someone running into the stairwell. That's when I found a gash in my forearm was gushing blood. I bolted into my room, grabbed Tawfi's still wet towel and wrapped it around me then called the front desk. The concierge was at my side in twenty seconds.

The police were called but I wasn't much use. I hadn't

seen the man who jumped me so could offer no description. I checked my things; nothing was missing. Then Sir Monte showed up and asked for video from the hotel's CCTV cameras. We reviewed them as paramedics treated me.

We found the guy who'd done it. He was big and buff. Dressed in a black hoodie and jeans with Nikes on his feet. Running down the stairs. None of the cameras got a look at his face.

We backed up to find where I exited my room to head for the office and saw him waiting down the hall in a doorway. He bolted over to my door but didn't reach it before it latched closed. He waited ... and shortly after, a maid came up with fresh sheets. He quickly put something on the floor to prevent the door from closing all the way then waited until she left to slip inside the room. Going back further we saw him enter the elevator with a group of people and ride up to a couple floors above me then head down the stairwell.

Sir Monte gave me a sideways glance filled with disbelief. "Very neatly planned, with precision," he murmured so no one but I could hear. "Did you arrange this with al Qasimi?"

I glared at him. "Yeah, right, I set myself up to get stabbed for some stupid reason I can't figure out, yet."

"Perhaps I should put you under surveillance as well," he said, his voice dry and laced with anger.

"Jesus Christ," was all I could think to say.

I was taken to a nearby hospital to have the cut stapled. Took 15 but no serious damage, fortunately. Then I was put in a new room on the top floor that overlooked Heathrow's runways. I sat by the window to watch the planes come and go until three am before I could even think about trying to sleep.

And wished to God I'd wake up to find this had all just been a nightmare.

EIGHT

I don't normally remember my dreams, but that night I had one that included both Reg and Tawfi and the black shadow of the figure that attacked me. And for some reason I was thinking a burning snake with wings was involved, like it was coiled around them and slowly squeezing them into nothing as I tried to get to them but couldn't move or even breathe and —

I jolted awake, not from the dream but from the hotel phone ringing. I grabbed it. "Yeah?"

It was the front desk. "Mr. Pope, a Mrs. Colin Pope is here to see you."

"Here?" I looked at the clock. 9:53 am.

"Yes, sir. Shall I send her up?"

"Uh, yeah, fine. Sister-in-law."

"Thank you, sir." And he hung up. I grabbed a hotel robe and wrapped myself in it then washed my face. I remembered I hadn't bathed the night before but figured I wouldn't be too rank yet. Then came the knock at the door.

I opened it to find my brother's wife looking at me with an expression that could be amusement or bemusement or a need to use the toilet for all I could tell. She was in her casual chic mode and looked like she'd just finished prepping for a ladies' lunch, not having spent all night on a crowded plane. I let her in with a growl of, "You got here fast."

"I was invited to a baby shower, Dev," she said. "I wasn't sure I could make it but my mother changed her plans to watch the boys and Marci said, *even though she's really busy, she'll handle*

Colin for Monday and Tuesday. So, here I am."

"Good ol' Marci. No bags?"

"Downstairs. I'm staying with friends."

"You talk to Colin ... "

"When do I not?"

Oh shit, this was gonna be rough. "I'll order coffee."

"Tea, please." She looked at my arm. "Rough night?"

"My room got broke into," I said. "Not even worth Channel Four takin' note."

She just nodded.

I put in an order for a full English breakfast and to hell with the cost, then I sat on the bed as she eased into a chair, her eyes locked on me. I'd seen that look before when I'd done something she didn't approve of, like a mother disappointed in her child. I took a deep breath, grabbed a pillow and shifted to lie back, my eyes watching her eyes watch me. "Okay, let's have it."

"Glass always half-empty with you, isn't it?"

"Diana, I ache all over. I didn't sleep well. And I'm still freaked out at getting attacked last night so cut the crap and get down to — "

"Some of our dealers have been interrogated by FBI agents," she said. "About you. Two in Los Angeles. One in Chicago. Three in New York."

Shit. "Why?"

"The FBI's questions were regarding an extortion racket. FYI — Griffin Faure is behind the complaint."

I laughed. "You're not gonna tell me he came back to the States to admit what happened?"

"He's been back a while," she said, causing me to sit up. "And yes — he's telling his version with the suggestion there may be others who've been, oh, *caught in the same trap*."

"Griffin Faure, bullshit; Papa's pushin' this and he's just pissed 'cause golden boy and I had some fun," I snarled, then added for good measure, "and I recorded it."

"I know. I know *all* about that."

"How?"

"Devlin, please — I know people, too."

"And do I need to guess who told you?"

"No. He trusts me and he's worried. Federal agents trying to find out more about you and The Faure Group, and pushing hard? Hitting informants? Questioning how *certain people* got repaid for losses cause by that criminal family? They've even been to West Nyack. Lots of huffing and puffing but no arrests. So far. But he couldn't find you so he contacted me."

That made me blink. "You haven't seen the videos have you?"

"You can be sure the FBI has. What's more — I also hear a certain Congressman is helping the Faures push this."

"Aw, fuck," shot out of me, followed by, "Sorry."

"Don't be, Dev. It's just you and me. Now ... what you did with that shit, Faure — I really don't care. He stole from us and nearly drove Colin to suicide. He got off light. What I want to know is why this shit is coming down on us now and what you did to cause it."

That made me look closer. She had her mommy eyes on; I'd seen them when one of the kids was trying to pull a fast one. "How'd you find all this out so fast?"

"Please! I used to be a party girl in the city that never sleeps and could teach Vegas a thing or two about keeping it there. Once I make friends they're friends for life. You never know who'll come in handy when you need some help."

"You think you can offer any?"

"Depends on how you answer a question."

"Oh, jeez, that crap again?" I sighed and leaned forward. "Okay ... hit me."

Her smile widened. "I just need to know — did you ever know someone named Kenneth Tavelscha?"

Oh, son-of-a-bitch, it was worse than I thought. I just nodded.

She nodded back. "Have you kept up with him?"

"Not since college."

"He's that Congressman. Republican. Bought and paid for by The Faure Group and they've been cross-referencing. Apparently for a while because less than an hour after you'd been arrested by the Metropolitan Police — " I shot a look at her. "Yes, I do know about that."

"Christ," shot out of me. "You didn't tell Colin?"

"Devlin! With me about to leave on a trip!?"

"Right. Sorry. Guess I'm freakin' out."

"You should be, because Tavelscha had the TSA add your name to the no-fly list, and an hour after that the FBI opened up that investigation, calling it a *blackmail* racket."

"Oh, fuck!"

Fortunately room service arrived and I was able to shift focus away from my inner chaos. I let them set everything up, signed the bill and tipped them and got them out, the whole time trying to figure out what I should and shouldn't say to her. Didn't do any good; she had her mommy eyes on me the whole time.

She calmly poured out tea for herself and coffee for me then set up a chair beside the tray, took a slice of toast and piece of bacon, and sat back in her own chair.

I kept standing by the door, unable to move, my brain spinning.

After another minute of watching me and sipping her tea and nibbling at her food she said, "Dev, you know how Colin and I met, right?"

I had to nod. "He ... he got lost and you ... uh, you found him. Brought him home."

"You know where I found him?" I shrugged a *yes*. She smiled. "I always thought it interesting you never said anything."

I sighed and glanced at her, my mind beginning to focus. "I didn't need to."

Her smile widened. "Y'know, the only reason I approached him was I'd heard my usual connection got busted and that I should assume the new guy's a cop. So when I saw Colin —

no way did he belong in that neighborhood. *Fuckin' rookie*, was my first thought so I went over to play. Be a real bitch. But he looked at me with those lost dark lovely eyes and the first words he said were, *Oh my God, you're so beautiful.*" She sighed. "I wasn't. I was at the tail of a party weekend. But his attitude ... his whole manner ... it was so simple and straight and honest and sweet ... I fell apart. Sobbed. He said he was sorry and gave me a handkerchief. Cheap white cotton. Buy 'em by the half-dozen. I still have it. Wouldn't part with it for anything."

I turned to her. "You're good for him. For both of us."

"Thank you for that." She smiled and pulled out a tissue to dab her eyes. "It took me ten minutes to find out he'd met with a client and parked his car in a cheap lot to save a few bucks, but couldn't remember which one and was close to falling apart. I offered to call someone but he panicked and said you were at school and your father off on business and no one could know how he'd screwed up. So we went to every lot I knew — and found it at the fifth one. By that point, he was shaking so badly he couldn't drive so I got behind the wheel. And I stayed. And we have three beautiful perfect sons." Then she looked straight at me to add with a near growl, "And I will never, never, never let anyone — anyone at all — hurt him or them. So if you don't give me the complete and absolute truth, I'm here to have fun at a baby shower for an old friend, and then back to New York."

Where they would build walls to protect the business and I would be fucked.

Of course she was right. I'd just been trying to postpone the explosion till I was back in the states and had our own attack dogs lined up, ready to rumble. Hamilton could get just as down and dirty as the other side but he needed my version of the story and no way was I spilling it in a phone call or email. Now it looked like I was going to be stuck in the UK for a lot longer than I thought.

It must have shown on my face because she kicked the chair away from the tray and said, "Sit."

Like a well-trained mongrel, I did.

"Now tell me all about Kenneth."

"What good would that do?"

"Dev, this son-of-a-bitch is messing with my family. I want to know why and you'd better fucking tell me."

I jolted at her anger. Warrior Queen all but flared from every fiber of her. It was to be the truth, the whole truth and nothing but the truth or God help you.

That's when the beast gave a short huff and let out a long sigh and lay down to sleep. So I focused on my breakfast, and as I ate I laid it all out about Kenneth fucking Tavelscha.

****

He was a blond jerk of a football jock who was too sun-bright and asshole-ish for my taste. We only had one class together since mine were advanced and his mainly remedial, him being a scholarship-baby who also played rugby, squash and baseball; one of those no-watt types who're good at sports and wearing athletic gear and not a damn thing else. Me, I looked straight and acted straight so his type was usually shocked to learn that a guy built like a wrestler instead of a girly-glam-boy happily preferred dick to pussy, which is why I made damn sure generic-homophobes like him knew it.

Now he wasn't bad-looking in a linebacker sort of way and his legs were just right for those shorts. Blond hair swirling over suntanned skin and catching the morning rays so perfectly you'd think they were CG'd. He only wore nylon half-length that clung to his thighs and his just-bubble-enough-for-my-tastes ass along with workout shirts that showed off beefy arms carved from granite. Even in the middle of winter he'd only wear another layer of light Nike crap with a hoodie that made his tight face look like he was thinking really hard when he was doing nothing of the kind. What's sad about it is, he wanted me to give him a blowjob. But rather than just ask, he thought he was being clever with his hints at it.

Of course, my friends thought he was hot. We hung out at this bar near campus, a made-over gas station with a thousand tiny lights covering the ceiling making it seem both day and night inside. He started showing up at the same time as us. My male-pack would notice and snark about the signals he kept sending me, signals a blind man could see, while the girl-pack would just sigh or shake their heads. But I ignored him. Some instinct was telling me to be careful with ol' Kenneth.

Sure enough, one day I was there alone sitting at a corner table and relaxing after my final mid-term ever when he busted in with three of his jock buddies. It was a Friday just past three and they plopped around a table at the opposite end of the room, yapping their typical sports crap and whining about how hard the tests had been in voices loud enough for the dead to hear. I tried to ignore them but it was impossible; there's something about a pack of dicks that brings out the too-obnoxious-to-bear in them all.

Most of me wanted to head on, but I felt casual and lazy and my legs just didn't feel the need to move, so I popped in my ear buds, cranked up some *Imagine Dragons* and half-closed my eyes, making like I was dozing as I gazed at them like a cool cat eyeing its prey and trying to decide if it was hungry enough to go hunting. A couple of Kenneth's buddies were just what I like — solid bodies, dark hair, nice frat-boy faces, legs like a man should have instead of stick-figures — but even that couldn't rouse me beyond a light purr. Not till Kenneth deliberately strolled up near me to buy a round.

He stayed there, leaning against the bar, letting the form of his back dive down to that perfect ass draped over by those ever-present nylon shorts emphasizing his amazing legs. I let my eyes wander over them. Wondered why I didn't just jump his bones already. Show him how much he wanted a man to use him like the whore he wished he was. And if his cock was nice ...

Then he cast me a sly glance to make sure I'd noticed how gorgeous he is — which irritated the shit out of me. I'm not big on being in the closet. If you want dick, go for it. Don't be all cute and cagey so you can deny who you are. That's when I noticed his buddies were casting me quick little smirks, like they figured I'd love to grab ol' Kenneth's butt the second I had the chance and were just waiting for me to try something.

Critter's purr became a growl of *They're up to no good.*

I shifted online with my phone and checked to see if there had been any gay-bashings that I hadn't heard about but nothing came up. Then I got to thinking — *Sojourner Week* started that night. That's when the fraternities and sororities at my college had all kinds of games and parties and events after midterms leading up to Spring Break. All to *raise money for the less fortunate.* In reality it was just an excuse for the privileged few to be even bigger drunken assholes than usual. There'd been word last year of a homeless man being led around by a dog collar and leash while wearing nothing but a diaper as part of a scavenger hunt. Nothing had come of it because, as the gossip went, he'd been given some nice cash and dumped back in his gutter. He'd vanished soon after.

So could it be that these little fucks were planning something for *Sojourner Week*? Did their sniggering glances mean I was going to be part of it? Did my paranoid self tell me to get the fuck away? Yes. I huffed and shifted into a sitting position, planning to leave ... but critter growled, *Wouldn't you like to mess with their little frat selves? Especially Kenneth Fuck-all?*

To which I purred, *Why not?*

First order of business was to find out what they're up to. So I deliberately made eye contact with ol' Kenneth and smiled at him. Sure enough, like an overgrown puppy he brought over a toy to play with — an already open beer.

"Hi-ya, Dev," he said, grinning. "Got ya 'nother one."

"Thanks." It was pisswater in comparison to what I'd been drinking so I pretended to sip some.

"You been keepin' to yourself a lot lately."

I shrugged. "Just finished mid-terms and still got two papers to write."

"But you're already set to graduate, right?"

I nodded. "Then comes Grad School."

"Y'know, we're havin' a party, tonight. *Sojourner Week.* Why don't you come?"

I damn near said, *In your ass? Sure.* But I only muttered, "Wish I could but I gotta get home. Workin' this weekend."

"You work too hard."

I chuckled. "Can't leave everything for my brother to do."

"Oh, right. Heard about your dad. Sorry."

I smiled my thanks, my eyes locked on him.

"C'mon, join us tonight; guys'd love to have you."

I'll bet hit my brain but stopped before it hit my vocals. I just glanced over at the other table. They were trying their best not to look like they were smirking and nudging each other. I raised my beer in acknowledgement of them. Kenneth set his beer down to glance their way so I used that moment to exchange his beer for mine before he looked back at me. What made it great was how his beefy body hid my actions from them.

"Y'know, we're goin' on a beer run."

"Thought your parties were catered."

"Fuckin' freak wants to serve nothin' but wine. We had to make him add beer. So just to be sure we got enough we're gettin' a keg or two." Then he downed half his/my beer.

I guzzled mine then stood up. "Sounds like fun. Lemme think while I take a leak."

Then I winked at him and half-licked my lips. He blinked and offered me a lopsided grin. He was hooked. I headed for the men's room. Kenneth drank more of his beer and, not realizing he was reflected in the glass on some framed things on the wall, held up a thumb for the guys to see. Then he followed me.

I slipped into one of the toilet stalls and peeked through the space between the door and the wall. A moment later Kenneth sauntered in and stopped, startled at not finding me at a urinal. I opened the stall door and yanked him in with me then grabbed his ass and groped him. He gasped.

"Shit, Dev — cut it out!"

"It's what you been after all year!"

"No, I — I — "

"You're a junior, right?"

"Uh — yeah — stop it — "

Now that I had my hands on his hot muscles?

No fucking way.

"You took this long to figure out you want a man's lips on your dick?"

"No — no — "

Which was bullshit. I did a quick grope-by to find he was getting fat and hard. I pinched his tits. He gasped. Then I crushed him against the partition wall.

"Don't lie, Kenneth ... "

"I — just — just a blow job, that's all I want. See what it's like with a guy instead of a girl."

"Girls give you blowjobs?"

He nodded. "Sometimes. But they make it tough — "

"Okay. Let's go back to my place. Or we can do it here."

"No, better go — I — shit, not now. Okay? Not now."

"Why not? I'll make you happy faster'n that piss-water you drink or any dumb bitch who thinks she knows how to suck cock."

"Dude, you don't understand — I — shit, I snuck something in your drink."

"What?" I asked it like I wanted to know what it was.

"Roofie."

"What?! Why?"

"Party tonight. Naked fag in a cage. In the bathtub. Piss on him for a buck. Money goes to charity. Now it sounds dumb."

"And illegal."

"Only if you remembered ... but you'd have been out of it and, man, c'mon — that — that stuff's gonna — it's gonna — " His eyes grew confused. He looked at me.

"Gonna put you out cold," I smiled. "I switched our beers.

How much did you put in?"

"Just — couple — "

"A double dose? Are you fuckin' crazy?"

"Naw, just makes it easier — last longer ... "

"You've done that to girls?"

"Naw you — you're bigger'n them."

"You have?! Fuckin shit, Kenneth, you dumb fuck, that's a jail ticket and no more football. You stupid shit!"

He was feeling it, now, and his ice-blue eyes grew big. "Didn't mean anything — just fun and — and — oh, shit — just a joke — you — remember — aw, shit. What you — gonna — do?"

I snarled and grabbed his butt and decided to have some fun with him so I pulled him tight to me. "Show you what roofies are all about, asshole — using yours." Then I ground my crotch against his.

His eyes grew wide. "Shit — no — " He tried to cry out but I put a hand over his mouth to muffle him — and then he passed out. And was he as heavy as he looked? Holy shit.

Okay, now what? I hadn't planned on doing anything more than leaving him in the bathroom with his shorts around his knees ... but I got to thinking — Kenneth and his buddies would know I was just fucking with them. They might retaliate and that could mess up me graduating. But what if I got him back to my apartment and he woke up there? Not so easy to blow that off, and if they tried anything with me I could yell I'd been gay-bashed after one of their guys made it with me. That brought a wicked grin to my face.

What's good is the bathroom doors were down a hallway that led to the parking lot entrance and was out of sight of the tables, and I'd been smart enough to keep my phone with me. I could call the bartender, later, and make some excuse about leaving my backpack; tell him I'd come back for it after my last test. So I called up an Uber, slung Kenneth over my shoulders and staggered out, one hand wrapped around one leg and traveling up to find he was a jockstrap kind of guy — and that those sweet golden hairs swirled all the way up to and over his ass.

Uber pulled up nice and quick, so I spit out, "Already started *Sojourner Week*," and flopped him in the back seat then checked around to see if anybody had seen us. Midterms were still keeping the campus like a ghost town. Perfect. I sat next to Kenneth and we drove to my building.

I tipped the driver, got a wink in response so cast him a grin, then dragged Kenneth across the back seat to pull him up into a fireman's hold and carry him off.

I was in the back of this u-shaped building, on the ground floor. Rent was cheap and included utilities, which was perfect since my asshole father'd never given me enough allowance to really live on. I'd come close to getting a better place when he died, but I only had a semester left and figured his life insurance would do better for grad school; now I was glad I had the joint.

I propped him up against the wall, to open the door, then half-carried him in to fall onto my double bed. My only other furnishings were a messy desk, a recliner and TV. The kitchen was complete even though it was rarely used and the bathroom just had a shower stall, no tub. About as basic as they come, but it worked for me.

I looked at Kenneth sprawled across my unmade bed. Beefy calves hanging over the side. Shorts draped across his thighs and crotch. Available for anything I wanted.

Anything.

And deep inside my critter rumbled.

I sat beside him and pulled his shirt up to find he had a belly that was as trim and golden as the rest of him, with neat tan nips that were big and round and pointed. Damn, he was a hundred times hotter now than when I saw him strutting around campus ... and before I knew it I was running my hands over him and caressing him with my lips ... and feeling it in every part of my body, especially my dick.

I removed his shirt and used my phone to shoot pictures of him then maneuvered him completely onto the bed. His shorts rode down his hips, adding to his beauty. His shoulders flowed into well-formed pecs then trimmed down to his waist to join his hips before becoming two legs that would make Michelangelo's David's look like twigs in comparison. One of those jocks who'd set out to show how defined his muscles are but still managed to keep just enough softness on him to make his body elegant instead of merely rock solid. I kicked myself for not taking Kenneth up on his hints.

I rolled him onto his belly and slipped his shorts off to reveal a really nice white ass framed by the jock's straps. I caressed it. Snapped the straps. Ran my fingers along his crack, but found myself more fascinated by the tan-line the shorts had made. White creamy skin melding into golden brown in soft measures, not sharp lines. The jockstrap seemed to contradict it so I rolled him onto his back, fondled him for a few minutes, then slowly ... slowly removed it, taking photos every step of the way, revealing his cute little penis was surrounded by sandy hair.

I shot dozens more pictures of him — on his back, on his side, on his belly, half-covered with a sheet crushed around him, everything you can think of. It was almost like I was making love to him. In fact, I found myself lying on the bed between his legs and stroking his dick as I massaged his balls ... and nuzzled his pubes ... and licked along his shaft. Man, I was having all kinds of fun.

It didn't take long for him to grow into something nice. Not the biggest I've ever had or even the most impressive but fat enough and long enough to be more than acceptable. I took photos of him rock hard. Took more of me sucking and stroking and licking him. I didn't even thinking of slowing down as he grew harder and fuller. The veins around his shaft began to pulse as it turned dark and red and his ass flexed and he gave a soft grunt ... and he came. There wasn't a lot; it mainly dribbled back onto his belly, but I got pictures of that, too.

He moaned a little but didn't wake up.

A ray of sunlight began to filter in through a window near

my bed so I shoved it closer and posed him in some beauty shots. His long body exquisite in how it lay on its back and then on its sides and then on its belly, with his lovely butt smooth and white in contrast to his tan. Man, I was still having lots of fun ... and I was still telling myself that's all it was.

What I didn't realize I was no longer thinking but was only acting from animal instinct. So after more caressing of his ass and kissing of his cheeks and doing close-ups of it all ... I set the phone on a tripod, programmed it to take a photo every five seconds, stripped down in a place where it caught me undressing, lubricated his hole with a slop of Vaseline and straddled his ass.

Still telling myself it's just for fun.

I gripped his cheeks and lay my hard-as-fuck cock between them. Ran it back and forth, loving the feel of my balls pressing against his butt. I thought this was all I'd do.

Still telling myself it's just for fun.

But then I pulled back and smoothed a condom onto my dick and slowly, slowly, slowly pushed it deep into him.

And fucked him.

Hard.

For at least ten minutes. Huffing in and out and in and out, his cheeks quivering from my rhythm and him giving off soft moans until I was close to screaming from the tightness of him around me. I pulled out, yanked off the latex, took three quick rubs along my dick — and fired all over his back, screaming from the sensations and jerking and gasping as I released load after load. Some even got in his hair. God-DAMN, it was good — better than I'd ever had. Better than any orgasm I'd had, since, really.

Until Reg.

I managed to step back. Take a hundred more photos. Leave Kenneth sprawled on my bed and covered with my cum. Caressed him a bit more. Then I took a shower as everything downloaded to my laptop.

A couple hours later his buddies came looking for him. They'd tracked down my apartment through the school's records, which I didn't like and raised a big stink about. Once I knew who it was, I grabbed a paring knife, opened the door and let them in to see him in his glory. They tried to threaten me. Swore I raped him. The knife was the only thing that kept them from jumping me.

I let them know I knew about the plan for me and told them if they attacked me in any way I'd file hate-crime charges and tell the world Kenneth had come to my place and we'd fucked like bunnies. Flat out dared them to say otherwise.

They just pulled his shorts back on and took him away.

I never saw him again.

****

I finished just as I mopped up the last of my eggs with the final piece of toast, then pushed back from the tray and glanced at Diana as I said, "And that's all there is to it." I poured out the last of the coffee. "I'm amazed his buddies kept his secret this long."

"Kenneth did well for them," she replied, no change in her tone of voice. "One's on Fox and is known to get exclusives with Mr. Tavelscha, who is a *rising star in the party*; the other two have a business that's been awarded a surprising number of government contracts. I get the feeling those boys kept quiet so they would have some leverage in the future."

"But why? Kenneth was out to go pro in football."

"His father wouldn't let him. Instead he wound up with a degree in political science and a post on his own Congressman's staff. He's now married, has two daughters and snatched that Congressman's seat because *he wasn't conservative enough*."

"You got better sources than the CIA."

"Amazing what some glasses of wine and soft reminiscences will get you." She rose and set her cup on the tray. "Now I need to go."

"So what are you gonna do? Got a room here?"

"No, I'm staying with friends. They have a nice big flat overlooking the Thames. There's a cocktail party tonight and the bridal shower's tomorrow." The look in her eyes told me she intended to get the best info anyone could possibly get.

I smiled. "Hope you have fun."

"Won't be thanks to you. Colin is very unhappy you're still here." Her fingers caressed my chin, making me look at her as she whispered, "You know, Devlin, he relies on you too much. I've been thinking ... the boys are old enough to where I could start helping with the business. I don't know much about it ... but I could learn."

"That's a good idea," I said. "It'd let me be on the road more."

"I'm glad you agree." She headed for the door.

I followed her. "You know where you're goin'?"

"Underground into town, get off at Hammersmith then grab a 391 bus. Lets me off a block from the flat."

"Diana, c'mon, you gotta be beat. Take a car; I'll pay."

"I slept on the plane," she said, then patted my cheek. "I've got my cell phone with me. I'll do what I can to find out how to settle this. And while I'm here, young man, you will behave yourself or you'll wish to God you had."

"Hey!"

"Bye." Then she left.

I couldn't believe it. She'd calmly taken full control of my situation and let me know I was a fuck-up beyond measure, all with a smile and a quiet warning. Even though I knew she was right, my critter growled and I stormed around the room, all but howling and snarling and spitting ... until I couldn't handle it, anymore, and slammed my fist against the wall. Hurt it. Big-time. Stupid thing to do.

But shit, I hated being controlled.

NINE

I needed to blow off some steam or I'd explode, but I hadn't brought my running clothes with me. Just sneakers. Fine. I yanked on a pair of briefs, pulled my sleeping shorts on as well as a tee-shirt and hoodie, slipped my feet into my runners, made sure I had my key and ID note and headed out.

It was brisk, but in a few minutes I'd have myself warmed up so after stretching I decided to circle Heathrow. Talk about stupid? My average run is five-six miles a day and that damned airport is a good ten or twelve, in circumference. Because you can't just run the perimeter; you have to go down this street and across that roadway and around another circle and along a back road and over another thoroughfare and on and on. But the good thing about it was by the third turn I was more focused on just not stopping than on the turmoil in my brain.

It was Diana's parting crack that had slammed me — about me behaving myself. My father'd said crap like that to me too damn many times. Usually accompanied by a slap or a punch or his fucking belt buckle across my back. I still had some scars. In fact the last time I saw him he tried the same shit, trying to get me back under control.

Now my father was one of those people who won't believe what they don't want to believe. Since I didn't fit into his idea of what a faggot looks like ... he never thought I could be one, even though I never dated girls. But then one day he called and demanded I come home. He didn't say why, just get my ass there.

I hopped a train after my last class and got to the house

about six. Dad was sitting in a chair in the living room, four empty beer cans and half a fifth of Bourbon gone. The second I saw those I knew he'd be trouble. The second he saw me, he was.

He got up from the chair, unsteady, and glared at me as he said, "It true you suck dick?"

I'd been dreading that question for years, and the words cut deep into me, but all I did was give him a shrug of *Yes*.

He downed another bourbon and drank some beer, his focus on something I couldn't see. He was bigger than me by two inches and thirty pounds but most of it was a gut he was building. Still his hands were solid beef, as were his arms, and just because his hair was more gray than black didn't mean he was too old to be a hard-assed bastard. So I kept my eyes on him. Waited for the first swing so I could duck.

He shifted his glare onto me. Moved closer. Looked me over like I was something he wanted to buy. "You do this to get at me?"

I snorted. "I do it 'cause it's who I am."

"Fuck." More beer. "Your brother know?"

"Colin's got nothin' to do with this."

"He suck dick, too?"

"What the fuck? He's married and has twins. Where the fuck you get off wonderin' that?"

"You think I'm gonna keep payin' for some faggot's fancy-ass college and all that shit?"

"I got grants and scholarships; your part makes up about a third of my tuition and half my livin' expenses."

"Fuckin' expenses, cocksucker. Convincin' stupid college kids to let you fuck 'em."

I laughed without thinking. "You think I don't get hit on by guys? I'm told I'm pretty hot, a real otter."

"What the fuck's this *otter* shit?"

"Young. Stocky. Built. Hair on him. Not old enough to be a bear, yet, or even a cub but gettin' there. Lots of guys want me to fuck 'em." Then my voice dropped into a growl. "But I only wanna fuck the ones who look like you."

"Me? You fuckin' sayin' you wanna fuck me?"

I smiled and winked and —

The first punch caught me off-guard. I stumbled around as he roared at me. Landed another punch in my side. My wrestling took over so his next swing gave me the momentum to roll him over me and across the floor into the couch. He wound up sitting half on his ass and half on his side. He was so stunned by the move he didn't even try to get up; he just looked at me, his face a mass of drunken stupid.

I backed out the door and headed for the subway. I didn't notice my nose was bleeding till I was halfway there. I stopped in a mom and pop and bought a bottle of water and used that to clean myself off. By the time I was on the platform I looked normal — as normal as you can when you've disowned yourself and added to your debt load by way too much money. Sure, it wouldn't have to be for the full tuition; I'd been as cheap as I could so all I really had left to worry about was the Spring Semester. But Grad school would be a bitch to pay for. I wondered if I could really afford to go.

I got the call just after I got off the train.

From Colin.

"Dad's had a stroke. Get here as quick as you can."

I debated not going, but that would leave my brother to handle everything and he was already hard-pressed to take care of his family and the company. So I showered, shaved, packed my nose and went back. By the time I got to the hospital dad was dead.

The doctor called it a stroke. Colin accepted it as a stroke. Diana comforted him as she juggled the twins ... till her mother arrived to take them over. I was offered sympathy by everyone, but I shrugged it off.

Colin was pretty shook up so I handled the funeral arrangements and probated the will. The company was split between him and me as was dad's life insurance — a hundred-and-fifty thousand bucks total. I rearranged the next semester's classes so I could come in to help twice a week and weekends.

I know I should've felt bad about the *passing of my father*, but I didn't. All I thought was how his death took care of my tuition. And may have brought justice to mom.

What I couldn't figure was how dad had found out. He'd called me the week before to bitch about Colin and demand I come help with the business, and not a word. Then this guy named Noel expressed his condolences and revealed he was the one who outed me.

Fucking Noel. Another trust fund baby whose daddy was high up in one of those too-big-to-fail banks and mommy was editor of a national fashion magazine. We'd met in the student union and I'd thought he'd be a fun one-nighter, but talk about a control freak. He started off by telling me how to suck his nice-enough dick, which took all the fun out of it. Then he insisted I eat his ass, which I don't mind doing to the right kind but his was small and boring and needed to be cleaned first. The final bit was he wouldn't let me fuck him and only gave me a hand-job, so I blew him off after that.

Oh, but one didn't ignore Noel. Once we shared a bed my life was supposed to be his and his alone. So if I was in class and he texted, he'd toss a fit if I didn't answer right off and would send a long nasty message about how irresponsible and immature I was. Stupid little bitch couldn't accept that I really wasn't into him.

Don't get me wrong, he was good-looking enough. Brown Hair. Broad shoulders. Ice blue eyes that were just as cold. One of those taut-bodied Upper East Side boys who would happily pay as much for a shirt as I did rent because it was the latest thing, then would blame the poor for being too lazy to work five jobs to make ends meet. Even if everything had clicked between us in bed I'd have blown him off, my dad was the only asshole I'd tolerate in my life.

Once he realized there was no way in hell I was going to pay attention to his sense of entitlement, he called dad at the office. Then the little bitch let me know what he'd done by complaining about how much detail he had to go into to convince my father he was telling the truth and flat out said it was my own damn fault for not being nicer to him. What surprised me was, all I did was shrug.

Yeah, part of me was pissed off but another part was happy he'd done it. What made it better was, since Noel was still interested in another night together my critter hissed a happy growl and I decided to ... oh, *give in*.

Till we got to his condo.

He started with his directions so I tore his overpriced designer crap off him, used it to tie his little bitch ass down to the bed and fucked him for hours. In his ass and his mouth. And I played with his dick till he was so hard and ready he was begging me to finish him off. Then he went nearly catatonic when I finally did. After which I dressed, untied him and left.

He begged me for another night but I never went near him again. When he started his harassment crap up, I had Hamilton file a restraining order in a very public way. That embarrassed mommy and daddy so he vanished *into rehab*.

Of course, remembering dad's death and figuring I'd caused it with our fight made me wonder if the Faure's bullshit might be a sort of karma against me. But considering the chaos that fucker had caused and changes we made for the better in the company, and the fact that I finally got full reimbursement from the little shit, I convinced myself it didn't fit the parameters.

Remembering that brought a smile to my face. And even though it took my fourth and fifth wind to make it all the way back to the hotel I was still on my feet when I stumbled into the lobby — pouring sweat and rubber-legged, but I was also feeling the amazing nirvana that comes from a good run.

I was back in control.

****

Of course, there was a gangly guy waiting in the lobby when I returned.

"Mr. Pope? Trevor Laughton, of the Express," he said as I headed for the elevator. "Here's my card."

"So?" was all I could spit out as he shoved it in my hand.

"I'd like to talk with you about the attack on you, Friday night."

I was too breathless to speak. "Don't wanna. Talk about it."

"But this also concerns the possibility it's connected to why you were detained earlier in the day and — "

"Do I look like. I been arrested?" I snapped as I entered the elevator. The doors closed on him and I zipped up to my floor, kicking myself left, right and center as it slammed in on me that I should have done something to placate that asshole's interest. Explained it away somehow, or just put him off. Now they're honing in on me so they might go after Reg. If they were anything like the animals in the States they'd dig until they'd destroyed him. I had to stop that ... but how?

Shit, Diana was so fucking right. I was in way over my head. She'd found out the FBI was being pushed by Faure-pere and his mongrels, and Kenneth was assisting them, and got it without any trouble looked like. Her connections were way beyond my feeble network so no question I'd need her help. Maybe her taking control wasn't a bad idea. Besides, she could be a much of a hard-ass as I could be, and two New Yorkers on you? Give it up, baby.

Don't get me wrong — I liked Diana. She had my brother's back. Hell, she's the one who got him on the road to normalcy.

I'd graduated and been working with the company for six months and on more than one occasion had bolted into Colin's office to disconnect a call before he shifted too far into rant and rave mode. This was while we were still dealing with the Faure mess and having trouble trying to keep things together, so I was torn between fury at dad for the abuse done to Colin and irritation at my brother for not being able to get back on track and handle the company better. On top of that I'd begun to feel like Diana was trying to take over completely. So when she'd called to suggest I should also get an MRI to see if my anger issues were due to brain damage I'd snarled, "Fuck off, *Mrs. Queen-Bitch-Pope,*" at her and hung up.

Marci had overheard, of course, so sweetly slipped into my office and told me, "She's right, Devlin." Before I could explode into one of dad's outbursts her eyes filled up with *shut the fuck up* and she leaned against my desk to tell me a story.

It was during my last year of college. Diana and Colin had been married about six months and she was five months pregnant with their twins. Somehow he'd kept dad's abuse secret from her — until she walked in on dad berating him with words and slaps over a messed up order. In his office. Where everybody could hear what was going on. Even as Marci was trying to calm dad down. Diana had simply stepped between them and told dad, "You'll stop this shit right now."

Dad had snarled, "It's my fuckin' business, not yours, bitch," and tried to shove her aside, but she wouldn't budge. Then he tried to shout her into submission, but she wouldn't budge. Then he threatened to slap her and Colin got between them, but she would not budge.

She just got cooler and calmer and more stuck to the ground as she glared into dad's hateful eyes and said, "You *will* stop this shit right now, motherfucker, or I will have your fucking ass thrown in jail. Then I will tell everyone you hit a poor pregnant lady and will make fucking sure your fucking balls are cut off and shoved up your fucking ass. And don't think I can't do it, asshole, because I know people in there. Do you fucking understand me?"

Dad got red in the face and snarled and growled and spit but stalked off, tossing a few choice words over his shoulder. Marci quickly followed him and quietly closed the office door so they'd have a semblance of privacy ... but she made damn sure she could hear every word.

Diana didn't move, not until Colin started bawling behind her. Then she sat him on a couch he had in his office, kneeled before him (Marci swore she did but how she could in her condition made no sense to me) and held his face in her hands till he regained control. That's when she finally learned the real reason he'd been coming home depressed, with cuts and bruises. Dad had sensed she wouldn't tolerate his outbursts so had confined them to the office. Then Colin would tell her he'd run into a door or fallen or whatever lie he could think of.

He'd started blubbering an apology when she stopped him, whispering, "You were trained to fear that man. I was not. From this day forward I will be at your side and he will never lay another hand on you. Nor will he raise his voice again. I promise you." And she was good to her word.

Then after dad died she started Colin on rounds of seeing doctors to find out if his problems might be physiological. I think half the reason she was doing it was to give him hope that he could be fixed in the face of the Faure disaster. And sure enough, the discovery that lesions on his brain were short-circuiting some of his synapses *did* give him something to cling to. Diana had just received the results of the scan and figured some of my anger might be attributable to the same thing. That's when I'd snarled at her. And now Marci was eying me with this serious *Momma Hen* glare.

"Devlin," she said. "I've known you since you were two. *Sweetness-and-Light* has never been your nickname."

I was still angry enough to snarl, "You knew what my dad was doin' all this time and did nothin' to stop it, so what gives you the fuckin' right to mess with me now?"

She'd just looked at me and said, "Get the scan." Done in a way that told me if I didn't I'd regret it.

I'd never liked or trusted Marci. She's one of those people who will swear she never butts into someone else's business but, by God, she knows every bit of it and is perfectly willing to use it against you when she wants to. So I did it, half to keep Marci on my good side and half so I could use it later to find out why she'd never done this with dad.

She has yet to even acknowledge me when I ask.

Turned out my brain wasn't as severely damaged as Colin's so the doctor said, "You seem normal for New York born and bred. If anything starts happening that's out of the ordinary, let us know and we'll dig deeper."

I'd nodded and smiled and said nothing about Kenneth ... or any of the others. Why ruin the good doctor's illusions?

Meanwhile Diana had found a guy who worked with people suffering from PTSD and brain injuries from accidents and abusive spouses. Between that and Diana's backup — and his kids turning out to be sunshine and light instead of obnoxious brats — while Colin could still have his moments, he was at the point where he could apologize for exploding at one of the piss-ant dealers who used and abused us.

Looked like he'd be doing more of that now that I was going to be in-country for God knew how long. Which meant the problems would suddenly explode. It's like a law of nature and had already started with that phone call from New Jersey.

Meaning I'd have to let Colin know about it so he could provide the DNA sample.

Shit, that was a call I did not want to make.

****

I took a nice long steaming hot shower and the hell with the bandage getting soaked. It was one of my calming methods. Plus, remembering Tawfi washing himself relaxed me enough to let me decide what my course of action should be.

To start with — make my lie to Colin truth and with as much noise as I could, so when the press got to digging around that's what they'd find first. Also that was all he'd know if they asked him about anything.

Next — find out what the hell Sir Monte wasn't telling me about these murders.

I wrapped myself in that robe then slammed online to find

out more about the Queen's pin people. There wasn't much; in fact the most helpful article was a snarky bit in *The Globe* that talked about the cheapness of the Royals for using slave labor in Myanmar. The Palace gave a non-response about the rights of all people to make a living, *even in a former colony like Pakistan.* That told me where the factory probably was — Lahore. It was owned by a guy named Hassan-something who'd been trying to get us to use him, but I'd seen his work; it felt rushed and unattended. *Guess I was right,* I thought with a snicker.

I sent out emails to some dealers asking if they'd used him and what they thought of his factory's quality. I wouldn't hear back till Monday at the earliest so I dug a bit more into the ceremonies where pins like theirs might be used. Before long I had a couple files packed with PDFs.

Then one article about a ceremony held a familiar name.

Lieutenant Reginald Brewster Thornton was being pinned with a medal for heroism in Afghanistan. He wasn't the focus of the photo; Prince Hot Ginge was, and even though he wasn't what I go for he looked good. But he paled in comparison to Reg's stiff-upper-lip demeanor and at-attention stance. And if anyone was born to wear that uniform he was, the way it fit him. I paid minimal attention to the story — something about rescuing a member of his platoon after the man was wounded — because that photo made him look even more like a brother to the men who'd been killed.

I'd torn up that card the reporter gave me so pulled it from the trash and looked at it. *Trevor Laughton of the Express.* I wondered if I could offer a quid pro quo — interview with me in exchange for information about the killings. I pulled up some news reports. They ranged from the *we hate to discuss this sort of story* articles in *The Times* to *Hate-filled Muslims are out to kill us all* in *The Sun.* Several with Laughton's by-line accompanied by a really bad photo of him. The gist was similar all the way across — *married heterosexual men were being raped, stabbed and strangled by a deranged faggot, leaving their poor wives without a husband and defenseless children without a father*! The usual types crawled out from under their rocks to demand fags be sent to jail, castrated or exterminated. We had those screamers in the States so none of it affected me.

Then I found a story with a map showing the locations where the bodies were found. The first one was near Knightsbridge, the next was by Acton, the third was Northfields, the last — Hatton Cross. All not far from the Piccadilly Line of the underground. For some reason that struck me as weird ... almost precise.

Information on the murders was less detailed than Sir Monte had told me. He'd slammed the lid tight. In place of that were photos of them as living human beings. Men with blond to light brown hair and general huskiness enjoying their wives and children.

This may sound callous but the only one I thought was really attractive was the last — Martin Perriman. He'd been a Staff Sergeant so the photo used of him was in his uniform, looking beefy and smug. Next to it was one where he'd been caught in mid-grin as he tickled one of his kids, a tenderness in his face that was missing in the others. His happy eyes hurt me.

Something else that story verified was that Sir Monte had lied by claiming he'd still be alive if I hadn't gone after Reg. By omission the article revealed he hadn't taken the underground the day of his death; only the first three had. And his body was found in an open parking area behind his office while the others had been in parking garages not far from where they worked or lived, as if they'd been dumped there. And the timeline for his death was odd; the coroner put it at between two and three hours prior to the body being found at 8pm. He was probably already dead when I grabbed Reg. Sir Monte had used this to fuck with me.

The relief I felt at realizing it told me it had worked; I just hadn't noticed. What's really odd is how I felt vile at being relieved. The man had been killed in a hideous manner; how could knowing more details of his death make me happy?

Then another thought hit me — didn't that exonerate Tawfi? He was on the same train as me. I Google-mapped it and saw it was conceivable he could still have done it. The train would've reached Hatton Cross about ten, maybe fifteen minutes after I got off then Perriman's office was a ten minute walk from the station. That kept his death within the realm of possibility but it was tight. Tawfi did not strike me as the kind of guy who would rush anything ... well, except for sex when in need.

I watched a quick segment on BBC online about Perriman that included video of him playing with his kids and comments about how his business had been failing. Money was so tight the family needed help to pay for his burial. A fund had been set up so I donated twenty-five pounds Sterling.

Big of me, I know.

Without thinking, I began to sketch Perriman's face, using a fountain pen I had. A pen that once belonged to my father. It laid down nice dark lines when I wanted and soft ones when I needed. He'd slapped the shit out of me when he caught me using it once. I was twelve. It was the only thing of his I kept just so I could keep using it the way he didn't want.

What's crazy is, as I sketched I started to weep. Not crying or sobbing, just tears slipping from my eyes. A couple hit the ink-work and smeared it. I thought about trying to correct them but couldn't do it. They seemed right for the moment.

This guy ... these guys ... all going to work or headed home from work ... they didn't know what'd hit them before they were dead. But Reg had known what to expect. He had courted it to try and stop it. He had actually thought I was going to do the same thing to him. Had deliberately aimed for that apartment block with its sub-level parking to try and force the issue. Jesus, he must've been terrified, and the idea that I'd caused him such pain and anguish cut deep. I didn't realize till I was done with the sketch but it really looked more like him than it did Perriman.

I set it on the desk to dry and sat in a chair by the window to watch the jets come and got at Heathrow. Tried to sort out the chaos in my thoughts. Didn't work. All I could think about was Reg and what I'd done to him.

It made me sick.

And horny.

Sir Monte and Four-buttons had left his photo on my cell phone so I looked at it. His hands bound behind his head. His exposed chest. The flow of his body. The smoothness of his skin. When I'd made that comment about not killing a man because I might want to use him, again, I'd been spitting shit. But the beauty of Reg lying on that dirty floor — I wanted to touch him again. Hold him. Bring him to nirvana.

I thought of the photo of him being decorated by Prince Hot Ginge, again. Closed my eyes to better picture it. You couldn't see a lot of Reg's face but his body was perfect under that uniform, his broad shoulders with his military stance and ramrod straight back. Elegant legs straight and exquisite. The flow of his coat over the hump of his rear. I leaned back in the chair and —

He opened the door and entered my room to straddle me, still dressed for that ceremony. Undid his tie and slowly pulled it away. Let me slide the coat off his too-fine shoulders. Slow and tender. He unbuttoned his shirt and pulled up his clean white tight t-shirt and let me play with the feathery hair on his pecs and his lovely nips as he moaned in ecstasy and stood to undo his pants and lowered the zipper inch by inch to reveal another pair of those striped briefs, his dick pressing against the material, his pubes fanning out and around as he pulled the elastic band down to reveal his beautiful self and I took him in my mouth, running my hands up the back of his legs and up and over his beautiful ass and trailed higher and higher under his shirt and coat along his sides to toy with his elegant nips and drift back down to wander around his perfect thighs, the hair on them tickling my fingers, then whispered around them back under his pants to his glorious ass, over and over and over and over and —

I came. Fired hard. Straight into the air so it fell back onto my face and belly. I gasped and gulped and nearly laughed for joy.

It was almost as good as him being there. Almost the same as I'd felt when he came in me. Almost the same as when I'd held him.

He was mine again.

He was mine.

And I almost felt completely at peace.

****

I sat there not wanting to move. I'd skipped lunch — that's the one great thing about an English breakfast; it's all your meals rolled into one — but it was past eight and I was hungry. Only I'd have to do room service, delivery or catch the tube to go someplace. Which meant leaving and coming back to my room. Which meant cleaning up and getting dressed. Which made me remember I was out of clean clothes. The hotel had laundry facilities so I forced myself up, showered off, again, then ordered a pricey burger and a Fanta, pulled on some jeans and a tee-shirt and headed down to eat my dinner on a tray while I washed my crap, playing Solitaire on my phone as the machinery whined, letting my brain sort everything out in my subconscious.

My phone rang just as I was shifting my wet things into a dryer. It was Diana.

"Out and about?" she asked in a voice that was too sweet.

"Doin' laundry. All by myself."

"Sure."

I heard people talking in the background so asked, "How's the party? The gossip?"

"I'm trying to remember if I sounded that stupid when I was a party girl."

"Probably."

She chuckled. "Mr. Glass-half-empty. I got some fun dirt."

"Such as?"

"Well ... I met this one woman from Canada who is very into Andrea Dworkin's writings."

"Don't know her."

"Radical feminist. Hates porn. Thinks all sex is rape of women. Even gay sex. Get the picture?"

I snorted. "Sounds like the nuns mom told us about."

"I doubt even they would say they're glad men're being raped and murdered instead of women for a change. That it might put teeth in the sexual assault laws. Who knew Canadians were so blood-thirsty?"

"*Can* we blame Canada for this?"

"Only if he's a gay Canadian Muslim. Another woman's husband is high up in New Scotland Yard and she said they know the killer's from the Middle East."

"As are Christians and Jews."

"Doesn't fit the narrative, Dev."

"Hell, I could've told you all that."

"Which you didn't."

"Touché. Did you get anything better?"

"Depends on what else you haven't told me. When the Canadian sex-hater made her comments, a woman who is very-very anti-gay and working in Parliament said word had spread through her crowd of how a young married constable had been sexually assaulted by someone believed to be American." My heart dropped to my feet. She kept on with, "He's currently in seclusion but that won't last long."

"Why — why not?"

She gave only the slightest pause before continuing, "The British Home office is stirring things up over a surveillance operation begun by the Metropolitan Police. They don't know who, yet, but Parliament is looking into it. So you can bet they're feeding reporters the rumors. There are strong hints it's a Middle Eastern country's embassy being watched and that it ties into the killings. And there might be other victims besides those they know about. Some who lived. Consensus among this crowd is the Met is keeping it quiet because they think a home-grown Muslim Jihadist closet-case is seeking his own sick revenge on Her Majesty's Anglo Christian subjects for daring to assist in the invasions of

Iraq and Afghanistan and theft of their natural resources, with the assistance of countries like Saudi Arabia and Dubai and on and on and on."

"Was this a cocktail party or a meeting of the KKK?"

"I'd say both but it is England."

"That why you're not mentioning names?"

"You can be so silly. What's up on Monday?"

"Running back over to Ghadir's to check into some decent backup factories, sound him out about the Royals. Got some good leads on some big business if it pans out."

"Colin mentioned something about that. Does anyone in the states manufacture pins like ours?"

"Not that I know of."

"Might be worth looking into. Maybe we could even set up our own factory."

"That'd jack the costs up."

"Colin showed me how much we're paying in freight and duty for our orders, Dev, and it's not cheap. If we also remove tariffs from our American orders, factor out Mr. Mihn's profit, even if we double his base costs it's not that much more and you don't have lots of overseas calls to make or a language barrier. Plus *Made in the USA* has a lot of caché. In the USA."

Her response took me by surprise. "I ... I'll sound Ghadir out about it."

"Give me call when you're free. We'll do dinner."

"Why not tomorrow?"

"Tomorrow's the shower. Starts at two and, as I understand, will be more than a few hours."

Meaning, *Lots of drinking and lots of gossip and more to tell you that I haven't told you*. "You got it."

"I'll talk to you later."

She hung up. Truth is, she hadn't learned a damned thing, so far. The anti-Muslim crap was already a concern of Sir Monte's and the anti-gay crap had already flared up. Plus I was on top of worrying about the media digging up what I did to Reg, though this did get me to decide I'd call that reporter, Laughton, tomorrow and see if I could send him down a fake trail. Still I figured she'd been kind of arrogant thinking she could figure things out in a country she'd never been to before.

But then paranoid kitty snuck in with, *You dumb shit, why do you think you know what she's learned? You're under surveillance and she probably suspects your phone is tapped so she just let the bastards know reporters are aiming for Reg and did it as cool as can be. She doesn't care about dinner; she knows you're holding back and wants to pump you about the real shit.*

Of course. Diana's not dumb. I had to laugh at myself for being a condescending idiot.

I called Trevor Laughton right that moment.

TEN

He lived in Wembley so said he'd pick me up at the hotel for lunch, on Sunday. Indian food, to which I always say *yes*. There is *nothing* like a good curry.

I called Mr. Mihn just after midnight to discuss the gold flaking. He apologized and said the order had gone to the wrong level of craftsmen, but he would FedEx us new ones immediately. I also discussed the possibility of expanding business with him but got the feeling he'd have trouble doing it at the level of quality we'd need. Still, I knew he could handle orders of up to five-thousand pins with little trouble so we'd see how things went.

The next morning I did the hotel's free breakfast buffet then searched online for more technical info on nano-chips as ID tags. Not a lot to be had, just links to a few stories and papers that had been published a couple years ago. I was about to Google up some techies to get their input when I realized it was time to meet Laughton downstairs.

He was waiting as I stepped out of the elevator, very thin, very casual and with a salt-and-pepper beard over pasty skin.

"Hope you weren't waiting too long," I said as we headed to his car.

"No, just arrived," he said, handing me his card, his hand shaking slightly. And he had a Geordy accent.

"Sorry about brush-off," I said, as if I hadn't apologized over the phone. "But I needed to hit the toilet and — well, you know how it goes."

"Right. Been there."

He had a new Mercedes C-Class, not high-end but not cheap for a reporter, and very clean. For some reason this made me decide to keep my nail clipper in my hand, its filing tool ready. This was not really adding up.

We drove less than a mile down to an old pub in the middle of a parking lot, which made me even warier, but then I caught a whiff of the best aroma ever so followed him in. We sat at a booth, ordered a couple of curries and pints, then when the drinks were delivered he got up to *wash his hands* and —

Griffin Faure came up from behind me to take his place, verging on flabby but still human, with a touch of gray in his hair.

Why was I not surprised about this?

"Pope," was his way of greeting.

"Hi, Griff," I said in a gueeny voice, "long time no see. Hear you're back in the States to rob widows and orphans. What else you been doin'? Anybody we know?" Then I batted my eyes at him and smiled.

His cold dead eyes did not change expression. "I hear you're suspected of killing four men."

I grinned. "Wrong. Got an alibi for all four. Sorry."

"Yes, and one of those alibis is a cop you raped, just like you did me."

"Griff, Griff, Griff," I moaned, as sad as I could make it, "what you and I had was special. I'd never do *anyone* else like I did you."

"Liar. I know of three others and even know who you worked with to kidnap me, right down to where you got a Porsche that was like mine. You were really stupid about it all."

His hands were folded and he was leaning against the table. I reached across and caressed his fingers, saying, "If I'd been stupid, you'd be dead. Instead, I hear you're married again. Got kids. Back in daddy's good graces. Life is so hard at the top."

He didn't move. "You heard right."

"So what you doin' here?" I purred with as much insinuation as was humanly possible. "You miss how intense it was when you came all over your suit? Want another session with me? I notice you let the hair grow back on your hands; does that mean it's on your chest and belly and legs, again? I find that really hot, so I'm free this evening." Batted my eyes at him, again.

He still didn't react. "I always knew your shit would catch up to you. I just wanted to gloat a little."

"You came three-thousand miles to do that? Wow, you don't have enough to do at work. Daddy must still be wary."

"My father has nothing to do with this. I have business here. You being in this shit is just the perfect beginning to what I'm sure will be a great week. Thanks for verifying the rumors."

"You're welcome. And if you want better info, contact Sir Monteith St. James of the Metropolitan Police Force. I'm sure he'd love to keep you up to date."

"Don't need to." Then Faure winked at me, pulled his hands away from mine and rose. "My business'll be done in a few days, but I may stay over just to see what happens."

"Sell tickets?"

"You know, Pope, you really are a stupid man. You've always underestimated what my family can do and how patient we can be in doing it."

I grinned. "It'd be nice if you learned some self-control. You had so little when we were together. I honestly didn't think you'd cum in my mouth as quick as you did."

He smiled. "Have fun. I know I will." Then he headed off.

"Griff," I called after him. He glanced around at me, so I continued, "You filled out nice, so I mean it — if you want another session you know where to find me." I cast him a kiss.

Still no change in expression or body language or anything to indicate I'd affected him in any way. He just turned and walked on. His skinny boy left with him, a to-go bag in hand.

Well ... here was proof-positive Griffin Faure and Kenneth Tavelscha were working in tandem with the TSA, Home Office, Foreign Office, MI5, MI6, Parliament, Sir Monte and the FBI. Looked like I was totally fucked.

Totally.

But what's funny is, I was almost relieved. I finally knew exactly where I stood, now, and that's half the battle.

My meal got delivered a few moments later and I ate every damn bit of it as casually and happily as I could ... till I found out the fuckers left me the bill for both meals.

Fucking cheap-assed son-of-a-bitch.

Since I'd been dumped less than a mile from the hotel I walked back, still nice and casual. Now that I knew I was under surveillance, and not just by the Met, I'd be damned if I let them think I'd been freaked out about this.

Even though, to be perfectly honest, I was. Big-time.

****

I spent the rest of the day on research for the pins, sent off emails to a couple of techies who seemed knowledgeable in the Nano field, hopped over to Hounslow West on the underground for dinner, sorted through my notes and ideas, writing them down on a pad in my briefcase, and did nothing else. If my phone and laptop had been made available to the Met and, thanks to them, to everyone else, I wasn't going to do anything through either device to give anyone a clue as to what I was planning.

So ... what *was* I planning? To know what the hell was going on with the murders and do everything I could to show I was not involved with them. They probably already knew I was looking into them, but I could pretend that was only a segue due to the pin research.

Still ... the next step? Get another phone with a good data plan and use that for researching and calling, as need be. But do it in a way so as not to draw suspicion, meaning I had to wait till I was in the middle of London and find a kiosk that wasn't too obvious to a guy tailing me. Second, I'd saved some of the news stories as PDFs so got the names of a couple of real reporters at the newspapers to contact and give interviews to. What I'd say ... hell,

I had no idea, yet, but it would be to point out I was no killer. In fact, I began to see how I could suggest the Met thought I might be the guy because, through an innocent misunderstanding of the differences in American and UK gay mores, I'd thought Reg was interested and wanted some fun and that's what my trouble stemmed from — public indecency. They needed to investigate to make certain I hadn't done this to help the killer, and I now realized it was just a stupid unfortunate move on my part. I also decided I would agree to any deal offered on my kidnapping and rape of Reg if the Met would agree to that story being the public one.

And I'd make damn sure that's all Faure knew about, too.

Once I'd accepted my new terms, I hit the bed and slept like a baby.

I skipped breakfast and called Ghadir for a lunch appointment. On my phone to make it all official. If we went to his favorite place it would mean a good five courses of elegantly spiced meats and sauces and I wanted to make sure I had room. He was quick and cool about it, very unlike him, first wondering why I was still in town. I laid the groundwork for an excuse by saying I'd been contacted about supplying pins for a high-level personage but couldn't tell him who or what till I saw him in person. That got his attention and he even asked if Jamil could join us, again.

I had to bite my thumbnail to keep from chirping, *Oh, for God's sake, honey, yes! Please.*

Hell — I can be as queenie as the next faggot.

I left straightaway so I could hop off the underground and grab the water taxi from its stop at The Tower of London. That would take me under Tower Bridge en route to Canary Wharf, giving me a massively gorgeous view of The City as we pulled away. That puts me in a great mood, and this time I even hummed the music from the opening of Hitchcock's *Frenzy* as we passed under it. Seemed appropriate seeing as how I was now mixed up with a serial rapist-killer.

It also gave me time to read over my email responses

from techies and dealers. More fodder for the surveillance crowd.

To my surprise, Ghadir had lunch delivered to his office and we ate in his six-chair conference room overlooking the Thames. Jamil, gorgeous as ever in tight black slacks and a fitted maroon shirt tucked in, showing him off in ways no straight man should ever consider being seen, served us and sat in but said very little. However, his beautiful eyes never left me, like he was guarding his father.

I told Ghadir I had an *in with the Royals* and he assumed that was why he'd been interrogated by Sir Monte's people.

"If there is anything to do with them their protectors become like angry hounds surrounding their flock," he said.

"That's why I've come to speak with you," I said. "You know England far better than do I. Your guidance on this will help us to make the correct impression." My grammar was always better around him, and my willingness to flatter him helped even more.

"This is true," he nodded. Never let it be said the man had no ego. "But you say they wish to have them be electronic?"

"Tiny ID chips in each to identify the one wearing it."

"That makes no sense. A pin can be easily transferred from one man to another."

"A technology expert I know in Palo Alto says a chip can be worked to recognize only the person who is supposed to wear it by using weight and movement and voice."

"But these can be altered."

"Alterations by anyone but the approved people would be noticed and the pin deactivated."

"This sounds rather precise," Ghadir murmured as he pulled out his set of our samples. "And delicate. I do not think they will accept having such technology built in another country."

"*Can* we do it in the UK?"

"I know of no one capable, but I will ask. I do know of someone in Germany who may be able to."

"I doubt that would be acceptable either, these days."

"Perhaps not."

I finally realized what he'd said and asked, "Are you planning to move?"

"No, I think only of opening an office in Berlin." He cast a glance at Jamil. Guess he was moving. Dammit ... or not. One-on-one with him in Berlin? Pitter-pat went my heart.

Ghadir set the pins on the table. "These styles would work best. No gems. No cloisonné. Simple and quiet. No attention drawn so you cannot tell what they are for. These are very popular in Poland, you know."

"You do business in Poland?"

"I also looked there. Perhaps *they* could insert the chips — no, no, again, it is not in the UK. That would hurt your chances of gaining the job."

"Didn't there used to be a Motorola plant near Derry, in Northern Ireland? That's part of the UK."

He nodded. "I will look into this. The costs would be much less than in England."

I picked out a couple of pins — one a silver-plated arrow with red and blue stripes painted on as feathers, the other a molded lion wearing the Union Jack as a vest. "I don't have samples of these. May I borrow yours?"

"These are older issue," he said. "You should have Colin find out if the molds are still available."

Jamil then left and brought back a small pin of crossed flags — one the Union Jack, the other a coat of arms.

"What about these, Da?" he asked, his accent very South London. "Standard issue. Safe."

"This actually would be good," Ghadir said. He handed the flag pin to me. "Put two chips in for safety? Backup?"

"Cross-reference." I nodded, grinning at Jamil. "Great idea."

"Thank you," Jamil said as he sat back down, his eyes still locked on me. It was beginning to make me uncomfortable.

We talked more about the possibilities and I mentioned

Diana's thought about opening a factory in the US. Ghadir wasn't too impressed, mainly because he thought Ireland would be a better choice. Part of the EU but still solid with the UK and US both, no matter what. I let it go.

We finished after three and I was horny as hell from Jamil's beauty and attention, but not for a second did I think he was interested in me; it seemed more like he was on guard than anything else. Even as he escorted me to the elevator he struck me as merely wary. So I asked him about it.

His expression didn't change as he said, "I was questioned separately from Da. They asked me things that're ... that are unimportant to Buckingham Palace's need for insignia."

I grimaced. "Sorry about that. The English are so damn funny about — well, you know I'm gay, right?"

"Yes."

"I think they wanted to make sure I can't be blackmailed or something, in case we do get the order." He merely nodded, his eyes still locked on mine. I continued with, "Are we okay about this?"

"So long as your intentions remain with the pins."

I'd nodded. "They will." Then I got on the elevator, turned and couldn't help but glance him up one side and down the other and add, "Unless you say otherwise."

He shook his head. "I won't."

And the doors closed.

Man ... when a guy says that to me I usually take it as a challenge. But like I said, Ghadir was too important to our business so I let it slide, stopped in a high-end mall to find a kiosk was right next to a very busy Cafe Nero, got coffee I didn't want, a phone that I did, then headed for Knightsbridge, hoping to have another session with Tawfi.

****

I got there with no trouble. It was at one end of a

refurbished old red brick and white filigree building that covered a full block, with insides of nothing but mahogany and brass. I introduced myself at reception and sat in a plush chair by front windows of cut glass. Moments later, Tawfi glided down a full staircase to greet me.

And he looked like hell.

Oh, he was dressed as elegantly as before and his posture and attitude were still as precise, but his eyes were unfocused, his aura of invincibility was gone and that solid power-builder block of a man in a black suit was right behind him. After the barest of greetings he led me back up the stairs through another reception room to an office decorated to within an inch of reality, not saying a word until we reached an ornate door; then he motioned to the bodyguard and said, "Abdel ... "

The man nodded, looked me over with a hidden sneer and took a seat by the upper receptionist.

The moment Tawfi had closed the door behind him, he sagged and wandered to his desk ... and collapsed into its chair.

"Sit, Devlin, please," was all he could say.

I did, asking, "Are you okay?"

Tawfi said nothing for a long moment then looked at me and sighed. "A friend has died."

So now he knew. Of course he would; Perriman's name was in all the papers and broadcasts. Shit, I hadn't thought about that and how it might affect him.

"I'm sorry. It must've been someone very close."

His eyes bore into me. "Do you follow the British news?"

I nodded and deliberately gasped, "Martin Perriman."

Tawfi tensed, took in a deep breath and looked away. "I am at a loss, Devlin. This is the first time in my life I cannot comprehend what has happened. I am sorry, but this may not be the best time for us to meet."

"I understand. I'm so sorry." Then I decided to check on something. "Wait, didn't he die last Thursday? It was all over the papers on Friday and you and I — "

He put up a hand to stop me, frowning. "I pay as little attention to the media as possible. I have assistants for that, and they inform me only of stories deemed important. I learned of Martin's death when I returned to my flat. Saw it on BBC. To know what happened to him ... and what I had just done with you ... I have barely slept since."

Okay, now I felt like shit for asking.

He sighed, again. "It is the manner of his death that so troubles me. I am devastated, yes, but also very angry. It appears he had taken up with someone else and they ... they destroyed him. These emotions are confusing to me. I do not know what to do about them."

"It was a serial killer, Tawfi. Martin just — just had the bad luck of lookin' like the kind of guys that creature hates. I don't think he hooked up with anybody else."

Tawfi let out a soft, sad laugh. "How good to know."

Okay, Dev, open mouth, keep inserting foot.

"Hey, I'll come back some other time," I said.

"No, I have already sent for Mahjub. He knows of these pins and can inform you. But my flat is close by and I had planned for dinner. Now ... "

"I, uh," I shrugged and muttered, "I had plans, anyway." I stood. "Look, here's my card. Call me when you're up to it."

The door buzzed. Tawfi pressed a button on his desk and a slim young man with sandy highlights in his black hair entered. He was cute and nicely dressed but not on the level of Tawfi.

"You called me, sir?" he asked in a soft well-modulated voice.

Tawfi slipped back to in control mode and nodded to me. "Mahjub, this is Devlin Pope, from America. His company makes commemorative pins such as these."

He showed the boy the pin.

"Is there something wrong with these, sir?" Mahjub asked.

"Not that I know of," Tawfi said, perturbed.

Mahjub stepped back, subservient. "I meant no disrespect, sir." Then he turned to me. "My only difficulty with this agent is, the order does take a long time to arrive."

"I don't want to take business away from anyone," I said, pulling out the three pins I'd taken from Ghadir. "I'm offering something different. We're looking into putting micro-chips into pins such as this to help identify people, and I'm checking out what sort of market there might be for it."

Mahjub took the flag pin and eyed it. "That is interesting. I had wondered when nano-technology would approach this. If the metal is a bit thicker and the clasp more secure, it would be very useful."

I looked from him to Tawfi, who gave a light smile. "Mahjub is our resident I-T person. Computers, security, internet service, international hook-ups for conferences, everything."

That brought a gentle smile to Mahjub's face.

"That's fantastic," I said. "Maybe I could pick your brain as to how best to do this." Mahjub glanced from me to Tawfi and back, so I added, "Not today, of course. But later in the week?"

He nodded. "Yes, please. I am completing a project now but will be done Wednesday."

Tawfi looked straight at me. "Or Thursday?" he asked.

I smiled. "Thursday's better for me. Would that be okay?"

Mahjub nodded. "I arrive at nine."

"He is always on time," Tawfi chuckled, soft and easy. "He has a flat on the top floor. His commute is via the lift."

The guy just nodded. We set up an appointment for ten, then Tawfi escorted me to the lobby, where he shook my hand.

"Thank you for stopping by," he said. "Mahjub is the best person to work with on matters so technical and I'm sure you will — "

"Am!" cut him off. We looked around to see a pair of dark-haired boys bursting through the entrance, arms outstretched.

Tawfi's glorious smile exploded across his face and he squatted to embrace both of them, now chattering in a language I had no hope of understanding.

A burly young man with a strong resemblance to Tawfi, wearing upscale gym clothes and sandals over black socks, followed the boys in. A lovely woman in a high-couture Hijab was right behind him, rings on her fingers and bells on her ears not to mention a dozen bracelets and a Mark Cross bag that probably cost as much as Colin's and Diana's house. I glanced out the entrance to see a new Range Rover with a *Wallingford Livery* sign set under the windshield on the dashboard, its older reed of a   driver removing several packages from its tail.

The chatter continued in what was obviously a happy vein — the only words I found understandable being *Paris, Hermes* and *MacDonald's* — until Tawfi jolted and turned to me. "Devlin, I apologize. Allow me to introduce my brother, Hamad, and his wife, Leila. Just returned from Paris." He turned back to them, smiling. "This is Mr. Devlin Pope, from New York. He's come to work with Mahjub on upgrading our embassy pins."

Hamad wore the same pin as Tawfi while Leila, if she had one it was hidden by that mass of jewelry. I offered my hand and said, "It's a pleasure to meet you."

Hamad ignored me while Leila merely smiled and glanced me over in a way that was more like an inspection than a greeting.

Tawfi noticed and his smile froze in place. "My apologies, Devlin. It is my intention to make certain my nephews are raised with better manners than my brother and sister-in-law."

Hamad and Leila glared at him and snarled in that language, but Tawfi snarled something right back, nice and simple and both went silent. I may not know what form of Arabic they were speaking but *Shut the fuck up* pretty much sounds the same in any language, and he had the power behind it to mean it. So that's when I made my farewells and got the hell out. Let family deal with family.

I found a Starbucks on Brampton and used their Wi-Fi to set up my new phone then started digging more ... specifically into

Tawfi's brother. I don't trust my senses with Middle-Eastern guys ... at least, those I don't know ... and I was getting a weird vibe off him. Not like he was interested or even uninterested but like he was deliberately refusing to even consider me as a human being worth paying attention to. While that was more than a little insulting, it also reminded me of the last time I'd sensed that off a guy. A good-looking muscle queen I'd met in a bar and almost hooked up with. Instead, something in me snarled, *Back away from him*. Later I learned he'd beaten another man to death. With his fists. All because the guy had called him a fag. On top of that, Hamad was close to the same size as the man who was in my hotel room, the other night, so paranoid kitty was growling.

Well ... I found out why Sir Monte was treading carefully with Tawfi. The al Qasimis were a royal family worth hundreds of billions, thanks to oil, banking and transportation, and they ran their country like a sheikdom, just with modern skyscrapers and Bentleys instead of tents and camels. The sheik had been in power for nineteen years and modernized his people in ways not even Saudi Arabia had managed to do with even greater wealth. Tawfi was the oldest and next in line to the throne, so to speak. Then came Hamad, with two kids by Leila, and seven more brothers and sisters. I found no mention of his mother, just a photo showing her behind the senior al Qasimi in a beautiful, stylish Hijab, being properly subservient.

Call me cynical, but if any member of the al Qasimi family was behind the killings I doubted they'd even be so much as charged with the crimes.

The alarm went off on my phone, so I called Diana about dinner. "There's a Pizza Hut on Regent at Jermyn if you're up for somethin' that's tryin' to be American."

She all but laughed at me. "I'd die for a good slice, right now, but Pizza Hut?"

"I know, I know, I know, but in a pinch ... "

"Where are you?"

"Knightsbridge."

She hesitated before asking, "Why?"

"Possible client. For some new pins, with chips. In fact their I-T guy's interested in helpin' make it work."

" ... Tell me about it over dinner. Can you make it by six?"

"See you there."

I arrived at five-fifty; Diana strolled up a minute later. She greeted me with, "Are you really desperate for a slice?"

"Of Tony's on Millbrae, yeah."

"There's a pub around the corner. I'd love to try their fish and chips."

We headed for it then shared the biggest, greasiest, best meal I'd ever had in England. She downed hers with two Shandys while I had a couple pints of Guinness. The joint was noisy enough to have to speak in above-normal voices to be heard, so no way could anyone record us there ... and just to be sure, I turned off my phone.

Diana was interested in Ghadir's comments and Mahjub's interest. I didn't mention Tawfi's embassy; got her to talking about the shower, instead.

"Just like one in Brooklyn," she said, "but with gifties from Harrod's instead of Macy's. I bought a Tiffany spoon for ten times more than it's worth so I could have it in their box. Big hit." Then she took a good swallow of her Shandy and said, "Marci told me about the call from New Jersey."

Shit, I'd forgotten about that. "How'd she know?"

"When the local boys called the troopers, they figured you wouldn't show and called the office, and Marci called me. I told Colin and he's on his way over."

"He is? How ... how'd he take it?"

She took a sip, this time, then sighed. "For the first time since I met him I have no earthly idea. And you cannot believe how happy that makes me. The circumstances are horrible, but I ... I honestly think he can handle it. All by himself."

I found myself smiling. "God, I hope so."

She leaned on the table, clasped her hands and rested her chin on them. "But you, Dev. Can you handle *your* self?"

"What do you mean?"

"You didn't tell me about your visitor, the other night," she purred.

Shit. "Just a guy I picked up. Get my mind off the crap."

She sighed, in response. "Devlin, I know you like to sketch the men who mean something to you and you use your fountain pen for that. There was still some ink on your fingers when I showed up."

Shit, and I'd washed my hands. "Mommy don't miss much."

"I learned from my mother how to keep track of everything. She had to, just to keep me alive."

"Okay, okay, but it really was a pickup. I just ... I liked him. Even got his info for a repeat. Stupid, ain't it?"

She grew very still. Her eyes tore into me. "I already told you — gossip's hot about the Met being in an uproar — the egg-on-face kind. That a British cop might have been *molested*. Then today I hear that it happened in the middle of a bungled attempt to catch a killer, letting another man get butchered. And considering when you got busted ... "

I drew in a deep breath and nodded. "It's nowhere near like you think. Trust me on that."

"You don't know what I think." Her voice was like ice.

I leaned against the table, rubbing my temples, fighting a sense of horror welling up inside. I noticed a waitress passing so stopped her with, "Excuse me, do you carry Jameson's?"

"Black Label."

"Bring me a shot, please."

She nodded and zipped off.

I looked at Diana and could all but hear her mind screaming, *Oh, my God, as bad as that.*

I said nothing until the shot appeared and I'd downed it then chased it with a gulp of Guinness. Her eyes were so sharp on me I had to say, "I'm not turnin' into my father. I don't usually do this ... but it's been a nightmare and I — I just need somethin' to ground me."

Her voice was careful as she asked, "Is it working?"

I took in another deep breath and shook my head. "Nothin' is. Every time I turn around, it gets worse."

She nodded. And waited.

The pub's noise was oppressive — men and women scream-chatting and clinking glasses and singing songs. The one positive thing was, no one could record us in here. So I ordered another Guinness. And took a deep breath.

Then I laid it out about Reg.

Right down to the hole he left in my heart.

Whoever said that confession is good for the soul is a fucking liar. Because once I was done I felt empty and alone and two milliseconds from breaking into sobs. It was like I relived the whole damned thing and now felt twice as guilty and ashamed ... and wondered if I *had* contributed to Martin Perriman's death. My hands were shaking and my last Guinness hadn't even been touched yet.

Diana let out an endless sigh before saying, "Jesus Fucking Christ, Dev, what the fuck is wrong with you?"

"I — I don't know." I was about to lose the battle against tears.

She sat there and said nothing more for several minutes, her eyes locked on some distant point. Then she gave a soft half-laugh and said, "At least you feel guilty about it."

I took a swallow of Guinness. "Guilty? Shit, I fuckin' hate myself, for the first time."

She took a deep breath. "How many others were there?"

I shrugged. "That cop in Chicago."

"Ryan something — "

"Orriagio." Then I cast her a sharp look. "But he deserved it."

"Judge Devlin."

"You gonna tell me after what Griffin Faure pulled, he

didn't? And Kenneth plannin' his bullshit? And what I could tell you about the others — "

"Others? Lots of others?" I just looked away. She nodded and said, "You know, you're not coming home."

"I know. I'm on bail right now, but — "

"No, they won't let you. At the very least you're guilty of molesting a cop and making the Metropolitan Police look like idiots. They'll want to save face, and there's talk about six other men who might've attacked in the London area."

"That's bullshit; I don't go for English guys."

"Not a good defense, considering Constable Thornton."

"His name's Reg."

That made her lean back, her mommy-eyes hard on me. She let out a long slow sigh. "Devlin, they will turn over heaven and earth to see who else they can find to charge you with, on both sides of the Atlantic. Don't even begin to think they will care whether or not it was justified, or even if it truly happened."

"You can thank Griffin Faure for that. He's in town and let me know he's enjoyin' the show. Probably helpin' Sir Monte with pointers and possibilities."

She nodded. "Well then, as things currently stand if you don't wind up in prison, here or there, it'll be a miracle."

"Thanks for the pep-talk."

"It's reality, Dev. You know how to face that, don't you?"

I sighed and nodded and sipped some of my Guinness.

"What we need to do is change how things stand." She finished her Shandy. "Do you still have Tavelscha's photos?"

"Yeah."

"Please tell me they're not in your condo, because the FBI's already searched that. Thoroughly."

"Shit. SHIT! No ... I ... "

"Your office? That's been searched, as well."

"I have a safe deposit box. In mom's name. Maiden name. Here's the key." I pulled out my keychain, took a green one off and handed it to her. "They may not've figured that out, yet."

"Sometimes paranoia is useful. Are Faure's there, too?"

I looked at her for a moment then said, "Yeah. Hamilton has Orriagio's."

"Any others?"

I swallowed. "You'll see."

"A serial rapist's souvenirs," she sighed. "What about Constable Thornton?"

" ... Reg ... " She just looked at me. My hands began to shake, again. Hell — I was quaking inside like a 9.9. "They ... they're on my cell phone. I'd rather not turn it on right now."

She took in a deep breath. "You better get yourself ready. Find a psychiatrist. Someone here who can explain this — these actions of yours. We'll pay for it. I'll talk to Hamilton about an attorney here, too."

"You hate me now, don't you?"

Her voice became a hiss. "Begging for sympathy, Dev? After this?" She jabbed at the phone then continued, "I'm helping you because you're my husband's brother and I love him, and the only way I can protect him, right now, is by protecting you."

"Protectin' me? By havin' me tell you about Kenneth in the hotel room? Knowin' the cops were probably listenin' in?"

"Yes! That way your side of the story's known before opinions get set in stone, and it lets the bastards know there's more going on than they've been told by the American side." She stood up to pull on her coat. "Y'know, speaking of Kenneth — I think it'd be a good idea for you to call him, tomorrow, and ... oh, *make amends*. No, make it Wednesday. Aim for about 10 am, our time. I think Kenneth reads his e-mails by then. I'll send you his phone number."

"How do you know all that?" She just smiled, tight and cold, so I said, "Diana ... you sure you want to get into this?"

"No, but have you ever known me to back down from a fight?"

"I've never seen you in one."

"Well, you're about to. And something I learned a long

time ago is, always play by your opponent's rules."

"Jeez, wish I knew what made you into such a hard-ass."

"Ask my mother sometime," she said, grabbing her purse. "Like I said, she had to become one to keep me alive till I was old enough to find someone I cared about more than me."

"Colin."

Her smile grew warm again.

I leaned back in my seat, unable to look at her. "How'd you know he was the one?"

"Because I hurt for him," she murmured. "Didn't take me a minute to see he was special. That he needed someone to hold him. Just ... hold him. By the time we got to his apartment I was ready to kill anyone who hurt him."

"Good thing you didn't find out about dad till — "

"I knew. But I wanted Colin to tell me about it. Work with me. I didn't know what else to do or how to handle it in a way that wouldn't make things worse for him. Then I saw that SOB slap him and ... " Her voice trailed off and she gave me a slight shrug. "You can't change the past, Dev. All you can do is accept it and, if you're lucky enough to get a second chance at becoming a decent human being, take it. I got lucky."

I finally looked at her. "He thinks he's the lucky one."

A gentle smile crossed her lips. "What about you?"

"Me?"

She nodded. "You've changed."

"Oh?"

"Normally there's an edge to your voice. Taut, like an overstretched wire. It's not there when you say that cop's — "

"Reg."

That softened her expression. " ... His name."

I sagged, a little. "You know how you feel about the kids? And Colin? That's how I feel about him. And I don't get it."

"Don't you?"

"You're not gonna tell me this is love."

"No. Only you can decide that."

"But he's straight!"

"And your voice grows gentle when you talk about him. But you do have a point; I can't see how you'll ever make it right with *Reg*. Not short of another miracle."

Then she walked away.

I sat there to finish my Guinness, kicking myself for my stupidity in falling for a man who probably hated me. Mingled in was wondering why I hadn't told Diana about the link between Tawfi and the murders. But I think, even then, I needed to be sure about him and that the Met was wrong.

I returned to the hotel and did a quick Google search on Kenneth Tavelscha. I found lots of photos of the right-wing bastard at functions and events. He didn't look a bit different now and usually had his very fake-blond wife in tow, sometimes his three daughters with them, and squawked a lot about family values and trickle-down economics and the homosexual agenda and liberals and on and on, but nothing more than what Diana had already let me know.

Until I found a recent photo of Mr. and Mrs. Tavelscha at a gala fundraiser in Washington, DC.

Hosted by Faure-pere. Griffin and a nice-looking woman identified as his wife were also in it. Some cross-referencing told me her father was high up in a company called Seluruh Dunia, in Singapore. They were heavy into oil in partnership with The Faure Group.

A little more digging and I found more photos of Griff and Kenneth chatting at that same party with a Russian oligarch, who owned Ves' Mir Energy and was also big in oil; it was a Russian paper so I had to use Google Translate to work that out.

Needless to say, I was seeing something of a trend here.

Then in another photo, one from a financial magazine based in Saudi Arabia, was a man who looked so much like Tawfi it had to be him. Full name? Prince Tafiq Murtada al Qasimi.

Once again Google Translate helped me work out that they were having a wonderful time at a gala in celebration of an oil venture Tawfi and Griffin had partnered on that had begun to pay off. Bigly. Thanks to Kenneth getting a bill passed in Congress allowing US Corporations to avoid sanctions on Russian oil so long as it did not come directly from there.

Finally I found photos of that party on Pinterest and after scrolling through a few dozen pages found one of Tawfi and Kenneth by a gaudy wall, laughing, Kenneth looking at the drink he was holding, all bashful and sweet, with Tawfi's right hand resting on his left arm as he spoke to him, his head cocked a little to the left.

Just like he had when he realized I was coming on to him the other night.

That made me laugh for a good minute, thinking what I was thinking would be way too rich to be anything but true ... until my brain caught up to me and I choked on the realization.

Kenneth was solid and fair-haired.

Like Perriman ... and Conescieu and Hanlon and Goughan. And Reg.

Okay ... I had a feeling I'd be sounding Kenneth out about a lot more than why he added me to the no-fly list.

ELEVEN

The next day I went to the British Library and used their Wifi. I stayed in the technology area where they had thousands of books relating to nano-tech, pouring over them and using my laptop to research online stuff. At the same time, my new *mobile* helped dig up more connections between Tawfi, Kenneth and Griffin. My hope was this would keep the Met's spooks focused on my pursuit of a pin order and not let them know I thought Sir Monte had pulled some shit with me.

All that came up was the usual fluffy business crap about Tawfi and Griff and political crap about Kenny, without any new link to any political maneuvering. All very inspirational. All very positive. The mainstream media loved the two good-looking billionaires and offered not a single solitary critique of Griffin's business practices (tho' there were several on the liberal sites, online v-logs and Facebook). Plus, since Kenny was a first-termer and had already *achieved more than most second termers had*, everyone was cutting him a lot of slack for the few *misspoken words* he'd uttered against gays and *those other people*, figuring he'd calm his alt-right rhetoric down in the next election.

As for Tawfi — or Prince Tafiq, as he was referred to by his country's media — he was the COO of the family's business, Khayr Enterprises, with daddy the CEO and two younger brothers in major roles ... but nothing for Hamad even though he's second oldest and the only son with children. A bit more digging found stories that he was very athletic and very much pampered. He'd won a Medal at some Olympics-style competition so that gave him plenty of slack since he was also, apparently, not the brightest bulb. I guess every family has to have at least one idiot.

They had three major projects going — expanding and updating their refineries to handle more Russian oil; working with China and Russia on rebuilding the commercial prospects for the old Silk Road path, both physical and electronic; and using desalination plants to help reclaim desert soil for agriculture, which they'd had a lot of success with so far. Nothing going on in the States for them ... not that I blamed them for avoiding us after Czar Snowflake showed we couldn't be trusted, but it was interesting how The Faure Group was also shifting away from the country that had enriched them.

At the same time I used my new phone to let a couple of reporters know where I was, *anonymously*, so they could *find me*. One did just after eleven and I was shocked, *shocked* to be approached. *I thought everything was being kept quiet.* I told him ... no, *insisted* my arrest was due to a *misunderstanding*. I'd thought this guy I saw was hot and up for some fun so followed him off the subway (making sure to use American words for everything) then grabbed his ass when we were alone. I didn't know he was a cop, so when he jumped me, yelling words in some weird language (also pretending not to understand British idioms) I fought him off and ran, thinking I was about to get mugged or beaten up. That's why I was arrested at my hotel. I let the guy catch a glimpse of the bandage on arm but told him I couldn't talk about that and ended the interview by telling him I was hoping I'd soon hear from my attorney telling me we'd come to an agreement with the cops. I don't think he believed me, not completely, but it did give him a different avenue to go down, and my willingness to talk *as much as I could* helped get him past some wariness hurdles.

I had a late lunch in the library café. That way I could call the office about nine because Marci would be in ... only she hadn't arrived yet. Very unlike her. So I called Colin at home.

The second he heard me, he said, "It's her, Dev. It's Mom." And his voice was spooky.

"Oh, Jesus," whispered from me. "Are they sure?"

"They're gonna run DNA but ... "

The breath left me, long and slow. "Colin, I'm so sorry you're the one who had to deal with this." No response. It took me a moment to continue. "Well ... at ... at least ... now we know she didn't abandon us."

He gave a soft huff. "She died. They showed me her locket. Wasn't around her neck. Chain was broke. Had it tight in her hand, they say. Way the bones were. Like she knew she was dying. Hoped she'd be found, some day. They let me see it. You and me. Picture inside. We were smiling. I don't remember smiling."

His voice sent chills through me. "Colin, Diana's on her way home."

"Yeah. Lands in a couple hours. Wants me to pick her up."

"Do it. But don't drive; take a cab or Lyft or something. Where's Marci? Let her drive you."

"The office, you know that."

Really? Hmm. "Okay, um, Colin, listen to me, *listen to me*. I ... I ... I can't believe how strong you are in the face of this." He snorted a soft laugh in response. Words poured out of me. "No, really, I always thought you were the weak one, that you took after mom and ... and she let dad get away with so much and I was so angry over it because I thought she was weak but now I see how it's how she tried to protect us when the cops and the fuckin' church wouldn't, and when she was gone you took over for her and you let dad hit you and I thought ... I thought it was 'cause you were afraid but now I see you kept yourself between him and me and ... and ... and now I really do see it ... see you were the strong one. Ten times stronger than me. You're facin' what happened to mom and I ... I ... I just couldn't. I got myself into a scrape here where I couldn't go home, so I wouldn't have to face it, so it wouldn't be my choice ... but it was because I was scared. Scared of what I might do, 'cause I'm the weak one, but you — you're facin' it like a man, not a scared wild animal." I ran out of breath. Could think of nothing more to say.

Colin just sighed. "Dev ... can I ask you something?"

"Anything." I had to whisper, I could barely breathe.

"Were you home the day dad died?"

I did stop breathing, for a moment, then I nodded. "Yes."

"He hit you?"

He knew? Son-of-a-bitch. A deep breath. "Yes."

"When you left did ... did you think he was dead?"

"No. He was on the floor. Sittin'. Drunk — shit, too drunk to get up."

"Yeah," he sighed. "His alcohol level was .25."

"It'd been that since we were born." I let out a deep sigh. "How long've you known?"

"Neighbor saw you leave. Blood on your face."

"Since that day!?"

"No. Marci told me. Yesterday. When she told me you'd been arrested so couldn't go to ... to view the ... "

Oh, that fucking bitch. I had to grip the table to keep from screaming.

"I told you," I croaked, "I got into a situation where I can't come home. Not yet."

"Arrested? Really?"

" ... Yes."

"For what?"

"Indecency." If he found out I was lying I could explain that away, then.

"Oh. Diana know?"

"Yes. When she got here."

"I see." His breath just whispered on the phone, for a few moments. "When I get into the office, I'm firing Marci. Having the books audited."

"What?!"

"Diana says some of it don't look right. Some of the figures."

"Do it. Diana can take over. She's sharp and she's got some good ideas for the company."

Another soft chuckle. "More'n I ever had."

"Cut it out."

"Dad was gonna leave it all to you. Said I'd fuck it up. Said you're twice as capable as me. Damn near proved him right."

"Colin, tell me seriously — has anything gone to shit since we dealt with the Faure family?"

"No. Thanks to you."

"Wrong. You kept it goin'. I was on the road half the time. You kept the business goin'. Made sure the dealers got what they needed when they needed it. And if I brought in new ones, you made 'em feel at home. I'm good at handlin' problems; you're good at preventing 'em. You're the strongest of us. You had to be."

"Yeah. Right. I'm Bloomberg, reborn. Gotta go. Talk to you later."

I didn't want to end the call but I said, "Okay."

Then I snapped.

"Colin. Colin!"

"What?"

"If you do anything stupid, I will commit murder!"

That caught him off guard. "What?!"

"If you do anything stupid, I will kill Griffin Faure." I let my voice be as harsh and cold as I could. "He's here in London and I will find him and I will cut his fucking throat."

"What the fuck's wrong with you?"

"I'm a mean motherfuckin' bastard, like dad, and if you do anything stupid, I will blame Faure and track him down."

"Don't be a dumbass, Dev. Jesus." I could hear him breathing steady, again, and for some reason that made me feel okay. Made me feel he'd make it through. Then he finally said, "I'm ... I'm not gonna do anything ... "

But just to be sure, I snarled, "I mean it, Colin. I fuckin' mean it."

He was silent for several more seconds then asked, "Are you drunk?"

"No. I almost was, yesterday, but I ... I felt like shit this mornin' so — "

"So you're not like dad. So stop making this about you. I gotta go."

He ended the call.

I sent Diana's phone a text and sat in the café drinking enough tea to float a battleship and having too damn many pastries just so I could keep from running amok. It wasn't till I got a text from Diana that Colin was at JFK with the car that I was able to relax.

But just to be safe ... maybe as a way of making sure Colin would be okay ... I called half a dozen Five-Star hotels, telling them I was FedExing some documents to Griffin Faure and wanted to make sure he'd still be there when they arrived at ten am tomorrow. If they said he wasn't a guest, I'd respond, "Oops, sorry, pulled up an old itinerary." Then I'd go to the next one.

Until I hit a hotel in Mayfair that said, "You'll be fine." Meaning I knew where to find him ... at least till Wednesday.

I hopped the underground to Green Park to do a quick reconnoiter on the hotel — one of those big, gray, Victorian things with attitude. The second I saw it I turned around and headed for Hatton Cross. Something was tugging at my brain about the dead men and I needed to go over my files to see what it was.

Because if I was right, while I didn't know who the killer was ... I had a good idea who it wasn't, and Sir Monte was focused on the wrong man.

TWELVE

Since I'd eaten so damn much waiting for Diana's text, I just bought a pack of beer and took that up to my hotel room; fortunately, I like British beer warm. Then I dug into my files — and in the fourth story, I got it.

Victim number three, Stuart Goughan, had worked for Masterson Livery Services, not Wallingford. His body was found in the back of one of their SUVs under a small apartment block in Northfields. CCTV had caught it driving in. A few minutes later a stocky man in a hoodie and overcoat left; no image of his face. No clue, yet, as to where Goughan had been grabbed, just that he had been called to a client but never arrived.

I pulled Wallingford's page and history up, deliberately using my laptop. They were one of those old and venerable companies, established 1837, and offered a wide range of higher-class vehicles; I mean, we're talking Range Rovers, Maseratis, Bentleys and Jaguars. Masterson, it turned out, was an upstart company established only a few years ago and offered passenger sedans like Vauxhalls and Mercedes along with SUVs and the like, but nothing in the class Tawfi and his family would use. They had a page showing who their drivers were — all male, all races, all religions and —

There was a familiar face — Trevor Laughton, whose name was really Jonathan Nettles. Another two minutes and I knew they were part of The Faure Group.

I laughed for ten minutes over that. This made one link to Tawfi even more tenuous and was beginning to pull Griff into it. I entertained the thought of him being the killer but he's not of Middle Eastern origin. Nor could I find any connection between him and Verlag Restaurant, where Etan Conescieu worked. That link was anything but tenuous; the restaurant was only four blocks from the embassy and his body was found in an underground parking garage close by ... next to a dumpster ... blood everywhere so no question he was killed there. And again, CCTV wasn't helpful, catching nothing but a shadowy figure grabbing him as he left the underground station before dawn and forcing him down the ramp to the garage. The killer emerged twenty minutes later. The cameras in the garage had not fired up, yet; which was considered a bit too convenient to have been anything but planned for.

I had to dig more to find out Liam Hanlon's company was Crofton-Parkes-Meade Investments & Banking in The City and that he lived in the Limehouse area, which was to the east. CCTV only showed him running about Covent Garden, where he had an appointment, then entering the Holborn underground station during the lunchtime crush. He vanished until his body was found in Acton, the other end of town and opposite to the direction he was supposed to go. There was a lot of blood, so he'd been taken there to be killed and the one camera that might have caught some of what happened had been smashed.

Perriman was killed in a spot that had no CCTV coverage and, once again, the figure thought to be the killer passed through what cameras wearing a hoodie to hide his face.

Official word from New Scotland Yard was these were crimes of opportunity ... which was bullshit. Even the press was having questions about it. They were all too similar and well-planned, and word was slipping out the Met knew there were connections between them that extended beyond physical type and —

The room's bell rang. I think I jumped five feet. It took me a moment to catch my breath, and I wasn't even sure I should answer it. Then it rang again, more insistent, so I got my nail clipper ready, went to the door and opened it to find —

Reg.

Standing there. Hands in pockets. Clean black t-shirt over new jeans, a new faux-leather jacket over them. Same tennies, though. He was watching me, wary and lovely and lost as ever. It took every ounce of willpower I had to keep from pulling him into an embrace and just ... just holding him.

I managed to form the words, "Come on in."

He entered and stood in the middle of the room, his hands still in his pockets, showing off his magnificent ass to its best advantage, though he didn't know that's how I saw it. Or maybe he did. Maybe Sir Monte had noticed my research and sent him over to play the fag for as much more info as he could. Maybe they knew I had another phone and wanted to keep better tabs on me. It made for a cynical beginning and I hated myself for thinking that, but I was still in paranoid mode.

"How you feelin'?" he finally asked. "Your arm?"

"Fine. You ... you off duty?"

He shook his head. "On leave. Boss won't let me come back yet. Wants me *evaluated*." He all but spit the last word out. "It late for me to drop by?"

I shook my head. "I never hit the sack till midnight, one, somewhere in there. Want a beer?"

He nodded. I grabbed one and opened it for him. He downed half of it, his hand shaking. I watched its sharpness bring him back to his center. His eyes grew sharp on me. "Y'know, you did a right job of mucking me up."

"Sorry." I sat on the bed.

"Are you?"

I nodded. "For the first time in my life, I ... I'm sorry for what I did."

"You say that but ... "

"Yeah, I know, it's just words. Bullshit stuff."

"Then why you sorry now? Why over me?"

"I've explained that." I chuckled. "Tried to. But it don't make one fuckin' bit of sense to me, either, 'cause you're not even the type I want to ... to go for ... "

"Yeah, right, nothin' makes sense."

I leaned forward, resting my arms on my knees. "Reg — you mind if I call you that?" He shrugged. "Would you tell me — did you really think this decoy operation'd work? Or surveillance? Whatever the fuck it was."

He sipped his beer and sighed, not moving from where he stood. "I thought it might, but the target — he barely even looked at me."

I nodded. "Tafiq Murtada al Qasimi."

He cast me a sharp glance. "I hear you know him."

I nodded. "Now."

"Not before?"

I looked him straight in the eye. "No."

"Don't look that way."

"I know," I sighed. Obviously, Sir Monte had kept him out of the loop regarding what I was doing. "But what I don't get is — there's cameras everywhere in the UK. How could you not get good video of him goin' to Perriman's?"

"Hoodie up. Head down. Stayed in shadows, like he knew where the cameras were."

"But that's not what he was wearing. He had on a regular suit and overcoat and — "

"Could've been under 'em."

"Bullshit, the way that suit fit. So why'd you put him under surveillance?"

"He had some weird comin's and goin's. He's always out with that bodyguard."

"Abdel."

Reg looked at me, frowning. "Yeah. But *not* always. Those times — he was on his own and we matched 'em to the first three murders."

"His Oyster card — ?"

"Don't have one. His type gets drove everywhere. But that night — the night you ... um, that Abdel guy was off and he bought a return ticket to Zone Six. Got the Boss' attention, so we put everything into action. I wasn't the only man they had on tap, but I — I was closest."

"So you've been plannin' this for a while, and that night on the underground you were tryin' to get him to come after you. That's why you had that brace on."

He shrugged and sipped more beer. "Dr. Herries-White thinks he stabs 'em to get control, then strangles 'em as he — as he has his way."

I had a sudden flash of Reg being attacked like that, his face caught in the same agony, his lovely eyes going cold and empty, and it made me jerk in a sudden breath and I couldn't think and blurted out, "And you thought — you thought I was gonna do that to you."

He looked away. Gave me another shrug.

"Jesus," I muttered then bolted up and opened myself a beer and downed half of it before leaning against a wall, unable to face him. I finally murmured, "Reg ... I am so sorry. I am so fuckin' sorry ... "

"Are animals ever sorry? Really? Dogs, even?"

I looked at him. He was staring out the window, watching the jets land, beer hanging from his hand, down his side. I sat back on the bed, my eyes locked on him. Neither of us spoke for a couple of minutes.

"Reg," I finally whispered, "why're you here?"

He took in a deep breath and looked back at me. "I — I talked with Dr. Herries-White. He — he told me the same crap as you. 'Bout how I — how I *reacted*."

"It's not crap."

"I know. But I still don't understand it. Understand why. Those men in the report. The ones you — they all look alike."

"Yeah. My type."

"So how many are there?"

"A few," I sighed, then said, "But they all messed with me so ... "

"You said that. So what'd I do to you?"

It took me a moment to say, "Nothing."

He backed away from me. "You really mean it? You ... you just took me from impulse?"

I didn't dare speak, so I shrugged a *yes*.

"But that makes no sense!"

"Does it have to?"

"Yeah, to me!" he cried. "I been stalkin' about, all over, tryin' to figure it, for days, and you — you're — you're tellin' me there's no reason for it? That it's really just about the bloody tats on my neck? But that don't explain why ya didn't — ya didn't ... didn't ... " He couldn't continue.

The hurt and confusion in his eyes smashed through the wall and, once again, I lost control of my words.

"Why I didn't fuck you?"

The sharp look he cast me verified my guess. "You ... you were gonna. I could tell."

"You're right. I was."

He looked away, irritated but still confused. "I thought we had it all wrong. That you were him, y'know. On the train. We're waitin' weeks for the right time to try and get him to — get al Qasimi to — and then he's there and I'm doin' my routine and he's lookin' at me, I can see him lookin' at me and it's goin' like we wanted — but then he shrugs me off and you — *you* start watchin' me. Tight on me. And I ... I ... I couldn't believe it. I wondered if you and al Qasimi had a signal and he turned away."

He leaned against the desk in the same position Tawfi had, but confused and uncertain instead of casual and in control. "Were you workin' with him? Have you had lads we don't know about? Was it your turn, that night?"

"With Tawfi? No."

"Toffee?"

Shit. "Tafiq. When I picked him up on Friday, that's the first time I spoke with him."

"Another bloody coincidence? Right?"

That made me look away from him. "I can't explain that. But I swear to you, I haven't killed anybody. Haven't helped anybody kill anybody. You know this is true, just by when the first three murders happened."

He nodded and relaxed a little. Jesus God, he looked so beautiful with his legs slightly parted, one hand gripping the edge of the desk, the other still holding his beer, his elegant face letting reality filter past. He finally said, "Yeah." He downed more beer and sneered at himself. "Wanna know the real reason the Boss dropped me? Me. Thinks I'm a coward."

"Bullshit."

"I was supposed to lead him off at Boston Manor, if he took the bait. Cross the road. Head for Blondin Park. It's fair open there and we had lads on tap ... and 'cause of who he is we had to catch him in action. We had an idea what to expect and knew he'd go quiet with us. But then you started lookin' at me. Hard on me. Bigger 'n him. Just as dark and ... and angry. Your eyes so fuckin' angry. I got — I got scared. Nearly lost my shite, I did, thinkin' we had it wrong. I been in fuckin' combat but you just lookin' at me — not al Qasimi, but you — you maybe bein' him ... it shook me. I ... I texted the Boss and he said I should still lead you off. But I ... I couldn't move. We passed the station and the Boss were yellin' at me to get done with it, but I couldn't move."

"I noticed your texts weren't happy."

"Yeah ... and that's what made you decide to pick me. I'm scared and I'm fightin' it and that's what made you — made you go for — that's what made it happen. That's what fuckin' made it happen and ... "

Oh my God, I wanted to hold him close and tell him it was a lie, but I couldn't move.

Because he was right.

What I did was evil.

He sipped more beer and said, "I ... I told Boss I ... I grew up in Hounslow. Near the east depot. The ASDA has an underground car park so you'd probably make your move there."

"That building down the end of the street. And the others were found in parking lots. Makes sense."

"He ... he didn't like it. Didn't have any units close by so had to bring in Hounslow Station, for the lot of good they did. I didn't care. That's what let me move. That's when I exited. And you bloody followed me. I had to keep me hands in me pockets so you'd not see 'em shakin'. The area we went into, it's bein' rebuilt, houses redone. I figured fewer people in there, easier for backup to find us, two blokes walkin' alone. I could handle one bloke, no matter what, but no sign of 'em and we're walkin' and walkin' and I'd told the Boss where I was and they've got fuckin' GPS on me and he said they'd find me, but ... but ... "

His hands were shaking. I rose and moved closer to him, feeling so fucking ashamed of myself I almost couldn't stand it. He downed more beer.

"Then you jumped me. And I couldn't breathe. And before I could think, I was bound, hand and foot, and you got me into that bloody house and still no sign of 'em, not till you were naked and on me and they shot some torch light into the foyer and then they left, they bloody fuckin' left me there and I thought I was dead! But then you didn't. You did that to me. And I did it and I was still so scared and I can't believe it but I did it and — and the doc says it's okay, it's normal, but it's not it's not, it's not and — "

"You're not a coward, Reg."

"Tell Boss that," he shouted. "The looks he gives me."

"You thought I'd killed three men but you still decoyed me away from people. You were smart to wait till you got to an area you knew. You did what you had to do to stay alive, even after your backup let you down. You're not a coward. As for your Boss, that motherfucker used you to dig information out of me because he knows how I feel about you."

He bolted away from the desk, furious. "FEEL ABOUT ME?! What the fuck does that mean? How can you bloody feel anything about a man you fuckin' raped!?"

"You're right — and your Boss knew that. And he used it

to mess with me. And it fuckin' worked."

"What d'you mean, it fuckin' worked?"

"That man with him — Herries-White — he saw it. Saw me lose control. When your boss used you to mess with me — "

"I messed with you? You think I'm bloody messin' with you?"

I couldn't speak. He looked at me like I had four heads.

"You — your presence did, and it still does and I don't know what to do."

"What're you sayin'?"

"I'm sorry," I whispered out, feeling lightheaded.

"You already said that."

"But you *are* the first man I'm sorry for. Sorry for doin' that to him. You didn't deserve me goin' after you."

"The other blokes did?"

I nodded.

He sat on the windowsill, lost. "You mean that? They all — they did something to you?"

I nodded, again.

"What?"

"One was a cop who manhandled his wife," I said. "Another swindled me. My family. Another stole clients from us. I took down one guy who yelled at a barista I liked because he didn't get the cream in his double half-caff mocha just right. He was trying to hail a cab in the rain. Never had a chance to take even a sip of his fucking coffee. Another was being an asshole at a gym I go to."

"You ... you did to them what you did with me?"

I couldn't keep the words from whispering out. "I told you — them, I fucked."

"What'd I do to make you want to do that to me?"

"Nothing! Nothing. I just wanted to hold you but then watching you walk — I wanted more. Until I did hold you. Then everything changed and ... and I ... I had to make myself let go."

"That why you cried?" I nodded. "And why you left me

that scratch? It's not like you — you thought I was a rent boy?"

I jolted. "No! No, Reg, I broke your phone."

"Piece of shite. Police issue."

"Still, it wasn't right. I owed you for it."

"Boss didn't believe me when I told him what you did. Had me checked. Doc collected your — your DNA and he ... he verified that I wasn't — that I hadn't been — that I wasn't hurt. Hurt in that way." His voice dropped to a bare whisper. "It don't make sense to me. I never even thought about bein' with a bloke before. I ... I play footy and there's lots of grabbin' arse and bein' the maggot in the showers and such, and not once did I think of it as more'n that. But then you fuckin' jump me and tie me down and — and now all you're sayin' is *you don't usually do that* an' *you're really, really sorry*. Fuckin' sick, it is."

He slid down to a crouch. Bit at a nail. I still couldn't move.

"Reg, can I ask you something?" He sort of shrugged a *yes*. "How did you feel when I — I was finished with you?"

"I'm not a poof," he snarled at me, his glare sharp.

"That's not what I asked."

He rolled his eyes, hesitated, then whispered, "Drained. Of everything in me. I've not been with me wife since. Can't."

"You ever feel that with her?"

He gave me another vague shrug. "When we was first married. Every night. But then the kids come and we got busy ... "

I gently moved to kneel before him, my eyes locked on his. I was not thinking about what I was doing. "And lonely?"

He gave a slight shake of his head. "No time ... "

"But alone?"

It took a moment but he finally said, "Yeah."

He leaned against his knees and laid his face in his hands, his breath ragged. I carefully touched his honey-colored hair, my own hands shaking. I was in zero control of my movements.

"Reg, you're not gay or queer or any stupid label like that; you're just a nice, normal, everyday kind of guy. And I'm not sayin' that 'cause I think there's something wrong with sex between men. I don't. I'm a real asshole when it comes to homophobes. But I hate labels and I like to be honest. Face facts. And the fact is, you're just like any other guy."

"Like you?" he whispered.

"No," I said, letting my fingers travel in light circles over his scalp. "I *am* an animal. Worse than one, sometimes. I don't think they even know the word revenge, but I bet they understand the concept of it better than us. Understand it's counterproductive. You can get lost in it. Wind up destroying yourself instead of your target."

He began to breathe deeper and leaned into my hand, his voice thick and uncertain. "Why does that feel so nice?"

"Because it's tender." I shifted my fingers up a little to take in more of his head and whisper over the scars in his scalp. "You want to know why *I* think I didn't violate you?"

"You don't know?" he whispered.

"Just a guess. I may ask Dr. Herries-White to recommend a psychiatrist so I can understand it better. Still interested?"

He sent me the slightest of nods, unwilling to do anything that might make me stop caressing the hair on his head.

"The tattoos on your back. They reminded me of tenderness. My mother's tenderness. And I'd just learned that ... that without question, she was dead. Had been for more than twenty years. The chaos in my mind was overwhelming, so when I saw your tattoos I remembered she had one on the back of her left shoulder in some kind of sign and she'd always been so tender and at that moment, I saw you were in turmoil and I — I thought — thought you needed tenderness. And I needed someone who needed that. I'm selfish and greedy and impatient, like most people, but sometimes I stop bein' all about me and think about someone else. Without meaning to."

I let my fingers trail around to his right ear and whisper around it then back to his left. "You're a beautiful man, and when I saw you on the tube your beauty made me look at you, but it was your pain and confusion that made me need to — to be with you. Hungry to be with you. And I was starving for you every second until I had you. Then I saw deep into your eyes. Saw your turmoil and it made me hurt too much to hurt you."

He cocked his head a bit to give me a wary look. "You talk about me like I'm a woman."

"How could I, when you're anything but?"

Then I let my fingers drift back through his hair and grip it to shift his head back just enough to open his beautiful face up to me and I looked into his sad eyes and his slightly parted lips and without a thought I moved in to let mine connect with his in the most tender way possible.

The electricity I felt the second I kissed him — it was as if I'd been fired into orbit. His lips matched mine so right. His breath carried a hint of mint. I didn't chew on him or ram my tongue against his; it was just a moment of Zen elegance worthy of all the poets who've ever written anything ever. Fire roared inside me. My heart nearly filled to explosion. I'd never kissed anyone like this before — with complete openness and tenderness and patience — and I never wanted it to end.

But Reg gasped and shoved me back with a cry.

I fell on my ass and he staggered to his feet, his eyes locked on me in shock and — shit, and horror. He glanced around, breathing hard, then yanked the door open and bolted from the room.

I hated seeing him go like that, but what was worse? I was barely able to hold myself back from chasing him down and grabbing him and dragging him back and throwing him on the bed and having at him again. Yanking his jeans out of the way and plunging deep into his exquisite ass like some mongrel fucking his bitch or tom raping a feline in heat, and this time I don't think I'd have stopped till I'd owned every part of his body.

The body of a man I felt guilty for having already harmed.

In a room bugged by the Metropolitan Police.

Who were probably hoping I'd pull something like that.

Shit, Diana was right — I needed help.

****

I didn't sleep much that night. I called myself every diseased name in the book and even made up a few. Mixed it in with reliving that kiss. Sighing over it like some stupid teenage girl who'd snuck her lips onto *her-favorite-boy-band-singer's*. I wanted more of those kisses. Wanted to be worthy of them.

I wanted Reg.

I loved Reg.

I fucking loved him.

Yeah, right — could I get any more obnoxious without finding a bodice somewhere to rip open? Jesus.

But it was reality. Diana was right; I'd found someone I cared about more than myself. More than I did Colin and my nephews — my own blood! I have never felt this way about anyone. Ever. Even mom; my love for her was colored by hate for her not taking us away from dad. And it was shredding me inside.

Because I also had this animal need for him, to join with him and find release with him. It was a tidal wave of horror and desire and lust and selfishness, and I couldn't get rid of it.

I tried watching the planes come and go ... but that only reminded me of what I could not do and ... yet ... might eventually do. That one day I'd have to face the horror of the idea Reg might be out of my life, completely ...

As if he was in it now. As if he could ever be in it. A married man, obviously happy with kids all over and made the old-fashioned way, not by artificial means. All of them looking like both him and her and happy as kittens. And yes, I know I'm making assumptions based on just a glance at the photo on his mobile phone ... but it fit him. And I ached to be part of it.

Part of him.

I finally gave up on sleep and got back to my research on nano-tech and pins, reading through the PDFs I'd downloaded and files I'd photocopied. It was mind-numbing but not even that put me to sleep. I'd just go brain dead and wander through memories of Reg walking down the underground platform. Or lying on that dirty floor after I was done. Or facing me down in that interrogation room. Or standing in the doorway, watching me, wary as a street cat you'd love to pet and hold. Or looking at me before I kissed him. And my heart would go soft and my breath shallow and I'd have to remind myself to pull enough air into my lungs to stay conscious and not collapse to the floor like some nervous fainting bitch in a Victorian novel.

Okay, this had to stop. I needed to be back in control.

Well, the first thing to do was get Kenneth Tavelscha off my back. Have him reverse the travel ban or whatever so that if I did get out from under criminal charges in the UK, I *could* come home. If I could make myself do that. No, I'd have to — just so I could remove myself from the temptation of forcing myself onto Reg, again. That also meant handling the FBI's inquiries and settling down the dealers they'd spoken to.

I sent Diana an email asking for their names then hunkered down to work out some bullet points in explanation — that I was working with the UK government on a new project and they'd asked the FBI to check into some gossip about me, emphasis on the word *gossip*. And I determined to officially came out to every one of them. No more of this *I don't like to share my private life* bullshit to protect the company. I now am who I am, as the song sort of goes.

But the truth was, I'd been cowardly about it. Hiding it. Not no more.

Then there were my questions about the whole murder set-up. I'd shared some with Reg — and Sir Monte, by default — but it was time to stop sharing and start pushing back ,and those would be my tools. I'd also do what I could to help Tawfi in this, since he was as much the focus of this crap as me.

To begin with, the whole situation bugged me. We got a killer who's smart enough to avoid being seen on camera yet winds up brutalizing and killing the same type of man every time? Men linked to Tawfi's embassy? All of them? It's obvious that's deliberate, but why?

Tawfi's a diplomat. He's got immunity, so as I understand it he could just walk out of the country without charges. The story might be embarrassing, but it might also help him. He's Muslim so he could easily claim it's just some stupid Western plot to hurt a strong Islamic leader and steal their country's resources. His country's media would go along with it as would the mullahs or imams or whatever he had in his patch of land. Plus he's rich as shit and probably has lawyers even nastier than The Faure Group's so that could be as vicious as world war three. What could anybody gain from that?

Unless he *was* the killer and was just arrogant enough to think all of the connections didn't matter. But I still didn't buy it. Stabbing someone then raping them as they're dying and — and then *strangling* them? That's way too psychotic for him. Plus he's richer than Jesus. If he'd wanted those guys that bad he could've bought them. *Here's a hundred K if you'll be gay for pay.* Serve it up right there's no man alive who'd turn that down, not in the tax brackets the victims were in.

Of course there was the question of blackmail, but that works both ways. All the men were married with kids so that would've been solid leverage against them. And that was something else — picking married men with children, every time? That made the crimes seem a hundred times worse. Hell, the media was already screaming about widows and orphans at the hand of a deranged faggot; mix in a Muslim guy and it'd go nuclear.

Then there's Griffin Faure. Him being in London at the same time as this all coming down and knowing as much about it as I did, if not more. Him also being connected to one of the victims as well as Tawfi's company? I know it's a small world when it comes to billionaires but that's still a bit too much to accept as coincidence. So I started wondering if he'd been in London during any of the murders.

I sent Diana an email, deliberately using my laptop, and asked her to find out if Griff was in London recently. Since we both knew Rio I didn't bother telling her how to do it. And now Sir Monte would have a new avenue to wonder about. Let's see if he's as sharp as he likes to think he is.

Now I was ready for lunch so strolled back to the Indian food pub to see if I could find out more about that cloak-and-dagger crap Griff pulled, Sunday. I had another great curry as I flirted with the same tiny waitress — a recent émigré from Mumbai who loved the attention of a good-looking American dude. I managed to find out Griffin had been sitting in a back room for an hour before I arrived, on the phone the whole time, had ordered nothing to eat just lots of Scotch, and his helper had been panicky about getting his food ready to go before Griffin was done with me. And the son-of-a-bitch left no tip on his bar tab. I know you don't need to in England but still — that's just plain tacky; I doubled the cost of my meal to make up for it, kissed her hand in the old-fashioned way and headed back to my hotel. I think she'd have sold me the business by that point, whether she owned it or not.

Then I called Griffin's hotel to *see if he'd collected my FedEx envelope* only to be told *it hadn't arrived.* I said I'd contact FedEx, *very irritated.*

By this time, it was after ten am in Washington. Diana had sent me Kenneth's email address and phone number so I gave him a call ... and got his voice mail. I left a simple message — *Hi, Ken, this is Devlin, from college. Just calling to say hello and discuss your deal with Khayr Enterprises* — and left him my number. I wasn't sure what I'd say to him, yet, but sometimes the best thing to do is just wing it; makes for flexibility.

He returned the call fifteen minutes later.

"Dev," he said, his voice cool and controlled. "I figured you'd be calling."

"Oh?" I said. "Why'd you think that? I haven't seen you in eight years."

"Stop it. I know damn well you're just trying to get home and can't get a flight and — "

"I'm not headed home, yet. I'm workin' on a deal here in the UK. Special pins for an embassy, and I was researchin' it and found that you know the ambassador. Just thought I'd ask you about him. See if you're willin' to give me some info."

"What're you talking about?"

"Well, the guy I'm dealin' with is Prince Tafiq Murtada al Qasimi and he comes across as pretty easy-goin', but he is as smart as they come and said somethin' that I don't know how to answer. I was tryin' to figure out the best way to deal with that by diggin' into his company's history and I saw he was at a fundraiser of yours in DC, a few months ago. Handled by The Faure Group. That's some high-power backin' you've got. Way out of my league. But I was hopin' you'd help — "

"After what you did to me!?"

"What'd I do to you?"

"You know damn well."

"Oh. That. So ... did Prince Tafiq do it, too?"

Silence. Just the sound of him breathing. "Give me another number."

I gave him the hotel's number and the room I was in. He ended the call and five minutes later the phone rang.

"Kenneth?" I asked, the second I picked it up.

"This line's scrambled. If anyone tries to listen in all they'll get is a fax signal. Now what're you up to, Dev?"

"Protecting my brother. You wanna come after me, fine — have at it. I can understand why you'd want to. But you leave my family out of this."

"I'm not after your — "

"You got the FBI messin' with the dealers we use to sell our pins. Now they're afraid to work with us. My brother's life is tied up in our company and if it goes under, I don't know what he'll do so — "

"Not my fault you're part of that — "

"Don't do it, Kenny! I'll turn into a mean motherfuckin' son-of-a-bitch. And with those pictures — you'll be lucky if you can get elected county clerk after — "

"What pictures?"

Uh-oh. "Haven't you read your emails, yet?"

"We had last-minute conference meetings. My staff checks my emails and no one said anything about pictures or — "

"Private email, Ken. Personal."

I heard him ticking on a keyboard. A few moments later he gasped out, "Oh, fuck."

"Yeah," I said, wishing like hell I knew which ones Diana had sent him.

"You son-of-a-bitch."

"Told you." He was silent. Just his breathing audible. I waited a few moments then said, "Ken, all I'm askin' you to do is back off."

"Give in to blackmail."

"I'm not askin' for money. I'm not usin' this to enrich me, not like your *buddies* are." I heard a near gasp when I said that. "All I want you to do is back off so my brother and his family'll be all right. If you do that, I'll be happy ... and I'll get your buddies off your back, too."

I could almost see the frown on his face as he tried to understand what I'd just said. I could tell he didn't want to ask ... but, "How?"

"You needed money for some new equipment or something and I — I took some glamour shots of you. Made it worth your while. I'll sell those to some rag like *The Enquirer*, under another name. Let 'em know I need money for a defense fund. Make it as sleazy as I can. But I'll also *let slip* I tried to take things to the next level and *you refused*. Said you weren't into that."

"But you said — I mean, it shows here — "

"What I told your buddies and what can be proven are two different things ... so long as I withhold those photos."

He was silent, for a moment. "How does this help me?"

"Gets the story out there, makes you look human. Face it head on. Tell 'em just about every man you know has dick shots on Instagram and Tumbler, includin' your buddies. And all I'll release is the nice pretty ones I shot; no frontal. You'll get a solid following in the female crowd, even right wing, and it kills the leverage your buddies have over you."

"But they — they saw me passed out and — "

"I don't know what you're talkin' about. They came to pick you up and you walked out, fully clothed, cash in hand to — oh, wait, I remember, to pay for that stupid-assed party. And I'll forget about what you planned to do to me. By the way — did you find someone else to pull that crap on? Like one of my friends?"

"Naw, it was a stupid idea. I was a stupid kid."

"It's college. I think that's a requirement." I sighed then added, "Truth is, I'd noticed your hints and I was sorry I hadn't taken you up on them. You're a damn good-lookin' guy, Ken, and you do have one beautiful dick."

He chuckled. "Oh ... you're sick."

"You're not the first person to call me that."

He was silent, for a moment. "You don't think this'd work?"

"Your buddies being demanding?"

"Not really. It's just — shit, it goes against everything I believe, giving in to blackmail."

"You're not givin' in to me. We're workin' up a compromise. That's the art of politics, right?"

"That's what they say."

"Kenneth ... I thought you were gonna turn pro when you graduated. Why didn't you?"

"I got hit pretty hard in a couple of games. Last one, I got knocked out. Doctors said I had the beginning of CTE."

"Shit."

"Yeah. I was gonna go on and just not get hit but my dad talked me out of it. He's my campaign manager, y'know."

"Do you like doin' this? Bein' in politics?"

"When I was in the legislature, yeah. But DC ... " He took a deep breath and said, "How'd you know about Tafiq? He tell you?"

"No. I only met him a couple times but I read him, and while he is gorgeous I'm not what he's drawn to. You are."

"Yeah, he's smooth. That fundraiser — Toni was tired and went home early — that's my wife, Antoinette — and he was staying at the hotel and we went up for a couple drinks to talk and one thing led to another ... " His voice trailed off.

"He's a beautiful man," I said, carefully. "Eyes to drown in. Confidence to spare."

"Yeah," he sighed. "Y'know, I — I wasn't really all *that* out of it with you, Dev."

"I wondered why it was so easy to get you goin' ... "

"When I got off — shit, it was good. Even when you ... when you ... y'know ... took a lot to keep still ... "

I took in a deep breath, not sure what to say. "Ken, I — look, I shouldn't have done all that to you. I knew you were curious and — well, I was in asshole mode. I should've just taken you up on your hints and worked with you. We could've had a lot more fun, that way."

"Yeah, could've," he whispered. "So are you out?"

"Completely. Now. Thanks to you and The Faure Group."

"Got anything in your bag of tricks for them?"

I jolted. "They know about you and Taw-uh, the prince?"

"I think so, some of the things Griffin said. But I hear you got some kind of leverage on him. Even got him to pay up on some money he owed. That's a big deal with those guys."

"I'm from Brooklyn. I know people who know people, know what I mean?"

"Doesn't do me any good."

"Kenneth," I sing-songed, "you know *me* ... "

His voice grew hopeful. "Really? 'Cause the shit they want me to get passed — if you do this I'll kill the FBI crap along with the no-fly stuff. And ...uh, y'know ... maybe next time you're in town ... "

I had to chuckle. "I'm open to it but better not in DC. That kind of thing always gets found out in that town."

"Yeah ... gotta keep it quiet. My father-in-law's big in the GOP and he hates Democrats and liberals and queers and everyone who likes them. He and my dad get along great, and Toni's daddy's daughter."

"So come up to Brooklyn, sometime. I got a condo in Red Hook. Nice and private. Plenty of space to do whatever the fuck you want, and nobody gives a shit in my neighborhood."

" ... That sounds nice, Dev. Bye. And thanks." He hung up.

I started laughing. This was turning out to be fun.

I found out from the desk that there was a FedEx office within walking distance, so just to be as big an asshole as anyone in The Faure Group I hopped over and overnighted a note saying, *I know what you're up to, Griff. Maybe we should get together again and ... oh ... discuss it like we did before, sweet cheeks — just you and me this time.*

My only regret on that was I wouldn't see his face when he opened the envelope.

THIRTEEN

The next day, I scooted on over to Tawfi's embassy to meet with Mahjub. I arrived in time to see Abdel and a pair of beef-meisters like him escorting five men and two women down the front steps, and they were not being gentle. They shoved them against a car, used a few words in Arabic that I'm fairly certain translated to *Fuck off*, then headed back up the steps. I scurried after them.

I heard some of the ejected guys call after me, "Wait, who might you be? Who're you!?" I ignored them.

"What was that all about?" I asked as Abdel led me into the building.

He glared at me with barely concealed contempt then he and his twins stormed down a side hall. I'd have felt insulted if it hadn't all been so silly.

I turned to reception in time to see a huge TV screen in a padded frame being carried down the stairs by four more powerhouse guys, Mahjub right behind them.

He saw me and hurried over, saying, "Mr. Pope."

I nodded and motioned to the door. "What's goin' on?"

He glanced outside and shook his head. "Those people — they tried to sneak in, claiming they had an appointment with Prince Tafiq, but he was called away so ... "

"Oh. Will he be back?"

He cast me a quick glance. "Perhaps by noon." He turned back to the men carrying the crate down another narrower flight of stairs and cried, "Careful! That bannister has been crafted from mahogany and would cost more to replace that a year of your wages!" He spun back to me. "I apologize for the confusion. These were supposed to have been collected yesterday but the conference went long. The screens are too large for our lift so must be carried down to the back entrance, but this is the last of it."

"Looks like a lot of work," I said.

He didn't smile. "Three weeks of set-up for what supposed to be two hours of talk, but it is done. Till next time. If you don't mind following me downstairs, when this is loaded we can hop straight back up to my office."

I shrugged an *Okay* and we headed down to the ground floor. The last crate had to leave by a door too narrow for two men to fit through, so it was carefully shuffled out onto the back alley then lifted into the back of a truck using a massive tailgate. Inside held four more of the crates along with rolling cases of what was labeled as computer equipment. Mahjub signed off as they strapped the last crate down then watched the guys drive away before breathing a sigh of relief.

He led me back inside, locked the door and set the alarm for it, then we headed to a small elevator stuck in a corner and rode up to the third floor.

"This is your transit system, huh?" I asked, smiling.

He nodded. "We have a number of flats on the top floor."

"Saves on rent and travel expenses."

He nodded. "London prices are ludicrous."

"Abdel live here, too?"

"Security has its own wing, on the first floor."

"What about Prince Tafiq?"

He grew tight. "A prince does not usually mingle with those who work for him," he murmured as we exited the lift.

"I'm surprised Abdel and his boys aren't with him."

"They will collect him when he is ready."

"And still face those reporters when he gets back."

He gave me a little smirk. "There is more than one entrance to this building. Here we are."

He led me into a nice-size room with electronic equipment covering tables, shelves, workbenches and even the floor. One monitor had a dozen windows gleaming in it, each showing an image from a CCTV camera. Another bank of monitors showed constantly changing script flashing up the screen, line after line, and another set was updating a security system. A soft hum whispered around us.

"Wow, you are I-T," I said, wandering over to the CCTV monitor. "Are you part of security, too?"

"I handle only the cameras."

"How long do you keep video backup?"

Mahjub gave me a sharp look. "Why do you ask?"

"Curious, that's all."

He eyed me for a moment then sat in a swivel chair, his eyes even harder on me. "Are you truly who you claim to be?"

Bam, straight to the chin. I chuckled. "Look us up online. My profile's on there."

"I have. I also know that you're investigating Prince Tafiq and Khayr Enterprises and their links to The Faure Group ... as well as the murder of Martin Perriman."

At that shot, I blinked. "What makes you think I'm doin' that?"

"It is not so difficult to arrange to be notified of searches aimed at certain words or certain people when they occur. Do you deny this?"

I took in a deep breath. "No."

"Do you work with the police?"

"No."

"Why should you be believed?" I just shrugged. He continued with, "Our embassy is under their surveillance. Has been for weeks. They were rather clumsy with it, as if they wanted us to know. They have tracked me, Abdel, his assistants, Prince Hamad — when he was here, last — and a dozen male employees as well as Prince Tafiq. Now it seems they only follow him. Why?"

"Does he know?"

"Of course he does. Has this to do with a dead man?"

"Man, I should come to you for information."

"You do not answer my questions."

"If you're investigatin' me then you must've noticed I'm lookin' into makin' pins for the Queen and her Court so ... "

"So your research is too wide-ranging for what you claim, and you still do not answer my question. Do you work with the police?"

"I told you — no."

"Then do you plan to disrupt Kahyr's business alliances?"

"No."

"Are you aligned with The Faure Group?"

"Hell, no!"

He grinned at how I spit those two words out then offered a vicious smile and whispered, "Do you think you will work your way into Prince Tafiq's bed?" That one jolted me. He noticed. "You are not the type he is attracted to."

"You know that, first hand?" I growled as I looked straight at the blond highlights in Mahjub's hair.

He noticed, tensed and touched a hand to them. "I used to be completely blond. A girl I liked suggested it. But it was — it was a mistake."

"Because the prince likes blonds ... "

Mahjub took in a deep breath. "You know him. This is interesting."

The critter was still growling so I took in a deep breath. "A prince don't mingle with the help unless he wants somethin', does he? Did he ... uh, force you?"

Mahjub frowned at me. "Not in the way I think you mean. It is only ... he is a powerful man in my country and it is better to have his favor than not. And I like living in London."

I exhaled. "Sorry. So why're you tellin' me all this?"

He frowned, "Because Prince Tafiq *is* what you like, and if reports are to be believed — well, it would not end nicely for you. Most certainly not if you tried to force the issue."

"Aw, gimme a fuckin' break; I'm not a dumbass." I

leaned against a table. "You got an in with the cops?"

He smiled and caressed his laptop. "I have no need of one. I can find out anything I wish to know."

"That how you knew about him and Perriman?"

He nodded to the CCTV screens. "One time I saw Martin Perriman arrive after embassy hours. I watched and a few times Prince Tafiq would leave. Always on a Thursday, when Abdel is not working and his assistants are too casual. This was when he said I could return to myself. It was not difficult to understand what was happening." He gave me a sharp look. "He did not kill the man."

"I know."

Now he frowned. "Then why is he still under surveillance?"

"Cops don't agree with me."

"But you disagree with them." I nodded. "How do I know you mean this?"

"They thought I was helpin' him."

"Is that why you were arrested?"

"Whoa ... I want you to teach me how you do your research 'cause I am way behind the times."

He gave me the most perfect condescending frown I'd ever gotten from an IT guy. "As I said, it's not so difficult to triangulate information."

"Says the tech whiz."

He gave a soft laugh then asked, "Why do you think Prince Tafiq is innocent of Martin Perriman's death?"

"He didn't know about it Friday night."

His expression shifted to incredulous. "You *have* been with him." I grimaced. "And he has asked you to return."

I shrugged. "All without bleachin' my hair."

He relaxed a bit, turned to his workbench and opened his laptop. "Perhaps you will keep him busy. Happy."

"Did Perriman?"

"Why else would he continue meeting with him?"

"Are you okay with this? What your prince did with you?"

He frowned at me again. "Am I allowed not to be?" Then he held up the crossed flags pin and shifted to, "Here, I have a preliminary idea of how this might work but it would entail something more intensive than merely programming the chips and having them monitored. That may prove to be exorbitant in costs as well as manpower so ... "

I let him chatter on in a language called *computer-speak* that I didn't even begin to understand. He was kind enough to take pity on me and say he'd send me a couple of links and PDFs to help explain his ideas. We kept this up for hours, ordering in Chinese, drinking tea by the gallon and coming up with a hundred different ways the chips in the pins could work. By the time Tawfi appeared in the doorway I was so loaded down with techno-info I felt like a cyborg.

"I thought I might find you here," the prince murmured. "Is all going well?"

I'm sure my eyes were spinning when I looked at him and said, "I now know the secret of the universe. Number Nine."

He chuckled. "And I thought it was Forty-two." He shifted to Mahjub. "Burn a DVD of yesterday's conference and send it here." He handed Mahjub a card; the logo on it was for Griff's hotel. "There is still disagreement on what was agreed to."

"I put a copy on our secured site, sir," Mahjub said.

"Which I showed them, but they wish to *study it*. Send one to our attorneys here and across The Pond, as well."

"I'll get it straight over."

"Tomorrow will be sufficient. They don't depart until Saturday. And once they have it I would not be surprised if another meeting is demanded, despite my insistence it is ... oh, unnecessary."

Mahjub nodded, his eyes never meeting Tawfi's. "Sometimes the recording process is very slow, sir. One has to make certain there are no glitches or missed moments. I may not be able to get the copy to them till early afternoon. Or late."

Tawfi smiled. "What a pity. Has my father accessed the video?" Mahjub nodded. "Then tomorrow *will* be most interesting. Are you finished with Mr. Pope?"

Mahjub looked at me and I nodded. "One more detail and I'll turn into C-3PO, but without the manners."

"Consider yourself fortunate," said Tawfi. "You have been schooled by a master. This young man is the future of our country and her best defense against those who would abuse her. We are very proud of him."

Mahjub stood straighter and blushed. "Thank you, sir. Oh, I notice you have yet to open this morning's news feed. Would you like me to update it?"

"That's not necessary. Do you know where my brother is?"

Mahjub turned to his laptop, did three clicks of input and up sprang a map of London with a red flashing dot on it. "At his gym, sir."

Tawfi rolled his eyes. "Which means his wife will be at Harrod's with my nephews and their nurse. Mahjub, you may wish to retire before they return. And warn Abdel and his men, if they are still here. The driver will bring in the packages."

The boy hid a smile. "As you wish."

Tawfi turned to me. "If you'll join me ... " Then he led me away from Mahjub's room.

"Buyin' spree, huh?" I asked Tawfi as we reached the elevator. "Paris wasn't enough?"

"My beloved sister-in-law believes money is a tool meant to bring her happiness. I fear for us all if it ever runs out."

I chuckled. "Well that's not beyond the realm of possibility if you join forces with The Faure Group." He looked at me, wary, so I continued with, "Just a guess. But I know Griffin Faure; saw him a few days ago. And you're havin' a video sent to his hotel, so ... "

"Don't be *too* clever, Devlin. It doesn't suit you."

"Hey!" But I saw his eyes were laughing so huffed and added, "Just an FYI — they don't have a very good reputation in the States."

"Is that so?"

The elevator door opened and we steeped inside.

"Of course ... you already know that. Very clever, Dev."

Tawfi cast me a sly look. "I do hope you don't mind joining me in my flat. After spending all day in discussions I'd rather stay in than go out. The embassy has a cook who is quite good; she could work something up. Not high-end, but not eggs on toast, either."

"Sounds great. Are we being served? Or do we greet the delivery guy at the door and tip him with a blowjob?"

"You are delightfully vulgar," Tawfi chuckled. "I have neither maid nor butler, so we shall have to serve ourselves."

"A man in your position?"

"I cherish my privacy, and if one has servants one is never alone."

"Can I have dinner with you, *Prince Tafiq?*"

"I can think of nothing that would please me more."

Then he hit the button for the elevator to go up.

****

Tawfi led me down a corridor of blank painted walls punctuated by faux columns in the Egyptian style and lit by a never-ending row of minimalist but fussy chandeliers. There were five doors on the left, three doors on the right, all presented as full scale entrances, with ornate tables and mirrors across from them that had long vases of colorful flowers on either side. On top of all this, the carpet was so lush I felt like I was walking on marshmallows.

"Living quarters for our staff," he said.

"You don't hire local?"

I asked it like a joke but he gave me a simple look as he

said, "For lesser positions."

We reached an even more ornate door and he led me into a flat that was the polar opposite of everything else in the building — open and airy with modern and classic mixed just right. Chaise lounges flanked a low coffee table, ottomans at each end. Light Persian carpets protected the original hardwood floors. Tall windows were visible behind sheer gauze curtains tenderly flanked by silk drapes of many colors blended together to make them inviting instead of standoffish. The walls were painted cream, with only a few elegant framed pieces on them, and were accentuated by flowers and plants just where there needed to be and not one spot more.

The first words out of my mouth were, "Your embassy built this for you?"

His smile almost broke through his solemnity as he said, "No, for my grandfather when he was in my position. My father stayed here, as well." He removed his suit coat and hung it on a simple coat-stand. "I had it remodeled. Redecorated. Modernized. The electrical wiring, alone, required complete replacement. But it may surprise you to know the carpets and the furniture are original. Shall I give you the Cook's Tour?"

"How long's it gonna take?"

His gaze did not change. "Are you hungry?"

I looked straight at him. "Starving."

He chuckled. "Devlin, you are as impatient as a child."

"It's the American in me." I gave him a goofy smirk but his expression didn't change so I added. "Are you still messed up about — ?"

He put a finger to my lips then helped me off with my own suit coat and hung it next to his as he said, "Yes, I am. It's odd, but I now feel ... disloyal wanting to be with you. I had no such concern the other night ... "

"It's natural. I mean, you and he were an item for a while, right?"

"Three months. Then contact ended."

"Just stopped?"

" ... Yes."

"Sorry, I shouldn't have brought him up."

"Why not? It is part of the reality we must face." His hand caressed my cheek. "He was not as lovely as you in physical appearance. Nor was he as ... advanced in his lovemaking." I had to chuckle at that. "But we enjoyed each other's company and I never left him unhappy. I thought that referred to both of us. But now? Now I think I advanced things more quickly than he wanted and that led to the problem between us."

"How'd you meet?"

"A package being couriered to my embassy was stopped in customs. He handled its release, brought it here and my signature was required."

"Customs can stop a diplomatic pouch?"

"If someone is foolish enough to send it via DHL rather than by hand. He and I struck up a quiet conversation and kept in touch. And a few weeks later, he met me here."

"You were close to him."

"Somewhat. I feel it would be a dishonor to bring another man to the bed he and I shared. Dishonor to his memory, so soon after his death." He shifted his head to look at me. "Funny thing to think, isn't it?"

I took his hand in mine and kissed his fingertips. "No, I think it's perfect. So, if all you want is dinner, that's fine."

"I didn't say what I wanted."

He hooked a finger through one of my back belt loops and pulled me towards a door flanked by Egyptian-style statues. I tried to turn and follow him but he wouldn't let me, so I wound up walking half-backwards-half-sideways like a dyslexic crab.

"C'mon, Tawfi, this is awkward."

"Hush."

We wound up in a fair-size room with a canopy bed that was drowning in the most luxurious comforters and pillows and draperies I'd ever seen. Silk covered walls. Sheer panels before a pair of tall windows looking out over treetops. A low mahogany cabinet sat between them and plush chairs were positioned perfectly.

"Grandfather slept on this bed?"

"No, this is the guest room," he said as he stopped me at the foot of the bed, "and you are my guest."

"Is this where you and Martin — y'know?"

He circled me, saying, "Devlin, it's unseemly to be jealous of a dead man." Then he nudged me up to one of the bed's posts.

"I'm not."

"Shh."

He undid my tie and stepped back. God, the beauty of him. The glide of his legs. How his waist shifted, oh-so-slightly with each step — like a panther strolling through the jungle, sure and aware of himself. He would never be as beefy as me, but on him that wouldn't have looked good.

He stretched the tie out then drew close to nuzzle my neck and nibble at my skin, sending shock waves through me.

"I can see why vampires are considered erotic creatures," I giggled.

I tried to twist away but he held me in place. His eyes bore into mine.

"Clasp your hands behind you."

I did without even a thought. I would never have done that with anyone else. Nor would I have let him bind them with my tie, tight but easy.

His eyes locked on mine, saying, "I am not open to a full repeat of our night together. Not yet. I feel it would be improper to share that sort of intimacy now."

"Tawfi, I mean it — if you'd rather not — "

He put his elegant fingers to my lips, caressing them as he whispered, "Shh. I do what I wish. Martin would never allow me to put him in this position so this ... this is acceptable." He unbuttoned my shirt. Slow. Teasing. His voice a whisper. "We would dine. Talk of nothing. Then he would let me have him." He shifted the shirt aside to reveal my t-shirt and gave my nips a light pinch.

Holy shit, good thing he had me tied 'cause I was ready to jump into animal mode. My voice cracked as I said, "So you — you fucked him like you fucked me. Right?"

He chuckled. "Still so vulgar. But no. With him I took more care. Less haste." He pulled my t-shirt up to let his fingers drift over my pecs and around my nips and down my belly. "He was hesitant. Cautious. But always giving."

"Did — did you love him?"

He hesitated then shook his head. "I enjoyed him."

He kissed me as he removed my belt. Twisted it around and around one hand as the other caressed my chest and arms and sides. Then he undid my pants, lowered them a little and shifted all his attention to my Jockey briefs. Barely touched me as his fingertips curled around my bulge. Let my dick strain against the white cotton. Made my ass clench and my balls scream in ways I never knew they could.

"It is difficult to believe something so basic could be so right," he whispered, his voice husky.

I half-gasped out, "Glad you approve. I work at — at keepin' my belly flat and — "

"This is more than your physical appearance, Devlin. Martin fit my usual preference in a man." He nuzzled my neck, drawing his lips down my throat and his fingers up my sides. "But something in you hides from me. Cries to be caressed. Cared for. Tamed. Perhaps even owned. I want to be the one who takes you from frightened creature to gentle companion. I want to be the one who owns you. And that surprises me, because we will have only a few nights together, if that, before you leave."

He shifted my pants down just past my ass, his fingers tickling the hair on my legs and gliding over the white cotton still covering me, making me gasp in as I said, "I'm — I'm in the UK three-four times a year. Maybe ... "

"No. I am too demanding and you too impatient."

I was about halfway to Mars with need. "So can I — can I join the fun now?"

He looked at me, his beautiful lips slightly parted, his eyes half-closed, his breath deep, and he shook his head. He caressed my crotch again and again and again as he whispered, "You want this inside me, don't you?" I nodded. "You'll have to be a very special man to achieve that."

"Are you a — you a virgin?"

"I'm very particular. And I think tonight you felt you could force the issue. But that is not going to happen. All I want for myself is to hold you. Feel you. Nothing more. I'm not ready to go even as far with you as I did on our first night. It is too soon after Martin. But a creature is not tamed by ignoring its needs, wishes or desires. You must gain its trust. Caress it. Pet it. Show it why you should be its master."

"Companion."

"Shall we see?" Then he grabbed my briefs and tore the front open, releasing my dick. I damn near came from the sudden release. Then he cupped my balls and ran a gentle finger up and down the base of my shaft. "Is that acceptable to you?"

That made me blink. "Huh? Uh ... I dunno ... I ... I don't like not being in control."

"So if you were not bound would *you* try to tame *me*?"

"Maybe." I worked at my tie. Tried to undo the knot.

"Maybe?"

"Yes. I'm the guy on top."

"You weren't with me, the other night." He looked at my dick and gave me a sly grin. "Just now you let me bind you, which has had no effect on your readiness. Does this?" Then he tore my t-shirt in half.

I yelped. "Tawfi, in about two seconds I'm gonna get my hands free and grab you and — "

He put a hand to my heart, circled his fingers through the hair on my chest and let his smile take over his face. "Devlin," he murmured, "take pleasure in anticipation."

He stepped back and slipped off his shirt and pants, revealing an AX tee and boxer briefs that made him hotter than hot. Socks went away. Then the tee. Then he slowly, slowly guided the briefs down to reveal he was close to full attention. He came back to me. Pressed himself tight to me, his dick rubbing against mine.

"Try this, first. Intimacy without complete intimacy."

He slipped my dick under his balls and between his legs, his own dick now rubbing against my groin. Then he rocked over it, working me with his thighs. Rubbing back and forth and back and forth again and again and again as he nibbled my tits and ran his nose and lips over the hair on my chest and I lost contact with my mind and clenched at him and pushed back and growled with each thrust and I felt him growing harder and harder and the hair on his thighs connected with mine and his pubes mingled with mine and nips rubbed against mine and his lips held tight to mine and I pulled at my tie but I couldn't get loose to grab hold of him and make him mine and it went on and on and on and on until I tensed and pushed harder and harder against him and jolted and cried out and I fired and saw dancing lights and every nerve in my body was screaming and I was ready to faint from the beauty of it all.

Finally he leaned against my chest and whispered, "Now would you let me do with you as I wish? Now would you?"

I gulped nuzzled his ear. And bit it, softly, then kissed the skin I'd bitten and whispered, "I would stay here for you."

He sighed deep and nodded, then he looked at me, pleased, and stepped back to show me his lean lovely body with its fans of hair and glorious legs and nips worth nibbling on for centuries and amazing fucking dick, and I realized he'd cum on my belly and it was trailing into the elastic band of my ruined briefs and that brought me back to the point of wanting more and more from him. I pulled at my tie and still couldn't get free, dammit. I nearly howled.

He chuckled, his voice low and deep and vicious in its eroticism as he said, "You need to clean yourself and dress for dinner."

Then he left me tied like that as he pulled out his phone, still displaying himself before me, and called down an order to the cook.

FOURTEEN

Tawfi didn't untie me until I was back in control, then he led me into a bathroom as big as my condo and joined me in the shower. He washed me from hair to toenails, using soaps I'd never seen before with scents I'd never smelled before, leaving me feeling cleaner and gayer than I've ever felt and so fucking turned on I fired another load as he rinsed me off.

He chuckled and dried me with a towel that was big enough to use as a toga, saying, "You were very hungry."

"And I wasn't even on a diet," I chuckled back.

"Really?" he said, his voice dripping with a smirk. "I think I prefer the look of your penis to Martin's. It's larger. A nicer shape. Rather like mine ... "

"Thank you, sahib," popped out of me.

He slapped my naked butt, making me yelp, then said with a smile, "I do not consider that word to be an honorific. Please do not use it, again."

He pushed me into the bedroom, neither one of us in a stitch of clothing yet. A pair of white AX briefs and T-shirt were on the bed next to my pants and shirt.

"To wear home," he said as he pulled his own pair on.

"Just goin' to my hotel."

He rolled his eyes as he pulled on clean briefs. "A well-groomed man must always have something between him and his suit. Otherwise he is nothing but a beast dressed in human clothing. And I did tear yours."

"I've torn a few of my own. Never paid for 'em."

He smirked, stepping into his suit pants. "Oh? Have we stories to share?"

"Not something you'd want to hear." I held the briefs up. "Jockeys don't cost anywhere near this much."

He just smiled. I slipped them on and even snug they felt like silk caressing my skin. He turned me around and smoothed them over my ass then wrapped himself around me from behind. Held me close. Nuzzled the nape of my neck.

I chuckled. "Careful, you'll get something goin' again."

"I know," he whispered then released me with another pat on my ass. "I snuck three more pair into your case. Wear them in remembrance of me."

"Tawfi, c'mon — "

"Devlin, in my country it is considered rude to refuse a gift. Please don't insult me."

I sat on the bed to pull on my socks. "Yes, sir. And thank you."

"Thank *you*." He gazed at me and whispered, "Thank you." Finally he sighed, "Martin would accept nothing I gave him. Oh, he never refused my gifts; he merely hid them in a desk drawer at his office. I discovered this by accident the last time I saw him. I asked him about it. He told me his company was having difficulties and his wife would wonder how he could pay for such extravagances. A Polo shirt is an extravagance? A Dior belt? I was so very angry. And insulted." He took in a deep breath. "Now you know the reason we did not see each other again."

"I know where he's comin' from," I said. "I been there." I almost added *Thanks to the Faure Group*, but held it back.

He nodded. "It took me three weeks to accept the truth of him. He had a wife. Children. And he was frightened he might lose them." He let out a long sigh. "I suppose he is no longer afraid."

I rose and drew him tight against me. "I *do* know him."

"You? What have *you* ever been fearful of?"

I meant to just shrug but words drifted from me.

"Myself, lately."

He shifted back to look at me. "How do you mean?"

"Things've happened that — that got me wonderin' if I *am* nothin' but a beast in a nice suit."

He gave me a hesitant smile and picked up my suit pants. "An *adequate* suit. If you want a nice one we should visit a tailor I know."

"I wear what I can afford, Tawfi. Briefs like these, they cost more than most of my pants."

He pulled away and leaned against a canopy post, wary. "Are you rejecting my offering?"

"No. But please don't give me any more. I — I might grow to like them too much, and that ... " My voice trailed off.

A hint of confusion filled his eyes as his smile crossed his face. "I'm not sure what you mean."

"I just mean ... I'm buyin' dinner next time," I said as I pulled on my pants.

"That will be a novelty. I always pay the tab."

"Not with me."

He cocked an eyebrow and let a mocking tone enter his voice. "You said I could do as I wanted with you."

I gave him a long look then sighed, "Is that part of the deal? Am I your courtesan?"

He let his fingers wander through the hair on my chest as he murmured, "We can discuss this later. Dinner has been ready for the last twenty minutes."

Not on the table, though; it was warming in the oven and chilling in the fridge. So he and I set it out and damn, it was kick-ass. Baba ganoush. Tabbouleh. Shirin Polo. Fatteh with roasted pine nuts. Mahalabiya and Kahnfaroosh. Bottles of icy Lebanese wine. Tawfi told me what each one was and I feasted on it all and felt so fat and happy by the time we were done, I thought I should order an ambulance to slop me on a gurney and ferry me home flat on my back, like some ancient Roman bitch.

"I'm gonna have to run all the way 'round Heathrow," I said, as we headed for the door, "so I don't pack on twenty."

Tawfi laughed. "I am pleased you are pleased."

"Doin' anything this weekend?"

He hesitated. "That depends on tomorrow. I may have to return home. I may have to travel to the States. I may be able to stay here. But I won't know until late in the day."

"The Faure Group, right?"

He eyed me for a moment then asked, "How well do you know Griffin Faure?"

"A lot better than he'd ever admit."

His smile threatened to become pleased. "Interesting how you put it."

"I could sleep over. Gossip all night ... "

"Let me see what tomorrow brings. I may take you up on your offer, then. But not here."

"Gotta keep undercover?"

"At least the appearance of it." He kissed my nose. "This lift will take you to the lobby then you merely walk out. Take care traveling back to your hotel."

I said my last good night then headed down the elevator. It let me out into a nice-enough lobby filled with overly plush chairs, dozens of support columns, filigree trim and black-and-white checkerboard marble floors half-covered with bland Persian carpets. A couple of fussy chandeliers threatened to actually give off just enough light. Not at all impressive.

I stepped outside and saw I was at the far end of the building from the embassy's entrance. Mahjub wasn't kidding; I now knew of at least three entrances and there were probably a dozen more. I wondered if the entire friggin' building was the embassy.

It was a lovely night, just past ten, and there was a hint of fog in the air — the crisp chilly kind, not thick in that Sherlock Holmes way. I hopped down the steps, halfway wishing I'd brought an overcoat, but I'd walked home from a conquest's apartment in a blizzard dressed only in a shirt, jeans and boots and made it alive so —

"Mr. Pope?" jolted me around.

Tawfi's sister-in-law, Leila, was approaching, a bag of groceries in one hand, her cellphone in the other. I was less surprised at her appearing than at the fact she'd been shopping for food in her Chanel ensemble.

"Mrs. al Qasimi," popped out of me. "Or is it princess?"

She grinned and shook her head. "I am not royalty."

"Yeah, I guess. You're out late. And alone."

She held up the bag. "Breakfast for my sons, tomorrow. *Coco Pops* and *Frosted Shreddies*. Hamad does not like them to have this so the embassy staff will not order it. I have to sneak it in after they are gone and he's to bed, then I feed them before he wakes. It makes for more pleasant times."

"Grocery stores're still open?"

"There is a Sainsbury's close by. You also are out late."

I held up my sample case. "I worked with Mahjub on some pins and lost track of time. That boy is intense. Prince Tafiq was kind enough to have me fed. The embassy's cook — whoa!"

She smiled, glanced up at the entrance and nodded. "My husband's brother is very accommodating. We often think, too much so." She looked back at me. "But he is the oldest and the favorite and so much like his father no one argues with him."

" ... Oh?"

"Yes. Did you know our king has very ... eclectic tastes, and did not marry until well into his thirties? He sired a dozen children in ten years, five of them male and two sets of twins."

"Whoa, I've got twin nephews. Is your husband a twin?"

She cast me a condescending look up one side and down the other. "No, both sets are female. Now Prince Tafiq is the last unwed." She all but purred as she said, "He takes after his father in so many ways."

Okay, I both did and did *not* like the direction this was going so shifted it by saying, "I'm told I take after my dad even though I'm the youngest."

"Of how many?"

"Two. I try not to hold it against people when they make the comparison. I hated him."

She laughed. "You speak like Hamad when he deigns to speak. But I shouldn't disparage my husband. His sole aim is to build his body for the next Olympics."

"Looks like it's workin' nice."

"Yes." She gave me an odd, appraising look. "He began before we married. At that time he looked more like you and was thought to be quite the catch."

WTF? Why was she telling me this? And the looks she was giving me — I felt like a co-ed at a frat party being sized up for that night's entertainment.

It must have shown on my face because she huffed a laugh and smiled, saying, "But it is late and is an hour back to your hotel. The Millennium is close by and they have a taxi rank."

"I'm just hoppin' the underground."

"At Knightsbridge? Do you know how to get there?"

"Yeah. I was here Monday."

"Of course. Then I'll let you get on." She started away but spun around. "Oh, and about Monday — do let me apologize for our manners. Prince Tafiq was correct; they were not proper. One should treat all people with respect. Even *tradesmen*. Safe journey."

She cast another glance over me then headed on to the embassy entrance before I had a chance to come up with a reply that didn't have *you fuckin' bitch* attached to it. Man, it's women like that who make me glad I'm queer.

I started away and almost forgot to go left then right. After a few minutes I found myself on Sloane Street. A look around showed me a building down at the other end that I knew was across from the station so towards it I went.

This area was made up of high-end shops that were closed by seven so there was next to no traffic on the street. Nor was there foot traffic. The fog grew thicker but that lightened my mood because I started picturing *The Wax Museum*, with big bad Vincent

Price, and could just see *Princes Leila* winding up as one of his figures. It got me back to where I could think, *So she's a self-entitled bitch who likes to toy with those she sees as her inferior? So the fuck what? Her type's a dime a dozen in New York, male or female. Not worth the agita.* And I had to admit, her comments about Tawfi's father were more than a little interesting. I decided to do a lot more research into his family. Find out if she was bullshitting me and he was a twin. Two princes for one; oh, did that send my mind to the land of the wicked as I closed in on Brompton and —

I was grabbed around the neck and yanked into a narrow walkway like I weighed nothing, but I twisted and rolled and kicked us back onto the street and slammed the guy around against a store window, shattering it as he held onto me and crushed me against the wall. I grunted and fell and he piled in on me, hard and heavy, and was choking me so I dug in my pocket for my nail clipper and kicked and we tumbled across the pavement as I pulled the clipper out and he was back behind me and choking me more and something flashed and I used my sample case to deflect it and shifted the clipper's file around and jabbed him in the wrist and arm around my neck, over and over, and he jolted and grunted but still held on and —

"Hey! Police!" was screamed at us.

The guy spun and shoved me into the gutter and ran.

A moment later Reg appeared. "You all right, Pope?"

I was on my back, water splashing around me as I looked at him, confused, and managed to grunt, "Yeah! Yeah."

He raced after the guy.

I staggered to my feet, my back dripping wet, and could just make out that he'd reached Brompton and stopped and was looking both ways. He threw his arms up in anger then jogged back to me.

I leaned against a wall, shivering, and heard the whine of a siren approach. Reg and the squad car reached me at the same time.

Two cops piled out, one barking, "What's happened?"

Reg showed them his ID and said, "This man was attacked. Looked like a mugging."

"You all right, sir?"

I checked myself. Saw no blood. No scratches. Knew I'd have some nice bruises in the morning, but that was livable — until I saw a nice slice through my suit jacket. "Shit," popped out of me. "Motherfucker ruined my suit." On top of it, there was a hole in my case.

More cops came, Reg gave them a description in more detail than I could have — stocky, dark gym pants, dark jacket with a hoodie, weighing about 100 kilos. They roared off but I didn't expect them to find anything; the fog was getting thicker by the minute.

I was taken to a nearby police station, made a statement along the lines of *I got no idea what happened*, got checked by an EMS medic who found nothing broken, then Reg popped me into a blue and white car and drove me back to the hotel through the swirling fog.

It took my brain half the trip to catch up to me and realize we were alone and I finally said, "What the fuck?"

Reg glanced at me. "Yeah, what was that?"

"A mugging?"

"The lads think so."

I looked at him. His eyes kept on the road, high beams and cop flashers on. Finally I asked, "Do you think it was the same guy who jumped me the other night?"

" ... Could be."

"Why were you there, anyway? I thought you were on leave."

"I am. *Officially*."

"Shit. Sir Monte's workin' you on the sly. Tailin' me."

He glared at me. "*Boss* has me keepin' an eye on you."

"He doesn't trust me."

"Why should he, after what you did?" he shot back.

"Then why're you drivin' me?"

" ... Doin' me job."

"Still watchin' me. I dunno if I should be pissed or flattered."

"How 'bout neither?" he snarled, then after a moment he added, "You were in that embassy for near twelve hours."

"You were out there all that time?"

"I'm not the only person on the team."

I sighed. "Then you know Prince Tafiq didn't show up till nearly five, and I'm pretty sure you know where he was."

"So what were you doin'?"

I leaned back, uncomfortable as shit in my soggy suit. I pulled off the jacket, wincing as my side let me know its displeasure. "Buildin' trust. Gettin' info. Findin' out what I could."

"And?"

"Oh, you trust me enough to share with you?" No answer. I sighed. "Prince Tafiq is not your man."

" ... Boss says you said that."

"He was involved with Perriman for months but all of a sudden he's killin' men who look like him? And not just any guys but guys who can be linked back to the embassy? Plus Tawfi's dumb enough to leave behind DNA? C'mon."

"*Toffee*? He's your sweets, is he?"

I huffed a laugh and spelled the name for him, adding, "I think he's bein' set up. Dunno why, but ... "

"But you'll work something up. Right. Got it."

He said nothing more till we were at the hotel and he'd seen me up to my room. As I opened my door he murmured. "I maybe shouldn't tell you this but we think he was being blackmailed, your *Toffee*. By Perriman."

"Why do you think that?"

"Some big deposits were made to his checking over the last few months. Routed through a dummy company owned by Kahyr."

"Prince Tafiq's company."

"Yeah. We're wonderin' if the first three men were killed just to mix up Perriman's murder. Like Agatha Christie does."

"Jesus," and I laughed the word out. "There's a business deal goin' on between him and The Faure Group, so this timin's all off for that kind of shit. Unless they're the ones pullin' somethin' on him ... "

"Oh, bloody hell, are you some conspiracy freak?"

I sneered. "From the guy who refers to Agatha Christie's plots! Gimme a break." I threw my ruined coat into the room. "Just between you and me, I do *not* think 9-11 was inside job or that there was a second gunman at Kennedy's assassination. But I have had dealin's with The Faure Group and I wouldn't put a damn thing past 'em."

"So you said. Yesterday's conference was between them, Kahyr, and three other companies — Seluruh Dunia, Quán Shìjiè and Ves'mir. So far just seems to be a normal partnering of people working on oil and gas exploration. Spread the costs."

"But not the profits. Right."

"All nice and normal."

I shrugged and started to enter the room then stopped. "Seluruh Dunia — that sounds familiar."

"Based in Singapore."

"Griff's wife's from Singapore."

"Second one, yeah. But a British expat. Her da's high up in the company."

"You boys *have* been diggin'."

"Same as you have. Gotta cover every corner and you keep raising awkward questions."

I nodded. Eyed him. He was stronger than the other night. More assured. Sexier. I had to swallow in order to say, "Come on in; let's discuss."

Reg stayed in the hall. "After what happened last time?"

"I'm not gonna try anything with you."

He shook his head, his eyes locked on me. "No."

I stepped back out of the room and closed the door. He

took a wary stance.

"Reg," I whispered, "are there cameras in my room?"

He hesitated then said, "Just mikes."

"Then come on in; make your report from here."

"Why?"

"I ... I just like bein' around you."

That brought an incredulous look to his face. "Why!?"

"I don't know! But — but ridin' with you in the car, I felt safe and — "

"Well, you're back here, now. I'd not leave again, were I you."

He started away but I grabbed his jacket sleeve. "Y'know, you liked the kiss."

He yanked away but didn't look at me. "You got me by surprise."

"Reg, you liked the kiss. I could feel it."

His breathing grew faster. "What're you up to?"

"Come back in. Let's just talk."

"What — your candy boy wasn't enough for you tonight?"

"You have his apartment bugged!?"

"No! But it don't take much to figure — and thanks for verifying."

"Well that's not what I want, right now. I just want to be with you."

"You wanna turn me queer, like you."

"No!"

He shook his head, fighting himself, then backed away, whispering, "You are a devil," as he spun and stormed over to the elevator.

I watched him get on. Watched it close. Heard it whisper away.

And deep inside my critter purred, *We've got him. He's ours.*

FIFTEEN

I fired up my laptop to find a dozen emails from Diana with information about the dealers who'd been spooked by the federal spooks as well as Griffin Faure's trips out of the US — a lot of them to the UK in the last six months. I hoped seeing me checking onto the bastard would get Sir Monte's crew harder on his trail.

Well ... business came first, so I called all the dealers on the West Coast and filled them in with my bullet points — *wanting to do business with the crown, MI5 asked the FBI to look into rumors, Diana was joining the company to assist with customer service*, the whole nine yards. I used every sales technique I could think of, including the confessional, and I'm pretty sure they were still a bit leery of me, especially after I revealed my sexual orientation. Didn't matter; what counted was I convinced them well enough to continue working with Diana and Colin. I'd do the same with the East Coasters and Mid-western folks tomorrow afternoon.

Then I hunkered down to compare Griff's schedule to the dates the first three victims had died. Only the first one matched exactly; the rest were off by a few days.

Dammit.

I was too keyed up over everything so set it aside and took another shower, long and hot, and started thinking of the one I'd had a few hours earlier with Tawfi. And wished Reg was here with me. And then I remembered the one the Neat mustache had taken with Griff, years ago. How much pleasure he'd gotten from it. Which led me back to the kidnapping of the little shit. Which reminded me Griff was a sort of celebrity. A good-looking guy dating supermodels. Heir to billions. In a swinging town like London.

I dried off, wrapped a towel around me and started scouring the local gossip rags for photos of him. By limiting it to the last six months I found a couple hundred in the *Mirror* and *Star* and *Google Images* and *Instagram*. Half of them were with that nice-looking woman from the fundraiser photo, whom I found out was his current wife. She dressed up well but she was nowhere near the level of beauty as he'd been doing in NYC. I didn't know what I was looking for; it was one of those ideas that just sort of nudges your brain but dances away before you can catch hold of what it means — until I saw a Mercedes Mr. and Mrs. Faure were getting out of for a gala.

Masterson Livery.

No label or sign on the car but I knew because behind the wheel I could just see Trevor Laughton, in uniform, bright and crisp —

And the idea exploded in my head.

I went back over the other photos of Griff getting out of a car or limo or taxi, anything. Dozens and dozens ... and then I saw him.

A guy who reminded me of Reg.

Stuart Goughan.

Same crisp uniform as Trevor. Same damn Mercedes as he'd been driving.

I checked other photos of that gala and Tawfi showed up, but in the Bentley, and if I was reading the timeline of the photos right he was twenty minutes behind Griff. Plus, Leila and Hamad were with him.

I dug into the basic info I had on Etan Conescieu to find out what event was being catered at the embassy then searched out photos of that, as well.

Griff was there with his wife. And Trevor Laughton — no, no, his name was different and I really had to look the guy's name up — John? James? Shit — he was the driver again.

Now overtly it made sense; if you own the company, use it. But that locked me in. I found three more occasions where I could tell Laughton was Griff's driver but not one more where Goughan had ferried him anywhere, even going back two years.

But dammit, Griff wasn't here for three of the murders.

I dug like crazy but could find nothing showing Griff with Liam Hanlon, The City victim. No stories to connect him except what I'd been told. It wasn't till I found one back-page article with Hanlon's itinerary on the day of his death that I had the name of the company he'd gone to see. They were not affiliated with The Faure Group in any way I could tell. Nor with Kahyr.

Shit.

By this time, it was getting light outside. I was still too keyed up to sleep so I dressed, went down and had breakfast and a half-dozen cups of coffee. I could already tell this was going to be a bear of a day.

The only person over here that I could even think might get me the information I needed was Mahjub, but I had no idea if he'd do it for me. In fact I had a feeling he'd tell me to fuck off, in Arabic, because he suspected I worked for the cops.

Of course I knew Sir Monte's crew could get it. Hell, they could get CCTV pulled from every part of the city if they wanted and —

Wait — CCTV showed the guy leaving Goughan's murder scene.

I bolted back up to my room and dug into my info. I had a PDF of a news story with video capture of the killer leaving — black gym clothes, black tennies, bulky.

Except his legs weren't right. Seemed out of proportion. I'd thought it was just a bad video capture but I dug into news stories on BBC and ITV and Channel One and found two that played different parts of the CCTV video ... and I would swear those legs were thin, not bulky.

I thought back to Abdel, yesterday. He and both his guys

had legs like tree trunks. The one time I'd seen Hamad climbing the steps on Monday his legs were obviously solid and well-formed. I thought about Tawfi's legs with their gorgeous lines and watched both videos, again. No, he would have filled those pants better.

I managed to find CCTV of Conescieu's killer. The angle was different and the image grainer but I would swear this guy's legs were bulky. Solid.

Okay, I knew Sir Monte's guys were monitoring my laptop but I had to make clear what I was doing. So I called him.

I'll give him this much — he listened as I laid out what I'd found then said, "I'm sending a car 'round for you. Should be there in fifteen minutes. Please be waiting in the lobby. I'd like you to come in and see the rest of what we have."

Pudgy boy showed up and took me back to the same station I'd been held in. I was led to a room set up with computers and piles of files and photos on boards and everything you could think of that would help a murder investigation. They were no longer even trying to keep the evidence and details under wraps.

Sir Monte was standing over a laptop, looking a lot more haggard than when I'd last seen him. He motioned me over. I saw Reg rise on the other side of the table, his eyes locked on me.

"Here, Pope," said Sir Monte. "I want you to look at these videos and tell me what you see."

The first was of the figure heading to Perriman's office in Feltham. It was dark and grainy and too far to really make out anything but the man's form. And the way he walked.

"That's a swagger," I said.

"A what?" Sir Monte asked.

"The way the guy's walkin' — that's a swagger. Butch. I'm in control kind of shit. That's not how Prince Tafiq walks. Do you have CCTV of him? Like the underground? Compare 'em. You'll see."

Instead, Sir Monte brought up Holborn underground station and showed me an image of Hanlon entering — bulky, brisk and easy in his three-piece suit — and kept it going.

"Do you see anyone here who might be *swaggering*?"

"Are you kiddin' me?" I snapped. "Are you fuckin' — ?"

Bam! I saw him.

"Stop. Stop it! Back up! BACK UP!"

Sir Monte did as I asked back to when Hanlon entered then he let it go forward till I cried, "Pause! Slow. Slow ... "

He did. I looked closer to make sure I was right.

And I was. Son-of-a-bitch, I was.

I pointed at a man who was racing to the entry stiles and said, "Trevor Laughton. He works for Masterson Livery, which is owned by The Faure Group. He's the guy who ferries Griffin Faure around town."

Pudgy guy piped in with, "No one named Trevor Laughton currently works for Masterson, Boss."

"No, it's not his real name — he's John something. I've got the notes back at my hotel."

"They have photos of the drivers."

I spun to look at his screen. He scrolled down and I found him. "Jonathan Nettles."

I told them about the sneaky meeting Griff had arranged and what I'd learned about him and Masterson. Sir Monte did not seem convinced it had any merit.

Until Reg said, "Boss, hasn't that named come up somewhere before in the investigation? Nettles?"

Sir Monte froze and turned into the perfect illustration of mental gears going into overdrive. Then he turned to Pudgy and asked, "Who dispatched Goughan to his last job?"

Pudgy pulled up a PDF and looked. And turned to Sir Monte, murmuring, "Nettles, Boss. He fills in sometimes."

"Did we check him out?"

"Says he was working when two of the murders occurred."

"Doing what?"

"He was collecting a client when Hanlon vanished and he

was — well, he — um, dispatch. For Goughan. Conescieu was early in the day so he was home a-bed."

"Have we verified any of this?"

"No, boss. He wasn't the focus of our — "

"Then do it now!" Sir Monte snapped as he turned to another cop to snarl, "Have Mr. Nettles brought in. I want to speak with him myself."

"Sure, Boss," the guy said then hurried from the room.

Sir Monte turned to Reg. "I want you to go back to Pope's hotel and bring us his notes. All of them." To me, he said, "I'd like you to return with him and explain to us what you've been doing the last few days."

"You got it, Boss," I said, grinning.

He did not grin back. "Sorry? Did I hear you right?"

I grimaced, saw Reg hiding a smile and I said, "How 'bout I call you Sir Montieth?"

Sir Monte's glare was still cold but he said, "Yes. Do."

Reg came around the table to say, "Boss, the man who killed Conescieu — he was fit. Rugby kind of fit. Nettles is like a twig."

"I know," Sir Monte replied, "but this is too close a connection not to follow up. Berridge." Pudgy guy looked around. "Did we check other CCTV monitors to see if Hanlon came back out of Holborn with anyone?"

"He used an Oyster card, Boss; it don't show him exiting, anywhere."

"Did. We. Check?"

" ... Not that I know of."

"Then do so. All around the station. That might explain why he disappeared."

"But, Boss, he's got to use his card to get back out."

"Do what I tell you! Carlysle!" A rough-and-tumble guy in his early 30s jolted to attention. "Find out everything you can about Nettles, including if he has an Oyster."

Reg nudged me, snarling an, "Oi!" and motioned for me

to follow him. We hurried outside, piled into a squad car and roared back to my hotel, lights flashing and siren whining.

"I told Boss what you said," he muttered as we whipped around two massive trucks ... um, lorries. "We were lookin' into it when you called. Not finding anything."

I snorted, holding on for dear life. "Why would you? Everything pointed to Tawfi. Very neatly, too."

"That's why we didn't like it. You were right, it's comin' together too neat. Say whatever you want to say about him, that prince ain't a stupid man. This is more the kind of thing his brother'd pull."

"Yeah, all muscle, no brain, but the right size."

"He wasn't here for two of the murders. Passed through London but just to drop off the wife and kids and head up to competitions in York and Glasgow. Ruled him out, fast."

"You guys weren't very subtle in your checking. Tawfi knows all about it. Knows you're followin' him."

Reg glanced at me. "That why he didn't go for me?"

"No. He was headed out to see Perriman. To make up after an argument."

We pulled through a light, making cars swerve and stop, as Reg said, "Told you that, did he?"

"Yes," I said, once I could breathe again.

"You know how to work your way into men's minds."

"Just 'cause I can look at a guy and tell what he's up to? What he wants. What he needs?"

"Like you did with me?"

I groaned. "Fuck, are we on that again?"

He said nothing more until we'd stopped in front of the hotel and hit the elevator.

"Reg, I meant it — I didn't see anything in you that wanted anything to do with me. Anyone like me."

"Then how'd you get me to — ?"

"Stop it!" I was pissed. "You never heard of gay-for-pay? Give a man enough money he'll get it up no matter how deep into pussy he is. He'll even let you fuck him and swear he likes it. Loves it. Will cum with it."

"Bloody hell, you gotta talk that shite?"

"Then stop makin' it an issue. Shit."

We slammed into my room and he grabbed my laptop as I pulled together my notes, not another word between us. In fact, he didn't say anything more till we were back at the police station and handing everything over to Sir Monte.

"This is all of it, Boss," he said.

"Good work and fast, Thornton. Go into his laptop and copy everything he's done since Friday, last, inclusive of the links in his browser's history. Carlysle can print it up."

Reg looked at me. "Any problem with that?"

I shook my head. "I want this done as much as you."

I logged in and let Reg get to work then stepped back to watch them focus in on their new suspect. A printout of Nettles' face was now on their incident board and info had been set up beside it — 38 years old, married, one child, never went to university, no major bills, no illnesses known of, according to NHS, worked for Masterson for six years, clean record, and on and on.

I looked at the other boards and saw a massive amount of info on Tawfi — height, weight, schedule, history back to kindergarten, everything he'd done with Kahyr, what his current business was up to, even details on who was at the conference on Wednesday. Hamad, Abdel and Mahjub also had profiles but none of it was very detailed; I knew as much as they did. But someone was missing so I stopped Sir Monte as he was striding between boards.

"You don't have anything on Griffin Faure," I said.

Sir Monte hesitated. "Not yet. To gather anything more than public information on him we need far more reason ... a great deal more evidence ... "

"But you got so much on Prince Tafiq ... "

"Pope, on him, we had evidence and he — "

"BOSS!" Berridge cried. "Bloody hell, Boss, I got him! Got Hanlon."

We all bolted over to look at his monitor.

A camera positioned across the street from the Holborn entrance showed Liam Hanlon exit with a crowd, stop at the corner to put something in his mouth, then jaunt across the street and out of sight.

"Run it again," Sir Monte barked.

Berridge did.

"Pause."

He did, right at the point Hanlon fiddled with a package.

"Now frame by frame."

Berridge ran the video in slow motion as Hanlon put a white capsule in his mouth, chomped on it, slipped the package back in his pocket and headed on.

And I felt a sledgehammer crush my gut.

"Thornton," Sir Monte barked from a thousand miles away. "Was there anything in the coroner's report about drugs in Hanlon's system?"

I remember hearing shuffling behind me but it wasn't necessary. I let myself whisper, "It's gum."

I think Sir Monte glared at me. I only caught him in my peripheral vision because I was too locked on that image of Hanlon, bright, smiling, heading straight for — Jesus, for his death.

"Pope, answer me!" Sir Monte snapped, cutting through the fog in my brain. "What do you mean?"

"Chewing gum," I muttered. "He's gonna. Meet somebody. Somebody important. New client. Maybe. Can't have ... can't have coffee breath."

"Here's the report, Boss," Reg said. "Nothin' about drugs."

"Chewing gum?"

"Um — half a packet in his trousers. Peppermint."

"Was he still chewing it? Was it still in his mouth?"

" ... None was found on him, Boss. Nothin' noted at the crime scene, either."

I think I stopped breathing. I couldn't tear my eyes away from the image of that doomed man. I heard the words but could make no sense of them.

"Berridge, High Holborn's single direction there, correct?"

"Yeah, Boss."

"Find CCTV down the next block. Check every vehicle that passes through from this point on for the next twenty minutes. No taxis or lorries, just hire cars." He nudged me and I almost looked at him. "Pope? What's wrong? You're white as a sheet."

I gasped in some air and said, "I've done that. Thousands of times. Pop some gum before. Before meetin' a new. Client. I — I can't — I can't stop — stop thinkin' what he — what he's — "

Sir Monte knocked me onto a chair. I landed hard and it jolted me enough to where I could focus on him. And breathe.

"Thornton, are you done?"

"Yes, Boss. Just transferred the last to Carlysle."

"Take Pope back to his hotel. See him to his room."

I managed to understand what he was saying and rose to my feet, but I was wobbly. Sir Monte took my arm, saying, "Devlin. Devlin! I'd like Dr. Herries-White to speak with you. Is that acceptable?" I think I nodded. "I'll call you with a time." He turned to Reg. "Take the laptop. We've no further need for it."

Then Reg guided me out of the building.

I didn't say a word as we drove back. My mind was blank. Completely. I couldn't see or hear or anything. I know Reg led me out of the car and I vaguely noticed he had parked in the lot then I was blank, again, until he was digging out my wallet for the room key. He bopped it against the handle and opened the door to lead me inside.

I wound up sitting on the bed and heard Reg's voice echoing in my ears. "Pope, what's going on here?"

I looked at him and God he was beautiful. Like an angel. The world was pale in his presence. Unreal. Untrue.

I found myself saying, "How far. Holborn to Acton?"

"What? What're you asking — ?"

"How far?"

"If they took the A40, it's an hour in noonday traffic."

"They'd have to keep him. In the car. Hold him."

"Wait...wait, you think he knew? Knew what was planned? Hanlon? How could he?"

"He'd know something. Know he's lied to. Know they weren't ... weren't headin' back to The City ... "

"You think he knew what they were going to do? You think he knew and ... oh, bloody hell — you think he left that gum in it?"

"Someplace. That wouldn't be cleaned. *Here I was. When I was still alive.*"

Reg sank into a chair. "Christ, I don't want to think about that. It's like — I hope he did but, dear God, I hope he didn't. Isn't that the shite?"

"You thought I ... I was gonna do that to you."

His voice was a growl. "We been over that."

"I didn't understand it." I rose to my feet, swaying. "Didn't get it. But he's just a guy like me. Headin' for a meetin' and — and instead he's dead. And he might've known. He might've known for an hour somethin' was up. Was gonna happen. Oh, God I can't breathe. I can't think. I can't ... "

"Stop it! STOP IT!" Reg bolted up and punched me. Knocked me back on the bed. Loomed over me like my father had done so many times. "All the shite you pulled and you're just now gettin' what it's all about? You didn't know what the fuck you were doin' to people?! What the fuck's wrong with you?!"

There was hate in his eyes and anger and pain and they cut deep into me and tore me apart and I started bawling and grabbed him and pulled him onto the bed and held him tight to me as he fought me but I wouldn't let go because if I did I'd die, I'd die, I'd die ...

****

When I finally regained control, I was lying on the bed and Reg was sitting beside me, holding me like a child. My head on his chest. His shirt soaked by my blood. My nose — I could feel it still dripping. I shifted a bit. He noticed and murmured, "Pope?"

I didn't want to hear him. Didn't want to move. Just wanted to just keep lying next to him. Feel him breathe. In and out. Feel the tender warmth of him.

He trailed a hand around my neck to mingle his fingers in the hair on the back of my head like I did to him that night in the hotel. It was so gentle and right it hurt. I gulped in more breath.

"Pope?"

I nodded.

"Are you back?"

I nodded.

"In full?"

I shrugged, sort of.

"Dr. Herries-White's here. Will you talk to him?"

I nodded.

I heard the man's voice oh-so-carefully ask, "Mr. Pope, you mentioned you prefer to be addressed as Devlin. May I do so?"

I nodded.

Reg started to get up but I held him tighter. "Please, don't. Don't ... "

"Thornton, if you don't mind ... "

"Yes, sir." He settled back on the bed.

"Devlin, you feel very strongly about Constable Thornton, don't you?"

I nodded.

"Can you tell me why?"

I just gulped and sniffed and held Reg tighter and said, "He's not my father."

"The men you assaulted were?"

I nodded.

"The explanations you gave us for assaulting Thornton —"

"Bullshit. All bullshit. I wasn't really thinkin'. I wasn't plannin'. I was huntin'. Just an animal huntin'. Don't think about your prey. What it means to them. Just think, *empty belly needs filling*. Empty heart. Empty soul."

"But with Thornton — "

"Reg. Reg ... "

"You can call me that, sir."

"Very well. Reg. You did think about your prey, didn't you, Devlin?"

I nodded. "But was. Was just in. In my head. In my head. Till I saw. Saw ... "

I started breathing hard and shaking.

Reg gripped me and whispered, "C'mon, Dev, c'mon back to us. C'mon."

It was hard to fight back the chaos building in my heart. Took more than a few deep breaths and gulping in of reality.

I could hear Reg saying, "He was watching CCTV of Liam Hanlon exiting Holborn underground, sir, when this began. He paid particular attention to him putting a piece of chewing gum in his mouth."

"The gum that was found in the car?"

I jolted upright and looked around. Herries-White was sitting in a chair close to the bed, that same suit on him as before, his eyes hard on me.

"The car?" I gasped. "They found the car?"

"Half an hour ago," he said, his expression not wavering. "Located a chewed bit of gum under the back seat."

"Oh-my-God, it's his. His. He knew."

"We don't know that, Devlin. Forensics is analyzing it."

"He knew they were gonna kill him. Oh, shit — shit."

I was about to lose it, again, but Reg shook me, snarling, "Oi, oi, oi, don't do it! Don't you leave us, again. DEV!"

I slammed my eyes closed and used every bit of strength I

had to keep from breaking down. My head was pounding and my heart threatened to tear out of my chest, but I managed to take in enough breaths to nearly hyperventilate and force myself to ask, "How. How long. How long've I been like this?"

"It's half-four," said Herries-White.

"Three hours," Reg added.

I opened my eyes and looked at him. And saw his shirt was soaked with blood. I put a hand to my nose but it had finally stopped. I felt weak. Drained into exhaustion. A bit dizzy. I still touched his arm.

"Shit, I — I ruined your — "

"Shh-shh-shh-shh-shh, just a Tesco special."

"Sorry."

"No great shakes."

"You — you can't go home like that. T-shirts in top drawer. Dresser. Take the Armani."

"Yeah, me wife'll wonder where that come from. But you mind if I spend a penny and clean up? Will you stick around?"

I motioned for him to go so he rose and I watched him cross to the dresser and take one of Tawfi's AX tees and go into the bathroom. He stretched and flexed, stiff from having sat with me for so long, and became even lovelier. When I turned back to Herries-White, his eyes were still locked on me.

I looked away.

"You love him, don't you?"

I sniffed and huffed and shrugged then said, "I'd just kill anyone who hurt him."

He nodded. "I've seen many cases similar to yours. Soldiers in wartime whose fellows become more important than themselves. Men who were hard and cruel but upon becoming fathers gained a surprising level of empathy for any and all children, backed with a fierce protectiveness. You have nephews, am I correct?"

I nodded.

"Do you feel as strongly about them as you do Thorn ...

Reg?"

I hesitated. Then nodded.

"And your brother, Colin?"

I nodded. "And his wife. But they're family."

"So was your father."

I shook my head. "He was a monster."

"And your mother?"

"She abandoned us."

" ... I understand she was killed."

"She let him do it. Her way of suicide. Get away from us all." I didn't meant to say that but out it came. I couldn't take it back ... nor did I want to.

He smiled. "Devlin, do you know why I'm here?"

"Find out how crazy I am."

"No, actually, to keep you balanced, at lest temporarily. As I am also involved with this murder case as an associate of the Metropolitan Police, I cannot be your father-confessor. But I am willing to offer recommendations to others, if you wish."

I nodded.

"Very well. So I am here because Sir Monteith would like you, when you feel able, to return to the station and go over the evidence with him in more detail. Do you think you could do that?"

I looked at him. "What for?"

"You caught aspects on those videos the other officers on this case did not see. Officers trained to seek out details. Caused them to break free of their one-track minds and look closer at all of the evidence, not merely that which suited them. For what it's worth, thanks to you pointing out the differences in how two of the figures on the CCTV videos were walking, they now believe two different men are involved in these murders. At the least. Sir Monteith is not so arrogant as to think only his men are capable of handling this issue and would most appreciate any help you might be able to give. Are you willing to do this?"

"Haven't they talked to Nettles?"

"He hasn't been located, yet. But he will be; he has an appointment to collect Griffin Faure at Prince Tafiq's at six pm sharp. I understand one does not dismiss a member of the Faure family."

"No shit."

"Are you open to our request?"

I rubbed my head. "In a little bit. First let me double-down on some Advil and make a few calls. I'll do it on my cell phone so you guys can listen in. Okay?"

Herries-White smiled. "How long do you need?"

"Hour. Maybe less."

That's when Reg came out of the bathroom, fresh and clean and looking so perfect in that shirt I caught my breath.

Herries-White noticed, of course, and said, "Thornton — Reg, Sir Monteith would like you back at center. I'll bring Devlin over when he's ready."

"Yes, sir." He looked at me. "You all right, then?"

I just nodded.

"What'll I do with this" He held up his bloody shirt.

I motioned to the trash so he tossed it in and left. And I felt myself shrink, inside. The room felt darker. Colder. Words whispered from me. "All I ever wanted was tenderness. Why is that so hard to find?"

"Were you tender with the men you raped?" Herries-White asked.

His voice bore into me. I couldn't look at him but I knew — *No lies allowed*. So I shook my head.

"It's always been my belief," he said, "that in order to receive tenderness it must first be offered. Have you ever?"

I shook my head then rose and pulled a bottle of Advil from my ruined case. Saw the knife had punctured it. "Perfect," I muttered.

Herries-White saw the damage and came over to me. "Did this happen last night?"

I nodded.

"Have you something else to put these capsules into?"

"Yeah, sure. Why?"

"This puncture is good and clear. It might help us better determine what sort of knife was used to attack you."

I frowned at him. "Do you think last night — he was one of the guys who — who — ?"

"Where was your case when the knife struck?"

I had to think. "Left hand. Was in my left hand. Back. I twisted it up. So protected my lower back."

"All four men were stabbed in that area, on the left side. Viciously. Two or three times, each. If they hadn't been strangled they'd have bled to death."

I felt weak and leaned against the dresser. Pain shot through my groin and into my heart and I gasped for breath. It's a good thing Herries-White braced me because I'd have fallen. I was able to fight it back but it was still so damn hard to breathe. I looked at him and his eyes were sharp on me as he guided me into a chair.

"I like your reaction," he said. "I feel much better about you, now."

"What?!"

"All that you have said and done to this point could have been brought about by any number of other things, including fear of exposure. But just now you reacted physically, honestly and empathetically, all without the least bit of hesitation or thought. You felt the pain of those men and it horrified you. I no longer have any doubt you will assist rather than hinder our investigation."

I could think of nothing to say except, "I want those goddamn motherfuckin' bastards found and killed."

He smiled. "I'm sure you do. And I am also certain we will find those *motherfucking bastards*, as you so delightfully put it, and handle them in our own fashion. Now take your pills. Clean yourself up. Make your calls. We have work to do."

I nodded and did what he asked.

SIXTEEN

After a quick shower, I pulled on my last clean jeans and the other Armani t-shirt; it was snug on me. Tawfi's friggin' cook did me a number in the weight gain department. Tomorrow would be a good long run. By this point I was feeling human enough to face people, again.

The phone calls to the East Coast dealers were easy. I handed them the same bullshit I'd given the West Coasters, which seemed to go over well; one even commented that my company's new direction had already been put up on the message boards. The Midwest was more *Prove it* but I figured Diana could deal better with them.

I got a text from Mahjub that he'd had a breakthrough on the pins and wanted to show me. I ignored it and called the office to fill Colin in but got shut down fast.

Diana was there and they were in the middle of trying to figure out how much cash Marci had embezzled from the company — over what was beginning to look like decades.

Which brought a nice big, "What the fuck?" from me.

"It's crazy, Dev," Colin said. "A hundred-thousand a year since she was hired. She inflated Mihn's costs just enough for no one to notice, added suppliers who don't exist, made it all look real and we — we trusted her. Dad trusted her."

Before I could shut my trap, I snarled, "Trusted her or let her?" It would explain why she was silent in the face of his abuse.

"Aw, Jesus, you don't think she was blackmailing him?"

"You said Diana's there?"

"Yeah, right here."

"Put me on speaker; I want you both in on this."

"Okay."

"Hi, Dev," Diana purred, sounding a lot more in control than Colin. But when has she never been?

"Hi from the future, baby. First off — Colin, you remember our shippin' manager back when the Faure shit happened?"

"Yeah, Jackie something," said Colin.

"Check and see if he and Marci were workin' together, on that." I knew she'd hit Rio up rather than deal with our back-stabbing ex-employee. "Might also give you an idea as to where she's stashin' the money."

"We already have a line on that," said Diana. "She hopped a straight-shot to Jamaica, but so far as we can tell she isn't staying anywhere on the island. My bet is she did a charter to the Caymans."

"Sounds right," I said, finally noticing Herries-Whites was deliberately trying to look like he was not listening in. "Do we know people down there?"

Colin piped in with, "We know people who know people."

I damn near jumped for joy at hearing him say that. "Even better. Now we still got our reserves — "

"In treasuries," said Colin. "Only you can access those."

"Talk to Hamilton. Ask him what needs to be done to transfer them to you and Diana."

"But you — you're coming back, right? And besides, they haven't matured — "

"Doesn't matter, Colin," said Diana, "so long as they're the type that can be used as collateral."

"They are," I said. "I made sure of that."

"Then we'll be fine. I hear you talked with some dealers."

"Yeah, I told them you're handlin' everything with them from now on."

"Thanks for letting me know."

Okay, time to make it clean and clear. "Well, reality is, Ghadir and I are thinkin' of startin' up a factory in Northern Ireland to make pins. He's already looked at a spot I found and is talkin' to the locals. It'd make sense for me to stick around and help get things up and runnin'. And now that I've got that in with the Royals for their pins, well, that's gonna take some finesse and ... " My voice trailed off. I could hear Colin breathing hard.

"You're leaving the business?" he asked.

"No, no! Expanding it. Makin' use of the Brexit chaos."

"Colin, we talked about opening another factory," Diana purred. "Maybe a small one here, too. Now that we know what Marcy's been doing it even makes financial sense. We'd keep Mr. Mihn for the large orders, use ours for the smaller ones."

"You think that'd work?" His voice almost sounded steady.

I almost answered but for once was smart enough to keep my yap shut.

"I know it will," Diana said. "We need to do something."

"Yeah, I, uh — I guess we do, with more kids ... "

I jolted. "More kids? Diana?!?!?!"

"Oh," she said in all innocence, "didn't I mention? Another set of twins. Guess who's getting her tubes tied, after this."

I bounced up, startling Herries-White as I yelled. "Whoa, that's fantastic! Congratulations! I'd kiss you both if I was there."

"No need, Dev. Let's talk next week, once things are more settled."

"Yeah. Great. I-I-I'll call you, Monday. Whoa." I ended the call and grinned at Herries-White. "I'm gonna be an uncle, again."

He almost smiled. "So I take it you have regained your equilibrium?"

"Buddy, this Devil could face any devil there is, now."

"Then shall we?"

****

We got to the police station about fifteen minutes later, and Herries-White showed Sir Monte the damage to my case and Advil bottle.

He nodded, turned to Carlysle and said, "Take this down to the lab. Ask if it could be a match." Then he turned to me and said, "Unfortunately, CCTV will be of no use in locating your attacker. Bloody fog. Where's Thornton?"

I looked at Sir Monte, confused. "Excuse me?"

"Is he with the car? Did he drop you?"

I went cold. "He headed back an hour ago."

Herries-White joined us. "Yes, he left just before five."

Sir Monte froze. "He texted us he was staying. His locator's still at Hatton Cross. Berridge, when did that text come in?"

"Um — 17:12, Boss."

"Call him." He bolted to the door. "Carlysle, hold off on the lab. I want you to locate Thornton's car!"

Carlysle scurried back in and hit his computer.

Berridge looked around. "Goes to voicemail, Boss."

"Contact the hotel. Get CCTV for anything from five before to a quarter past."

Berridge got to it.

"Car's still at the hotel, Boss," Carlysle called.

"His phone?"

"Already looking — and here. Christ — Knightsbridge."

"Call in the closest units. Have them — "

"Got CCTV, Boss," Berridge cried. "Here's Thornton."

We all piled over to look.

Reg exited the lobby at 16:58. Another screen showed him heading into the parking lot. Another image showed his car parked down the side.

But he didn't appear.

He didn't fucking appear!

Berridge checked three other cameras and Reg wasn't to be seen. Without a word from Sir Monte, he focused on the exit gate of the parking lot.

A black Bentley drove out at 17:01.

And it had diplomatic plates.

"BLOODY FUCKING HELL!" burst out of Sir Monte with such violence I actually stepped back from him. "Citywide alert for that car! I want to know where it is! Right now! Focus between Hatton Cross and Knightsbridge. Berridge, I want all CCTV along any and all routes to that bloody embassy and around it." He grabbed a landline and punched in three numbers. "Carol, get me Sir Laurence at the Home Office. And Lord Fitzwilliam in Foreign. Patch them into me on conference, now! ... JUST BLOODY DO IT!"

Then he turned his eyes on me and they were the coldest, cruelest eyes that I'd seen since my father's. "I have yet to be fully convinced you and al Qasimi are not in league, so for your sake Thornton had best be found alive, because if he is not, if he is already dead and his body has been dumped between here and Knightsbridge, then you will never see the light of day, again, and I needn't kill you to make certain that happens."

"Oh, c'mon, Sir Monte," I snapped then bit my tongue when his glare got even more harsh.

His voice was like ice. "We agreed to Sir Mon*teith*."

I took in a deep breath. "Sir Monteith, I'm here helpin' you! I HAVE been helpin' you!"

He did not look convinced but at least he began to pace, breathing hard. "We've got to get into that bloody — "

"I can," I said.

He stopped and glared at me.

I kept on with, "I got a text from Mahjub. He wants to see me tonight. I can call him or — or text him. Tell I'm on my way over. You cleared him, said he's not involved, so I can get in. All nice and legal and now. Right now."

I could all but see the gears moving in Sir Monte's head.

"Pope, what sort of game are you playing?"

I turned to Herries-White. "Doc ... "

"I believe you can trust him, Sir Monteith."

I started inputting a text. *Just got your message. Finishing dinner. Be there soon.* I kept glancing between my phone and Sir Monte, watching the gears keep whirling.

At least the glare was gone as he said, "No, Pope, I can't allow it. You're a civilian and it would be too dangerous. Will you hold this?" He handed the phone to Herries-White and headed over to Berridge. "But as you are an American and not *currently* under arrest, I cannot actually forbid you to contact a business associate for a meeting, can I?"

I smiled. "I'm an asshole from Brooklyn; nobody tells me where I can and can't go."

"Typical American," he muttered, almost smiling. "Berridge, turn to me." He did. Sir Monte removed a pin from his shirt and spun to pin it under the collar of my jacket. "We have pins of our own, you know. I now have them on all my men, thanks to your destruction of Thornton's mobile phone."

Reality slammed into me. "Oh, shit, I know why you thought Reg was at my hotel. I got blood on his shirt, so he changed into one of mine and left his in the trash."

"Well ... it doesn't do us much good there, does it? May I advise you to not to remove your jacket? Berridge, CCTV?"

"They hopped the M4 straight to the A4, Boss, not enough time between cameras for them to have stopped, even considering traffic. I'm up to West Cromwell."

"They're taking him to the embassy. Fastest way there?"

"This time of day? Forty-five minutes to an hour."

"Carlysle!"

"Yeah, Boss?"

"Get us a chopper then a car."

"Where'll it land? There's no room by the station."

"Treaty Center has a multi-story car park," said Berridge. "Maybe the top level?"

"Good idea. Carlysle?"

"On it, Boss."

"We'll land in Hyde Park by the bandstand. Have a car meet us there and clear the area. Berridge, call in SFO. I want that bloody building surrounded, nobody in, nobody out without us knowing. But quiet as possible about it. Nothing on their doorstep, not yet."

"You got it, Boss."

He took the phone from Herries-White. "Carol? ... CAROL! ... When you get them both, patch them through to my mobile. ... TELL THE BLOODY LITTLE FUCK THAT A CONSTABLE'S LIFE'S IN DANGER AND I NEED TO SPEAK WITH HIS FUCKING BOSS, AT ONCE! Christ!"

He slammed the phone down.

Herries-White was shaking his head. "Sir Monteith, do you really think anyone would use an embassy car to kidnap and possibly kill a British Constable? With CCTV that might catch who was driving? This would cause a serious issue between two sovereign nations."

"You forget the Yvonne Fletcher incident with Libya — "

"That was three or four men who were returned to their country and, supposedly, punished for being idiots. Prince Tafiq is not that much of a fool, nor that low a level diplomat."

"What about Abdel?" I asked. "He's the one who's always drivin' him around."

Sir Monte glared at me. "He has an alibi for one of the murders."

"Iron clad?"

"As can be. He was with Mrs. al Qasimi."

"Oh, Jeez, Hamad's wife."

"Yes. He ferried her about while shopping."

"Which victim?"

" ... Goughan."

"What day?"

"Six-September."

"No, day of the week. Monday, Tuesday?"

"Thursday."

"Abdel's off work, Thursdays. One of his associates should have handled Leila."

"Christ, you're on first-name basis with the whole bloody family?" But his brain was back to working. "Found in one of Masterson's vehicles. Late in the day. Edwards?"

"Yeah, Boss?" I saw a slim young man in glasses pop his head over the top of a monitor, in a corner.

"Did we make a list of the shops we think Mrs. al Qasimi visited the day Goughan was killed?"

"I think so. Lemme look."

"I'm most interested in anything near Northfield." He wandered over to a map showing the locations of the bodies. "If she was inside the center and he went to get petrol or have the car washed ... Nettles left for dinner, about one, in a Masterson car ... and their office is in Chiswick ... " Sir Monte eyed me. "But why? What could either of them gain from this?"

"What if these're set-up murders? Done in as vicious a way as possible to blame on someone who can *not* be tried for them?"

"Pope, we've gone over that and — "

"But am I right about diplomatic immunity — that you can't arrest and try someone who has it if they commit a crime, no matter how awful? Even murders like these?"

"It depends on the country. At its most basic immunity can be waived, or the offender can be expelled and his own country might put him on trial."

"But what if what all you really wanted was to get a guy out of the way, just without killin' him. Because if you did kill him that'd put suspicion on you?"

"Where are you headed with — ?"

"Here it is, Boss," said Edwards. "From what we could tell, she stayed mainly around Hyde Park — Harrod's, specialty shops in Mayfair, Kensington. One of the DC's recognized a bag from a spa in Belgravia. It's a chain ... "

Sir Monte looked at him, wary. "Do they *have* a location near Northfield?"

"Checking — checking — oh, bloody hell — Ealing. Two miles from where Goughan's body was found."

"Wasn't Goughan's call for Ealing?"

Edwards shuffled some papers then said, "Train station."

"Do we know where Abdel Naifeh is?"

"No, Boss," said Carlysle. "He wasn't the focus of — "

"Berridge, have you any sort of idea who was driving that bloody embassy car?"

"Sorry, boss, he had the sunscreen down. But I got the car all the way there. The embassy has underground parking, accessed down an alley behind the building. Got a glimpse of it entering at 17:58. I'd say they never stopped, Boss. Straight drive."

"Oh, for God's sake, ANYBODY — any word on Nettles, yet?"

"No, Boss. Masterson's still trying to raise him. He never called in about the collection so they sent another driver to pick up Faure. He left seven minutes ago."

"Chopper's en route, Boss."

Sir Monte grabbed my arm and dragged me to the door, saying, "Tell me more of your thoughts on the way."

We exited the building just as a police car pulled up. Sir Monte shoved me in back and sat next to me.

As we roared off, siren screaming, I started yammering in my best sales voice, "Okay, so here's the deal — you can't call him out as gay because there's rumors his father was like that, too, till he got married, so it might backfire on you. But what if there's access to billions of dollars at stake and you're not allowed that access for some reason or other?"

"If you're suggesting Prince Hamad," he snarled like he's explaining the obvious to a child, "his alibis are iron-clad. He's visited several times in the last few months, but we've been able to ascertain where he's been during two of the murders and wasn't even in London for two others. Al Qasimi is still the only consistency, throughout." But the gears were going in his brain.

That's when I got my text from Mahjub. *OK, back door, like before, #14. Reporters in front. Text when here.*

Sir Monte watched as I sent an *OK* back to him.

"Which back door?"

"It's one they use for deliveries. I think the security is just basic there. But that building's got 'em all over ... "

"Yes, alarms everywhere. We know." His phone rang. "Yes?" His face froze. "Where was he? ... Hang on — " He put his phone on face-time and Carlysle appeared. "Go ahead."

"His wife found him in his shed, Boss. Hanged. He left a note and she verified it's his handwriting. And, Boss, they found it on top a box with a hundred-thousand pounds in it. Cash. I forwarded you a photo of the note."

"Yes," Sir Monte said, "I see it's come through. Hang on."

He shifted to a photo that showed a note written in a careful but shaky hand. It read —

Poor Stuart. I heard him scream. I didn't know ... but he's still screaming. He won't stop. And the others — the others scream too. I know they do. I hear them echo. I can't take it anymore. I'm so sorry.

"Jesus Christ," whispered from me.

Sir Monte's voice was subdued. "Carlysle, I want to you to go to his home and gather any and all information you can and inform me, real time. Have as little to do with his widow as possible; we'll send someone over to work with her. Oh, and before you go, arrange for a black cab to meet us at the landing site."

"On it, Boss."

"Good man." Then he ended the call and looked straight ahead, tight and unmoving.

I had to ask, "Black cab?"

"We can't have you show up at the embassy in a blue and

white," he said, his voice cool and even and hollow. "It might tip our hand."

Then his entire attitude screamed, *Now leave me the fuck alone.*

I did.

****

If it had been under any other circumstances the helicopter ride to Hyde Park would have been fan-fucking-tastic. The whole of London spread out before you. The Thames winding its way, not so very far below. Landmarks and skyscrapers and parks gleaming in the late evening light. History calling to you. This city had a magnificence that even New York, for all her splendor, could never have.

We aimed for an open space that had been cordoned off by a circle of police cars and unmarked sedans. Groups of cops and plainclothesmen stood around, watching us, with crowds of people outside the cordon — including what looked like a growing cadre of reporters.

Sir Monte took it all in and growled, "MI5's here. They took no time for a change. And still with no word from Home Office. All right ... " He looked at me. "You open your mobile with a numeric code, correct?" I nodded. "Then you go straight to the cab and leave; I'll handle MI5. Soon as you're at the door dial eight six on your phone. If we don't get some kind of signal from you within fifteen minutes after that, I'm sending SFO straight in and damn anyone who says we shouldn't. Are we clear?"

I nodded.

By this point the chopper was on the ground so Sir Monte hopped out one door then I snuck out the other and made a beeline for the black taxi. I heard someone yell at me but I jumped in the cab, told the driver the address and we headed off. The cops let us through.

It's a short drive to the embassy but traffic was snarled —

until a police car joined us and led us down a couple of sidewalks to where the street we needed was blocked off. They let us through then we passed a group of men in black outfits huddled around a van, their eyes watching us go. Despite the cordon, down the block you could see a gaggle of reporters milling about at the embassy's entrance. I guess the SWAT guys were letting things stay as normal as possible till absolutely necessary.

I had the taxi pass and round the corner then drop me at the mouth of that narrow alley. I hurried up to behind the embassy. It was nothing but shadows there, emphasized by the occasional lighted window, and barely any traffic noise from nearby streets.

I found number 14 by using my phone's flashlight to see the numbers. It was the same door where the TV screens had been picked up. I hit 86 on my phone then texted Mahjub ... and waited.

And waited.

I texted him again ... just as he opened the door.

"You came so quickly," he said.

I almost said, *No one has ever accused me of that before*, but shut it down and just chuckled, "I was having dinner with a client not far away," as I entered. I continued with, "Listen, Mahjub, I need your help — "

"Client?" Mahjub chuckled. "You were with the police."

Bam! Tape was wrapped around me, trapping my arms against my sides. Wrestling took over and I dropped into a roll — or tried to. Instead I got yanked up and slammed against a wall then shoved to the floor as someone the size of a gorilla sat on my back. I fought to twist away, but the gorilla held my legs as Mahjub wrapped more tape around my ankles so I couldn't get the leverage I needed.

The whole time I'm screaming, "What the fuck? What're you doin'? Motherfucker, get the fuck off me!" Crap like that, which did zero good, of course. Even my best wrestling moves were proving worthless.

"Good idea to use tape," Mahjub said. "Much better."

The guy then helped Mahjub force my wrists behind me

to bind with more tape. In seconds I was immobilized. They flipped me over and I finally saw it was Abdel helping him. Shit, no wonder they were able to take me down; he outweighed me by a good fifty pounds, all of it juiced up muscle.

"What the fuck's goin' on?" I snarled, trying to hide how scared I was. I saw his right forearm was bandaged and he was using his left to control me.

A napkin got whipped into my mouth to cleave-gag me. Oh, I could still curse and spit and howl in every four, five, six and hundred-letter word I could think of, but my volume was cut by seventy-five percent. Didn't stop me from snapping and snarling as they picked me up and set me over Abdel's shoulders to be carried, fireman style. I still fought and struggled but his grip was too damn tight.

Then Mahjub took my phone. When the numbers to input a passcode came up, he ticked over them with quick fingers and it went blank. Not off but quiet. A moment later a pulse appeared on it and he smiled. "Tracking system was installed. Did you know the police have been monitoring you? I think you did."

He grinned, opened the door and tossed the phone into the street then closed and bolted it.

Abdel carried me to the elevator, Mahjub leading, and we rode up to the top floor then headed down that long corridor. The little shit had another napkin twisted tight around my throat so I couldn't curse or yell, not that he needed to; by this point I'd stopped struggling because I was close to throwing up from the pressure of Abdel's unforgiving muscles against my not completely solid gut. Also, I was trying to dig for the nail clipper in my jeans pocket. I managed to get one hand just inside it then, as best I could, gathered the pocket's material closer and closer. If I could only reach it —

But before I was able to we entered Tawfi's flat.

I managed to twist and look around and I saw Tawfi lying on a chaise as if asleep. I started to kick and struggle and curse, again, despite Mahjub's stranglehold but it did me no good. Then we entered the guest bedroom.

The first thing I saw was Reg lying on the bed, face down. Unconscious. Still dressed in the AX shirt and his jacket, but his pants and briefs were around his knees. Leila stood beside him, wearing overalls and latex gloves, her hair in a bandana.

She snapped a question at them, in Arabic.

Mahjub replied, a bit subservient, and dropped me onto my feet then held me in place.

She sighed then cast me a smirk and pulled out a cell phone. She dialed a number then looked at it, smiling, and said, "Are you ready, darling?"

"Show me," whispered from the phone.

In Griffin fucking Faure's voice!

She turned it to show he was in the back of a car, Bluetooth in one ear, on FaceTime, and he was grinning ear to ear. "Hello, Pope. Welcome to hell."

I managed to spit out a coherent, "What the fuck're you doin', motherfucker?"

"Payback. I told you not to fuck with us. The only reason your cop buddy's still alive is because I want you to watch what happens. Know it's all your fault. All the others? They were just unlucky; nobody gives a shit about them. But your cop? Boom. Your whole fucking family's dead meat."

"And Prince Tafiq will have embarrassed our country so badly," said Leila. "I'm sure my father-in-law will banish him to a tiny office in the back of the palace forevermore. If he is allowed to live."

"You think that'll help your dumb-ass husband?!" I growled, making sure I enunciated every syllable. "He's too fuckin' stupid — "

"But he has me and two sons. Strong incentive to make him crown prince, I think."

Abdel yanked me in the air then slammed his left hand into my gut four or five times before I landed on the floor. I couldn't see for the stars in my eyes and the pain and the intense desire not to spew in front of these assholes. Then he grabbed my hair, pulled my head back and slipped a noose around my neck.

I heard Griff say, "You always were a stupid fuck, Pope. Now you're just proving it. Say hello to the devil."

Abdel dragged me up by the noose and whipped the rope over the hall door as Leila dropped the phone into a bag that was also on the bed. Then she pulled a used condom from it —

With a clear crystal phallus?!

She held the damned thing level and it gleamed in the subdued light, then she squeezed what looked like — wait, was that cum dripping out of the condom onto it? She smeared it over the tip and holy shit, it hit me — that break-in at my hotel wasn't to attack or rob me; it was to get Tawfi's condom! The dead guys weren't raped; they were sodomized by that thing after it had been smeared with his semen. That's why there were traces of a condom's latex in it. And she was gonna do that to Reg?

My Reg?

Mine?!?!?

NO FUCKIN' WAY, MOTHERFUCKERS!

I managed to snarl, "You crazy fuckin' bitch, you leave him the fuck alone or I'll fuckin' kill you!" before Abdel used the noose to yank me up off my feet then pulled the door shut to keep me there.

Son-of-a-bitch, I was being made into a suicide!

No, no, no, no, no way, motherfuckers! NO!

I forced myself to focus on the nail clipper. Fought myself to think about that and not that I couldn't breathe or the pain around my throat that was screaming through me, and I made myself shift the file out and I held it back-assed-wards and awkwardly jabbed at the tape around my wrists. It cut into my skin as I kept jabbing and jabbing and fighting to free my hands and my head was pounding and my eyes were shattered and I couldn't breathe and I was pissed as hell that I was going out this way then I sort of heard Mahjub say, "What's this?"

He came close and undid Berridge's pin, saying

something in Arabic. By instinct I made myself twist my shoulders to ram him, jolting him back, then yanked my legs up and dropped them over his head and Jesus Christ it tore into my neck but I used his shoulders to lift up against the rope and gasp in some air just as the tape around my wrists broke and I whipped my hands around and jabbed the little shit in his left eye.

He screamed and fought to get away but I held onto him, jabbing at the tape around my body and arms until I saw —

Leila stab Reg with the knife!

BAM! Instinct took over and I yanked my legs up over Mahjub's head and kicked him into her. He knocked her down and off the bed and bounced over her and slammed to the floor, still screaming.

Abdel shoved the door open and the rope slipped off it. I dropped to the floor and rolled, coughing and gasping. I jabbed at the tape around my ankles and it broke as he dove at me. I rolled aside and tore at the tape and scrambled to my feet and rammed headlong into his gut but he just grabbed me around the waist and lifted me up to where I was doing like a headstand and I could see Leila rushing over with the knife so I twisted and wrapped my legs around his head and grabbed his belt with my hands and jerked and we tumbled to the floor. He released me then I rolled back onto my feet and jabbed at the last of the tape around my body.

Leila lunged at me with the knife but I let myself drop to the floor as I freed one arm. She whipped around at me and I managed to grab her hand and twist it and when Abdel came roaring over I kicked up and used her to slam the knife into his chest.

Somebody screamed — don't know if it was him or her — but he stumbled back, blood spewing everywhere, then I freed my other arm, howling, and yanked Leila up and had the knife to her throat and —

"DEVLIN!" cut into me.

It was Tawfi. By the door. Looking drunk. Barely able to stand. But he still had his voice.

"Devlin. Let her go."

I looked at him. I knew what he was saying but I did not understand it. I was still growling and gasping for air and my head was splitting in half and I could barely focus my eyes and I'm sure I looked like some rabid animal while Mahjub was screaming and Leila was crying and struggling and the knife was still close to her skin and I think it cut her. I think. But I couldn't think enough to understand till Tawfi raised a hand in a gentle gesture of *stop*.

"Devlin — she is the mother to my nephews. Let her go. Now." Then he added in a near whisper, "Please."

I hesitated, still growling ... but I let her wriggle free and she staggered into the middle of the room, looking around in shock.

Abdel was on his side, motionless, a crimson pool gently spreading around him. Mahjub was letting out something between a cry and a moan as he rocked in a corner. Blood appeared from under Reg's jacket, staining the AX t-shirt dark and red. And I didn't understand it. I could not understand one damn bit of it —

Someone was pounding at the front door and men's voices were screaming, "Police! Open up! POLICE!"

Tawfi glared at Leila. "Go. Stay in your flat."

She looked at him, still in shock, so he said something to her in Arabic. Probably the same thing. She slipped on Abdel's blood as she circled around to the door, still crying and wanting not to get too close to Tawfi, but she had to pass him and as she did he grabbed her arm and snarled more words at her in Arabic. She froze. Her face drained of color. His eyes bore into hers. She nodded and raced off.

He rolled around to face the front entrance.

Moments later I heard the door smash open and the Met's SFO guys roared into the room, still screaming things like *Police* and *Do not move*!

I had enough presence of mind to drop the knife and raise my hands so they were easily visible. I was cold and shivering and my head was killing me and my mouth was sore as shit and I didn't want to give some trigger-happy cop any excuse to shoot first and worry later, like they do in the States.

Tawfi's hands remained in view but he did not move from the door — until one SFO member started down the hall. Then Tawfi barked after him, "Do not go down that corridor."

"You got no say, you bloody rag — "

"This is embassy property!" Tawfi snapped in a scream of a whisper. "You are in violation of its sovereignty."

"What's going on?" I saw Sir Monte rush in, flack jacket over him.

"My company owns this building," Tawfi growled, not looking at him. "We lease part of it to my country. These are embassy living quarters." Then he rolled around to look at Sir Monte and added, "But I am loathe to make an issue of it so long as your men stay in this area. In my flat. And go no farther."

Sir Monte took everything in with one glance then called out, "Other rooms?"

"All clear, Boss," drifted in from a couple directions.

"Medics?"

"Here, sir." Then a pair of men roared in with cases of medical supplies.

"You've work to do. Prince Tafiq, do you promise me there is no one else in this building who has participated in the attack upon my constable?"

Tawfi took in a deep breath and said, "I promise you that the only two men who attacked your constable are on the floor. There." He motioned to Mahjub and Abdel.

"Wesson." The SFO guy facing down Tawfi looked at Sir Monte. "Come help the others."

The guy did what Sir Monte said without a second's hesitation.

One of the medics cried, "Thornton's been stabbed, sir. Bleedin'."

I looked at him and shook my head, *no, no, no* ...

"How serious?" Sir Monte asked.

"It's like he was sliced ... "

Sir Monte looked at me. "Which one had the knife?"

Once again I knew what he was saying but had no fucking idea what he meant. I was cold as ice. Quaking. His expression grew confused.

"The young man," said Tawfi. "In the corner. Devlin took it away from him."

Sir Monte nodded. "Berridge, take a photo of Pope, right now. Then remove the gag and the rope around his neck."

Berridge appeared and did as he asked. It wasn't until he was untying the gag that I remembered it was there. Guess that's why I'd been growling.

"His neck's pretty raw, Boss," Berridge said as he lifted the rope off me.

Sir Monte turned to the medic tending to Mahjub. "He can wait. Take a look at our man." The guy rose and came over to me. "Thornton?"

That medic said, "I don't think it got any organs but A&E can check that. And there's a nasty gash on back his head, too. Looks like he's comin' 'round."

"Get him to St. Mary's, now."

"Yes, sir. With traffic, we'll hit A&E within half an — "

"You'll arrive in ten minutes. Take the SFO tank and if the bastards won't stand their cars aside, have them moved."

The medic smiled. "Right you are, sir."

Somehow I managed to croak, "So — so he's okay?"

The medic looked at me. "It's all good."

Good? Those motherfuckers nearly killed my Reg and all he can say at finding out they weren't able to was *It's all good*? It was fan-fuckin'-tastic. It was sense returning to me, the world returning to me, life returning to me. I think I started to laugh. And weep.

Tawfi straightened up and said, "Tell me, can your medics draw blood?"

Sir Monte looked at the medic tending to Reg. The guy

nodded.

Tawfi saw and said, "Then please do so from myself. I believe I was drugged."

"How?" Sir Monte snapped.

"I had a long difficult meeting, today," Tawfi said. He hesitated before continuing, "Mahjub brought us tea." Then Tawfi looked at me. "Devlin. You're bleeding. Rather badly."

My medic and I looked down and saw the cut to my arm was pouring blood through what was left of the bandage. He jolted.

"Sorry, mate," he said. "Thought it was from the dead guy so focused on your neck. Amazed you can still breathe."

I chuckled and croaked. "Shit, no wonder I was feelin' cold."

Then I passed out.

SEVENTEEN

They kept me in the hospital for a couple of days, *as a precaution*. My arm got stapled up, again, and I was given something lovely for pain. I still could barely speak, but overall I was fine. Considering.

Reg was kept in a different area but the nurses loved me and kept me updated on his recovery. He was in surgery for hours getting put back together, however no major organs were damaged beyond repair and it was believed by all that he would make a full recovery.

Sir Monte — no, Sir Monteith, I owed him that — he dropped by with Dr. Herries-White and had Berridge take my statement. I had to speak slowly and carefully but laid out everything that happened. They accepted it without a squeak, which surprised me. They'd been so unwilling to believe anything I'd told them, before. They didn't share any information with me, but being alone and having nothing to do but think for hours at a time ... I pretty much worked out most of the whys and wherefores of what was going on.

Negotiations between The Faure Group and Kahyr were not going well. Griff's people were focused on building a new oil pipeline and refinery, but Tawfi wanted to focus on upgrading the lines and facilities already in use while focusing on re-establishing the ancient Silk Road trade route, which would benefit his country just as much and mean more to his people. One method was developing a southern extension of the Trans-Eurasia-Express to avoid the brutal Russian winters, which would include the Pearl

River Delta in its routing. (I got this from a couple of articles in the *Financial Times*, *The NY Times International Edition* and a few sources that needed *Google Translate* to make sense to me; Sir Monteith was kind enough to have my laptop brought to me.)

Seluruh Dunia were on Faure's side, especially as regards oil exploration and transport of it. Ves'mir in Ukraine, and Quán Shìjiè in China, were open to both but were leaning to Kahyr's idea. Negotiations started in earnest just over a year ago but the big boys didn't come in to finalize agreements till the last few months ... and that's when the egos made life difficult for all.

During the second partner conference, in Montreaux, Hamad and family were also on hand for one of his bodybuilding competitions. That's when Griff and Leila either joined forces or started an affair ... I'm not sure which. My bet is both Leila and Griff wanted Tawfi sidelined but weren't sure how to handle it, yet. Then she saw how Tawfi reacted to Martin Perriman when he delivered the diplomatic pouch, and my guess is Griff remembered how Tawfi was with Kenneth, so she got Mahjub to do his techno-magic and investigate him. When they saw he was having financial trouble, the plan began to form using their knowledge of Tawfi's preferences and Griff's money.

My guess is they paid Perriman to have sex with Tawfi and pass the used condoms along to them. The poor guy must have been desperate to help his business and just didn't realize what he was getting himself into.

Leila also knew Abdel was a very conservative Muslim who despised gay men so worked on him to *help remove an apostate from the throne*. According to a one-column story in *The Sun,* comments he made to his assistants suggested he thought the throne could then be replaced with a true Islamic government, and the paper's reporter *was sure he would not have hesitated to kill some infidels in order to further it.*

I don't know how she and Griff got Mahjub into it, but money sent him by The Faure Group was manipulated into payments being made to Martin Perriman by Kahyr, seemingly at

Tawfi's behest. Perhaps this was Mahjub's revenge for being used as Tawfi's playtoy.

Then Leila saw Etan Conescieu moving in the catering supplies and step three of the plan was put into motion. Mahjub sourced out that he worked from 6am to 2pm so he could go to school, so Abdel jumped him on the way to his job, killed him, sodomized him with that crystal phallus after smearing Tawfi's semen on it and snuck back into the embassy, with Mahjub's help.

I'm convinced Griff pointed them to Stuart Goughan and Liam Hanlon as the next two victims and tricked Jonathan Nettles into luring them to their deaths. Then Griff paid him too much cash to not keep quiet ... even as what he'd done tore at him. Through all of this Mahjub kept tabs on the police, so when the car that carried Hanlon was impounded he spread the word and that pushed Nettles over the edge and he took the easy way out. What's sad is since the money was part of a crime his wife and child wouldn't get to keep it.

Perriman was supposed to be the last murder because by that time Mahjub knew Tawfi was under surveillance. But they had to wait because of that silly argument. Then when Prince Tafiq indicated to someone, somehow, he'd be unavailable that Thursday evening, they'd seized their chance. Nettles drove Abdel down to Feltham, Perriman was killed, then Nettles made an anonymous call from a prepaid phone to complain about an *odd Muslim guy sneaking around Perriman's office*. I what turned out to be a very shaky, hesitant voice. Only I messed that up by jumping Reg and sending the whole force into high-alert to find him. No one remembered the call till after the body was found.

When Griff heard I was now involved in this he decided to kill two birds with one stone. Mahjub must have learned Reg had visited me so he was targeted, and this time the murder would be in Prince Tafiq's flat so he could be caught red-handed ... and I would be guilty by association, thanks to what I'd done to the guy. Their plan was for me to be jailed, but then I'd walked right into their little web and they figured making me a suicide would be even better. Jesus.

It almost sounds clever, doesn't it? Almost. But once the Met stopped focusing on Tawfi and started looking around the whole thing began to unravel, mainly thanks to CCTV being all over the city and Sir Monteith's techies being just as good as Mahjub, once they got locked and loaded.

I'd like to think that if Griff and Leila had known about Nettles' suicide they'd have scrubbed the mission and Reg would've been left alone — but I'm not willing to give them that much credit in the way of smarts. Now Griff was back in NYC using his attack dogs to keep from being linked to the mess ... *just because he had a meeting with the Prince immediately prior to the murder* ... and she was God only knew where.

Anyway, that's my take on it all. And I have to be honest — I was rather enjoying the outcome. Because on top of their plans getting so totally destroyed, Griff was having to deal with the media calling me a hero for putting my life on the line to save a cop and end a serial killer's reign, especially since big-bad-brave me was also damn near killed. That almost made the whole thing worthwhile.

Almost.

However ... that was not the public version of these events. What the Met handed out to explain what happened would send anyone reeling into bizarro-world.

The situation with Reg and my arrest was touted as part of a deliberate scheme by the Met *to confuse the killers*, hoping to force them to make a mistake, and they were oh-so-pleased with themselves that it had worked. How it worked was never really addressed. Or asked about. Or explained. Or commented upon. All that mattered was the reign of terror was over.

Now here's where it gets fun — Abdel was hailed as a hero for trying to stop Mahjub! Slim little Mahjub with the blond highlights in his hair was fingered as the one and only killer and neither Griff's nor Leila's names were mentioned once in connection with the deaths. They said he stabbed the men before raping them to gain control then strangled them as he fucked them, something that was put far more delicately by all except the *Daily Mail* but that was the real gist. Abdel had happened onto his next travesty and been killed by him.

In the underground parking garage, not Tawfi's flat.

Okay ... there were so damn many holes in that explanation you could've watched a wide-screen movie through them and lost nothing in the visuals. For example, Tawfi's DNA being on the victims ... but that was somehow shifted to be Mahjub's. And there was Nettles' suicide, which clearly linked him to Goughan's murder. That was shrugged off as him *being sensitive and horrified that he had directed the call that led to his best friend's murder*; the only thing good about that was his widow got to keep the cash. Same for the money Perriman got from Kahyr; no question, no comment, no confiscation.

Which I guess is good.

There were a hundred other ways the story was a mess, but apparently all that mattered was the public was swallowing it. Dr. Herries-White came on a number of talk shows to discuss how Mahjub was in *a heightened state of agitation when he hunted his victims* and he had fixated on tradesmen he'd seen at the embassy. I hated them calling him *a self-loathing homosexual closet case who was ashamed of his desires and feared his family's rejection*, but to balance it they pointed out that I was gay and he'd planned to blame all of the murders on me before returning to his country, the implication being that he planned to continue his reign of terror in the north since that's where the blonds tended to be. So he'd kidnapped Reg to lure me to the embassy then knocked me unconscious and strung me up to slowly choke to death. As Sir Monteith put it, my *hard head prevented my blacking out completely, and seeing him kill Abdel and stab Constable Thornton had fired up my sense of survival and we'd fought till I disabled him and the police were able to find me*.

Jesus, all of this was such bullshit it was downright embarrassing. Of course the British press was going nuts trying to make contact with me, all of them wanting interviews. I begged off by telling them I couldn't speak very well yet so be patient. Most were. A couple still tried to sneak into the hospital room but they quickly found that's the fastest way to piss off a British nurse, something you do NOT want to do.

What's great is — it got me a visit from Prince Hot-Ginge, and he looks even hotter in person, might I add. He came to thank me on Her Majesty's behalf. I barely restrained myself from giggling and telling him it was nothing then asking if he had plans that night. Without the wife.

Barely.

Then we did some chit-chat and I managed to get the name of their purchasing officer for the pins through joking about not wanting a medal since I heard they sometimes break and *my company did much better work than that* and bullshit, bullshit, bullshit. He knew I was handing him some salesman crap and went along with it. Damn, I liked him. Wished he could be king.

When I finally was released and escorted through the pack of reporters back to the hotel, Reg was still under critical care. I wanted to see him but his wife and four kids had full-time priority; they'd come too damn close to losing him and he belonged with them. Naturally the press was loving any and all photos of him and her and the kids together and filling every space they could with them.

And it tore me apart to have to let that be.

I was set up in a lovely suite at the Met's expense, given my passport back and told my name had been removed from the no-fly list. I could return to the States as soon as I felt up to it, the hint being *sooner than later, got it?* I did, even though I didn't really want to or, to be honest, really plan to anymore. I wanted to stay in London.

No ... I had to.

For business.

Honest.

I had a couple of nice long FaceTime conversations with

Colin, Diana and Hamilton. The FBI had dropped the investigation into my blackmail racket but a couple of dealers were still wary of us. Diana shrugged it off with a simple, "I'll get them back."

I believed her.

Colin had the impression the police were going to shove mom's death into their cold-case file even though the truth of what happened was obvious. Those bastards do keep covering each other's asses and it being decades after the fact was beside the point. However, we could have her remains now and bury her when we wanted. For that, I did have to be there, so I set up a flight home for Saturday.

Ghadir and Jamil dropped by to let me know they'd found someone in Northern Ireland who could work with us on designing and fitting nano-chips into the pins and was open to starting a factory if we wanted to back him. I told Ghadir about the purchasing agent for the Crown and he nodded.

"I have been trying to get to this man," he said. "Perhaps your celebrity will help us."

Jamil just kept his cool wary gaze on me the whole time.

I finally gave out a half-dozen interviews to make the media happy, including a couple of BBC and Channel Four video feeds from my hotel room, playing up the hoarseness. Lots of questions that barely counted as marshmallows were lobbed at me along with great praise. They even liked seeing the sketch I'd done that looked like Reg. I could have grown a head the size of Montana if I hadn't found it all so fucking funny.

The last interview ended about four on Thursday and I was beat, so I stripped and lay down for a short nap and —

The door buzzer jolted me awake. I got up and wrapped myself in a robe and went to open it and —

There was Reg — neat shirt, neat jeans, neat jacket, hood hiding his face from most observers, so lovely. I started breathing soft and my heart went still. It was all I could do to smile at him and step back to let him in.

He entered, careful about his movement but grinning and

looking around the room. "Touch of déjà vu goin' on here."

I shrugged, my eyes locked on him. "I thought you were in critical care."

He chuckled. "That was to keep reporters away from me. Sent me home, last night. Nice sneak-about. Hurts like a bastard if I reach too high or bend wrong." He took in a deep breath and sighed, "Oh, but it were good bein' in me own bed."

"I'm surprised your wife let you out."

He looked at me. "Just saw her off at King's Cross. Taking the kids up to her parents'. Be back tomorrow, then we're off to my folks in Spain. They got a cottage. There for three weeks to recuperate."

"I'm glad. Use lots of sunscreen."

And could I have said anything dumber?

He just looked at me, grinning soft and easy. "Boss filled me in. You're the reason I'm still around. Thanks."

I let my smile widen. Actually felt bashful ... and was I blushing like a teenage girl? Jesus!

Then he took my robe and drew me close, whispering, "C'mere," just before he kissed me.

Oh ... my ... God, how perfect it was. The wonder of him pressed against me. The beauty of his lips caressing mine. Nothing else in the world mattered at that moment. Nothing. Just him with me.

My Reg with me.

When we broke apart I had to lean against a wall, I was so dizzy.

"I owe you that," he said. His eyes did not leave mine. His lips stayed partly open. Wet. Oh-so-fucking-beautiful I had to draw him close and kiss him, again.

And he winced in pain and grunted. I'd touched his injury.

"Sorry," I said, then gently drew him close and pressed my lips to his and let his breath become mine and his heartbeat join mine and his body mold to mine and it built and grew in intensity until I had to break away from him and nestle my face in the crook of his neck and breathe and breathe and breathe as his hands caressed the back of my head and he held me closer.

"Bloody 'ell," he murmured, "that were a corker. Maybe I am queer."

I heard myself whisper, "Stop it. That word is nothing but a label put on something natural in order to make you afraid and controlled. You're just a man. A beautiful man. Who deserved so much better than he's gotten." A soft chuckle came from him so I had to ask, "Can we stay like this for a while? Just a little while?"

He gave me the slightest of nods. I found myself close to weeping.

"You almost died savin' me," he murmured. I just sighed. "I saw the room when I come to. 'Fore they carried me out. You on the floor, blood everywhere. The body. That kid crying over his eye. I know the official line but that little guy couldn't kill a man twice his size. Not even with a knife. Not in the front. But you ... you're all argy-bargy, ain't ya?"

I took in a deep breath and looked him right in the eye and he nodded, his face bright and open.

"Dr. Herries-White said you told him you'd kill anyone tried to hurt me. That's how me squaddies and I felt about each other in the 'Stan. I never felt closer to anyone than them, even me wife. But now? You. It's all turned on its head. You backed up what you said and ... and ... "

He pulled me into another kiss.

I was joyous beyond belief.

This time when we parted, I murmured, "Reg, if we never do anything but this. Just hold each other like this. I'll be happy. So long as I know you don't hate or fear me anymore, I'll be happy."

"That right?" he murmured then pulled away from me, completely, his smile mocking me. "You gonna get me to wonderin' about it all and then you're just gonna leave me to work it out on me own? Yeah, I'm still invalided out but ... "

He slipped his jacket off his glorious shoulders and down his elegant arms, the material caressing every inch of him. He dropped it onto a chair then he stepped back. Let me take in the full view of him.

Sleepy gray eyes under honey-colored brows. Thick hair covering a classic skull and cropped close. A couple of scars in his scalp. Aquiline nose. Taut lips. Strong neck under a clean chin. Smooth cheekbones. His shoulders broad. His chest full and round under a shirt that fit him just right. His legs filling his jeans in ways too perfect to be real. Those same basic tennis shoes splashed with paint. All the complete opposite of what I like — and a man I could never live without, ever again.

I guided him onto the couch. He carefully leaned back on it and looked at me with a crooked grin. I sat beside him. Nestled my head in the crook of his neck. Man, I loved just being next to him. Feeling his breath entering and leaving him. Accepting the warmth of him. I ran my hands over his shoulders and across his chest and down his abs, wishing he was doing the same to me. His shirt had come unbuttoned by his pants, revealing some of his heartbreaking treasure trail and some of his bandage, so I lay a hand on his belly to slip through the opening and let my pinky toy with the downy hairs as we kissed again. Long and leisurely and so complete and wonderful.

He let me unbutton his shirt, so slowly, oh so slowly, then travel down his side to flow around his thigh and trail up to his crotch. I could tell he was getting full and rich. I drew my hand back up over his belly and opened his shirt even more, tickling the short soft hairs as I maneuvered it completely out of the way.

He tore his lips away from mine, gasping for air. I kissed his neck. Kissed his ear. Kissed around to his eyebrows. Caressed the hair along his scalp with my nose. He smelled so fresh and wonderful, tears trailed down my cheeks. I loved the sensation of his light hairs on my fingertips. Felt joy at the quivers of his skin as I caressed his sides. My heart was so light it seemed ready to float away. I had to keep reminding myself to breathe. I let my hand travel back down his body to unzip his jeans and reach inside to feel the beauty caught in the cotton of his briefs.

He groaned and clenched his ass then yelped and started to back away, so I quickly moved my hands up to pull him back into another kiss. He let me.

After a few minutes I broke away and looked at him. His face so close to mine. His eyes so confused and lost and needy. I found myself saying, "I mean it; I'll stop when you say so."

Something I had never said to anyone ever in my life.

He touched my face and nodded. "I know. Which is mad 'cause I don't really know you."

"Neither do I, anymore."

I took half an hour to just caress him, fingers touching his bandage, soft and unsure, then playing with the hair on his chest and his lovely nips. Then his sneakers and socks were gone followed by tickles and caresses on his feet. Jeans worked off in stages — first unfastened completely to fondle his crotch, then pulled down to his knees to toy with the hair swirling over his thighs, then to his ankles so I could focus on his sturdy hairy calves, then off, followed by a few moments of savoring his loveliness. Then I dropped my robe and kneeled before him, feeling him and holding him and letting him tentatively explore me, hesitant but soft, not retreating not once no matter what they brushed against.

The only time he broke away completely was when he examined the bandage to my arm. Caressed it. Looked from me to it with hurt in his eyes. I just shook my head to keep him from speaking and moved back up to him and kissed him again.

I'm not sure what he really felt throughout this, though he would choke back gasps when my touches became too intimate, but the feeling of his fingertips traveling down my back or across my ass or along my arms was bringing me close to insanity. I began to shiver and make gasps of my own. And when he reached down to whisper them over my dick and balls I felt as if the gods had sent him here to drive me mad with desire.

By the time I pulled his briefs away to reveal all ... he was fat and full and ready, so I slipped my lips down all of him, making him damn near scream the moment my tongue began its magic. I had to be careful; he was too close to firing. So I focused on kissing and caressing his lovely balls and nuzzling the hair on his legs with my nose.

He'd rub my back and clench his ass and dig himself deeper into me, wanting to catch that final wave, but I wouldn't let him. I planned to make him want to come back again and again, if I could.

I finally got him to let me slip a finger between his beautiful cheeks and caress his hole. Toy with it. Show him how erogenous a zone it can be. He actually gasped when I started to slip a finger in, but he didn't stop me. I worked it for a little while. Then I snuck the Vaseline from my briefcase and dribbled some on my finger and slipped it deeper into him, locating his prostate and massaging it. He grabbed my hair and damn near shot his wad right then.

"Christ," he growled, "what you doin'?"

"Showing you why every man should like this kind of thing," I snickered back. Then I began sucking on one of his tits and watched his lovely dick bounce around as he squirmed under me.

He was nearly into madness from the sensations. I worked him softly. Gently. Slowly stroking his dick as I pushed my finger in and out and in and out and he grabbed my arms and dug his fingers into my flesh and grunted and cried and lost control and fired, clenching his ass so tight I lost it too.

Without touching myself.

I damn near blacked out from how perfect it was.

Somehow I managed to crawl onto the couch to lie beside him, his whole being shivering next to me. I held him close and he wrapped his arms around me and pulled me against him.

We did not move from the position for nearly an hour.

****

I finally returned enough to myself enough to whisper, "Was it good for you?"

He chuckled. "Bloody hell ... "

"Can I ask you something?"

"What?"

"What did you think about when I was on you?" My fingers traced a circle over the hair on his chest. "That night? When I had you fuck me? What did you think about to help you?"

"What d'ya mean?"

"What thoughts went through your head? Your wife? Your kids? Anything?"

He sighed and finally said, "Girl I knew in school. Levara. Gorgeous. Black as night. She loved ridin' me. Bein' on top. First girl I was ever with. I pictured it being her on me."

"What got you to go along with me instead of fight?"

"Those other blokes fight you?"

"Tried to."

"Were they scared, too?"

I nodded.

"Did you make 'em get off?"

I nodded.

"Your finger up 'em? Is that how?"

"Sometimes."

"That were the weirdest bestest feelin'."

"You didn't fight me. You went along with me. Why?"

He took a long moment before answering. "Your eyes didn't hold death. I saw that in Afghanistan. Old men, young men, women even — there's a look in their eyes just before they're gonna kill you. My best mate told me of it; he was on his second tour. Saved us a couple times." He didn't say anything for a few moments then continued with, "He's proprietor of a pub in Brighton now. Took the wife and kids down to see him. His wife. His kids. Got along famous."

I held him closer. Let my fingers whisper through the hair on his scalp. Then I drew my fingers along the hair on his arms.

"Liked it more on me head," he murmured, sounding like a child close to sleep.

I moved my right hand up to his skull and began running my fingers through it. "Like this?"

He drew in a deep, happy breath. "Me mum used to do that till I got too cool for it. Is this what blokes do? Touchin'. Holdin'? Talkin'?"

"Sometimes. This sort of love used to be normal. Used to be accepted. Used to be encouraged. One more powerful. One that fills you to the core. It built a civilization of warriors and men who would fight to the death for each other."

"We're bloody Spartans, eh?"

I hesitated. I didn't want to answer him but the fact was, "Yes. I feel about you like I've never felt about anybody, ever, in my life. I've already shown how far I'll go for you."

"Guess that makes me your woman, don't it?"

"No!" My voice was sharper than I'd intended. He gave me a sideways look, his hurt eyes wary. I couldn't stop myself from saying, "It makes you the first man I've ever felt this for. I've been with so many other guys. Guys who were more than willin' but who were just — just gratification. With you — Reg, I dunno. I killed for you. I risked prison for you."

Confusion filled his eyes then he smirked. "You just wanna get your dick up me bum."

"No. I meant it when I said if you told me to stop I would. And I won't touch you, again, not till you want me to. I hope you will but you're so much more than just a bed partner."

"Why?" He was fighting to understand. "Why me? What is it about me that makes you think I want that?"

"I don't know what to say to you. I just know I could stay like this ... just holding you like this ... forever and be happy."

" ... I don't think Mandy and me ever felt that for each other," he murmured. "Mandy's me wife. I always been hot for her. Shite, we fucked like bunnies even 'fore we was married." He looked hard into my eyes. "I love her. Still do."

"Good."

"But I never felt so deep for her. Like what you say. I do for my kids but her — she's me wife."

"I don't want you to change that. I don't want you to change anything about you."

He let a chuckle loose. "I'd say this is a bloody big fuckin' change."

I took in a deep breath and forced myself to ask, "So what do you want to do?"

He shrugged. "I dunno. I dunno what I feel. There's somethin' there but I dunno what it is." He chuckled. "Maybe it's me happy I'm alive. Or gratitude to you for savin' me."

"God, I hope it's not just that."

He looked away, still lost, then leaned in to me. Rested his head against my chest. He didn't move, again, except to breathe.

I finally had to ask, "Are you sorry this happened?"

He hesitated then sighed and said, "I'm kind of sticky. Can I do a quick wash?"

"What about your bandage?"

"Not a shower; just a hand cloth."

"Have at it."

He straightened and maneuvered up to his feet and went into the bathroom to pee. Watching him stand there, his back flowing into his ass flowing into his legs — I felt an even wilder sense of protection for him. He was part of me now, someone I loved more than I loved myself, even more than family, and it didn't matter how he felt about me.

"You, uh, you hungry?" I called to him.

"I could eat," he called back.

I ordered fish and chips through room service then grabbed my pad, pulled up a chair to sit and sketched a light loose picture of him as he washed. Different from Tawfi's. Simpler, more elegant. Not as erotic. Filled with everything I could feel at the moment. My hands were shaking from the intensity of it all but I got a good one. He glanced back and chuckled at me doing it.

The buzzer rang and I said, "Food's here," then wrapped myself in the robe and opened the door to find —

Tawfi.

My mind actually went blank.

"Hello, Devlin. May I come in?"

I jolted and said, "Yeah, sure, Tawfi. How you feelin'?" I noticed the bathroom door was closing.

"I am quite well," he said. "The effects of the drug wore off rather quickly. It was an organic recipe from my country's mountain tribes. How do you feel?"

"Pretty good."

He drew me close to kiss then pulled back just a little to eye me, almost amused. "Ah, do I detect the fragrance of a lovely young constable?"

"His name's Reg," popped out of me before I could stop it.

That made Tawfi blink then he said, "I hope he will give me the honor to address him as such." That's when he heard Reg in the bathroom then saw the sketch, picked it up and smiled. "This is very good," he said. "Looks exactly like him." He set the sketch back down. "He's a very attractive man."

I chuckled, uneasy. "C'mon, Tawfi, you're not gonna get all jealous, are you?"

He laughed. "Devlin, who do you think you are? A Padishah with his concubines? Have to be careful to keep his harem happy? You disappoint me with that attitude."

"Sorry, it's just — "

"I know, I know, Americans are rather childish when it comes to sex. Even those as adult as you. But jealousy is an emotion a man in my position cannot afford. It becomes far too easy for your enemies to distract you and, thereupon, remove you. My father insisted I read not only *Sun Tzu* and *Machiavelli* but also

Othello. They come in quite handy in my world."

"Understood. Sorry I said anything."

"Don't be. I ... I merely dropped in to personally invite you to the embassy, tomorrow. About three? I think you may enjoy what happens."

No insinuations behind his words, meaning it was something other than sex he was offering.

"So what's it all about?"

He brushed his fingers through my hair. "You are as impatient as a child. Wait until tomorrow. It will be like Christmas for you. I promise. Unless you prefer to be with your young constable."

"He's leavin' town," I said with a sigh. "With his wife."

Tawfi eyed me. "And that displeases you. Interesting."

I took in a deep breath and thought, *Don't lie to this guy; he'll know and hate you for it.* So I said, "Tawfi — with Reg — it's not about sex. The way I feel about him is different in ways I don't understand. With you I'm hungry. Horny. You're what I like and I like being with you. Fuck, do I like it. But with Reg — I dunno. I feel protective. Scared. For him. Of him. I feel a connection with him that's drivin' me nuts because I know, I know, I know he'll never be mine. Not completely. We haven't been together once, not all the way. But what's crazy is I don't care. I can't let go of him. I want both of you in my life."

Tawfi nodded. "Greedy as a dog who, when bowls of food are put down for it and its sibling, devours all leaving nothing behind."

"Whoa — rough way to put it but ... yeah, I guess."

He chuckled. "Devlin, as I once told you, I will marry some day. Not because I must but because I wish to. As wonderful as men are, until such time as they can bear children the female sex is necessary, and I wish to leave behind many of my progeny. But for them to be legal they must come from a traditional Muslim marriage. Which I do not mind; I am not averse to women."

"Guess that makes me odd man out, 'cause no way in hell

am I ever doin' a chick."

He laughed. "In which case my father would probably have you beheaded, the old hypocrite. I understand Leila told you of the rumors about him. They have been circulating since before I was born, but he ignores them. Of course he thinks I know nothing about him and a certain captain in the Imperial Guard, who in his day was startlingly beautiful. So have no fear ... of him; so long as we are in London you are safe."

"What about Leila? She may still pull some more shit."

"She is back in my country and will stay there, tending to my nephews. Do you know what I said to her as she was leaving, that night? *On the day I die, she dies.* I think she will help me live a very long and prosperous life."

"Man — I don't ever want you pissed off at me."

"Not possible," he said as he caressed my chin. "For what I have learned about you in the last few days has made you a very, *very* special man, to me. And dangerous."

He kissed me on the nose and smiled.

I could barely breathe as I said, "I'm leavin' Saturday. For a while. My mother's funeral. Finally." He nodded, understanding. "You ... you got plans Friday night?"

His smile widened. "I shall arrange for dinner to be served in my flat, my greedy little dog."

I gave him a grin and a soft bark.

He cast another glance at the bathroom door. "Ask your young constable if he will join us, tomorrow, before he leaves. If he wishes he may bring his wife."

"Okay, so ... so what's so big about tomorrow? What're you gonna do? I gotta give him a reason to show up."

"Very well, a taste. My beloved brother's wife confessed everything, so at ten am New York time I will take full and complete control of The Faure Group and all that they own. And I will kick every member of that family into the street. It has taken until now to arrange, and it is my hope you will attend their funeral."

"That's all you're gonna do? Griff was part of gettin' four men killed and — "

"Ah, yes, Griffin Faure — you must not yet have heard. He, um, *leapt to his death* from his father's penthouse. In New York. Two hours hour ago. As his father, shall we say, *watched*. I heard just before I started over here. I believe his father had ... *suspicions* as to what is about to happen and held his son responsible."

"*Had suspicions?*"

The expression on Tawfi's face was so completely unreadable, I shivered.

"Whoa," I said. "I *definitely* don't ever want to get you mad at me."

Tawfi gave me a gentle smile as he asked, "Whatever do you mean?"

"Nothin'," I chuckled. "Your concubine will be on site, sir, and on time."

He caressed my chin and said, "Courtesan." Then he winked and left in the elevator that brought up our food.

That's when Reg came out of the bathroom with a towel wrapped loose around him, adding to the eroticism of his casual beauty, murmuring, "Took 'im long enough to leave. Bloody hell, I'm starved," as he took a plate. "So what's that talk of concubines and harems? He thinks I'll be in his bed, too?"

I barely kept a wicked grin off my face. "You are his type."

He snorted. "Yours, his, everybody's, eh?" Then he carefully sat on a chair at a table, his left leg stretched out, and dug into his food, muttering, "God, this is brilliant."

I watched him, loving every movement he made. And for some stupid reason I was immensely pleased he'd washed without getting his bandage wet. Next thing you know I'll be cutting photos of him out of *Hello* and *OK* and taping them to my bedroom walls. Jesus.

"What time're you leavin', tomorrow?" I asked.

"Mandy's back at five; flight's at nine."

"Well then ... our *audience* with Prince Tafiq is at three pm ... if you can make it."

Reg shrugged. "I'll wear me best dress." That made me laugh so he looked at me and snarled, "Uniform! Bloody arse. And don't think for a second I'll toss it off."

I just gazed upon him. The line of his body made my heart almost stop, something deep and troubling welling up behind it. I took in a long breath, cast the feeling aside and found that even the mushy peas smelled good. Which reminded me I hadn't had lunch, so I pulled a couple of beers from the mini-bar to give him one —

And froze at how beautiful the three tattoos on his neck looked, all but glowing against his smooth skin. I put the beers on the table and let my hand trail down his spine ... feeling something quite animalistic building behind my heart, again.

I whispered, "What do these symbols mean?"

He reacted to my touch like a cat. "What's that?"

"Tattoos. On your neck. Down your spine."

He nodded. "Top one — that's *Live*. Middle one's *Love*. Bottom means *Laugh*."

"I don't have any tattoos."

"I noticed. But there's some scars on your back. What're yours from?"

I hesitated then sat and whispered, "My father had a belt with a hook in the buckle. Sometimes he'd whip me with it. My brother also has them."

" ... Oh. Is your brother a — well ... "

I grinned. "A *poof* like me? No. He's so into his wife I don't think he'd even look at another woman, let alone a man."

His expression grew distant. " ... Unlike me."

"No, not like you at all," I said, "I'll tell you about Colin, some day, but trust me — it's not an apt comparison, you and him."

He stopped eating and leaned back, shifting to stretch his

left leg even more. Rubbed a gentle hand over his wound.

The animal in me grew silent as I took a deep breath and said, "Reg, you're not cheatin' on your wife. You're not cheatin' on yourself. What I bring you is somethin' different from what you can get with a woman. A different kind of love. But it is still love." He looked at me and with no hesitation in my voice I said, "And I do love you."

He hesitated then leaned forward and toyed with his peas, murmuring, "I can't say that to you."

Not yet, I thought then said, "Doesn't matter. You're the one in control. I've never said that to anyone, not even my father, but you are the one in control and whatever you say, so be it."

He looked at me for what seemed like forever then a hesitant smile flitted across his lips and he lifted his beer and tipped it to mine before taking a sip, then he dove back into his meal, muttering, "Bloody arse."

I nearly wept.

I sipped some of my own beer and dug into the best fish and chips that had ever been made in the history of the universe, because now I knew it was all gonna be fine. I knew it. Tawfi would be mine in his own way, one where he thought he was in control and I was there for him. And sooner than later we'd become equals in bed because now I knew he trusted me — two wolves happy with each other as we howled at the moon. Our own little pack.

While with Reg — with Reg I knew — I finally knew deep down inside he felt the same way about me as I did him. He might not be willing to admit it, yet, but he would. Someday. I'd already become his squaddie and that brought me to a glorious world of chaotic perfection. I also knew that eventually we'd do a lot more than what we'd done, tonight, but I could wait till he was ready. I knew I'd always have to share him with the mother of his kids, but I didn't care. I'd have to do that with Tawfi, someday, and reality is — so what? That would be completely apart from what I owned of their souls, so all that mattered was —

Tawfi would be mine.

Reg would be mine.

And the only thing that could make my greedy little beast happier would be getting them together in the same bed, full and complete, so they could also be each other's. Three of us one in the same pack.

Father, son and Holy Ghost.

Perfection.

I chuckled at the thought, making Reg look at me. I winked at him, in return. He shook his head, still smiling a little.

And for the first time in my life, I felt complete and total peace ... all thanks to my Underground Guy.

THE END

Kyle Michel Sullivan is a writer and self-involved artist out to change the world until it changes him...as has already happened in far too many ways. He has lived in London, Los Angeles, San Antonio, El Paso, Kansas City, Honolulu, Austin and Houston, and now resides in Buffalo, NY.

He has won multiple awards for his screenplays and has written books of every sort — from sunshine and light (*David Martin*) to cold and dark (*How To Rape A Straight Guy*, which has been banned a couple of times) to dark mystery (*The Vanishing of Owen Taylor*) to romantic comedy (*The Alice '65*) to flat out insane (*The Lyons' Den*).

He uses Tolstoy as his guide, and tries to build characters as vivid and real as possible. He has a lot of fun doing it mixed with angst, anger, and amazement...but that's the lot of a writer.

OTHER BOOKS BY THE AUTHOR

General Novels:
THE ALICE '65
THE VANISHING OF OWEN TAYLOR
THE LYONS' DEN
BOBBY CARAPISI
NYPD BLOOD

Fable:
DAVID MARTIN

VERY Adult Novels:
RAPE IN HOLDING CELL 6
PORNO MANIFESTO
HOW TO RAPE A STRAIGHT GUY

Printed in April 2019
by Rotomail Italia S.p.A., Vignate (MI) - Italy